THE WINDWEAVER'S STORM
TJ YOUNG & THE ORISHAS

ANTOINE BANDELE

EDITED BY
FIONA MCLAREN
CALLAN BROWN

ILLUSTRATED BY
ARTHUR BOWLING

BANDELE
— BOOKS —

Publisher: Bandele Books
Interior Design: Vellum
Editors: Fiona McLaren, Callan Brown
Illustrator: Arthur Bowling
Cover Design: Mibl Art
Ornamental Break Design: Bolaji Olaloye

ISBN: 978-1-951905-20-0 (Ebook edition)

ISBN: 978-1-951905-21-7 (Paperback edition)

ISBN: 978-1-951905-22-4 (Hardback edition)

First Edition | September 4, 2022

CONTENTS

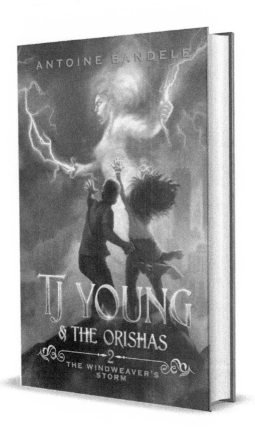

The Windweaver's Storm is the second book in the *TJ Young & The Orishas* series, a collection of stories based around lore and mythology from West Africa and the African diaspora.

If you enjoy this story and are interested in the rest of TJ's adventures, you can join Antoine Bandele's e-mail alerts list. He'll send you notifications for new book releases, exclusive updates, and behind-the-page content.

Visit this link:
antoinebandele.com/stay-in-touch

Read the free prequel short story to
The Windweaver's Storm!

What happens when a deity needs to reconnect with humanity?
They go to New York City, of course.

Oya, the deity of storms, must convey a message. But how can she
do it when no Orisha has communicated with a mortal in
centuries? To succeed, she must break the ancient rules that have
shackled her for ages.
The world's hope rests on the shoulders of her holy child, young
Manny Martinez, but she's proving fiendishly hard to reach with
a crowded mind full of family reunions, social media, and a city
rife with distractions. If time runs out, an all-out war could break
out between mortals and immortals alike.

Visit this link to read the prequel story:
https://www.antoinebandele.com/when-the-wind-speaks

PRONUNCIATION GUIDE

Characters

A·de·o·la - ah'day'yo'lah
A·de·ye·mi - ah'day'yea'me
A·yo·de·ji - eye'o'day'gee
Bo·la·we - bow'la'way
Du Bois - do'bwa
E·me·ka - eh'meh'kah
E·ni·o·la - eh'knee'o'lah
I·fe·da·yo - ee'fey'die'yo
Man·uel·a - man'well'ah
Ti·ti·lay·o - tee'tee'lie'yo
To·mo·ri Jo·mi·lo·ju - toe'moe'ree joe'mee'low'jew
Gra·vés - gra'ves
U·mar - oo'mar

Orishas

Ba·ba·lu A·ye - ba'ba'loo ah'yay
E·shu - eh'shoe
I·be·ji - e'bae'jee
O·ba·ta·la - o'ba'ta'la
O·du·du·wa - o'do'do'wah
O·gi·yan - o'gee'yan
O·ko - o'ko
O·lo·du·ma·re - o'low'do'ma'ray
O·lo·kun - o'low'koon
O·lo·sa - o'low'sah
O·ri - o'ree
O·run·mi·la - o'rune'mee'lah
O·sain - o'sane
O·sho·si - oh'show'she
O·shun - o'shoon
O·ya - oi'ya
Shan·go - shon'go
Ye·mo·ja - ye'mo'jah
Ye·wa - ye'wah

Terms

A·she - a'shay
A·so o·ke - ah'so o'kay
A·zi·za - ah'zee'zah
Ba·ba·la·wo - ba'ba'la'woah
Da·shi·ki - da'she'key
E·mi - e'mee
E·re I·da·ra·ya - eh'ray e'da'rie'yah
I·fa - ee'fah
Im·pun·du·lu - eem'poon'doo'loo
Ki·shi - key'she
Ma·mi Wa·ta - mah'mee wa'tah
Og·bon - og'bon
O·lo·shi - o'lo'she
Zo·bo - zo'bo

Locations

A·bu·ja - a'boo'jah
I·le-I·fe - e'lay e'fay
La·gos - la'gos
Man·da·wa·ca - man'de'wa'ca
O·yo - oi'yo

*This story is
a work of fantasy fiction
and not an accurate depiction of
the living practice of Ifa
and its many branches and followers
in the Motherland
and the diaspora.*

This one is for the 14-year-old Antoine
who had his head in the clouds.

1

OVER PROMISE, UNDER DELIVER

Everything should've been perfect for TJ Young. He had just had the best summer of his life. Camp Olosa for Remedial Magic had accepted him. He stared down giant alligators, took on more than one of the ancient Orishas, and then got an invite to *the* magical school of West Africa: Ifa Academy for Tomorrow's Diviners.

But there was this *enormous* weight hanging on his shoulders.

His promise.

The stupidest promise he could've ever made.

It was all he could think about despite it being summer, a teenager's prime vacation. Despite a soothing breeze coming in from his bedroom window, that promise festered in the wrinkles of his brain.

Sure, he totally broke the illusions of Yewa, the Orisha of Cadavers. And yeah, he found an ally in Eshu, the Gatekeeper. But he didn't have the stuff to bring down Olokun, the Orisha of the Deep Blue Sea. So, instead of getting eaten by a horde of sharks and eels that swam around with Olokun like minions, TJ made a deal: a favor for a favor.

TJ had told Olokun that, one, he could restore the praise the great deity had lost over the centuries, and two, that TJ could do away with Eko Atlantic.

Now, that first one was pretty simple. If all TJ had to do was go around and preach the good word, run a few fundraisers or whatever, that wasn't so bad. Sure, the big guy was probably looking for praise from more than just a handful of people, but TJ could *at least* manage that much. No, it was the second condition that really twisted his stomach in knots, a request that meant tearing down a city of skyscrapers that had been building up for as long as TJ had been alive.

You see, Eko Atlantic wasn't some underwater fortress, as TJ had assumed when he first made the promise. It was a human settlement near Lagos, Nigeria, the largest land reclamation project of its time, and a huge no-no for a deity who called the ocean waters his rightful domain.

A flash from TJ's laptop winked in and out, bringing him out of his stupor. Well, it wasn't TJ's laptop. It was his little brother's. TJ's junk of a machine was too slow, and his brother's had all these fancy plug-ins and notifications only a whizkid like him had access to. And *because* the laptop wasn't his, TJ was spending most of his time looking over his shoulder at the closed door.

The webpage he had up at that moment was a secret site only diviners could access, called *Evocation*. For weeks, TJ had been refreshing it to see if any sightings of Orishas in the real world had come up.

Olokun in particular.

When TJ refreshed the page for the dozenth time, an itch came at the tip of his index finger. He scratched it with his thumb and glanced down at the faint tattoo that was baked there. It was shaped like a forked line on a cross, the symbol of Eshu, another reminder of the divine contract he had tied himself to. Besides the tattoo, the blinking light of the countdown app on his phone was a pretty decent reminder as well. And at the moment, it read:

Eko Atlantic's Doomsday in 25 weeks, 1 day, 6 hours, 23 minutes, and 39 seconds

TJ had had two weeks to think it over, yet he couldn't, for the life of him, even *start* to work out a plan that would make the deity happy *while* preventing the breakdown of years' worth of Nigerian efforts and labors.

TJ let out a very long and *very* loud grunt as he leaned back in what was once his sister's desk chair. Had he still been sharing a room with his little brother, his frustrated outburst would've earned a "get over it" or "could you vent somewhere else?" followed by his brother taking his laptop back. Mom and Dad had given TJ his older sister's room when he got back from summer camp. TJ still wasn't used to it; it was like he was invading his sister's space.

These days, he wasn't so sure what to think about his sister. For the entire summer, he had tried to uncover how she died—how she was killed—but instead of an answer, he had an eventful run-in with the Orishas and some of his sister's old friends. A handful of words kept pressing into his brain:

"*Ifedayo was a Keeper, Tomori,*" that traitor, Mr. Bolawe—no, Bolawe had said. "*Your sister was one of us. She was our promised child.*"

TJ still couldn't believe it. Everyone had said Dayo was the Hero of Nigeria, the promised child meant to bring the Orishas back into the world. Not some Keeper who dealt in death and destruction. Nothing in Dayo's journal said anything about being a radical magical terrorist, and she wrote everything in there— even left it for TJ to learn from. Bolawe was just trying to throw him off. TJ had experienced the Keepers' wrath only a few months ago when they *attacked* Dayo's funeral. Bolawe had to be lying. If Dayo really was some Keeper, why would they attack one of their own?

All said, though... TJ still couldn't find a reason Bolawe would lie, either.

Pinching his temples, TJ turned from the blinking reminder on his phone and stared at the bedroom wall instead. Mom said he could change whatever he liked in the room, but TJ preferred it the way it was—how Dayo had decorated it.

The wallpaper was a constellation of stars in the shape of several Orishas. TJ had stared at it more times than he could count whenever he felt overwhelmed. Since coming back from camp, he had started silently critiquing Mom's interpretations of the Orishas. The painted Eshu didn't look quite the same as the real one, who was more pudgy than toned. And Mom had *not* drawn Olokun to scale. In reality, he towered over Eshu ten or twenty times over, but the painting only had him twice as big.

A buzz vibrated against TJ's thigh. He slipped his hand into his jean pocket and pulled out his phone. His screen revealed a text message from the one person who always made him forget about his worries: Manny.

If TJ could make a highlight reel out of last summer, meeting her would definitely be at the top. Well actually, number one would probably be surviving a trip to the Aqua Realm, but a very *close* second would definitely be meeting Manny. She was sort of the best: kind, compassionate, into all the geeky stuff TJ was into, and yeah, yeah, she was easy on the eyes too, and *maybe* TJ had acquired a *teeny tiny* crush on her.

But who could blame him? Manny was awesome.

Opening his messaging app, he scanned his friend's text, which read:

> Manny: U know u're way funnier over text
> Manny: Ur GIF choices are...

She had sent him an animated picture of a chef kissing his hand and blowing it into the delicious air. TJ scanned through their previous conversations. It was true many of his responses were in the form of silly GIFs, but he couldn't help it. Words just couldn't correctly communicate what looping images could.

Still, he couldn't help reading Manny's text in the worst possible tone imaginable. Rational thought would've had him reading her message with that slightly husky Brooklyn inflection, one almost always laced with humor.

But TJ couldn't help reading it as a jab.

Did she mean he wasn't funny *unless* he was sending GIFs? Was he a total bore when they spoke to each other in person?

The gentle hum of Manny's next text broke TJ from his self-destructing reverie.

> Manny: btw have u ever seen the dusk of the blood moon movies b4?

TJ sat up straight in his chair and did a lightning-fast Google search for the "Dusk of the Blood Moon." The results popped up with posters of shirtless teen boys played by men in their thirties, one with blood caked around his mouth, the other with wolf's hair sprouting over his back. TJ's thumb flew over his app and swiped back to his text with Manny.

> TJ: thats not that 🧛🐺 stuffz is it?
> Manny: yup yup im gonna buy some copies for us right now 😊 theyll be waiting for you in brookyln

Waiting for me in Brooklyn? TJ thought curiously, though he couldn't help feeling a pang of joy that Manny had basically invited him all the way from Los Angeles to visit her and watch so-bad-they're-good movies. *Yeah, that text message about the GIFs was definitely just a joke.*

But why had she said Brooklyn and *not* Nigeria, *not* New Ile-Ife, where Ifa Academy was?

Letting his thumbs fly free, TJ replied:

> TJ: brooklyn? dont you mean NII?
> TJ: u're going to IA aren't you?
> TJ: i mean with u-kno-who being a u-kno-what that puts you and ayo in top 2 in the camp standings right?
> TJ: u're not gonna accept the invite??

TJ really needed to get out of the habit of sending single lines instead of one long text.

That summer at Camp Olosa, TJ's friends were all in the top three. TJ didn't even make it to the top twenty, and Ifa Academy still accepted him. The top student was a kid named Joshua who actually turned out to be the Orisha Eshu hiding in a human boy's body. Sort of unfair and totally against the rules. That put his friend Ayo, the Nigerian man-bun wonder, at the top, and Manny just behind him. So the academy invited them right away.

In fact, now that TJ thought about it, Manny had barely mentioned Ifa Academy all summer. She had always gotten real quiet whenever the magic school was brought up in conversation.

TJ just thought she had gotten over whatever kept her from the place.

TJ sat staring at his phone's screen. There were no three little dots showing Manny was composing a response.

Shit... is she really not going to Ifa?

TJ started typing another message but deleted it immediately after. If there was one thing he knew about texting girls—despite his very limited experience—it was to never look too eager; never send a question after another question. Maybe Manny got caught up with one of her four brothers, or perhaps her mom had her running an errand.

But as the minutes snailed on, the bottom of TJ's stomach emptied.

He didn't want to go to Ifa Academy on his own. Sure, Ayo would be there, but he wasn't the same as Manny.

It took all of TJ's willpower not to pick up his phone and blast Manny with a stream of texts—GIFs and all. Instead, he put his phone on his desk just as Mom called out, "Tomori Jomiloju! Come down here right quick."

TJ shuffled out of his room. As he swung the door open, the savory smell of the fried plantains Mom had cooked that morning blessed his nostrils. Motivated by a watering mouth, TJ jogged downstairs, but Dad waved him over from the bedroom door down the hall. Dad's bald head glinted in the afternoon light from the hallway window. "Psst, son. Can you get this to your Mom for me? I'm sittin' on this eBay bid right now. Cain't miss it."

TJ took a thick envelope from Dad. If it weren't bursting at the seams, TJ would never have seen the dollar bills poking out.

"What's this?" TJ asked.

"Ah, nothin'. Just get it to your mother, please."

TJ took a peek over Dad's shoulder. He caught the image of a Kobe Bryant rookie card on a computer screen before Dad closed the door partially.

"You're not selling your cards now, are you?" TJ asked, crushing the envelope a little. Last summer his family had hit a few financial woes, a lot of that stemming from the tuition he needed to pay for summer camp and now... with Ifa Academy.

"Hey, you said not to sell family heirlooms," Dad answered,

catching TJ's frown. "I've been meanin' to sell my collection for years, you know that."

"Dad..." TJ gritted.

"Get that to your mom, like I said." Dad closed the door all the way and his slippers *pat-patted* away behind it, then the *click-clack* of fingers over a keyboard followed, and finally a shout of, "Oh, yeah! Up to five-hundred. It's not even mint condition!"

TJ groaned. He climbed down the stairs as quickly as he could to stop himself from pounding on Dad's door and telling him to *un*sell that Kobe rookie card. In his haste, he nearly bumped into Tunde, his little brother, who was balancing precariously on an old ladder in the foyer: one foot tip-toed and the other in the air. He stretched out as long as he could with one of his fingers touching the underside of a light bulb, which pulsed on and off.

Unlike TJ, Tunde hadn't hit his growth spurt yet.

"Wouldn't it be easier to just get a new bulb?" TJ asked as he craned his neck up to Tunde.

With tongue out and sun-baked dreadlocks hanging, Tunde strained a, "This... is one... of the few times... Mom lets me... use magic... in the house... so... *no*."

TJ laughed. "What charm are you trying to use?"

"Orunmila's Glow."

"Got it." TJ closed his eyes, focused the Ashe in his chest, and searched for the Ashe within Tunde's own. At the moment, he was like a second battery for his brother's magic, which feebly roiled through the dying light of the spent bulb. Thanks to TJ, though, in mere moments, brightness filled the whole of the foyer.

You see, *that* was TJ's unique ability. The one that didn't have any scholarships he could apply for, a gift not shared by any diviner in the world. TJ was like a steroid of magic, an extra charge he could manifest to boost other diviners and channel into himself.

"You're welcome," TJ said, smiling. Tunde had always outpaced him with magic in the past, but these days it was often the other way around.

"Yeah, yeah, whatever, *Lucky Charm*."

Last year, heck, even a few months ago, TJ would've scoffed

at the nickname. At one time, he thought it totally sucked. And yeah, it was still pretty lame that his claim to fame was essentially being a glorified sidekick to all his friends and family, but still... it was nice being helpful and wanted—even begrudgingly.

With a little hop in his step, TJ made his way to the living room where Mom held her hands aloft. Several long dark dashiki with two gray stripes going down the chest hovered in the air. Their swirling shimmy bounced in rhythm with Mom's hands, like she was some orchestrator. And as she swayed, her towering palm-tree-like dreadlocks swung with her.

"Hey, Mom. Dad told me to get this to you." TJ waved the envelope in hand.

"Oh, just set it on the table there," she answered, and TJ did as he was told. "Now. Stand right where you are!"

Before TJ could ask what that meant, one of the long dashikis attacked him, forcing its way over his head and down his torso.

"Ah! What's going on!" TJ flailed his arms as the shirt fought to get its sleeve over his wrist. TJ was somewhere between the dashiki's neck opening and the arm slit when he caught a flash of Simba, the family dog, running into the room. Simba barked at the other sleeve that was trying to force its way down TJ's other arm. Mom snapped her fingers and Simba sat, but his tail still wagged, ready to pounce again if necessary.

"Oh, honey bunny, stop fighting. I'm just seeing which of these uniforms fits you."

Once the dashiki had settled in place over TJ's body, it stopped its wiggling. But the thing was tight—much too tight. Like, rockstar skinny jeans tight. TJ could barely breathe!

"Nu uh... that won't do." Mom flipped a finger and the dashiki squirmed back up TJ's neck. The fight to get it off was just as bad as putting it on. The next dashiki, however, was as easy as putting on a poncho. That is to say, it was *much* too large.

"Oh, that won't do either. *Po o rá sínú aféfé.*" Mom snapped her finger and the dashiki whipped away.

For what felt like an hour, TJ and Mom tried on every combination of clothes. Whenever TJ thought they had found a perfect fit, Mom would suck her teeth long and stretched out in her old Nigerian habit before saying, "no, no, the shoulders aren't right" or "no, the chest is too loose. You have to look sharp and presentable for your first day at the academy." And when TJ thought they were *finally* done, Mom spent an extra few minutes enchanting the dashiki so that it would "grow" with TJ throughout the year. With all the commotion dying down, Simba shuffled out of the room, probably to find a suitable spot to nap.

"I swear. I blink, and you're two inches taller." Mom shook her head but pinched TJ's cheeks. It was true, though. At the beginning of summer, he was just under Mom's eyeline. Now, he got a pretty good view of her forehead. "I can't believe you're really going to Ifa! Did you fill out all your emergency forms? Did you get all your labels on your belongings? Did you practice your charm work for self-washing towels? Did you—"

"Ma! Ma! I got it. I got everything on lock." TJ chuckled.

If he had to rank who was most excited that he was going to magic school, it would be Mom way up at the top and then him a fair few levels below her. Not because TJ didn't want to go—he couldn't wait either—but Mom had been waiting for that day for *years*.

"Oh!" Mom skipped to the table with the envelope. "I've got to remember to send this off tomorrow and exchange it for enchanted cowries. School uniforms aren't cheap."

TJ avoided Mom's eyes at that. She knew he didn't like it when she mentioned money around him, and at that moment, she was likely cringing for slipping up. So he just ran his hand over his school uniform, which indeed felt like an expensive material of whatever-you-called it. He touched his fingers to the embroidered sigil over his heart: the coat of arms of Ifa Academy, a collection of swirls and lines TJ didn't know the meaning of.

"What are these two gray stripes going down for?"

"Oh, those are blank until they're filled in with your two Orishas' colors at the start of term." Mom pointed up to her old school uniform, which hung in a frame next to her university degrees and other awards... right next to Dayo's countless trophies.

TJ still hadn't told his parents what Bolawe said last year about Dayo being a Keeper. Until he found out the truth, he wouldn't slander his sister's name, least of all to Mom.

"You see," Mom went on, "the left strip on the uniform is for my primary Orisha, Yemoja, so it's blue and white. But then my secondary Orisha, Orunmila, is green and yellow. See it there on the right?" Something on the TV snatched Mom's attention away. "Baby, what did they say on the news just now?"

TJ followed Mom's gaze to the TV, where an image of Times Square was plastered across the screen. Only it was a Times Square TJ was unfamiliar with. Instead of all the bright lights and flashing billboards, everything was smashed, glass shattered, poles overturned, and an enormous crowd spotlighted by overhead helicopters.

The horror of the image had Mom looking for balance on the nearby sofa. TJ's heart stopped on him. What had happened? TJ flitted his fingers in the air to magically depress the "volume up" button on the remote lounging on the couch.

"Breaking news," a Nigerian female voice said over the image. "Again, this is *Divination Today* breaking news. There have been reports of a blackout in Times Square. The cause is unknown, but early sources say a diviner child might have been the catalyst."

TJ bit at his lip nervously as he tried to convince himself that Manny wasn't involved. There had to be a bunch of magical children in New York, not just her. But TJ's thoughts tended to spring to the worst. It couldn't be helped when the images on the TV kept cutting between people running down streets and freaking out.

"Simisola," a male voice, also Nigerian, returned with a reporter's clean cadence. "Can you tell us when this occurred?"

"Unclear. It seems to have happened only five minutes ago. But *Divination Today* is always the first to report!"

"Oh, this just in from the studio. It seems like this all was a movie production gone wrong. Perhaps this was just — "

Mom's phone rang, and she answered it immediately. "Hey there, Manuela! We just heard the report on DT. Are you okay? You live in Brooklyn, right? You weren't anywhere near Times Square, were you?" There was a pause, and TJ strained to hear what Manny was saying on the other line. "Oh good! What? Oh yes, he's right here." Mom dropped the phone from her ear. "It's your friend, Manuela. She wants to speak with you."

TJ did an internal facepalm. He'd left his phone upstairs. Manny must've been calling him like crazy. TJ took the phone quickly from Mom and said, "Sup, Manny!"

"Play along," she said sharply in a hushed tone, then she raised her voice theatrically. "Hey, *Mamãe*, can you get somewhere private?"

TJ had no clue why Manny was addressing him as "Mom" in Portuguese, but that probably meant she was around people who couldn't know she was speaking with him.

"Yeah," TJ answered. "I can get my phone from upstairs. Sorry, I left it up there. What's going on?"

"Yes, I'm okay, Ma. Don't worry. The UCMP has me. I got a visit from an Orisha. *My* Orisha. Oya has a message for my friend TJ Young."

2

ETHEREAL ENTANGLEMENTS

HAND SHAKING, TJ GAVE THE PHONE BACK TO MOM AND asked to be excused upstairs. He still couldn't believe what Manny had told him. There were rumors across the magical web that Orishas were showing themselves to diviners, but there was nothing about them talking directly to mortals. And apparently one of them — the Orisha of Storms, for crying out loud — wanted a personal appointment with TJ himself?

What was up with that?

"What's got you all hot and bothered, honey bunny?" Mom grinned with a knowing smile. She knew about TJ's crush despite him saying nothing of it to her — motherly instincts or whatever — but TJ had said nothing to her about the promise he made to Olokun or the gargantuan predicament he found himself in.

"Nothin'," he answered. "I just gotta send something from my phone to Manny! I'll be right back down."

"All right then, dinner will be ready in an hour or two."

TJ gave Mom a swift kiss on the cheek, then raced up to his bedroom, slid his phone from his desk, and facetimed Manny straight away.

His video call barely rang a millisecond before Manny answered, "Hey, hey! Hold on, let me add *Dad* to the call." Her hair was already big and unruly, but just then it looked like a leaf blower had had its way with her thick coils. *"Dad, can you hear me?"*

A moment later, a second person, who was definitely *not* Manny's dad, slid into view. He had a pudgier face than Manny's dad, wore designer glasses, which sat snuggly atop his wide nose, and a neat little man-bun topped his thick head: Ayodeji Oyelowo.

"Yeah, yeah, I can hear you," Ayo groaned from his bed as he pushed his glasses up his nose. "Why you callin' me your dad? What's goin' on? I was 'bout to go to sleep. You do know it's one AM 'round my way, right?"

"Play along," TJ murmured, but it didn't matter when both Manny and Ayo had earbuds in.

"Sorry, Dad. I lost track of time," Manny answered, her breath labored. "But this is important. Was there anything on *Divination Today* about Times Square?"

"Yeah!" TJ answered. "Something about a blackout and a movie production... I wasn't really paying attention at first."

Manny shook her head. "That's not what happened. Oya was there. She did all that—or, I guess, I did all that."

TJ recalled the destruction of Times Square, all that broken glass, the people running. A sharp shiver ran down his back at the thought of what Oya had done.

"Where are you right now?" Ayo pushed his glasses up his nose. "Are you in a car?"

"Yeah, yeah. Two UCMP officers are taking me into their headquarters now. Tell *Tía* Teressa not to worry." It *did* look like Manny was in the back of a car. And her head kept jolting to what TJ assumed was the front seat.

"What's a 'tee-ya'?" Ayo asked.

"It means 'auntie' in Portuguese," TJ explained. "Well, in Spanish too." Heat rushed his face as he thought back to one of his first conversations with Manny, where he had mixed up the two languages.

"That's enough, young lady," a gruff voice said on the other end. "Just let your folks know you're all right, then hang up."

"Sorry, sir; of course, sir," Manny replied quickly.

"Wait, I'm lookin' up what happened in New York right now."

Ayo's eyes drifted somewhere off-screen. A soft light fell over his face, winking in and out. TJ caught flashing images of the Times Square destruction in his friend's glasses. "Daaayum, girl. You did all *that*?"

TJ flipped open his laptop too and searched up "blackout in Times Square." Hundreds of results popped up about New York city suing some movie production for unsafe filming conditions. Manny explained in a murmur that the story was just a cover for what really happened.

"Is that why you didn't text me back?" TJ asked.

Ayo snorted and TJ realized his voice had cracked with nervousness. Leave it to Ayo to point out TJ's shortcomings.

"What?" Manny said with a pinched brow. "Oh, right, right... yeah... all morning there had been all this weird stuff happening. First in my room with my Oya coins, then in this video store I go to... the TVs were actin' up, and they were singing a song with my name in it. Then at the farmer's market the eggplants started wigglin' around, and—"

"That's enough, Miss Martinez," that gruff voice came again. "You can speak with your parents at headquarters."

The line went dead.

"Well, that sucks," TJ said to Ayo, who filled the screen in place of Manny. "Why do you think Oya wanted to destroy Times Square like that?"

Ayo shrugged. "Maybe she's not a fan of their hotdogs. I can't even pretend I know anything about the Orishas after that stuff with Josh and Eshu."

"Is Manny gonna be in trouble?"

"Nah, she'll be fine. It's the UCMP guys who might be in trouble for allowin' her to stay on the phone for so long. Let's pull up some posts on Evo and see what's really going on."

TJ fired up his search engine again. He and Ayo went through article after article about what really happened. Many of the shady sites even mentioned Manny's full legal name, unlike the more official reports, which only used words like "alleged diviner child" and "unconfirmed youth".

After a short while, TJ thought he heard something boiling. But his bedroom was on the second floor, nowhere near the kitchen. He sat up from his desk—grabbing his phone with Ayo on his screen—and searched for the strange noise. His brief investigation led him to the shadow under his bed where a wooden bowl was hidden between his old baseball cleats and a long forgotten Star Wars Lego set.

"Uh, Ayo..." TJ said to his phone. "Are you calling me on that water bowl Adeyemi gave us after camp?"

"No," he said, his attention still locked on his research on the other end. "You should answer it, though. Adeyemi probably got an update 'bout New York."

TJ pulled the water bowl from under his bed to find bubbles materializing at its base from nothing. Then the bubbles shot up and combined like a waterfall in reverse. Slowly, a human face manifested within the murky liquid. But the image didn't show the familiar, aged face of Elder Adeyemi, but someone else...

"Dude!" TJ exclaimed, heart racing. "I think it's Manny!"

The dingy water had definitely formed around a familiar mass of hair. Even though her face was faded and rippling, TJ knew it was her.

"TJ?" Her voice came through like she was underwater. "TJ, can you hear me?"

"Oh, woah," Ayo said from TJ's phone. "Those UCMP guys let you use a water bowl?"

"Uh..." she trialed off, looking to the side. TJ only then realize she had been lowering her voice. "Not exactly."

"So what then?" TJ asked.

"They uh... sorta put me in a holding cell until my parents get here. Said my Ashe could combust or something. I'm calling from a sink in here and—" Her face turned around, and they saw nothing but her back.

"Did you just say something?" a muffled yet gruff voice came from the water bowl. It sounded the same as that officer from the car before.

"Yeah... I talk to myself sometimes," Manny lied. "Sorry, I'll keep it down."

"All right then," the man said. "I sent two of my people to locate your parents. Our files say your mom works at that Puerto Rican spot on Fifth Ave, yes?"

"Mmhm, yup," Manny answered.

"All right then. Sorry about putting you in there. Boss's orders. If you need anything, just shout."

"Will do."

Manny waited a few moments before she turned around and faced TJ and Ayo again, and, in hushed tones, said, "Sorry 'bout that, guys."

"How the hell are you using a sink!?" Ayo asked straight away. "A sink has no magical properties. And that jail cell probably has anti-magic enchantments."

"I don't know. Everything about my Ashe right now feels... different. But I can barely see y'all on the other end."

"So what happened?" TJ asked. "Did Oya try to communicate with you?" TJ was sure if this was only two months ago, he would've been joking. But ever since they crossed over to the Aqua Realm and realized one of their fellow campers was an Orisha, saying something like "Oya tried communicating with you" wasn't all that far-fetched.

"Yes, she did," Manny said. "I was walkin' back home when I *saw* her in a window."

A sharp tickle went down TJ's spine. Seeing an Orisha in their own realm was one thing, but to see them in reality, in the Mortal Realm, that must've been mad dope. And a little scary.

"You said she gave you a message for me... she spoke with you too?" TJ asked, his skin growing hot with nerves. Word must've gone around in the Orisha Plane...

"What she said was all jumbled up. I don't know what happened. One moment she was inside me, *literally* inside me, like some of the rumors other diviners are talking about. Then she said some stuff about travelin' to the Sky Realm, findin' her husband Shango, and somethin' else I've been tryin' to remember... it all happened so fast, I couldn't process everything. But she sounded worried, like, she was speakin' *mad* fast."

"She mentioned Shango!?" Now Ayo was fully awake, sitting up straight in his bed. After all, Shango was his primary Orisha alignment. "Oya didn't say nothin' else? She just lost connection real quick? Just like that?"

"I'm surprised she connected as long as she did, honestly..."

Manny trailed off, pausing a beat to peek over her shoulder. It was another moment before she turned around to indicate the all clear.

"My brother said the record someone connected with an Orisha was only a minute at most," TJ said. "Sounds like Oya was with you for, what, a whole half an hour?"

"Hold up, hold up," Ayo said. "What's this business about a movie production gone wrong and you being a child actor?"

"Mad clouded saw me, yo. I sort of... flew—you know, when Oya latched onto me and all that. But when her voice went away, I fell to the ground and hit my head. Next thing I know, I'm being carried away by dudes in baseball caps and vests. They said they were part of the UCMP, but they kept flashing those permits at the cops and saying they were shooting a movie scene."

"No way that worked," TJ said. "Too many people would've seen you... too many cameras."

"Nah, she's right." Another bright flicker fell across Ayo's face. "Damn, those UCMP officials work crazy fast. All the videos uploaded are doctored. They made it look like Manny was hung up by wires and all that."

TJ brought his laptop to the ground with his water bowl and opened a new tab on his web browser to see an article of his own. Sure enough, in a shaky cam video from someone's phone, it appeared as though Manny was part of a special effect gone wrong.

"Miss Martinez," the gruff voice came again. Manny's eyes went wide, and she twisted around again. "Do you take your coffee with sugar?"

"No, thank you!" she squeaked. Again, she waited a little while before continuing. "Okay, we gotta end this. This guy's gonna catch me."

"Okay, okay, we'll wrap it up right now. Damn... the Sky Realm, huh?" Ayo pressed a hand into his chin. "If we had to drown to get to the Aqua Realm, I can only imagine what we gotta do to get to the Sky Realm. Sky dive off Pearl Towers and hope we don't go splat?"

TJ rubbed the back of his Afro. "What does Oya even want us to do there anyway, and why?"

"All I know is that we need to find Shango," Manny said quickly in a low whisper. "That's all she could tell me, really. She said you needed to watch out for Olo... Olo..." Manny coughed on her words. She clearly wanted to say "Olokun" but her throat didn't want to cooperate. "Ah, you know who I mean — what? No, no, I didn't bring a water bowl in, sir. I'm just talkin' to myself, like I said."

It was probably smarter if Manny waited until she got home to call TJ and Ayo, but TJ knew she must've wanted to get it all out as soon as possible. Hell, if some Orisha came knocking at TJ's door, he'd call Manny straight away, too.

Manny's face completely disappeared from the hanging waterfall in his bowl. TJ could hear some rustling in the background and a deep voice, who sounded wholly unconvinced. "Let's see who you're talking to, young lady."

"It's just my parents! It's just my parents, I swear."

Before Manny could protest, a new face filled the waterfall before TJ. With Manny, he at least had an idea of what she looked like so he could fill in the gaps. With this UCMP officer, all he saw was a murky blob of a man. "Hello, this is Lieutenant Chiu. Who am I speaking with? Is this Mr. and Mrs. Martinez?"

A heavy silence hung in the air, pierced only by the slight bubbling within the water bowl. It was Ayo who spoke up first, though, clearing his throat. "Why yes, yes. My name's Mr. Martinez." He tried to deepen his voice, but it was barely passable. TJ hoped the quality of the call was garbled enough to not reveal Ayo's terrible impression.

"And Mrs. Martinez, is that you I see in this sink?" the man asked.

That was a problem.

TJ was a terrible actor, and to top it off, for the past two weeks, his voice was going through fits of cracks. Worst yet, he looked nothing like Manny's mom. Quickly, he grabbed for the first thing in reach — a t-shirt. Then he wrapped it around his head like a headscarf, took a deep breath, and put on an exaggerated falsetto. "Uh, yes, I'm Mrs. Martinez."

He could practically hear the eye roll from Ayo and Manny through the phone and bowl, respectively.

"Who is this really?" the man asked.

"Ugh!" TJ went on, trying his best not to break character. "I am so offended. This is Mrs. Martinez."

"Can you please put my daughter back on that magical bowl of yours?" Ayo added. "We are so worried."

There was a brief pause before the man said, *"Shuǐ, zǒu kāi."* Then the hanging waterfall in the bowl crashed down and disappeared, splashing TJ in the face.

That had been the first time TJ experienced a magical water phone being literally slammed into his face. He definitely preferred getting hung up on the old fashioned way.

3

HELLO, THRESHOLD, MY OLD FRIEND

"HELLO? HELLO?" TJ SAID IN HIS HORRENDOUS MOM'S VOICE as he wiped water from his face. "Are you still there, sir?"

"He hung up on you, Teej," Ayo groaned. "Remind me to never let you audition for any roles at Ifa's theater classes."

"Hey! You didn't give me a choice! I should've been Mr. Martinez! I've actually met him!"

"Yeah, yeah... whatever." Ayo waved him away on his phone screen. Now he was out of bed and sitting at his very expensive sci-fi-looking desk. "So, what are we gonna do about this Sky Realm stuff and Olokun?"

"I don't know, but we knew that stuff about Olokun already." TJ glanced at the Eshu painting on his wall, then at the tattoo symbol on his forefinger. "Wait, Eshu! Let's try and summon him. In the Aqua Realm, he said we could call him anytime, at any threshold."

"Well, shit, man. Get over to your door and try it out."

TJ propped his phone on his laptop, then placed his laptop on his desk so Ayo could still see him. He kissed his fingers, set them to his bedroom door, and prayed to Eshu. "I praise the mysteries and power of Eshu! You are the messenger of Olodumare, the Orishas, and the Ancestors. You are the owner of the four directions: North, South, East, and West. Grant me long life. Grant me peace. Grant me elevation of my consciousness.

Grant me the ability to use my own hands. Eshu, I salute you. Ashe."

"Ashe," Ayo repeated on the phone.

Nothing happened. Only the bell of the *elote* man outside TJ's window sounded off. "Spicy elote and candy!" he called out, then in Spanish he said, *"Elotes! Elotes!"*

TJ walked over and closed the window. The elote man was indeed rolling with his cart and ringing his bell like a madman. TJ couldn't concentrate with all that noise. He shuffled back over to his door and did his prayer again. This time, the elote man got even louder, like he was trying to be heard through the closed window. TJ closed his eyes and tried to concentrate hard. But no familiar voice of Eshu came, no sensation, nothing. TJ at least expected to feel some sort of rush going through his arms and legs.

"So... is something supposed to happen?" TJ asked Ayo, who was still on the screen of his phone, which was propped up on his laptop.

"What are you asking *me* for?"

"You're the expert on this Ashe and Orisha stuff. That's your whole thing in this group. I'm the battery pack, the blood. You're the CPU, the brains. And Manny's the..." TJ couldn't think of what Manny was.

"Motherboard?" Ayo offered.

"Don't ever tell her we said that."

"Deal."

TJ couldn't really tell from across the room, plus Ayo's screen was really dim, but he was almost certain the man-bun wonder was fixing him with a confused grimace. "Bruh, that's how you really think of us?"

"It sounds hella dorky when I say it out loud like that, but yeah... you're the smart one."

"First. Thanks for the compliment. Shit never gets old when this," he pointed to his forehead, "is appreciated for all its glory. Second. Yes... that's goofy. That's goofy as all hell, man."

"So..." TJ picked his phone back up, "As I was saying... what am I supposed to do here?"

Ayodeji shrugged. "I don't know, pray real hard? Look, it took us doing that whole-ass ritual to manifest Olosa at camp, but we had the power of an Orisha helpin' us."

"And... I'm an Orisha—"

"I thought they said you weren't an Orisha."

"Well, something in-between. Something similar."

It was still undecided what TJ actually was. Between the elders he encountered, the magical creatures he ran into, and the great deities themselves, no one had an answer for what was so special about him, why he was so different. A lot of the Orishas were indeed human at one point, venerated and deified after their passing. But there was no one like TJ who could do the things he did, like crossing over into the Orisha Plane and back again with his memories intact. Manny and Ayo remembered nothing from the Aqua Realm, only faint feelings and images in their dreams.

Ayodeji sighed, rubbed his eyes, and flicked on a light. His screen rocked around, showing an entire wall full of books, scrolls, and Nigerian masks. He basically had a whole-ass library off the side of his room. After a moment, he wiggled his fingers, and a book appeared in his hand.

"Elder Isola," he said to the book. "Pull up the page on Eshu rituals."

The book in his hand flipped to its table of contents and answered, "What would you like to have me read to you today, Mr. Oyelowo?"

"Uh... Eshu's offerings should work."

The pages on the book flipped and stopped near what must've been an opening chapter. Then Ayo read, "One must first ask Eshu before all other Orishas, blah blah. Eshu opens and closes all doors, blah blah. Oh! Here you go. Eshu's offerings are vices like sweets, rum, tobacco, toys, and spicy food."

"Well, that's not hard. My mom is making pepper soup right now. Gimme a second." TJ started off, but Ayo stopped him.

"That stuff ain't gonna work by itself, though. We'd need to do another big ritual and whatnot."

TJ peeked out his window and up through the clouds. "The moon will be full again in a couple more weeks. Maybe we can try something then?"

"Maybe... Ugh. But I want to talk to him right now," Ayo

groaned. "How can Eshu say all that stuff about thresholds and not give you a sign? I don't want to have to wait until we get to Ifa Academy."

"Yeah, yeah," TJ echoed Ayo's own grunt, "but what can we do right now?"

"Right. But at least now we have direction, unlike at camp." Ayo whistled long and slow before collapsing back onto his bed. "Man, and here I thought nothing could top this summer! It took us months to mess around with the Orishas. Now they're coming to *us* before term even starts."

4

A WITHERING WORRY

OYA COMMUNICATING WITH MANNY? THAT WAS MORE THAN nuts. Or maybe it was totally normal in this new world of Orishas coming up to you while you're taking an afternoon stroll. What was it like for ancient diviners, TJ wondered. Did warriors wake up for battle to consult Ogun directly before hitting the field? Did fishermen brave the seas by saying "sup" to Yemoja, who just hung out along the coast?

TJ stared at his laptop screen, still searching through all the stories about Manny. He even flipped open *Evocation*, which often had authentic information about magical goings-on, not the doctored stuff from *Divination Today*. But even *it* had nothing definitive about the "Times Square Debacle." Sure, they mentioned Manny by name a few times, but there was nothing about Oya or Shango or the Sky Realm. So TJ pulled out the wooden bowl from under his bed again, filled it with his own spirit water this time, and said the name "Elder Adeyemi."

The water in the bowl remained still. Then it occurred to TJ that it was early morning in Nigeria. Perhaps the Elder was sleeping like Ayo had been. After a few minutes, TJ was about to put his water bowl away and try again later when the liquid inside bubbled. Like a boiling pot, each burst of water shot up, and then little waterfalls in reverse sprang up until the mass of water all met as one. For TJ, each tiny eruption came with a cloud of blue mist that only he could see. Unlike other diviners, he could actually *see* the inner workings of Ashe at play as a physical thing.

Eventually, the streaks of water settled from miniature whitecaps to a clear and translucent image of a face—much more sharp than what he saw with Manny. With a slender jaw, kind eyes, and a grace that could be felt even through the water communication, Elder Adeyemi smiled that royal smile at him from the bowl. "Tomori Jomiloju. I didn't think you'd call me so soon on my personal stream."

"Sorry, ma'am. But you said I should call whenever anything happened with the Orishas. Did you hear about New York already?"

"Yes," she said calmly. "I just got into headquarters here in New Ile-Ife. It seems Manuela has had a visit from Oya, correct?"

"Yeah, and Oya had a message for me. Something about getting to the Sky Realm and speaking to Shango. Ayo and I tried calling Eshu, but nothing happened."

Adeyemi pressed her fingers to her lips thoughtfully. A long moment hung between them and TJ wondered if the water call had frozen until he noticed a wrinkle twitching on the Elder's forehead. "You've told no one of this, yes?"

"No, ma'am."

"Not even your parents?"

"No, ma'am."

"Good. Keep it that way. I'm sure your parents are trustworthy, but if we have the smallest of leaks—"

"The Keepers could know what we know."

"Exactly."

The room seemed to darken then, probably just a cloud covering the sun. But the darkness brought with it a load TJ wasn't sure he could carry. It had only been two weeks since he and Elder Adeyemi had agreed to keep information like this between the two of them, so the guilt of keeping things from his family hadn't quite settled. To avoid Adeyemi's wise eyes, TJ glanced down at his hand instead. The faint symbol of the Eshu tattoo pulsated a little.

"It's a wonder what Oya wants with you," Elder Adeyemi said. "If she says you must summon her husband, it must be most dire. The old stories say those two weren't on the best of terms before the Great Separation between the Orishas and mortals. What do you think, young one?"

TJ still wasn't used to being asked questions like this. Elder Adeyemi often treated him like an equal in conversation, rather than a student. "I don't know, ma'am. They're both associated with the sky. I was reading in one of my books that besides the Great Olodumare, Shango and Olokun are in contention for most powerful Orishas — my bad, most destructive, not most powerful."

Elder Adeyemi nodded in approval at TJ's correction. "These are my thoughts as well. Oya must not think we'll succeed, which is fair. We are only human. And Shango would be a great help. As you know from your summer studies" — her voice was accusatory — "water magic does poorly in the face of lightning."

"R-right! Right! Good point." TJ tried to play it off like he knew that already. To cover up his shaking voice, he changed the subject. "On the topic of magic… Manny called us from a sink at the New York headquarters. Ayo said she shouldn't have been able to with the anti-magic stuff in that place. Manny said her Ashe felt different."

Again, Elder Adeyemi took her time to reply. "This is not unheard of. She was mounted by Oya directly. She may have retained some of the Orisha's primal Ashe afterward. Quite dangerous. *Very* dangerous. From these reports we're going through here, it would seem Oya only connected for a few seconds. Anymore, and Manny could have gone into cardiac arrest."

TJ gulped and tried to force out the image of Manny convulsing on a New York city street and then not moving at all. To avoid the thought, he turned away from the water bowl to his laptop screen, which flashed a headline about the Keepers. Apparently Olugbala, their leader, also known as Mr. Bolawe, had said the "Times Square Debacle" was no debacle at all, but something that should be celebrated among diviners if the Orishas were trying to call out to them.

"Any news on Bolawe and the Keepers?" TJ asked, still staring at the article on his laptop.

"None yet." Elder Adeyemi frowned deeply. She always did

that when TJ brought up Bolawe. They were both deceived by him, but the betrayal cut deeper for her. TJ only knew him for a few months. Elder Adeyemi had known the man since long before TJ was even born. "That said, everyone is keeping an eye out for Olugbala and his Keepers." She rarely called Bolawe by his name these days. "Sleep well, Tomori Jomiloju. I'll see you when you touch down in Nigeria. The UCMP has us all working double on this Manuela Martinez situation."

TJ hadn't expected her to cut the conversation so short. But that had become par for the course whenever the topic of the terrorist group cropped up. TJ had noticed the subtle changes of Elder Adeyemi's tone and facial expressions, which were dismissive at best and condescending at worst.

"O-of course," TJ piped up. "Thanks for taking my call, ma'am. I'll see you soon."

With that, the water fell back into the bowl, and Elder Adeyemi's face was gone. This time TJ did *not* get splashed.

Oh, shoot, TJ thought, *I forgot to ask if Manny would be in trouble.*

Ayo said Manny would be okay, but Ayo's idea of "okay" differed greatly from TJ's. The wealthy kid might've gotten into mischief and laughed about it later, but Manny didn't have his family—or his money—backing her. TJ really hoped Manny didn't get into any trouble over calling him. In fact, he was almost certain there was a magical law about impersonating different people the way he and Ayo had… or was that only when a diviner stole someone's appearance, not just their voice? Ah, what was he thinking? His and Ayo's imitations were terrible. No one would come after them after *those* performances.

A WEEK AND A FEW DAYS WENT BY AND TJ DIDN'T GET ANY calls or visits from government officials. Maybe Elder Adeyemi had put in a good word. What worried him, however, was that there had been no calls from Manny at first. For that first week, he only got intermittent texts from Manny saying this mystical organization or that magical institution wanted to speak with her, asking a billion-and-one questions and putting her through endless tests.

It wasn't until a day before it was time to travel to Ifa Academy that TJ could have a proper face time with her. Manny showed off her school uniform—a similar long tunic as his own, though hers was wider at the bottom, not unshapely but modest enough for school. And the stripes going down her front were maroon and gold on one side for Oya, and blue with white on the other side for Yemoja.

"And my mom said she found a connecting flight through New York," TJ had said after Manny's fashion show ended on their video call. "Your flight number is 1314, yeah?"

"Yep, yep!" Manny beamed.

They spoke excitedly about their upcoming reunion late into that night, and TJ couldn't help but fall asleep with a smile when they did eventually hang up the video call—hours later.

5

A TAIL TO LOSE

THE NEXT DAY, ON THE FRIDAY MORNING OF TJ'S FLIGHT, Mom and Dad laid out a feast with one of their famous tag-team cuisines: Mom with her Nigerian fried yams, plantains, and eggs, Dad with his American oatmeal, sausage, and power smoothie.

"Sorry, the smoothies don't got no peaches in 'em," Dad apologized as he chewed away at a smokey sausage link. "There weren't none left."

Tunde pointed his fork in TJ's direction. "That's because *he* keeps eatin' them all. Gonna be better once he gets up out the house for school and I get to have some again, *finally*."

"Really, TJ?" Mom tilted her head. "I thought you hated peaches, baby."

TJ shrugged. It was true he had a new craving for the sweeter fruit lately.

"Ah, that's just a side effect of the Young growth spurt," Dad said. "Dayo gobbled up them peaches too at that age, remember?"

Mom ran her fingers through TJ's Afro with a measuring squint of her eyes. "My goodness, you might end up being the tallest of us all."

"I'm telling you," Dad said. "Boy's going to be six-two *at the least*. Too bad it's against the rules for you diviners to play in the NBA."

All diviners and other magical peoples across the world were banned from participating in professional competitions. It would be an unfair advantage when many young magic users could just float balls into a hoop from half court if they wanted to.

"Maybe we should get you onto a crossover team instead." Dad forked another link. "Your friend from New York plays that game, right?"

TJ cringed with a clench of his shoulders. Sure, crossover was fun, but he was always tripping over his awkwardly long feet.

"How about we focus on making sure he passes all his classes this year, eh?" Mom came to the rescue. "*Then* we can talk about his career as a crossover player, with his *tall* self."

TJ didn't really didn't *feel* all that tall. It was hard to, with Olokun's towering figure still looming in his mind. But soon he'd be back with his friends. Manny would know what to do about Oya, and by now, Ayo would've built out some scheme to get in contact with Eshu.

A buzz came at TJ's side. He pulled out his phone to see an update, which read:

Eko Atlantic's Doomsday in 25 weeks, 3 days, 1 hour, 4 minutes, and 5 seconds

AFTER BREAKFAST, DAD GOT BEHIND THE WHEEL AND DROVE them all to LAX. TJ was not looking forward to the actual trip to Ifa Academy. First, there was the flight to New York, which was five hours alone. Then there was the long trip between New York to Lagos, Nigeria, which was three times the distance. And apparently, once they landed, there was a multi-hour drive from Lagos to New Ile-Ife after that.

The one silver lining of it all was that TJ would travel most of the journey alongside Manny.

"What are you smiling at, simp?" Tunde asked in the seat next to TJ.

"Nothing," TJ returned as he hid his smile under a bit lip.

As they got on the highway, TJ wondered if there was an advanced placement test he could take so he could travel through portals like the adults did on their own. A glint caught TJ's eye from outside the window. A car beside them kept perfect pace with them, like, eerily perfect pace. And the driver, who wore a cap with a familiar symbol, had a camera in his thin hands. Both his hands.

TJ blinked twice, rubbed his eyes, and blinked again.

The car was driving itself, yet the man was not in some new-age self-driving car. He was in some clunker, straight out of the eighties. Unless he was some sort of mechanic who souped-up old cars with modern technology, that was definitely not a regular ol' person snooping around.

"Uh, Mom…" TJ trailed off.

Mom turned with a wide smile. "Yes, baby? Did you forget something at home? We can still go back real quick."

"No. I think… I think there's a diviner following us." TJ thumbed out his window.

Mom whipped her head in the direction of TJ's point. "What the—who is that?"

The man in the other car clicked away at his camera's shutter with no shame. Mom started to roll the window down, but it jammed a quarter way down.

"Sorry, Yejide," Dad said, "I still need to fix that."

Mom waved a dismissive hand. "Ah, no matter. *Epo pupa ìbílè mo ké pè ọ́ máa bọ̀ wá ṣọ́dọ̀ mi.*" A slimy substance coated the window magically and it slid straight down, letting in a rush of air.

"Remind me why you asked *me* to fix it in the first place again?" Dad grinned with a roll of his eyes in the rear-view mirror.

Ignoring him, Mom called out over the roar of the wind, "Who are you? What do you want? What if a clouded sees you!? You need to have your hands on the wheel, *idiot.*" Whenever Mom said "idiot" with that distinct Naija accent, it always sent chills down TJ's spine.

The man's eyes shot wide, and he put a hand to his steering wheel. Now that TJ got a better look at his hat and the design on it, he recognized it as Eshu's symbol, the same one that had been tattooed on TJ's finger.

They were on a wide street, so they had a lot of room, but with

Los Angeles traffic, that could change at any moment. Even if they were in a bumper-to-bumper jam, that might not have deterred this reporter dude.

"*The Eshu Messenger Press* just has a few questions for the boy!" the man shouted back.

"Then send us a bloody e-mail! Don't go tailing us through the streets!"

"I'm in my rights, Mrs. Young. Public spaces, public pictures."

"*Ìránù!* You also need to abide by clouded laws. And I bet that car isn't registered, is it?"

For the first time, the man lowered his camera, his expression caving with embarrassment.

"Whatchoo 'bout to do?" Dad asked as Mom spun her finger. TJ could see the Ashe of wind magic wrap its way around the steering wheel.

"I'm gonna show you how to lose a tail."

"Yes!" Tunde hopped in his seat next to TJ. "Let's go, Mom! Am I allowed to help, too? I can bust that dude's wheels! Or maybe I'll ice his breaks!"

"No, you sit back and watch your mother work."

Even if Tunde wanted to help, he wouldn't have been able to do anything. Using wind magic, Mom thrusted the car forward faster on the open road, which forced TJ, Tunde, *and* Dad back in their seats like they were on a roller coaster.

Tunde put his hands in the air. "Yes! This is so hype! Yeet his car, Mom. Yeet 'im! Yeet 'im!"

TJ could barely move his chin so he could see the car next to him matching their speed. But then, suddenly, the reporter's car slowed. TJ forced his chin to the side to see white smoke pluming from the hood of the old clunker.

Were it not for TJ's ability to see Ashe, he wouldn't have noticed the water magic that rushed through the other car's engine. The reporter certainly didn't see it coming as he banged on his steering wheel to keep his vehicle moving. After a moment of pounding as his car crawled to a snail's pace, the man pulled out a magic staff in his car and vanished the water away.

But the damage was already done.

Mom pulled away just as more traffic showed up ahead of

them. Her trick on the reporter would've worked if it wasn't for the—

"Red light! Red light!" Dad shouted in terror.

Mom shouted back, "I can beat it!"

"Run through the yellow, Mom!" Tunde punched a fist forward. "Run through the yellow!"

"There's a camera!" Dad reminded her. "We can't afford the ticket."

"Ugh!" Mom groaned, and she slammed on the brakes. Everyone got thrown forward. Invisible airbags—well, literal *air*bags in this case—saved everyone from severe whiplash. Mom was known for her water magic, but she was pretty killer with wind, too, apparently.

Very slowly, the reporter pulled up next to them, his car coughing fumes. "That was a close call there, Mrs. Young. What was that you were saying about the clouded seeing us? All those theatrics you just pulled wouldn't help your case. Pretty dangerous, wouldn't you say?"

The reporter didn't actually sound all that bothered, and TJ took that to mean he would've been safe no matter what. Mom's nose flared through the side mirror as they waited for the light to turn green.

"TJ Young," the reporter said, his camera back in his hands. "What do you know about the 'movie production' in New York last week? We just want an official comment from someone connected to the source."

The light turned green.

Even if TJ wanted to answer, he couldn't. This time, TJ jolted to the side instead of backward. Mom had forced the car down an alley. But it didn't work. The reporter was *still* right behind them, as though his engine hadn't suffered any water damage. TJ's Ashe vision flared to reveal that the reporter's car wasn't rolling along because of the engine, but because of wind magic rotating his tires forward.

"How is he still driving?" Mom gritted.

"His enginee's dead," TJ said, "but he's using Oya's wind to push him forward."

"Ugh, Moon of Yemoja, I hadn't thought of that."

"Honey," Dad asked, clutching his seatbelt, even though they were going much slower down the narrow path, "why you got us goin' down this alley?"

"So no one will see… this." Mom made a fist and then spread her fingers wide.

A loud *pop* sounded behind them. TJ and Tunde both turned to see ice spikes had lodged themselves into the man's tires, bringing the vehicle to a more definitive halt.

"That's how you lose a tail, honey." Mom gave Dad control of the car again, lifting the wind magic she had set around the steering wheel.

Dad gawked over his shoulder. "There ain't much traffic 'round here, but damn, Yejide. Someone's going to notice all that ice."

"It'll melt by the time anyone comes looking." Mom smiled and blew some frost from her fingertips. She made it look simple, but the precision of the magic she had just used was master tier. From the little reading TJ did, he knew that ice magic was hard enough on its own, let alone using it on rotating tires like that.

"Mom! Mom! Mom!" Tunde clapped with each utterance. "We gotta call you the ice queen!"

The short chase clearly left Tunde with an adrenaline rush, but TJ was more on his father's wavelength. Even after fighting against Orishas, Mom's magical rage hit a bit different, and it left TJ's stomach way back at that red light.

NOT LONG AFTER, THEY PULLED UP TO AMERICAN AIRLINES, where Mom gathered all of TJ's belongings with the speed of an eager concierge. TJ barely had time to hug Dad goodbye or throw a rebuttal back at Tunde after he said, "don't get kicked out of the academy like you did at camp" before Mom had grabbed TJ's wrist and pulled him away. He couldn't do anything but let himself be dragged along toward the terminal doors. Mom's tugging was apparently for good reason, because a woman with another one of those Eshu Messenger Press hats rushed up to them with a video camera in hand.

"Chika Ogunseye from *The Messenger Press*. TJ Young, good to see you again. Is it true your fellow 'co-star' Manuela Martinez was part of that fiasco in New York? Can you tell us what *really* happened at Times Square?"

TJ had met the woman once before. Only a few months ago, in fact, when she had spied on him in his own backyard, masquerading as living poison ivy.

"How dare you?" Mom gritted. "Here of all places, with all these clouded. You should be ashamed of yourself."

These reporters were insane, TJ thought. You lost one just to have another on your tail. How did they even know what terminal he and his family would be at?

A security guard near the sliding double doors moved forward. "Sorry, ma'am. These tabloid people do this all the time. Come on in, they can't bother you once you get through TSA."

Other travelers stopped and gawked, whispering to each other. Most of them stared straight at TJ. He thought he could make out one of them say, "oh yeah, I think he's that one kid from... from..." and then the other answered, "that one show on that thing, right?"

That was one thing about living in Los Angeles. Anyone, literally anyone, could be a celebrity. And at the moment, the crowd gathering around was convincing themselves TJ was some child star. It didn't help that the reporter kept asking questions about the "movie production" the UCMP used as a cover story for Manny and Oya in New York.

Even as the security guard ushered them into the terminal and away from the questions and crowds, a few younger kids—likely at the behest of their parents—asked TJ for his autograph. TJ got through his fourth sloppy signing and third awkward photo before Mom checked his bag and took him through TSA.

Grumbling under her breath, she said, "These reporters are playing fast and loose with the Code of Concealment. They're getting bolder every day."

TJ knew the "CoC" was a worldwide law imposed on all magical peoples, the rules and regulations about *not* showing one's magical self to the non-magical community. But the reporter had said nothing about any mystical business. Just like the "official" reports, she kept up the charade of the movie production. She never asked directly if TJ knew anything about why Manny flew a few feet in the air while shouting Oya's name at the top of her lungs.

"Did Dayo have to deal with stuff like this?" TJ asked as they approached the end of the TSA line near the metal detectors.

"Sometimes. Remember that year when that man kept slipping on wet surfaces behind us?"

How could TJ forget? That year there had been some guy who kept slipping in puddles all around the airport. An airport worker would always come and help him up, and a few moments later, the same thing would happen. Over and over again.

"Wait," TJ said, "that *was* you? You always denied it when we asked!"

"Yes, well, I didn't want your little brother getting any ideas."

"What about me?"

"You were older… and better behaved. And I'd have probably jumped out of my flats if you managed something like that back then."

That one hit TJ pretty hard. After all the craziness during the summer, he'd almost forgotten how much Mom wanted his Ashe to manifest, only to be disappointed every time. At least now he *did* have magic, so that disappointment had gone away.

"Anyway, that Chika woman is lucky that security guard came up," Mom winked, "or else I would've had a nice little puddle waiting for her, too."

6

CREEPER IN TERMINAL 4

THE FIVE-HOUR FLIGHT WAS EASY, NO REPORTERS, NO ONE asking for autographs—though one guy with a mole over his lip kept getting up to go to the bathroom, making TJ wonder, one, if he was a reporter as well, and two, how much he had to drink. The guy did nothing wrong, exactly. He didn't even look TJ's way. But TJ was on edge after the morning chase and the shenanigans at the airport.

"Don't worry yourself, honey," Mom told him when they were somewhere over Colorado. "If you can't take your mind off the coming term, you can brush up on some of your prayers. I know you still have trouble with Olokun's hymns."

TJ didn't have any trouble with those prayers, he just didn't know how he felt about empowering the Orisha through worship when he needed to figure out how to stop him. Plus, it felt like anytime he prayed, it was like Olokun could see him, reminded of the silly mortal boy who made a deal he'd never be able to keep.

"And I know you're still trying to figure out what's going on with Oya and Manuela," Mom said gently. "Don't worry yourself about that, either. Elder Adeyemi and the other councilors are sorting all that out. Your friend gave them everything she knows... unless," she nudged her shoulder into his, "there's something else we should know about?"

"No, nothing." TJ shook his head. "But yeah... studying. I

should do that. Yeah, good idea, Mom." TJ was a-okay with steering the subject in another direction. So he took out one of his schoolbooks and pretended to study the rest of the way until they landed in New York.

THEY ARRIVED AND EXITED THEIR PLANE WITHOUT SO MUCH AS a whiff of another reporter. With how persistent the ones in Los Angeles were, TJ assumed one in New York would buy a plane ticket just to get close to him and Mom, but no one came with their cameras or questions. Instead, he and Mom were met with that old-fashion New Yorker indifference from those they passed, as they made their way to the AirTrain. Mom pointed out the skyline of New York City as they transferred from the domestic terminal to the international terminal.

"Oh, a few years back there was an incident near the Statue of Liberty," she murmured to him. "Some crazy mage from France tried to bring it to life to attack the city. My cousin, who works for the UCMP branch out here, helped stop that mess."

TJ looked around to make sure no one was listening. But there was only one couple on the far end of the train, along with that same guy with the mole over his lip. Plus, Mom kept her voice very low. Even as they dipped into a tunnel, which blocked out the skyscrapers in the distance, Mom had more stories. TJ listened to keep his mind off of the nerves building in his gut as Mom described an indigenous fairy outbreak near the Brooklyn Bridge when she was a kid, and a potential zombie outbreak near Central Park that was mitigated in the nineteen-eighties, right around the time of Michael Jackson's Thriller video.

"New York goes through that kind of madness every few years. The stuff with Manuela was nothing in comparison," Mom explained as they came to a halt on the AirTrain.

The international terminal was far busier than the domestic one. Travelers zipped this way and that between the high ceilings and wide halls. Despite the large space, it didn't seem like anyone had room to maneuver with all the fancy art fixtures and vendors selling last-minute postcards. There was even a man playing a piano in the middle of one of the spacious rooms. American flags were strung up from just about every ceiling—never letting you forget which country you were in. TJ had counted his dozenth flag when a thunder of footsteps clamored behind him, followed by a very loud and stretched out, "Teee Jaaay!"

Before he knew what was going on, TJ was wrapped in a hug so tight his arms were pinned around his waist. A bundle of excitement had him locked in place, and a mass of curly hair appeared in his peripherals.

"Manny?" TJ gasped and hugged back awkwardly.

Manny let go, beaming and brushing her hair from her face. "God damn, yo! Were you always this tall?"

"It's the Young growth spurt." TJ wasn't exactly feeling confident, but a hint of smugness still edged in. A horde of butterflies was attacking his stomach at that moment. Manny was excited to see him and that made him, well... get all giddy and whatnot.

"Hello, Manuela!" Mom said with a knowing smile.

Manny gave her a small wave. "Hey, Mrs. Young. My mom and dad are—"

"Right here!" Mr. Martinez said, catching up with his daughter. A woman who must've been Mrs. Martinez followed closely behind him.

Mr. Martinez had very dark skin, which contrasted starkly against his solid white beard and hair. And even if she didn't introduce herself, TJ would've known who Mrs. Martinez was instantly. Just like Manny, she had thick coils sprouting from her head—though most of it was covered under a green and yellow headscarf.

"The moment she saw TJ, she took off," Mrs. Martinez said with bright eyes.

Mom put a hand to her heart. "Awww, how cute." Manny hid her face between her lion's mane. "Well, it's nice to see you again, Zé, and good to meet you too..."

"Renata."

"My goodness, TJ!" Mr. Martinez measured his height against TJ's own. "Are you taller than me already?"

"During the summer, Zé kept saying TJ should be in the NBA someday," Mrs. Martinez added.

Something about what she said made Mr. Martinez perk up. "Ooo... basketball. TJ, do you know why those courts are always so wet?"

TJ shrugged. He knew a dad joke was coming, though; it was Mr. Martinez's specialty. Manny's, too. And sure enough, it was Manny who finished the joke by saying, "Because the players are always... *dribbling*!"

Mrs. Martinez rolled her eyes with a smirk, but Manny and her dad laughed out loud. "I'll definitely appreciate a break from these two."

For the next few moments, as they waited for their flight to be called, the two families chit-chatted about the coming year, the business of what happened in New York, and the prospect of returning Orishas. Manny's parents were particularly interested in what Mom had to say, as they were both non-magical. TJ and Manny tried to get away so they could talk in private, but their parents kept asking them questions. It wasn't until TJ's stomach grumbled loudly that the conversation subsided.

Everyone turned to him.

TJ only realized then that his stomach growl sounded very similar to a fart.

Nervous heat snaked through TJ's neck and shoulders as he blurted, "It was my stomach, I swear!"

"A side effect of the 'Young' growth spurt?" Manny joked with a wink and a jab. Usually, that kind of laughter from a girl would make TJ feel bad. But whenever it was Manny busting his chops, he never took offense. Maybe it was the way she chuckled or something... he didn't know.

Mom pulled out her purse and handed TJ a few enchanted cowries. "Go ahead and get yourself something from the food court. But don't leave the terminal."

"Uh, Mom..." TJ eyed the magical money in her hand.

"Oh," Mom facepalmed, "so sorry, let me get you some proper money." She withdrew a few dollar bills and offered them to TJ.

"Can I go too, Ma?" Manny asked.

Mrs. and Mr. Martinez exchanged cheeky grins, then nodded yes, Manny's mom saying, "Be back in an hour before the flight leaves."

"Will do!" TJ and Manny said in unison.

Shortly after, they strolled along the tall ceiling-high windows, past the gift shops and currency exchanges until they met a long row of fast-food joints implanted neatly over the linoleum floors. Salt and processed meat slithered into TJ's nose, and his stomach grumbled loudly a second time.

Manny grimaced. "Uh oh, do I need to pinch my nose?"

"Shut up!" TJ rolled his eyes with a chuckle. "So, how are your memories coming along? Anything new?"

Manny shook her head. "Nothin'. The feelings are stronger, though. And I have a lot of dreams about my cousin. But I'm sure they'll come back, eventually. That's not important right now, though. I need to use you for something. That's why I wanted to get away. Is that okay?"

TJ spread his arms wide. "Use me as you wish."

"Good!" Her dimples sunk into her cheek. She grabbed TJ by his wrist and pulled him to a ceiling-high mirror near the food court. She and TJ only had one selfie together, one they took after camp a few weeks prior, so TJ wasn't always used to seeing them side by side. He already knew they got along great; of course they did. They took on Orishas together. But somehow, he always felt out of place when he saw them together like that. Manny was short, confident, and super cool, while TJ was tall, awkward, and super *not* cool.

"So, like I was telling you," Manny said. "I could see Oya in reflections. I've been trying to call her back again and nothing is working. But..." she said long and stretched as she leaned her forehead into TJ. It was a light touch, barely anything at all, but it sent shock waves through TJ's arm.

"But... you think my boosting powers will help?"

Manny smiled. "Yup!"

"As I said... use me away. What do I have to do?"

"Help me with the Oya prayer. We'll swap every other line. And look directly in the mirror and don't break eye contact."

"What about everyone else?" TJ glanced at the other travelers whipping by with their roller luggage trailing behind them.

"When Oya showed herself, only *I* could see her. The clouded people couldn't see anything."

TJ wasn't so sure why, but when Manny asked him to do something, he did it. Hesitantly, he said, "All right... But I don't know about this. Feels like we're calling Bloody Mary or something. If we get killed, I'm blamin' you."

"Deal." Manny nodded and started the prayer. "Oya, please guide and protect me..."

"... Open the doors of opportunity by removing obstacles from my path," TJ continued, funneling Manny's Ashe through his chest, elevating it. They continued to go back and forth with the prayer and Ashe bubbled forth from TJ's belly, solid and strong. In the mirror, the mists of Ashe cast off them like a fog.

Maybe this would actually work. Manny squeezed TJ's wrist. She could feel it too, he knew.

"I am ready for your winds of change..." Manny continued.

And TJ finished, "... That brings prosperity to our realm. Ashe."

"Ashe," Manny said.

They waited a moment with wide eyes. TJ imagined a warrior deity with a machete in one hand and a whip in the other looming over their shoulders, but no such image appeared in the mirror. As the seconds passed on, their broad expressions slackened into the dips of frowns. Just like with Eshu, nothing happened. TJ looked pretty devastated, but it was nothing compared to Manny, whose hands were balling into quivering fists.

A crowd of travelers spilled up and out from an escalator, a few of them brushing shoulders with TJ. TJ wasn't sure what to say to Manny to make her feel better. It was supposed to be up to him to make this work. But there was one thing he could do to make it all better...

"Hey, I'm walkin' over here!" TJ said jokingly to a couple speed walking by with their rolling luggage. The woman smiled a bit as she passed, but her husband or boyfriend, who was red in the face, grumbled about his distaste for JFK International.

Manny put a hand on TJ's shoulder. "Stop. No. Don't do that. Ever."

"But that's how they do it in the movies. What? Did I say it wrong?" TJ exaggerated his New Yorker accent. "Hey, hey, I'm walkin' over here!"

"Oh god…" Manny covered her face playfully. "You're not even walkin', yo."

TJ changed that and started to step off toward the food court. "I said I'm walkin' over here! I'm walkin'!"

"Real talk," Manny stepped alongside him, "you keep that up and I'm going to plug in my earbuds and act like we're not walking together."

"Oh, c'mon, I thought you liked dad jokes."

"Of course I do, but it's all in the delivery. And you…" Manny looked him up and down with judgmental eyes. "You need work."

"Fine, fine. So what do you want to eat?" TJ gazed up at the pizzeria nearby. He put on an embellished Super Mario-esque accent, then said, "You want-a piece-a pizza?"

"TJ!" This time, Manny blushed under her dimples. TJ didn't mean to *actually* embarrass her and was beginning to feel a bit guilty for his very lame attempt at being cool until she said, "If you're gonna do that, at least don't butcher it. You gotta put your hand-a up-a like a-this," she pressed her thumb into her fingers and lifted them in front of her face, "then say 'you want a-piece a-pizza.' You gotta extend your words at the end, ya know?"

Damn… she's the best, TJ thought as he caught himself staring at her — a habit he definitely needed to cut out.

"There you go again…" she trailed off, blushing and glancing to the side.

"Making it weird again?" TJ finished for her. "A'ight then, hold up. Let me make it *un*weird. So… what accents can *you* do?"

"Outside that one example? None. And don't ask me to do one."

"Oh, c'mon. I gotta teach you one, too. Let me hear your best Valley girl. After we get pizza we can, like, totes, grab a latte with caramel." TJ limped his hand and everything. "You see how I did that? You gotta make the end of each sentence sound like a question."

Manny rolled her eyes, but as they passed the cafe, she said, in a pretty terrible Cali girl accent, "I can't do latte unless it has, like, almond milk sourced from organic farms. Plus, that cafe is, like, totally basic and hella corporate. *I* only do local."

TJ sniggered. "Yeah, leave the bad impressions to me."

"Shut up! I told you I'm wack." Manny smacked TJ along his arm as they shared in their giggles. Then suddenly, Manny tensed. "Wait. Look behind us but don't look, you feel me?"

TJ, the idiot he was, peeked behind his shoulder with absolutely *no* discretion.

"Ugh, TJ! What am I gonna do with you?" Manny gritted, though she didn't turn her head, staring forward. "You see who I'm talkin' 'bout though, right?"

"I was looking for a *who*? I thought I was looking for a *what*."

"Two families behind us. Black hat. White logo. You recognize that symbol, don't you?"

TJ curled to a wall-mounted airport map and pointed. "I think the McDonald's is on the other side of the terminal. What do you think?"

Manny caught on. "Yeah, yeah, looks like it's on the north side."

As they continued their charade, TJ watched as the person described stopped with them, doing his own form of pretend as he ran his fingers through pink and purple "I Love New York" shirts hanging from a cart. He indeed wore a black hat and TJ definitely recognized the symbol on it: Eshu's symbol, the same one on his forefinger!

TJ sucked his teeth. "Ugh, it's another one of those *Eshu Press* reporters. How did you pull him out of the crowd like that?"

"Ever since I got these," Manny gestured to her front and back end, "I learned to watch out for creepers, especially in Brooklyn. Glad it's just a reporter, though."

It took all of TJ's willpower not to stare down at the "these" in question and he cleared his throat. "All right, so how do you want to play this? Circle back and tell our parents?"

"Yeah, but we can't be too obvious about it."

TJ surveyed the terminal. A large group was approaching them, foreigners being led by a guide holding up a Japanese flag. "You thinkin' what I'm thinkin'?"

"Cut through and get lost in the crowd?"

TJ nodded. "Cut through and get lost in the crowd."

"All right. Go..." Manny waited until there was a split between the ogling masses. "Now!"

TJ and Manny increased their pace, gliding through old couples and families. TJ bumped a few shoulders and said his "*sumimasens*" to the Japanese tourists. Manny split between arms and elbows like nothing. Then TJ realized she was using a subtle bit of Oya's wind magic to gently nudge people out of the way. Tired of bumping knees and getting rude looks, TJ followed behind Manny.

This was definitely going to work. There was no way their pursuer could get through the gaps they pressed between.

"TJ, through that stairwell. It'll break line of sight."

"Got it," TJ answered as Manny ducked under a vendor selling Statue of Liberty postcards and into the door leading to a musty stairwell.

When the door closed behind them, they stared out the slit of the door window to see the man trailing past them. He kept craning his neck and practically tip-toeing for a better view. Now that TJ could get a better look, he noticed a mole over the guy's lip.

"That's the same dude from my flight!" TJ whispered. "He kept goin' to the bathroom."

"Definitely another reporter. Looks like we shook him, though." Manny pointed to the man, who had turned the corner with a light jog.

"I'd say that's one to us, zero to the creeper." TJ lifted his hand for a high five.

Manny reciprocated with a loud smack. "All right, let's go straight down here. It'll take us right back to the boarding gates."

TJ hurried behind Manny, who was skipping every other step in her rush down the stairs. Then they looped around the railing and went straight for the door below. But when Manny pressed her weight into the door, it didn't move. "Shoot, it's locked."

TJ caught up, examining the wall for one of those disability push buttons. Instead, what he found was that familiar mist that came to him when Ashe was at play. The door wasn't locked; it was being frosted shut! Even before the telltale crystals of ice spidered from the door lock in reality, TJ could see it like an odd reflecting prism within the "magic space" of Ashe.

"Manny, we gotta go back!" TJ said, nerves spiking through him. "Someone's frosting the door shut."

"Stop," a meek, slightly reedy Nigerian voice came from behind. "I don't want to hurt you. I just have to tell you something."

Their pursuer stood at the top of the stairs where they had come from. His hands were out to his side, and he wasn't stepping closer. But the light rimming around him made him look like a living shadow.

"We don't know anything about a 'movie scene!'" TJ clenched his fist, ready for another of Manny's wind gusts. He needed to be ready to empower her if something went south.

"Talk to the UCMP if you want to know so bad," Manny added, her internal winds already roiling with Ashe.

"I'm not here about what happened to you at Times Square, Mrs. Martinez. And I already contacted the UCMP. They're no help. I'm here for *him*." He pointed to TJ, and Manny took a small step in front of her friend. The man spoke very quickly, like he needed to get the words out before he forgot them or something. "I just need to tell you that you should not go to Ifa Academy. You attending is only going to benefit the Keepers and what they're planning."

"Yeah? And what's that?" TJ asked, unconvinced by the story this guy was trying to sell.

"I don't know *what* they're planning exactly. I just know that they *want* you at that place, and that's enough to want you not to be there." He turned wild eyes onto Manny. "You, Oya showed herself to you, yes? I believe the Ibeji Orishas are trying to speak to me and my twin sister, too."

TJ racked his brain. The Ibeji were in reference to the twin Orishas, right? So those rumors about Orishas showing themselves, trying to reach out to diviners, were right!

"Sorry, man, but we don't know you." Manny crossed her arms. "We're not just gonna take what you say and believe you."

The young man put a hand to his heart. "My apologies. I am Dele Ogunseye, one of the writers for Evocation's top blogs: *The Third Eye*."

"*The Third Eye*?" TJ questioned. "Ogunseye? You're related to

Chika, that other reporter, aren't you? The one who invaded my backyard as poison ivy! If you work for *The Eye*, what are you doing with that hat?"

The man didn't have an answer, feeling at the symbol on his baseball cap.

Dele, if that was really his name, pulled off his hat, revealing a receding hairline despite him looking barely out of university. "W-well, y-you see, I-I used to work for *The Press* until a few years ago. The only way I could get to you was by wearing it. I was covering your sister and—"

"Save your lies," TJ cut him off. He tapped Manny on the waist as a signal of attack.

"We don't have time for this, Tomori Jomiloju. They'll be after me at any—"

A blast echoed through the stairwell and a flash filled TJ's sight. He threw his hand over his face to shield his eyes, which stung with an odd heat. When his vision cleared, the reporter, Dele, was implanted on the wall, a collection of tangled cables binding him to the concrete like a fly caught in a spider's web. TJ's heart raced as footsteps reverberated off the walls and three people dressed in navy blue uniforms raced down to secure the reporter.

"No! No! The Keepers must be stopped. The Ibeji have the golden chain. They have the golden—" A cable gagged Dele around the mouth and his shouts became muffled grunts.

"Sorry about that, Mr. Young," one of the uniformed people, a man with a thick beard and thicker dreadlocks, said. His accent sounded a little weird, like a mix of Nigerian and British tonalities. "Name's Johnson. Captain Windell Johnson of the UCMP security force. Apologies we didn't get here sooner."

TJ frowned. How'd they know to get there at all? Wait, was he being monitored? He wasn't so sure how he felt about that. No, wait, he *did* know how he felt about that. He didn't like it!

"Is the UCMP following me?" TJ asked, watching as the officers held back the struggling Dele.

Captain Johnson murmured, "*Ọ̀pá mi wá sọ́dọ̀ mi,*" and an iron staff manifested in his hand. The large man generated a portal made of fire at the top of the stair landing. "Of course we are monitoring you, young man," he said matter of factly.

"These are the same uniforms that picked me up at Times Square," Manny murmured at TJ's side.

Captain Johnson raised his eyebrows at Manny. "Ah, yes, Miss Martinez. You gave Lieutenant Chiu quite the headache with that." The Captain waved his staff and the fire portal winked out of existence after his cohorts and the reporter stepped through. "I'm not supposed to ask, but... how did it feel... seeing Oya like that?"

"Um..." Manny exchanged an uncertain look with TJ. "It was... um... weird."

"Of course, of course. Excuse the curiosity. Please don't tell my Deputy Chief. It's been so long since someone had a connection like that. Anyway, we need to get you back to your parents. Your flight just called for boarding two minutes ago."

7

TWO PEAS, ONE POD

EVEN AS MOM SMOTHERED HIM IN KISSES, EVEN AS MR. AND Mrs. Martinez kept asking if he was okay, TJ couldn't stop thinking about what that reporter had told them. So the Keepers *wanted* him to go to Ifa Academy? Why? How could that benefit them and whatever plans they had? Did they have someone on the inside like Bolawe and they were just waiting for TJ to show up?

"Everything is all right," Captain Johnson had said. Before coming out of the stairwell, he'd changed his clothes to look like a regular traveler, Hawaiian shirt with dad jeans and all. "We were right there."

"Please," Mom had said, "send Elder Adeyemi our regards."

"Of course, ma'am." He bowed, his dreadlocks falling over his face.

"Mom..." TJ got in when he had enough space to breathe. "Mom, I gotta tell Elder Adeyemi what happened. That reporter, that Dele guy, he said the Keepers wanted me to go to Ifa Academy. That they'd stop at nothing to get me there. Does that mean it won't be safe?"

"Keepers? Those radicals from Nigeria?" Mr. Martinez asked as he got done smothering Manny.

"But... nothing could breach the academy," Mrs. Martinez

insisted with hesitation. "That's what my sister — she's a diviner, too — that's what she said about the place."

"She's right. It's impenetrable," Mom added firmly, staring TJ in the eye.

Despite everyone's reassuring words, Mr. Martinez held to a more skeptical expression. So they all turned their shoulders to Captain Johnson, who said, "Yes, Ifa Academy is locked down tight. The Keepers couldn't do anything to it or you, Mr. Young, even if they tried. Besides..." He leaned in close, his baritone deeper for it. "I have it on good authority that that 'reporter' might be associated with the Keepers... trying to keep you two students away from the academy."

"Last call for flight thirteen-fourteen," the flight attendant called out. "Last call for flight thirteen-fourteen."

TJ and Manny's parents said their final thank-yous to Captain Johnson. The UCMP official bowed again and took his leave down the terminal. TJ watched him depart as travelers crossed between them. Eventually, he disappeared into the masses, and TJ suspected he hadn't simply gotten lost in the crowd.

As everyone gathered their belongings, Manny whispered, "You really think that reporter was telling the truth?"

"It doesn't matter. What we gotta do is get in contact with Eshu. He'll know what to do. He might even know the truth about what's going on with the Keepers."

"How's that been going?"

"Not great, I'll tell you about it later," TJ hushed her, since their parents were waiting for them just feet away. TJ and Manny followed their parents to the end of the boarding line. TJ couldn't help looking over his shoulder for another *Eshu Messenger* reporter to pop up. When their parents showed their tickets to the flight attendant, TJ murmured to Manny, "Communicating with Eshu has been just as bad as us doing that whole Bloody Mary thing with Oya. Eshu said to call him at any threshold, but I'm getting a whole lotta nothin' whenever I pray to him under my doorframes at home."

After a few moments, they passed the threshold of the airplane. Like always, TJ said a short prayer to Eshu but was met with absolutely nothing. And it was hard to listen to the call of an

Orisha when a flight attendant behind him kept reminding an older guy that while there was no smoking on the flight, liquor would be available to travelers.

"You'd think I'd at least *feel* something, right?" TJ murmured to Manny. "What if Eshu's in trouble? Like you were saying, Oya sounded scared before she went quiet in your head."

"Maybe..." She lifted her shoulders sheepishly. "No way of knowing, really."

"Maybe we just gotta find another lagoon and some giant alligators to help us drown in it."

Manny rolled her eyes. "Ugh, let's *never* do that again, can we?"

MANNY AND TJ SAT TOGETHER IN A TWO-SEAT SETUP ON ONE side of the cabin while their parents sat in the three-seat middle aisle. TJ had offered Manny the window seat but she just said, "You take it. My bladder is mad tiny, so I gotta always take the aisle seat."

The pre-flight wasn't long, and despite the pressing heft of Keepers, reporters, and Orishas on TJ's mind, he was surprisingly at ease as he and Manny fell into casual conversation while they waited. Twenty minutes in and the plane was lifting off, TJ's spirits right along with it. And the farther they traveled from New York, the more distance the whole ordeal in the stairwell seemed to go. TJ wondered if it was because he was actively trying to forget his troubles or because, at the end of the day, there wasn't much he could do about them. More likely than that, his stress had evaporated because his arm was totally brushing against Manny's—and she didn't seem to mind it.

"Ugh!" Manny said suddenly, two hours into their eleven-and-a-half-hour flight. "This is why you always scroll to the last page." Her finger brushed over the screen lodged in the seat ahead of them. It landed on a movie poster of a teenage girl between a hairy-chested dude and a pale-as-paste dude. "Perfect! This is actually the prequel that went straight to streaming instead of theaters."

A groan pulsed under TJ's tone. "That's not that vampire-werewolf *Blood Moon* stuff, is it?"

"You betcha bottom dollar it is. And we're gonna watch it. Now." Manny took out her earbuds and shared one with TJ. The wire was a little short, so they had to lean in close, which meant their cheeks brushed against each other, not just their arms. If the price for watching a bad movie was to be *this* close to Manny... TJ would pay the fee—and add a tip if he could.

To TJ's surprise, the movie wasn't all that bad. Well, correction. It was complete garbage, but so bad it was good, even funny. At first, Manny took offense at the little chuckles TJ let loose whenever the lead actress acted as though she was coming up for air between each of her lines, or anytime a dramatic zoom pushed into a character's face after a reveal—not unlike Mom's Nolly-wood movies—but after a while, Manny too was laughing along-side TJ. And by the end of the movie, they were straight up whooping and hollering, which earned them a few side-eyes and a "be quiet" from Mom.

All their laughing had left Manny drained, it seemed. Once the movie ended, they started another one, a nature documentary that put Manny straight to sleep. But instead of leaning her head to the right toward their parents, her chin seemed to magnetize to TJ's shoulder.

To say TJ locked up like stone was an understatement. He was stiller than still. His heart forgot to beat. And breathing was put straight on pause. How the hell did he find himself in that position? More than that... why did it feel so right? TJ would've thought he'd be freaking out about his bony shoulder, but Manny's pillow of a head made it feel like a cloud had decided to rest on him. There was no stress at all, besides trying not to wake her up.

TJ had never seen Manny sleeping before. She looked so peaceful with her mouth slightly parted and a light snore escaping her lips. It was a sight he could get *very* much used to.

A shutter sounded to TJ's right. He lifted his chin slowly to find Mom sneaking a photo on her phone. TJ gritted his teeth and gave her a silent, "Stop it!"

She didn't, of course.

She just snapped away, smiling proudly all the while. She even bumped Manny's parents' shoulders and showed them the photos she had taken. Mr. Martinez scrunched his face up, looking a bit bothered, but Mrs. Martinez covered her mouth and TJ could hear a muffled "awww."

Moms always seemed to love TJ. He figured they thought he was non-threatening and too sweet to do anything with their daughters, mostly because he was generally quiet and kept to himself. They were unfortunately correct, though. TJ's first and last kiss was back in first grade, and that was only because they were playing "house" at recess. It wasn't like he wasn't interested in girls; he was. It was just scary, opening up and being all vulnerable with someone like that.

But as he looked down at the girl sleeping on his shoulder, TJ decided... This year... this year he would change that. Manny was worth taking the chance for.

8

GATEKEEPER, WHERE YOU AT?

HOURS LATER, JUST OUTSIDE TJ'S WINDOW, EKO ATLANTIC stared up at him. Shining skyscrapers jutted from below like giant metal fingers reaching up to bring their plane down. Despite its gleaming glory and colossal structures, it still didn't compare to Olokun, who was taller than their tallest building by a good long way. For a moment, TJ imagined a scene from *Rampage*, an old arcade game his father always drifted to whenever they visited the Santa Monica Pier. In that game, characters like a King Kong-esque gorilla or a Godzilla-like dinosaur thrashed sky-high buildings with reckless abandon. Is that what would happen here? TJ desperately hoped not.

"This is your captain speaking. We are now arriving at Murtala Muhammed International."

A tightness curled through TJ's neck, down his body, and straight to his stomach.

Overpromise and under deliver, he thought solemnly. He withdrew his phone from his pocket, opened his countdown app, and read:

Eko Atlantic's Doomsday in 23 weeks, 1 day, 22 hours, 2 minutes, and 10 seconds

Oya must've had some sort of plan. Why else would she have a message for him? What could the plan be, though? Eshu was probably on good terms with her. He'd know what to do. TJ just had to find some way to reach him.

"Damn, that's it, huh?" Manny yawned at his side. "It's not like seein' the pictures online. Them towers are *stupid* huge."

Manny quieted down when TJ didn't answer straight away. Then she tried to lighten the mood by quoting god-awful scenes from the *Dusk of the Blood Moon* prequel, which only earned half a chuckle from TJ.

It had been a long while since TJ had been in Lagos—at least four or five years—and he could barely remember it from back then. One thing that always got him was that he was no longer a minority once he stepped foot on Nigerian soil. Not visually, anyway. As an American, he was as foreign as it got, but it was a different kind of feeling. In this country, he at least *looked* like everyone else.

Mom smiled whenever he mentioned that. "Trust me, you and your dad stand out like a pair of sore thumbs."

Another thing he was reminded of as they got their luggage, hopped in a cab, and rolled through the busy streets was that, unlike Los Angeles, there weren't a lot of homeless people in the traditional sense. There weren't a lot of folks asking for handouts, anyway. Instead, they were looking to work a hustle in one way or another, selling merchandise, shining shoes, or leading unsanctioned tours. TJ even saw some kids straight out of school selling food on street corners. But no begging.

The streets of Lagos were a mix of pedestrians, motorcycles, bikes, buses, and cars, all sharing the same street. Bright, traditional fabrics for sale lined the corners. Many of the people wore traditional clothing too, though others wore western-style shirts and jeans. Spices filled the air and TJ's nose, especially as their cab passed by the food stalls.

"That's the Naija Hustle," Mom said in his ear as they pulled into Oshodi Bus Terminal. A huddle of other locals surrounded the modern-looking building, shouting for fares and destinations. The place was large, with tall windows and slanted angles sticking out among the unpaved and litter-ridden roads surrounding it. That looming reminder of Eko Atlantic backdropped the whole of it in the distance.

Their taxi pulled into the thick concrete structure. Two adults wearing traditional aso oke stopped the vehicle and said they would "take it from here." The taxi driver got his pay, headed out, and the whole group was led into a private part of the terminal. TJ knew it had to be private because the moment they passed into the area, he saw a few kids tossing fireballs to one another like they were warming up for a baseball game.

"Yo! TJ! Manny!" It was Ayo. He called out from beside a collection of yellow buses parked near concrete pillars. He jogged over to them, and a new hairdo bounced with him: loose box braids falling down the sides of his face instead of up in his typical man-bun. Two kids with Ifa Academy uniforms rushed by, scuffing Ayo's white sneakers.

"Dang it, man!" he shouted. "Watch where you're goin'! You know how much these cost?" The kids just continued to chase each other through the buses until one chaperone grabbed them both by the collars.

"Sup, Ayooo!" Manny cupped her hands and stretched out the end of the boy's name. "I don't know, the dirt mark's an improvement to them ugly ol' Jays."

Ayo waved her away with a long sucking of his teeth. Now that he was back on his home turf, his Nigerian accent seemed to be returning a bit. Though his attempt at a Black urban dialect still dictated his cadence. "It's 'eye-yo', not 'a-yo.' But sure, nice to see you, too, *Manuela*."

"Just givin' your name a little extra *sabor*."

"Oh! Let me get that for you real quick." TJ kneeled to Ayo's Jordans and sunk into his Ashe. Usually, TJ would *not* volunteer to clean someone else's shoes, especially someone as rich as Ayo, but he was excited to use any kind of magic now that he was among other diviners. All around him, kids were sharing new spells they learned. One student wrapped his entire arm with water, then drowned it with fire, which swallowed his arm in a plume of smoke. Another student, a girl with bright red hair, had a talking raven on her shoulder. And some older students were showing off their new staffs.

Concentrating on his own task, TJ focused on the dirt caking Ayo's shoes. His vision alighted and he could see what magic could clean up the mark, a charm he learned in one of his books. The more he understood the magic at play, the nuances of mystical energy, the better he could boost his Ashe.

"*Ìdọti pínyà lára bàtà*," TJ murmured and he parted the dirt particles from the white rubber of Ayo's shoes. In just thirty seconds flat, Ayo's Jordans were as good as new.

Ayo dusted his sneakers. "Dang, TJ, look at you bustin' out that li'l Oko charm."

"Always the tone of surprise. You do know I got accepted to Ifa Academy too, right?"

"Yeah, I'm still trying to work out how that happened when you didn't even rank in the top twenty at camp."

TJ knew Ayo only meant it in jest, but he couldn't help the pang of guilt that sliced through him at the words, the doubt that he didn't belong at such an elite school alongside his friends. Manny came to his defense, though, saying, "If going to the Aqua Realm and surviving isn't enough to get TJ in, I don't know what is."

"It's gonna be great when our memories are back," Ayo said. "My personal healer said it can take as long as a year, though he can't be sure. Before us, no one has come out of the Aqua Realm without being crazy and shit. Maybe that's for the best. Every time TJ talks about his fight with Olo… Olo…" Ayo coughed like something was stuck in his throat. "Oof, somethin' went down the wrong pipe."

"Aqua Realm or not," a deep woman's voice came from behind, "Ashe is not allowed to be used in this terminal."

TJ seized up with fear. Were they really speaking that loudly? They all turned to see a familiar face approaching them, a woman with muscles so big—particularly in her legs—she looked more like a warrior goddess than a regular woman. It looked like she was actually *bigger* than when they had last seen her at Camp Olosa.

"Miss Gravés?" TJ's eyes widened. "What are you doing here?"

"I was offered a position for the JSS-level *Ere Ìdaraya* training." She crossed her toned arms. "But don't go changing the subject. Ifa might have locked down this terminal for the academy, but you should still refrain from using magic until we get to New Ile-Ife." TJ peered around at the other students to say they were all doing the same, but it seemed like other adults were telling them to calm it down, too. "That said, good charm work, Mr. Young. Very efficient. Anyway, I came over to tell you all your bus assignments. Mr. Young, Mr. Oyelowo, you will be on the bus marked for JS3 Boys. Miss Martinez, you will be on the bus marked for JS2 Girls."

"Can't I go with Ayo and TJ, Miss Gravés?" Manny whined. "Splitting up the boys and girls is so dated."

"It's tradition here in Nigeria, young lady."

"But boys and girls aren't separated in classes or anywhere else."

"You can take it up with the school board."

"I have! They don't answer my calls, like, ever. I can talk to some other boys, too, Miss G, I promise. Please, please! Can I go on the other bus?"

"Sorry, kid. We'll be leaving in a half-hour. We're just waiting for two more groups to get in from late flights." And with that, she walked off to check in with a younger group of children who had started up a magical version of rock-paper-scissors, which, by the looks of it, involved the elements of water, fire, earth, and air instead.

"It's all good, Manny," Ayo said. "The drive is *only* four hours total. We'll catch up at the rest stop. By the way, y'all figure out what's what with Eshu or Oya?"

TJ shook his head. "Nothing. But I just got a new idea." His eyes tracked with Miss Gravés. "It's sort of convenient that the drill sergeant is working at Ifa, right?"

Manny caught on quick, her eyebrows lifting. "Just like Bolawe at camp…"

"No, way. Miss G?" Ayo adjusted his glasses in an exaggerated fashion. "Never. You think she's a Keeper, too, or something?"

"Who's that she's talking to now?" TJ nodded to the woman, who, after breaking up the kids, transitioned to a conversation with a man who was aggressively bald, including his eyebrows. He must've been a parent, but unlike the other adults bringing their kids in with a smile, the man didn't seem to know how to do anything but grimace. Creepy look or not, it was the way the two of them leaned in close and glanced over their shoulders as they spoke to one another that did it for TJ.

"Mr. Bolaji?" Ayo asked with a tilt of his head that made his braids fall to his shoulder. "Yeah, he's kind of weird... but a Keeper? Nah. The reason he don't got no eyebrows is because he's a terrible alchemist. Burned them off when he was a student, according to his family. The Keepers would never recruit someone as incompetent as him."

"Yeah, yeah, but it's more to it than that." TJ pulled Ayo to a more quiet corner of the terminal near a huge abstract statue of some amorphous blob. Manny watched their backs to make sure no one followed them. "On the way here, we ran into this reporter who cornered us at the airport. He told us the Keepers *wanted* me to go to Ifa this year. Maybe it's because they have Gravés looking after me like they did with Bolawe."

"Which makes contacting Eshu all the more important," Manny added.

"Yeah, but how?" Ayo asked. "We have the full moon coming soon, but no way to get through to Eshu."

"Well," Manny cleared her throat. "We're headed to *the* best place to research all that, right?"

ONCE THE LAST OF THE STRAGGLERS MADE THEIR WAY TO THE terminal, all the students loaded up and headed off for New Ile-Ife. Mom had attacked TJ with another pecking of kisses but reminded him she'd be with grandma for a week and she'd see TJ once the buses arrived at New Ile-Ife. Like the other diviners, she went into a private room to portal travel straight to the diviner town—Mr. and Mrs. Martinez headed off with Mom as well. Some of the older students complained that they should've been allowed to portal travel as well—not wanting to go through the long drive, but instructors kept reminding them the trip on the bus was meant to be a bonding experience.

Manny had looked a bit down, a step away from all the other

girls who were assigned to her bus. TJ must've appeared much the same, as he was assigned at the back of the bus with the other students he didn't know. The students with last names ending in X, Y, and Z, which included him as Young, two other boys whose family names were Zakariya and Zainab, and the quiet boy who sat next to TJ whose family name was Yemisi. The boy next to him had very high cheekbones, not unlike Dayo's best friend from Ifa Academy, Adeola. For a moment, TJ wondered how Adeola was doing. Last he saw of her, he blasted her with a pretty strong spell that sent her to the hospital. But to be fair, he thought she was the bad guy. Babalu-Aye Medical was in New Ile-Ife. Maybe he could visit her when he had time off from schoolwork.

The bus started up and TJ glanced back at his seat partner. The quiet boy with the cheekbones kept mostly to himself, so TJ did the same as they pulled out of Oshodi Terminal and toward the long city highways. TJ was still getting used to all the signs reading kilometers instead of miles.

Ayo was a few seats ahead of TJ, and he kept looking over his shoulder to make sure TJ was all right. They quickly left behind the bustle of the city. The landscape changed from a concrete jungle with newer cars and Western imports to the more rural vehicles and broken-down buses that frequented the outer country. The lanes got smaller too and some of the roads were unpaved, making for a less than comfortable ride. When the landscape flattened out to long stretches of brush, the boy next to TJ waved at him.

"Hey, how are you? I'm TJ."

The boy didn't respond. Instead, he gestured his hands and mumbled. For a moment, TJ thought he was signing. There were a few phrases he knew in ASL—American Sign Language—but he recognized nothing the boy was gesturing. Then TJ remembered. It was likely the boy was trying to communicate in YSL—Yoruba Sign Language.

When the boy recognized TJ's confusion, he lifted a finger and pulled out his phone. He typed a few lines on his keyboard and handed the phone to TJ. The screen read:

Emeka: my name's Emeka. sorry, im deaf. u're american right?

TJ laughed a little, thinking of his mother and the "sore thumbs" he and Dad apparently were in the country. Was it really *that* obvious?

He typed in his response.

TJ: how can you tell?
Emeka: u came in from the airport with that girl with the big hair.
TJ: oh right. that makes sense. my name's TJ btw. short for tomori jomiloju
Emeka: i bet everyone messes up your name where ur from huh? my best friend is american too. he didnt get accepted back to ifa tho. said his grades werent good enough 😔
TJ: im sorry to hear that. is ifa really that hard?
Emeka: yeah if you dont study. and this year we have the JS3 exit exams to see if we can advance to SS.
TJ: ss... that's senior secondary school yea?
Emeka: yeah, o right... american. you call it high school or um... 10th grade, eh?
TJ: thats right
Emeka: dont worry about the tests. there's loads of study methods. i'll show you a few.

TJ didn't have much time to think about tests or actual school work. Not when he needed to figure out how to get to the Sky Realm or speak to Eshu. There had to be something he was doing wrong when trying to speak to the Gatekeeper. Then again, up until that summer, no one could speak to Orishas, so maybe it was business as usual?

"All right, boys, we are officially in diviner territory once we pass that nature reserve sign just there." The bus driver pointed to a weathered signpost at the edge of the highway hours later. It sounded like his voice was playing over a loudspeaker on the bus, but there were no speakers fitted in the vehicle. Even if the driver didn't make the announcement, TJ would've recognized they were in New Ile-Ife territory. A slight rush passed over his neck as the bus bumped across the rocky road. The sparse treeline view in the windows thickened into dense forest. Not only did he feel it, he saw it, too. A huge mist covered the land like a force field bubble, large enough to cover a mountain range.

"Last stretch. Just an hour and a half more. Before we go any farther, though," the driver slowed behind the other line of buses, "you kids should relieve yourselves."

TJ turned to Emeka and typed into his phone again.

TJ: did you get all that?
Emeka: yea this driver is telepathic so he doubles his words in my head. thanks for asking tho

They all got out and stretched under the orange hue of the setting sun. Some adults were asking the students to huddle together near a set of shacks that must've housed the restrooms. The rickety structures appeared as though they could tip over by the slightest touch of Oya's wind, and TJ didn't want to get caught with his pants down if that happened.

A woman with short hair and wide hips bellowed, "Students, before you all take your restroom breaks, everyone circle up so we can pray to Eshu for allowing us a safe journey."

Some of the students grumbled. Emeka went over to a girl with long braids down her back. He gave her a big hug and a kiss on the cheek. They held hands as they did their prayer to Eshu. A mass of bushy hair jumped up and down between the JS girls buses coming in, and TJ realized Manny was waving and pointing to the crowd.

Then it hit TJ.

The chant! I can use the chant to summon Eshu!

The rest of the masses all came together in the field and chanted in unison. There had to be at least one-hundred-fifty of them in that field and TJ could actively feel the energy they stirred in their hymn, even if a majority of the participants were halfway to the bathroom. As he had learned that summer, he pulled on the Ashe swimming among the group, letting it funnel through him and out again with renewed strength. To TJ, the experience was like eating a full meal after a whole day of being famished. It was like being given a sugar rush and his brain was lit with more power than it had any right to have.

Like all the other times... nothing actually happened. But this time, TJ felt something rock deep within himself.

Something was there, and that something was watching him, watching all of them; he knew it. Yet there was no sign in the clouds or some magical tree that spoke a message. TJ wasn't sure what he was expecting, but he was hoping for something more than that.

The chant finally ended and all the students scattered to the first available restrooms. When it was TJ's turn to go, he was already thinking up new ways he could get a group together to stir up the magic again for another try. Maybe that Emeka would help them, too. He didn't have to know they were calling Eshu. He, Ayo, and Manny could just play up that they were really into the Orisha.

The bone-white tattoo on TJ's forefinger grew warmer. That had to mean he was on the right track. He just needed to figure out the correct ritual or the right offering to get Eshu to show himself.

He didn't have to do any of that, though. Because once he got done washing his hands, Eshu was beaming at him through the reflection of the restroom mirror.

9

TWO-WAY MIRROR

TJ RUBBED HIS EYES AND HIT HIS ELBOWS ON THE WOODEN walls of the small shanty restroom. He wasn't sure he could believe what he was seeing. But after the dozenth rubbing of his eyes, he couldn't deny it.

Eshu was right there.

The Orisha beamed from the other side of the dingy mirror, waving his wooden staff in the air. It looked like he was saying "Hello, TJ," but TJ couldn't be sure. Eshu's lips moved, but no voice came out.

TJ became breathless. A lightness filled his chest. Weeks of trying to call to Eshu, and there he was, with his drooping, long hat, wide smile, and wooden staff in hand—a staff TJ knew all too well. Well, not exactly *well*. When he used it that summer, it had looked like his sister's staff, as Eshu had mimicked the design to cloak the true form of the trickster staff.

"H-How... How are you doing this?" TJ managed to ask in a hushed voice.

Eshu snapped his fingers and a flame birthed from their tips. Then he flicked his staff and a fountain of water sprouted from it. He stood there for a moment, as though waiting for TJ to do something.

Throwing up an eyebrow, TJ uttered, "I don't get it."

Eshu nearly rolled his eyes and nodded to the sink in front of TJ.

"Oh, you want me to turn the sink on?" TJ asked, already flipping up the faucet handle. He waited for something to happen. Perhaps Eshu's face would sprout in the liquid like a water bowl communication. But the water kept running like normal.

Eshu waved for TJ's attention again, this time rubbing his fingers together where his flame danced.

"Oh, right! The fire!" TJ snapped his fingers and birthed a flame of his own. It took a moment for the heat to do its work, but eventually, the mixing of fire and water manifested steam. A few moments after that, and the mirror fogged up. Eshu smiled, then put his finger to the glass and wrote a message:

You worked that out pretty fast, kid.

"Eshu! I've been trying to contact you for *weeks*." TJ's mouth flew a mile a minute. "You know, you could have done a better job of telling me how to contact you. All you said was go to a threshold and pray. I thought I woulda heard your voice, or you woulda given me a sign or —"

Eshu flipped his drooping hat over his shoulder, then more writing appeared on the foggy mirror:

I did give you signs.

The words disappeared and reappeared.

That man with the spicy corn cart outside your house.
You know Eshu loves spicy foods.

TJ shut his eyes, giving himself an internal facepalm. He should have known then and there. Ayo had even read off Eshu's offerings when they were trying to figure it out. How could he be so stupid?

Again, more words appeared on the mirror.

And on that airplane...

... I thought that stuff...
... about cigarettes and liquor...
... would've tipped you off.
Come on, TJ.
You gotta be sharper than that.

TJ sighed. "Okay, that's fair, but a little subtle, don't you think? Why didn't you pull the mirror trick when I was in my bathroom at home? I spoke to you then at least three times a day."

Had to learn this method from an old friend...
... who was a little tight-lipped with their secrets.
Ashe flows differently these days...
... didn't know about this neat trick before.
But it is quite fickle.
We've only got a few minutes at most.

That was probably true. Already Eshu seemed a bit more faded than he had before. Good thing he wrote out his messages quickly. He was wiping them away and redrawing them like a master of that old etch-a-sketch toy. *And* he had to write backward on top of it.

Must've been nice being a powerful Orisha.

So, what's going on?
This about the big day in February with Olokun.
Yes?

TJ leaned forward, slumping his weight against the sink again as Eshu's latest words wiped away. "I saw Eko Atlantic with my own eyes. There's *no* way all those skyscrapers are coming down by February. And there are *so* many people there. How can I keep them all safe?"

Before you get yourself all worried about the big stuff...
... Make good on your first promise.
It's a lot smaller.

"You mean regaining Olokun's praise? I haven't thought about that much yet. But that should be easy, right?"

Easier, not easy.
How long did it take for us to communicate?
It took all those students out there...
... to give us enough Ashe to do what we're doing now.
Olokun needs many more.

"Ugh... some help you are. This is never going to work, then!" TJ slammed his hands on the sink. This was a lot of stress to manage and it didn't help that the restroom had essentially turned into a sauna with all the steam. "I should have just let those merpeople stick me with their tridents."

Come on, kid.
You can make it happen.
Listen, this might not work...
... but there's something we can try.
Have you heard of Yemoja's Lost Gemstone?

TJ searched his brain. He knew Yemoja was the mother to several Orishas, wife to Olokun, and the overseer of the ocean's surface. But he had only cracked open the first few chapters of his books. He wasn't sure he'd heard of any lost gemstone before though, so he shook his head.

Olokun wants Yemoja's power back, too.

"That wasn't part of our deal." TJ gripped the sides of the sink tighter.

This is true.
But we must keep the ol' grump happy now.
Mustn't we?
Helping the wife out would be a good first step.

TJ didn't like it and had the feeling he was being finessed, but what other choice did he have? "Fine, what's this 'Lost Gemstone' anyway?"

Before the Great Separation…
… Yemoja was building a new Frost Realm.
It went unfinished, and she left behind…

"Let me guess," TJ finished before Eshu got done writing the rest of his message. "This gemstone of hers, right?"

Right on the money.
Ever since she left it behind…
… Her ice magic hasn't been up to snuff.
She's been so sad.
Olokun wants nothing more…
… than to make her happy again.

"Is that the reason ice caps have been melting?"

They were melting well before that…
But you mortals have…
… sure as hell sped things along.

"But what about the Sky Realm? I don't know if you know, but Oya showed herself to Manny. Said something about us going to the Sky Realm and speaking to Shango."

Oh, Oya's always got her head in the clouds.

TJ couldn't be sure in the fog but it seemed as though Eshu was stroking the crystal in his staff.

And she's busy during September.
Stirring up all those hurricanes…
… off the Atlantic coast this time of year.

That much was true. TJ remembered how on the clouded news they always talked about East Coast cities having to board up their storefronts to protect themselves against horrible winds and cyclones.

A pounding came at the rickety bathroom door, followed by a thick Nigerian Pidgin, *"I wan shit. Guy, why you dey wasted time."* The cracks in the bathroom were just large enough where TJ could see a brown eye peeking through.

"Yo, step off and give me a minute," TJ returned sharply. "I been holdin' it a while."

Eshu started to fade even more in the mirror, winking out like a dying light.

"Oh crud, we don't have much time left, do we?" TJ lowered his voice. "Okay, okay. I'll go to this Frost Realm. But are you coming with me? How do I even find it?" TJ imagined himself having to trek through Antarctica until he fell over with frostbite.

Somewhere in your world, there's a doorway...
... in the shape of an Ice Shard.
And since the Realm went unfinished...
... no deity can enter it.
But since you have your...
... little trick, then maybe...

"Okay, okay. I know what you're getting at." TJ rolled his eyes. That summer Eshu had essentially tricked TJ into being a key to unlock a portal between the Mortal and Aqua Realms. Perhaps that was the same thing TJ had to do now but for this unfinished Frost Realm. "Can you at least point me in the right direction here... Earth might not look so big to you, but for us mortals it's a pretty large place to search and I'm kind of stuck at the academy."

This was many, many centuries ago.
But look to the UK.
They keep all sorts of...
... neat stuff over there.

"I'll ask Elder Adeyemi. She's connected to our magical

government over here. Maybe she can get some of her people on it or something. Are you sure this will make Olokun happy?"

"*Guy, why you dey talk to yourself?*" the boy outside asked.

TJ clenched his fist. He forgot to keep his voice down. "I'm almost done. I... uh... need to psych myself up sometimes."

"What's a 'psych,'" the boy asked in Nigerian-accented English this time.

"Uh, never mind. I'm almost done." TJ turned back to Eshu. The staff in the Orisha's hand shook like it was trying to get away from him. "Olosa's gonna get big mad with you when she gets out of that thing, huh?"

Olosa?

"She's still in the staff, right?"

Oh, right!
Yes, not looking forward to that meeting.

"Well, at least we have the start of a plan. I'll start gathering support in New Ile-Ife." TJ leaned in closer to the staff. "We'll get you out soon, Olosa. Sorry we trapped you in there."

Eshu saluted TJ with his staff and disappeared. When TJ finally cut off the faucet and made his way out, the boy who had been waiting for him shoved him in the shoulder. "Took you long enough, guy."

"Sorry, man. I left it nice and warm for you, though." TJ tried for a friendly smile. It was true. He was sweating bullets. What would the boy think, though, that TJ had bladder issues that required so much effort it had cost pit stains and a damp forehead? The boy didn't seem to want to know, giving him a grimace and brushing past. He had a slight limp, and TJ thought he might've hurt himself, but noticed the kid was wearing ankle weights. Before TJ could ask what they were for, the boy slammed the door in his face.

"Yooo, Teee Jaaay!" Manny called from behind. TJ turned to find her near one of the buses, waving him over. She stood next to Ayo, who also gestured for TJ to come. Many of the students were huddled around a line of thick brush, backdropped by the silhouetted buses and the lowering sun. The late afternoon chill was a welcome one after being in that sauna of a restroom.

Jogging over through uncut weeds, TJ made his way between students catching up and chaperones making sure no one wandered off. When he got close to his friends and brought them in for a huddle, his voice was giddy. "Eshu showed himself to me in the bathroom."

"Ah, gross!" Ayo scowled.

Manny smacked him across the shoulder. "Not like that, idiot."

"I was jokin'. I was jokin'!"

TJ rolled his eyes, ignoring Ayo. "So... no need for the full moon coming up. I asked Eshu about Oya. She's busy with her storms in the Atlantic. But he'll get in touch with her. He told me to focus on building hype for Olokun in New Ile-Ife. He says there's this Frost Realm we need to get to. Some lost gemstone there that belongs to Yemoja."

"Yemoja? I thought you said it was Olokun we needed to keep happy?" Ayo asked, leaning casually on the bus they stood near.

TJ shrugged. "My dad always says 'happy wife, happy life.'"

Manny snapped her fingers and pointed to the sky. "Funny. That's how it works for my dad, too."

"Right?" TJ said. "And if we make her happy by getting this gemstone, it'll make Olokun happy. Apparently, it's tied to her ice magic, which has been weakened for a few thousand years or something like that. I didn't get *all* the details. My talk with Eshu was rushed and this kid kept interrupting me at the restroom."

"Sounds good," Manny said. "Yemoja's my secondary Orisha alignment. I could help with that Frost Realm stuff, too. Had no idea she messed around with ice."

Manny peeked over her shoulder at the students in the distance. It looked like most of them were all done with the restroom. TJ could even see the kid who had rushed him coming out. Oddly, he started doing jumping jacks and checking his pulse for no particular reason.

"And don't forget, we need to tell Elder Adeyemi about all this," Manny went on. "Bet she can help."

"I'm hoping so," TJ returned. "Because I have no idea where to find a gemstone that's been lost for who knows how long."

"All right, students! All students!" one of the chaperones called out. "Back to your assigned buses. Next stop: New Ile-Ife and Ifa Academy."

Ayo pushed himself off the bus he was leaned against, smiling. "Man. I love it when we have an *actual* plan."

10

WHERE THE MAGIC FOLK GO

BACK ON THE BUS, THE BOYS WERE NOW ALLOWED TO SIT wherever they wanted since the rest of the trip was so short and the "bonding experience" was essentially complete after that four-hour drive.

Ayo sat next to TJ this time, but TJ made sure Emeka wasn't alone, asking the boy to sit behind them. Apparently, Emeka and Ayo had already known each other, but when TJ asked how, Ayo lifted a sharp finger and said, "Emeka, I know you can read my lips. Don't. Say. A. Damn. Word."

Emeka signed back with a smile and zipped his lips. TJ logged it in his mind to bring up whatever had them so familiar later. Anything *Ayo* didn't want TJ to know, TJ wanted to know.

The bus wound a path through thick forest, and like TJ's trip to Camp Olosa with a mystical cab, the bus transformed. Though this time, instead of becoming a bayou boat, the wheels got monster-truck big to roll over the uneven path they went through.

For an hour, it felt like the bus' path followed a few circles. TJ was sure they had cut at least two figure eights; the driver even went backward a few times, but then on their dozenth turn, they pushed forward into a vine-covered thicket, and on the other side: New Ile-Ife.

TJ wished he could be on both sides of the bus at the same

time to see everything. It was like being at one of those Pan African festivals back at home. Streets were filled with cloths and Yoruba pattern designs hung from storefronts. Spices drifted through the bus' open window: curry, nutmeg, and *uziza* from several vendors. But the similarity of sights and smells stopped there. Everything else about the village was, simply put, magical.

Instead of flashing billboards like in Los Angeles, there were banners with moving images. One of them advertised a potion that elevated the senses called "Essence of Oshun." The Orisha of Sensuality was laid out across the bottom of the billboard in a position Mom would've never approved of. The tagline above her read: *find your inner goddess.* Many of the boys on the bus took particular notice. Another banner, this one tall rather than wide, depicted a magical staff that flashed with a crystal of blue and white on its head. Its tagline read: *Yemoja crystals primed and ready at The Walking Stick. Harness the power of Mother Ocean.*

Further along, an acorn-shaped building the size of a children's playhouse sheltered fairy people. Two of the flying creatures held hands as they flew from a window on the third floor. TJ gaped at their shimmering butterfly wings and pointed ears. He'd heard of fae creatures before, but never saw them up close.

"Aziza," Ayo explained at TJ's side. "They aren't native to this area, but we give sanctuary to a lot of them here. In fact, I think we host the largest population, outside of Benin."

TJ wondered why magical creatures needed sanctuary. Protection against the clouded community or from other magical creatures?

Emeka handed his phone to TJ, which read:

Emeka: the js3 elemental teacher is an aziza 🧚 *you'll meet her. she's really good with* 🔥 *magic.*

From the curves and twists of all the different roads and pathways, TJ could imagine the city from a bird's eye view looking like an enormous, warped hourglass. It seemed the city was built much like any other, with the housing on the outskirts and the shopping within. As the homesteads rolled into streets of vendors and storefronts, TJ caught sight of a shop whose entrance was a doorway framed by three staffs of wood, iron, and copper. A hanging sign above read: *The Walking Stick, run by the Bamidele family since 1620 CE.*

Bamidele! TJ thought, sitting up in his seat. "Hey, in the Aqua —I mean, at that pool last year—Eshu—I mean, that Joshua kid —told me to speak to an Elder Bamidele. He said he had my sister's staff. Her *real* staff."

"Oh, yeah. He's the staffmaster 'round these parts. But look…" Ayo pointed to the window near the store's entrance. A shimmering calligraphy stated the shop would be closed for a week. "SS1 students spend their whole year making their staffs. Bamidele is usually out in some forest looking for a good spot for them to start their crafting sessions. Don't worry. I'll take you over when he gets back."

TJ stared at The Walking Stick until they rounded a corner to what could only be described as the village square. The statue of an enormous head occupied most of its center. The face was lined from brow to chin, and its hue was obsidian. It was the head of Oduduwa, the great king deified as an Orisha. Drummers surrounded the statue's head, pounding on their instruments and singing Yoruba hymns.

But TJ barely registered the drum circle or the massive statue. What caught TJ's attention the most was an enormous mural painted on the side of a towering circular building with thatched roofing. The almond-shaped eyes painted there shot shock waves through his heart. Because he knew that loving, gentle gaze.

It was his sister, Dayo.

The artist had painted her just the way he remembered her: wide, straight smile, upper lip slightly bigger than the bottom, full nose, pointed ears. It was like someone had taken her actual face, blown it up, and thrown it on the mud walls.

TJ's eyes started to water, and he turned away from the other boys on the bus. It didn't help that his gaze settled at the bottom of the mural where Dayo's date of birth and date of passing were lovingly engraved with a sheen of emerald paint.

A gentle breeze wafted through the bus window and across TJ's neck, reminding him of earlier that summer when he'd sworn he felt Dayo beside him. In fact, all last summer he thought there was some sort of connection between them that he must've just imagined. That desire of wanting to see her again swelled in him once more. And he couldn't help it. A tear escaped his eyelid. He brushed it away before anyone could see, but Ayo was sitting so close; TJ couldn't hide it from his friend.

Jabbing a fist gently into TJ's thigh, Ayo said, "I never did say how sorry I am about your sister, man. She really was a hero 'round here."

The promised child, TJ thought.

If she was still here, she'd probably have no trouble stopping Olokun and keeping Eko Atlantic intact. Mitigating catastrophes was a Monday morning routine for her. Still, he might not have been his sister, but he had his own unique abilities; he could only hope they'd be enough.

"Thanks, man," TJ said, his palm over his heart. "I appreciate you."

"Wait, wait, you're Ifedayo's little brother?" a voice came from the side. It was the same boy who TJ had held up at the restroom. TJ recognized those sandbag weights wrapped around his boney ankles. And now that he got a better look of him, TJ realized he hadn't quite appreciated his unique appearance. He was like a walking contradiction: skinny except for the pudge at his stomach, tall, except his arms were short, and his thighs were longer than his calves. His face was stretched at the eyes but squeezed in below the nose.

"Shooot," he went on. "You should have said something, guy. Name's Umar. My older sister played on the crossover team with Ifedayo a few years back."

TJ hoped his eyes weren't too red as he rubbed them. "Oh, cool. That's what's up. Sorry about the restroom earlier. I'm TJ."

"Do you play crossover, too? You gonna try out for the team? I've tried two years in a row but got cut both times. My baba says I'd be on the team if I had my growth spurt already and these broom legs filled out. That's why I got the ankle weights, to make them stronger."

TJ could relate. Not so much with the growth spurt part—he was plenty tall—but he had chicken legs, too. "Nah, I don't play. But my friend Manny does. She'll probably be on the team."

"Oh! That Brazilian girl?" Umar perked up. "I thought she wasn't coming back. Hey, maybe you can put a good word in for me, eh?"

TJ shrugged with an exaggerated pout. "Maybe."

Emeka tapped TJ on the shoulder and showed him his phone, which read:

Emeka: be careful with him. he's a little crazy. all he ever talks about is crossover and working out.

"I actually live here, you know," Umar went on. "Just on the other side of the embassy in the Adebayo compound. I hate having to go way out to Lagos just to come back here because of 'tradition'. Oh! Looks like we're finally here."

Outside the window, the village square transitioned into another forest thicket. The bus bounced over a bumpy road, and ahead of them, the long line of their convoy rocked forward, each bus seeming to dip *into* the earth below. When they got closer, TJ realized they actually *were* sinking into the earth, like a roller coaster dipping downward.

Emeka tapped TJ on the shoulder and handed him his phone again.

Emeka: hold on to ur butt. this part gets crazy 😬

Just as TJ handed the phone back to Emeka, his stomach lifted all the way to his throat as they descended into a downward whirlpool of earth. It was like going through a corkscrew on a roller coaster and TJ found himself tumbling to the ground. After he figured out what was up and what was down, and after a long moment of Ayo helping him, he stood. But it felt like he left his stomach on the floor. He glanced down to see that was literally the case. Well, what was in the inside of his stomach, at least.

One of the chaperones muttered *"fọ lulẹ́ kó tú"* casually, and TJ's airplane breakfast and lunch got sucked up into the crystal of the elder's copper staff.

"You'll get used to it, young man," he chuckled.

TJ lifted his head in thanks, still too queasy to utter any actual words. Shadow filled the interior of the bus now. Peeking outside, TJ saw that they were in some underground cavern with red earth packed in on all sides and torches implanted every ten or fifteen feet.

"Young diviners!" the driver announced as he opened the door of the bus. "Welcome to the entrance hall of Ifa Academy!"

The boys gathered their things and filed out into the chill of the cavern. It was more than just a dirt-filled cave, but something straight out of the *Temple of Doom*. Fire lit the long path of packed earth, ancient pillars, and exotic neon plants that rhythmically glowed like tiny heartbeats.

Manny rushed up to TJ from behind and nudged him at his elbow. "Did you throw up? I bet you threw up."

Heat flushed TJ's face, and Ayo answered for him. "Yeah, he did. All over the bus seat."

Giggling, Manny brushed her hair behind her ear. "Don't worry. It gets easier."

Ahead, a group of adults and children lined both ends of the cobbled path. Their bodies made a line to a weathered stone cube that stretched up fifty feet to the cavern's high ceiling. Yoruba designs pocketed the cube, revealing different colors at each corner: blue, brown, red, and white. TJ actually recognized the structure from his readings. It was called the Great Summoning Stone. And just like his book said, it resided in the Ifa Academy entrance hall. TJ just assumed the entrance hall wouldn't have been underground. The colors that pulsated from each corner represented a different element, coupled with a statue that protected each edge: Yemoja for the wet and cold of water, Ogun for the cold and dry of earth, Shango for the dry and heat of fire, and Oya for the heat and wet of the sky.

As they shuffled closer to the welcoming line of children and adults, TJ recognized the song they were singing, a welcoming melody in Yoruba to wish the students good luck. More than their sung words, TJ pulled out a few faces he knew in the lineup: Mr. Martinez, Mrs. Martinez, Mom, and...

"Ìyá àgbà!" TJ held his hands wide, and Grandma wrapped him in a hug. She only came up to TJ's middle, and TJ could rest his chin on her scarf-wrapped head. She was a stout little woman with rosy cheeks that were never free from a grin.

Planting two kisses on TJ, she replied, "I am so proud of you, Tomori Jomiloju." She handed him a handful of candy wrappers, dark and milk chocolates. "You go in there and show them what the Abimbolas can do!"

"*E̩ ṣeun, ìyá àgbà.*" TJ thanked Grandma in Yoruba.

"*Ooo, your Yoruba is much better now,*" she replied in her native tongue. "*Your grandfather and I will be in the Amazon for a few months with Bamidele to make sure your sister's staff wasn't tampered with, but don't forget to visit us after!*"

TJ gave Grandma one last kiss, then continued walking alongside his friends as they approached the Summoning Stone.

"Here, take these." TJ handed them some chocolates. "They're too sweet for me."

"What?" Ayo pushed his glasses up and grabbed the candy wrapper. "You ain't gotta tell me twice. Milk chocolate over dark chocolate all day."

"Dark chocolate don't taste bitter to you?" Manny asked, taking her own piece of candy.

TJ shrugged. "Usually, but I don't know… this growth spurt has me getting all these weird cravings."

"It's okay, sister," a boy said from behind. "He'll come next year, I bet."

TJ snuck a look over his shoulder to see an older boy, probably an upperclassman, with his arm slung over a younger girl, likely a junior, possibly a first year, wearing a frown and slumped shoulders.

"What's got them down?" TJ murmured to his friends.

Through a bite of chocolate, Ayo took his own peek and shrugged. "Ah, those are the kids of that weird guy I was telling you about. The old man who burned his eyebrows clean off. He never shows up to Ifa Academy. Bad memories or whatever."

TJ narrowed his eyes at the other parents. It was true. The bald guy wasn't among them, but Miss Gravés was there, staring right at him from the back of the line at the end of the cavern.

I'm just imagining things, TJ convinced himself. *Just enjoy the ceremony. There's no Keepers here…*

As they crossed the threshold into the sole slit in the Summoning Stone, the hymns from their parents and friends cut off almost instantly, replaced by the cathedral-like ambiance of the inner chamber. Inside, like a mirror of the statues outside, stood the stone likenesses of Yemoja, Ogun, Shango, and Oya, each tall enough that their legs molded an entrance into their own specific chambers. At the center stood the stone image of Eshu with his hands held out wide, his staff in one hand, and a large key in the other. Below him and between his feet stood a woman in a red-and-black dress befitting royalty, an elder with the grace of a queen: Headmistress Adeyemi.

"Welcome, young diviners," she said soothingly. When she moved her arms, her dress shifted like lava, with red rising from its hem and flowing up to a deep, obsidian black. "I am so happy to see you all made the trip safe and sound. Welcome to the entrance hall's Great Summoning Stone. Most of our returning students will already be familiar with the next steps, but for those new to us, you will enter the chamber that calls to your base element or Orisha alignment. There, one of the instructors will help you travel through your respective portal onto the campus. Give the chamber you choose your true name, and you shall pass. After this, you will be led to your boarding rooms, given a tour of the grounds and classrooms, and then you are all to report to the Oracle Rock for your term assessment. Good luck to you all in the new year. You may choose your paths now."

"Well, that's Shango's Fire for me." Ayo hefted his backpack over his shoulder. "See y'all on the other side, eh?"

"Shooot! You already know," Manny replied as she made her way over to the Oya chamber. "You nervous, TJ?"

"Me?" TJ exaggerated his response. "If I can go up against Orishas, this is nothin'."

Manny laughed and walked off with the other students queuing for the Oya line. But in truth, TJ was all kinds of nervous. He didn't know which chamber he was supposed to enter. This was his whole issue during the summer at Camp Olosa. No specific Orisha or element ever called to him, so how could he choose? Maybe it didn't matter. He could probably just choose whatever chamber and anything would work for him.

Considering Mom was aligned with Yemoja and he needed to help get the Orisha's ice powers back, TJ entered the chamber of Mother Ocean first. The chamber was filled with water like a giant pool. But when he tried to enter the chamber's water tank, the portal didn't heed him, repelling him away like a force field. Then he remembered he needed to give his true name.

"Tomori Jomiloju Young," he said. But still nothing.

From the top of the water chamber, a serpent-like mermaid TJ recognized as a mami wata swam down to him and spoke in an odd thought-speech. *Maybe you should try the next chamber over, child.*

It took TJ a moment to answer her because he found himself staring. After he shook the shock from his face, he made his way to the next chamber over. But the Ogun chamber, which was filled with axes, spears, and swords of iron was no better. Neither was the Shango chamber, filled with its fire pits and lightning rods, or the Oya chamber, where storm clouds filled the space.

Embarrassment slithered through TJ's gut. If he wasn't allowed to enter the academy at all, did that mean he was unworthy? A few of the younger students who needed help to find their proper place started to whisper as they noticed "that TJ Young kid."

"Is he at the wrong academy?" one of them asked.

"Isn't that Ifedayo's brother?" asked another.

TJ wished he knew some of Eshu's illusion magic so he could disappear.

As the last of the students crossed over, TJ was left alone in the inner chamber with Elder Adeyemi.

"Is everything okay, Tomori Jomiloju?" she asked, piercing him with her gentle, old eyes. "Were you having trouble? Anything I can help with?"

"Oh, no. No trouble. I was just looking for the bathroom."

Elder Adeyemi threw up an inquisitive eyebrow.

TJ slumped. "No... I'm lying... I can't get into any of the portals, ma'am. It's like Mr. Bola—ugh... like Olugbala said to me..."

Elder Adeyemi gave TJ the opportunity to finish. When it was apparent he wouldn't continue, she finished for him. "The book hasn't been written for you yet. If I'm remembering that man's words to you correctly."

"Yeah…" TJ really didn't want to give Bolawe any credit after the man's betrayal only a few weeks ago. "Is this some rite of passage? Does this mean I can't attend the academy?"

Adeyemi lifted her hand over her mouth, cloaking a light chuckle. "Of course not, young man. There are occasionally students unable to cross over. I can help you along through one of the portals. But," she lifted a single, long finger, "I do want to try something first. Come, sit with me just along here." She gestured to the cobbled stone bordered by grass and moss below where she stood. As though in one motion, like a gentle cyclone, she dropped and sat cross-legged. TJ mirrored her movement, sitting across from her.

"Channel your Ashe inward; repeat after me," she started. "Eshu. First honored opener of the ways."

"Eshu. First honored opener of the ways," TJ repeated.

"Guardian of the crossroads, lord of choice."

"Guardian of the crossroads, lord of choice."

They continued the prayer. As Adeyemi recited her words, and TJ repeated them, each line brought with it an energy TJ had been familiar with since childhood, a tingle in his fingers that had always brought him good fortune. And as their prayer came to a close, he could feel both their energies roil into one another and blossom into something new, something he didn't quite understand.

"You who are called Eshu," TJ completed the last line. "I honor and sing to you. Please open the gate, accept my prayers, and carry them beyond the crossroads."

TJ opened his eyes to a smiling Elder Adeyemi. Backdropping her was a portal leading to a path of green and yellow, like a chartreuse halo around her head. But the portal did not appear at the head of the other chambers, but between the feet of Eshu's statue instead.

"Oh, yes," she almost whispered. "As problematic as Olugbala is. He was right. The book hasn't been written for you, young man. This year will be a most interesting one for you."

"I didn't know an Eshu portal was an option."

"It's not. This portal hasn't been opened for centuries, if the stories from the ancestors are to be believed."

"So... I'm aligned with Eshu, then?" That would make some sense. He did just speak to the Orisha not too long ago. If he showed himself to TJ like Oya apparently showed herself to Manny, that's what could've been going on.

"No, young man," she said. "But I am."

TJ's face brightened with curiosity. Elder Adeyemi didn't exactly come off as the Eshu type. But that brought forth another question. "If you're aligned with Eshu, then how come *you* couldn't open his portal?"

"Because the connection was too weak, as it has been since long before I was a child attending the academy myself."

The breeze from the other side of the portal brushed across TJ's face, nice and cool. "But... how did you get into the portals at all when you were a kid?"

"I had to use my strongest elemental alignment with the help of the instructors then." She gestured her hands to the other large statues around them. "Just as some of the young ones needed help today. But with you... you seem to be the *key* to unlocking the latent powers of Eshu's portal. I suspect it has something to do with your talent for communal magic. There's something more at play here, and we will uncover it in time. Together."

"Speaking of uncovering..." TJ started, then he explained everything that had happened that day from the airport to the restroom.

Adeyemi settled in place, so still it was like TJ was looking at a statue of her. "Thank you for telling me this, Tomori. This, too, will need time to process. And I shouldn't keep you anymore. You've got orientation to get to." She lifted up as neatly as she had sat down. She offered TJ her hand, and he took it. He was lifted up by her as though he were no more heavy than a small child. "Welcome to Ifa Academy, young man."

As TJ walked through the portal they created, his finger with the Eshu tattoo warmed a little. He glanced down at its faint glow, then stared back up at the statue of the Gatekeeper. Softly, he said, "Thanks, Eshu. I know you had my back there."

11

IFA ACADEMY OF TOMORROW'S DIVINERS

IFA ACADEMY FELT MORE LIKE A CONSERVATORY THAN A school. It wasn't built up as TJ expected it to be. It wasn't some castle, not some collection of huts, no Wakandan palace, not even a building at all, really. It wasn't built *up*, but rather, built *around*.

The forest the academy called home was completely undisturbed, each tree and their roots free to grow where they may, with every structure built around it.

The portal TJ walked through was like all the others, all of which funneled to the same entrance grounds of the academy. He peeked behind him to see a row of five statues just as tall as the ones at the Summoning Stone, with Eshu's statue in the center and the other pairs flanking him on each side.

"Young? Tomori Jomiloju Young?" A girl came up to TJ's side, but her voice carried the weight of many years.

"Yeah, that's me. Did you need help?"

"Help? *I'm* the one who will be helping *you*. It's your first year, so I have to give you the tour." She pointed to a path leading farther into the academy grounds. Manny and Ayo were waiting near the base of a large tree with a signpost that read: *Mess Hall This Way.* "These two said they want to join you. Is that okay?"

TJ waved over to his friends, and they waved back. "That'll be great!"

Their guide, who was named Oroma, gave them a tour of the campus grounds. She couldn't have been any older than TJ, maybe even younger, but apparently she was hundreds of years old with neatly woven braids in the shape of a basket halo. Absolutely none of the hairs in her intricate hair design was out of place.

"Never mess with her at night," Ayo whispered to TJ. "She, uh... changes when the stars come out."

"Yeah," Manny agreed. "Some girl found her with her head pulled off last year. That's how Oroma gets her hair done so well. She, um... does it herself."

"Wait so... is she, like, a zombie or somethin'?" TJ asked, keeping his voice down as well.

Manny gave him a so-so hand gesture. "No one is really sure, and it's not like you can really ask somethin' like that. But the legend is that some clouded girls in Lagos saw her at night when she took off her head and changed to her multi-arm form. Apparently, she owned a salon over there and was making a killing."

"That's half the reason I come here." Ayo thumbed to his own braids. "But after those girls in Lagos saw Oroma and freaked out, the UCMP had her locked down to the academy grounds to keep her existence on the down low."

"In other words, I'm under house arrest," Oroma said bitterly. "I might be headless sometimes, but I'm never earless, young mortals."

As they followed along between a winding path of whispering willows, TJ tried his best not to gawk at what probably *wasn't* just a scar-line around Oroma's neck.

The grounds were composed of several sections denoted by elemental alignments. Some classes, Oroma told them, were conducted within the trees where structures were built like tree-houses, others were given within tunneled mud huts, and some even underwater where a river flowed into the academy's single lake.

"Classes underwater?" TJ asked Oroma. "How does that work?"

"Those classes are only for the SS students," Oroma

explained. "You need to know the Drowning Draught for that. They're taught by those mami wata creatures."

Maybe the same one I met at the Summoning Stone, TJ thought.

The living quarters rested in the middle of campus. Just like everything else, the dwellings were hung from trees, tucked into bushes, and hidden under roots.

TJ and Ayo were given their bunk instructions, which led to a habitat that brought images of old cavemen's dwellings: A set of humped rocks huddled together like a family of beetles. That's where the Junior boys would sleep, apparently. Upon closer inspection, TJ noticed the landscape was not naturally designed by the stones. The clay structures were merely painted to look like rocks.

"Some of the guys actually call our dorms the 'man cave,'" Ayo said to TJ, who rolled his eyes as they approached the dwellings under the shadow of the giant trees.

Manny's dorm was a little higher up, way above in the canopy in one of the tree houses. It must've sucked for any of the girls up there who were afraid of heights.

After they put all of their things away and were given their room assignments—TJ was bunked with Emeka—they all followed their guide, Oroma, to a natural stone formation that she claimed was the highest point of all the campus grounds: Oracle Rock.

There, they linked back up with the other students, who were at the base of the path that led to the top. The first face TJ recognized was Emeka, who waved over happily. TJ, speaking slowly and clearly, asked what the Oracle Rock was all about. Through text, Emeka explained they and the other junior-level students were going there to figure out which classes and electives they should choose.

The climb up took nearly half an hour over narrow precipices and jagged paths. TJ did his best not to look over any of the edges, but it was almost impossible not to. It made him feel a touch better though when he saw Ashe barriers of wind that protected anyone from falling over.

Emeka turned to TJ and wrote out another message.

Emeka: my gpa says that Ifa is getting soft. in his day he said it was an actual journey and struggle to get to the top of the stone

The long path up gave TJ plenty of time to think, especially with students all around him mumbling about what their oracles would predict for their futures. TJ was nervous but a little excited to hear what his future held. He never got his future read before. Mom always said those services were expensive, especially the accurate, less vague predictions. And even then, the success rate for most was negligible.

Eventually, all the junior students arrived at the flat top of the Great Stone. It was true it was the highest point of the campus. TJ gaped at the three-sixty view he had of the tall trees, where he could make out the tops of some of the tree house classes and the twinkling of the lake near the willows. He nearly fell over a few times, though. The winds up there were *rough*. TJ had to take careful steps to the center, where several rounded animal-hide tents were set up.

"JS3 boys will follow me to the tent just there." Oroma pointed to a tent constructed from leopard skins. White smoke billowed from the slit cut in its roof. "In alphabetical order, of course." She read from a paper in her child-like hands. "Adebayo, Umar. You're first to see the Oracle."

The oddly-shaped boy walked forward with his bird chest puffed. When he passed TJ, he said, "Wish me luck. I'm hoping they'll predict me making the crossover team this year!"

But a little while later Umar returned with downcast shoulders and a frown, saying that the Oracle told him it's best to stay clear of physical activities, lest he wanted to be riddled with disappointment and an injury.

"I'm still trying out for the team," he said, shrugging. "Make my own destiny and all that, right? Plus, she told me it's better if I focus on my biology classes instead this year. She can miss me with that."

Next up was a boy named Falu Bankole who was told to focus on avoiding rough waters, which he interpreted as not enlisting in electives for Oshun, the Orisha of Rivers. Later on, a Jomi Davis was advised to keep his head in the stars, which to him meant pursuing advanced classes with Orunmila or Obatala, the Orishas who lived in the cosmos. One of the boys, Okan Ibekwe, was told success would be found so long as he avoided man-made liquid, which he was still trying to figure out.

To TJ, the Oracle sounded more like a guidance counselor. Then, thinking on it some more... guidance counselors were kind of like oracles to begin with, to varying degrees of success.

Each of the Oracle sessions ranged from a few minutes to a half-hour. To pass the time, Emeka invited TJ and Ayo to play a board game version of crossover. The whole board fit in the boy's pocket in a folded square. All he had to do was tap his finger, say the magic words, and the whole thing flopped out in the shape of a real miniature crossover field, miniature fans sitting in the stands and everything. Even the tiny players they used looked real, as they air-stepped and scored points just like their real-life counterparts.

Emeka tried explaining the rules of crossover after TJ's first loss, but TJ told him he was familiar with how to play, he just sucked at the sport in real life—and apparently, that translated to the board game version as well.

Each time TJ lost, he swapped with Ayo, but Ayo didn't do any better.

TJ was reminded of games he played with his father back at home. It was like he was playing NBA 2K on his Playstation with Emeka, only far more interactive.

After TJ's third loss, Emeka swapped teams with him—apparently, Emeka's little miniatures were almost leveled all the way to max. Despite having the superior team, TJ still couldn't eke out a win, and he suffered two more losses when Manny walked up to them.

"Oh, is that the new Major League Crossover game?" she asked.

"It sure is," Ayo answered, signing at the same time for Emeka's benefit. "Emeka's handin' us our asses right now, though."

"I got next." Manny sat beside them on the stone ground. Her shoulder brushed closely against TJ's as she tried to give him pointers. Her advice helped, but TJ was too far behind for it to matter much, and eventually, he took another big fat "L."

When Manny started to play, she busted out her own player set from her backpack, and the match between her and Emeka was well above anything TJ and Ayo could've done. Manny was doing combos only someone as familiar with the game as she was could manage, making her players work together for longer and higher air-stepping maneuvers that outmatched Emeka's plays.

"What predictions did you get?" TJ asked Manny.

Manny got in such a groove that she stopped paying attention. "Ugh, I hate Oracle Okoro. He gives me those fortune cookie predictions every year. So vague and busted. Like, what is 'if winter comes, can spring be far behind?' even mean?"

"That's what happens when teachers get tenure, my Baba says," Ayo said, staring at the crossover game as though he could figure out how Manny was doing so well just by watching. "They get lazy when their jobs are ensured and whatnot."

There were only twenty or so other boys along with TJ in the JS3 levels, but they were up on that rock for nearly the rest of the day. Each time someone got a reading, especially those with more difficult ones, the Oracle had to take a break and resume work a few minutes later.

When the next boy, Ekon Kabiru, came out, he said, "She's taking another nap."

Everyone groaned and went back to whatever social circle they were in. Apparently, all the napping was to refresh the Oracle's "divine palette" with Obatala, the Dreamweaver, and Orunmila of Divination. During these breaks, TJ noted the diversity of those visiting the Great Rock. It wasn't just students. Adults poked in and out of tents of all shapes, sizes, and cultures, from big Greek-looking dudes with bunched himations, blind Japanese-looking women with simple robes called *itako*, and Native American-looking people wearing moccasins and hides.

Ayo probably noticed the wrinkle creasing its way through TJ's forehead because he explained, "Ifa Academy is known for two things: elementalism and divination, specifically oracle readings. People from all over the magical world come here for predictions of the future. Even those Norse folks way up north. Baba says that's where most of our funding comes from."

"So, what's it like going in there?" TJ nodded to the tents.

"Ifa readings are like doctor's appointments."

"What do you mean?"

"It's like this… say you go to the doctor. What do they do? Give you a diagnosis and suggest treatment, right?"

"Right."

"Well, basically our oracles give you suggestions. It's not future-telling like you might be thinking. I mean, sometimes it can be like that, but not always."

Dayo entered TJ's mind at that moment. He could almost imagine a twelve-year-old version of his sister waiting ahead of the sea of tents, just as TJ was waiting now. Was she nervous, he wondered. Probably. That's what Dad had said before Camp Olosa, anyway. But Dayo couldn't've ever known what the oracles would predict for her… something far more compelling than what activities she should take after school.

To get his mind off his sister, TJ asked Ayo, "So I can ask what I should have for breakfast tomorrow then, right?"

Ayo laughed. "Nah. Readings are usually about nurturing good fortune you have now or warding off bad fortune that might come."

"Oyelowo, Ayodeji!" Oroma called out, patting her braids instead of scratching them out. "The oracle will see you now. Remember, no asking about trivial matters. Only questions about your placement in your classes, please."

"And I've got some good fortune coming my way right now." Ayo patted TJ on the back and skipped to the tent.

As Ayo slipped into the tent, Manny and Emeka's Major League crossover game ended, with Manny taking a blowout victory. They congratulated each other, but Emeka wanted to run it back to "reclaim his honor." In their second match-up, Emeka had an early lead, so he got comfortable, just as Manny had. During time outs, he even spoke with TJ through his phone.

Emeka: nervous?

TJ typed in his response.

TJ: only nervous the oracle might fall asleep on me lol
Emeka: itll be alr. youll do fine i bet. i like ur watch btw

TJ peeked down at his oversized digital watch. Mugen, Jin, and Fuu from the anime *Samurai Champloo* were painted over it.

TJ: u kno abt this show?
Emeka: ofc. we got an anime club on the weekends. u should
come thru.
TJ: say less, im there
Emeka: bet. holding you to that.

As Emeka took a victory against Manny, TJ and Emeka continued speaking on their favorite anime—TJ's being *Fullmetal Alchemist*, the Brotherhood version, and Emeka's being *Death Note* if it ended after its first arc. After a while, Ayo came back out to say he was advised to give an old interest a second chance where the bay rises, which he figured meant he needed to focus more on the spellwork of his water magicks.

A few more boys were called up, but their readings were very quick, only five to ten minutes apiece. Soon, Emeka was up next. He went in with a bit of a skip. Well, not a skip exactly, but certainly a happy little jaunt. But when he came back out, he held his head low and his shoulders even lower. TJ was about to ask him what happened when he heard his name from the side.

"Yes, the Young boy is up next," Oroma, the chaperone, said to a handheld water bowl. "You and the others should come over now." TJ pretended he wasn't listening when the woman-child spun around to announce, "Young, Tomori Jomiloju! You're next!"

Gesturing for TJ, Oroma waved her tiny hand into the mouth of the tent. A few of the other students stopped their chatter to watch what TJ would do. Was this going to become a common thing all year, TJ wondered. He certainly hoped not. He was nervous enough on his own, but with everyone else taking notice only made it worse.

Trying to forget all the eyes on him, TJ obeyed, stepping forward.

"Good luck." Manny gave him an awkward thumbs up.

"Yeah, don't blow it," Ayo added with a chuckle.

TJ waved back at them furtively as his heartbeat kicked up with each step. He reminded himself this wasn't a test, not like the assessment he got at the beginning of the summer. All he had to do was sit there and listen to the Oracle. Easy.

12

PERCEPTIVE PLACEMENT

ONCE INSIDE THE TENT, TJ FORGOT ALL ABOUT HIS NERVES, his shaking fingers replaced by a lifted, stilted brow. Where TJ had expected to find a lot of hanging herbs, African masks on walls, or incense smoke billowing within the tent, instead he found himself among whiteboards filled with mathematical equations, computer screens lined with code, and the low thump of lofi beats playing an ambient tone in the background—from a high-tech DJ-grade setup no less. The only thing traditional about the place was the *Opan Ifa*—diviner board—which rested at the tent's center over a threadbare rug. That and the woman wearing flowing, aso oke robes in the center of the room. Her back was turned to him and she was hunched over in what looked like prayer.

"Good afternoon, Elder—I mean—Miss—um..." TJ trailed off, not sure how to address the Oracle.

The Oracle turned around to face him. The features on her face were just as shocking as the rest of the place. She was young. Very young. Like, perhaps straight out of university young. In fact, she reminded TJ a lot of his sister's best friend, Adeola— very spunky-looking, with high cheekbones, though with a little pudge. She wore thin-rimmed glasses covering up small eyes. She had locs dyed green. Her body... definitely curvy.

She was, in one word, cute.

"Ruby is just fine, love," she said with an English accent. She flashed a very youthful grin, unblemished cheeks, perfectly white teeth, the whole nine.

"H-hello, I'm TJ Young."

"Young? You're not related to Ifedayo Young, are you?"

"Yeah... but shouldn't you already know that as the Oracle?"

"If I had a pound for every time I've gotten that response." Ruby shook her head with a chuckle. "But I do remember your sister had a very unique reading."

"I heard one of those readings back at the camp I came from. Well... maybe I didn't. Eshu—I mean—someone..." TJ was saying a lot of things he shouldn't've been. "Uh... it was made up, apparently. At least part of it. The one that goes 'a promised child will rise with the light of a dying, falling star—'"

"'And the Lost Monarch will return once more'," she finished as she leaned forward into what looked like another prayer. But she bent low to punch in some keys on a keyboard propped up on a pillow next to her.

"Yeah, that reading," TJ said. "But I was told that prediction was made by the Keepers, not by the oracles here at Ifa. How... how did you know it?"

"Oh... because I'm the one who did the reading initially." The Oracle said the words offhandedly as she typed away.

TJ stood frozen in place. He must've heard her incorrectly. Did that mean this Oracle Ruby woman—well, young woman— was the one who started it all? But that didn't make sense. She would've been barely out of Ifa Academy or wherever she graduated from to make that reading on Ifedayo.

"And don't be daft about those terrorists, love." Ruby snapped her fingers and waved them in front of TJ's face. "I'm not with the Keepers. Never was, never will be. They were just the only ones taking my readings seriously at the time." She gestured to their surroundings. "As you can see, my little spot here is a bit unorthodox. Looks more like a lab than the traditional tent preferences, and the ol' stooges couldn't have that, could they? The new-age methods were frowned upon back when I had just started my studies at the Institute of All-Magicks. That, and people found my Orisha wonder-combo of Orunmila and Ogun too confusing to wrap their heads around."

"Ogun? I thought he was into iron and all that stuff."

"More than just iron, which tends to get inconveniently forgotten. He's the father of technology and innovation as well. Hence... my mixing of the cosmos with," she lifted a laptop at her side, "computations and algorithms."

TJ knelt down to be eye-to-eye with Ruby. "Is that seriously why no one listened to you? Because you used a computer instead of a divination board?"

"Oh yes. Some of the old geezers in New Ile-Ife are quite entrenched in tradition. Hell, old farts, in general, tend to be that way." A new song played on Ruby's lofi playlist and she skipped it from something less rhythmic and more chill. "But I was quite interested to see how far I could push my new methods, and there was one group that allowed me to work freely... though at that time they weren't as radical as they have been as of late."

TJ was reminded of Adeola last summer. Didn't Elder Adeyemi say she had a change of heart ever since Dayo passed away? Perhaps there were more than a few who had turned away from the Keepers, like Ruby. Though with the latter it seemed she never was associated with them officially, to begin with. And through TJ's cursory research, he found out that the Keepers had not always been an extremist group.

"Tell me, TJ," Ruby intoned curiously. "What do you know of divination?"

TJ shrugged, thinking back on the "fortune cookie" reading Manny had received. "I don't know... Just that it's a bunch of riddles."

"If you'll indulge me before we begin, I can explain a bit about what I do that's so off-putting to some."

TJ nodded, leaning forward with interest. He tried his best not to get tangled in the wires strewn across the tent floor.

"You see, oracle work and our readings come in two parts, foundationally." She shifted on her knees to one of her white-boards and drew two boxes with a green marker. "One, of course, is the spiritual, the act of communicating with the divine and trying to decipher the messages given to us whether through a divination board," she gestured to the Opan Ifa sat ahead of her, "through dreams," she thumbed to the flat cot behind her, "or via the signs given to us throughout the day, such as omens or what have you. You followin' me?"

TJ nodded as he sat cross-legged across from Ruby, completely enraptured.

"The second part is specific to the act of predicting the future." Ruby wrote in the second box on the whiteboard. "As it has been for years and years before the invention of the modern computer, we oracles did this by listenin' to Orunmila, and transcribin' what we got through visions and the like."

TJ quirked an eyebrow.

"Think of it a bit like Google translate." Ruby faced her laptop to TJ, where she pulled up the translator site with a simple phrase. "If you send a certain phrase through the program enough times, the meaning of the original is almost completely lost. It's our job to unscramble that, thus—as you pointed out earlier—what would seem like a riddle. We oracles do not speak in puzzles for the fun of it—well, not us good ones, anyway—it really is just the best we can do with what we're usually given.

"Of course, there are other prevailin' theories, like the idea of these codes being muddled because they are intended for the one who the reading is about. And it's that person, and that person alone, who should be able to uncover the truth so no one else can. But the jury is still out on that one." She scratched at her eyebrow and scrunched her face. "But that's a tangent, innit? Apologies."

"No, no, this is interesting stuff." TJ sat up straight to look more interested. He really was keen to learn, but he might have zoned out a bit during her explanation.

"You're too kind, love." She smiled. "I'll try to speed it up. So, as a child, I took a liking to coding and algorithms. I was very interested in deciphering the inherent laws of prophecy. Just as there are laws of physics, I thought *surely* there had to be laws of divination as well. So I started looking at patterns from predictions across all cultures, all eras, everything. And I came up with a program." She slid her finger over her trackpad and the laptop screen showed a line of code that looked like a whole lotta gibberish to TJ. Laughing, Ruby said, "I swear not to get into the specifics for this part. Essentially, I've come up with some arrangements that have made my readings at least four percent more accurate than these other geezers that call themselves oracles. You see, futures are really just a calculation of probabilities within divine encryption. That's why certain prophecies and the like have," she threw up air quotes, "'expiration dates.'"

"You mean... old prophecies could just... go away?" TJ asked, thinking of Dayo and the business about the promised child again. If that were the case, what he heard back at camp could have been just that... an expired reading.

"Yes. Some can go bad, just like milk. It depends, really." She glanced behind her and an old-fashioned clock TJ hadn't noticed before chimed twice. "Anyway, let's begin. Today we'll just be looking to see what elective will be best for you this year. Do you already know your Orisha alignment?"

"I know it, as in I don't *have* an Orisha alignment."

"Very interestin'. Well, I do like a challenge."

The ritual started off as TJ assumed it usually did. Ruby gathered *ikín ifá*—sacred nuts—in her hand and cast them to her divining board. She asked TJ a few personal questions about his interests, like his affinity with water bubble charms, and his worries, like his having to play catchup that year. Ruby would *hmmm* under her breath, turn to her board, type away at her laptop and recycle the process. Twice she took naps after a few particularly difficult series of questions and answers that got her readings jumbled up—or at least, that's what she said. TJ was shocked she could sleep on command before she told him a sleeping potion was laced in the soda bottle she drank from.

But it went on like that: Getting into the ritual. Divine board. Ruby asking a few questions. All of that continued for what felt like hours before finally...

"Yep, you are very difficult indeed," Ruby croaked after a third cat nap. "Very murky, a lot of guesswork. But," she *clicked-clacked* a few keystrokes on her computer, "with the help of my program here... I think I have somethin'. Though I don't at all see how this can be related to your schoolwork. That said, you and I are quite familiar with some of the phrasing here: *The embers are stoked, but the falling star has yet to blaze its trail, hot and bright. When youth sprouts in a burst, look inward for your compass, your sight.*" Ruby blinked slowly, still tired. All that artificial sleep must've been catching up to her. "It's fun when they rhyme like that, eh?" She made a note with pen and paper set to one side.

What in the world did any of it mean? Even though Ruby explained that she never meant to speak in riddles, her reading was still pretty infuriating.

"So…" Ruby looked back his way with eyebrows raised. "Any of that make sense to you, love?"

Good, at least she's on the same wavelength as me. "Like you said," TJ began. "I've heard the falling star stuff before, but I don't know what that new message means. And um… the youth sprouting could be my growth spurt, maybe?"

"Maybe…"

If they talked it out a bit, maybe they could figure it all out. TJ was sort of a big fan of getting answers, so he asked, "Why don't we try again? Maybe you'll discern more in the stars — or, um, your code or whatever."

Ruby shook her head as she changed her playlist again to something that sounded more like alien-mutant whales mating than music. She scrunched her forehead into thin lines and rubbed her temples before saying, "Your readings will just be the same. Unless you're planning to make some big life change, like say, gettin' on an airplane and leaving Ifa Academy tomorrow. Do you have anything like that planned?"

TJ wondered if it would be a good time to bring up his little predicament with the Orishas or that reporter at the airport, but he wasn't sure he was allowed to. Elder Adeyemi hadn't given him the go-ahead on something like that, so instead, he said, "No, I don't have anything like that planned."

"Well then, since you don't plan on doing anything like that… any readings I do now or over the next few weeks or months will be the same. That's why we typically do these once before each term, when change is most prevalent in a student's life."

"I see… okay then." But TJ wanted desperately to be forthright with Ruby. She seemed so cool. Something within him stirred. Maybe it was some residual magic from all the divination that was going on in the room, but a balloon swelled in TJ's chest.

"Good, good," Ruby said, "all of this could be helpful going forward. I mean, there was nothing about your guidance for classes but..." A ding came from the laptop. "Oh," Ruby's shoulders did a little jump, "there's some more here. It says... *Do not be alone when the moon is brightest. The shadow between friend and foe is thick; keep your eyes wide in the fog. Your heart will rise with first love in the clouds of a celebrated region.*"

"In that order?" TJ joked, but part of him wondered if he had something to do with that new message on Ruby's computer.

"That is for you to experience and decide."

"Really, no riddle?"

"There is one I can give you that's pretty straightforward."

"Oh, yeah?" TJ sat up straight again. "What's that?"

"Put some pillows on the floor on the left side of your bed before you sleep tonight. And," she gave him a wink, "good luck this year, Mr. Young."

AFTER TJ GOT DONE WITH RUBY, HE STEPPED OUT OF THE tent to find a twilight sky above. Icy wind lapped across his face, making him sniffle. He stood before at least a dozen men and women wearing entirely different outfits. Elder Adeyemi stood as their vanguard. She was rocking yet another dazzling dress—this one looked like an actual sun setting within the fabrics of her silks or satins or whatever it was. A few women to her left wore grass-bell skirts with towering flowered headdresses, and next to them a group of very tall, dark, and thin men who wore red-patterned fabrics. To the right was a collection of men and women with thin robes and pointy hats that shimmered. The rest of the crowd were people donning the typical linings of aso oke native to the land.

Elder Adeyemi spread her arms wide, and the sunset in her dress rose with them. "Hello, Tomori Jomiloju. How did your reading go?"

"Um... are... um... all these people here to see me?" TJ realized his question might've come off a bit rude and conceited, so he reined in his tone for a more deferential one. "I mean... where's everyone else? Am I the last student? I didn't realize it was getting dark already."

A few of the others around Adeyemi whispered to each other,

their murmurs as chilly as the early night winds. The way they gave TJ sidelong glances made him certain they all indeed *were* there because of him, because of what Ruby said back in the tent.

"I've sent the other JS3 boys to their dwellings," Adeyemi explained, then lifted a hand to Oroma, who had been dozing off atop a jutting rock. The Headmistress cleared her throat. "Oroma... please, escort TJ back to his quarters while my cohorts and I have a conversation with Ruby."

What were they going to discuss with Ruby? TJ wasn't sure he was ready for a bunch of strangers to know what he thought was supposed to be a private conversation between him and his oracle. Wasn't there some sort of oracle-patient confidentiality or something?

Rubbing sleep from her eye, Oroma groaned, "Yes, Head-mistress. Of course, Headmistress. I'll take him now." Despite her clearly trying to hold it back, Oroma yawned; it made TJ yawn too.

Elder Adeyemi smiled, glided over to TJ, and put a hand to his cheek. "Sleep well, Mr. Young. And listen well when you dream. Obatala is always trying to communicate at night." She turned her head to the rest of the waiting group. "The Oracle is ready for us. Everyone, follow me, please."

Each man and woman in their foreign and not-so-foreign garb entered the tent. Ruby's spot wasn't small, but it also shouldn't have fit as many as were piling in. TJ was sure some magic was at work there.

"Well, don't just stand there being nosy," Oroma snorted, waving TJ over. "Follow me."

"They're the ones crowdin' in on *my* reading." TJ thumbed behind him, but Oroma had already set off, humming a tune on her lips.

By the time they made it back down Oracle Rock, across the flat bridges, through the shallow rivers, and back through the thicket leading to the JS3 rock dwellings, TJ forgot everything Elder Adeyemi told him about listening well to his dreams. Instead, he fell right into his soft bed and saw nothing but abso-lute black.

13

GET IN WHERE YOU FIT IN

In his dreams, TJ found himself climbing an endless golden chain through the clouds. Fatigue captured his arms. His legs were like lead as cold wind forced goosebumps from his skin. Sweat crashed down his forehead and into his eyes, and he wondered if the chain would ever end. But through the vapor trails, he could *just* make out the impressions of... floating mountains? Twin clouds in the shape of agba drums? He just needed to hold on a little longer to reach them...

His limbs didn't like that idea.

It was much better to just fall instead, they seemed to say.

Shut up, stupid arms, TJ said back to them in his head.

It was fear that fueled him against his failing arms. It was fear that snatched at his heart as the climbing became too much. His hold became desperate. Instead of grasping link after link, he was looking for holes to fit his fingers in for leverage. But there were none. Gut bottoming out, he gave in and went tumbling through the winds, falling and falling and falling...

"Tomori Jomiloju..." a voice rasped to him from way up high, though it sounded more like a drone in the wind. Above him, a face painted itself from the clouds. Was that... Oya?

As he tumbled, wind crushing in around his ears, he fought against the watering of his eyes as he tried to make sense of the cloud that looked like it wielded a machete and a whip in each of its vapor hands.

"Tomori Jomiloju..." the voice croaked again. "Find me... find me."

Just as TJ made sense of the figure billowing in the clouds, his back found very hard ground. Though the pain in his back was sharp, it was far less violent than what he'd expected from a mile's long fall. TJ was still between dream and reality when he realized he was splayed out, back first, on the stone floor of his dorm room. Above him weren't the bright hues of clouds and vapor trails, but the muted colors of stone and cracks.

Hadn't Ruby said something about putting pillows out next to his bed? TJ had forgotten all about it, or rather, had been too tired to care.

Already, his dream was inking out of his mind. The details of that long climb were already blurring into a kaleidoscope of imagery and feeling. But it seemed as though he woke up at just the right time because Oroma was standing over Ayodeji's bed... without her head.

"Wake up, young man," Oroma's voice came from nowhere. Where the heck was her head?

"Ah!" Ayo screamed. If TJ wasn't already awake, the shout would've woken him.

All the other boys—except for Emeka—shot out of their beds. Ayo scrambled straight out of his sheets, revealing Oroma's head on his pillow. The woman-child cackled a horrible laugh as her body set her head right again. "Haha! Don't lose your head!"

"What?" Ayodeji grabbed at his neck. "No! No! Guys, did she take my head!? Did she take my head? Ah!"

"Hah! Made you look!" Oroma continued her chuckling as she lit crystals along the dorm's stone walls. The room filled with gentle orange light, revealing bunk beds filled with boys rubbing their eyes.

After the commotion of Oroma's morning call died down, she advised them all to keep a dream journal, which most of the boys scoffed at. TJ jotted a note about the chain and the floating mountains. And when he and Ayo walked to the mess hall together later, TJ explained what he could recall from his dream.

"Oh, the golden chain!" Ayo exclaimed in an excited whisper. "How could I forget? Bruh, we don't need to fall off a skyscraper or nothin' like that. We just need *that* to get to the Sky Realm. Did you see where the chain started?"

TJ shook his head. "Nah, I only remember climbing, but not how I got on the chain to begin with."

"Damn... the location of the golden chain is lost to time. Diviners been steady lookin' for it. But nothin'."

"I'm assuming the golden chain is a one-way ticket to the Sky Realm, then?"

"That'd be our best way up there. Maybe the only way." Ayo nodded as the sun peeked through the canopy above and revealed the mess hall ahead with its open tables covered by thatched roofing. Students appeared from different paths leading to different nature-based dormitories. The strips going down their dashiki shined every color of the rainbow, denoting their Orisha or elemental alignment. TJ was the only one who wore a dashiki uniform with blank gray strips and he tried to cross his arms to cover them, embarrassed.

"If you think about it," TJ said as they approached the line for breakfast, keeping his voice low, "We *did* find our own way into the Aqua Realm. I'll ask Eshu when we get in contact again. Just not sure how to get another two-hundred-plus people to do a communal chant to call him again."

"Year and name, please," a very large man asked them as they came to a table near the front of the chow line. He had deliberate, thin lines of scars going down from his forehead to chin.

"JS3. I'm Ayodeji Oyelowo. This is Tomori Jomiloju Young."

The man's lined face lifted at TJ's name. "Oh? Young? You don't mean..."

Ayo slung his arm over TJ's shoulder and pulled him in. "Yup. My boy's related to the Hero of Nigeria."

"Shame what happened to her. I heard about the funeral and those Keepers early this summer..." The man slammed his hands down on his table, making papers fly in the air. The sheets of parchment fell back down gently and perfectly in neat stacks. "Don't worry, boy. We'll make sure the Keepers get theirs. We're all behind you, all behind the Youngs and the Abimbolas.

You ever need anything, you ask for Ozolua." He threw a chunky, flamboyant thumb at himself. "Anyway, here are the suggested papers Oracle Ruby drew up for you boys. Have yourself a fine breakfast." He handed them each a sheet of paper, then leaned in close, making the table screech along the ground. "And don't forget to ask for the egg stew. I made it myself."

TJ and Ayo thanked Ozolua and made their way to the chow line, where sweet plantains, fried yams, and egg stew simmered from chafing dishes. The scent of savory mixed with sweet filled TJ's nose, but he wasn't paying attention to any of the food — despite the thunder in his stomach. His eyes were plastered on his schedule, which read:

A-Block | Mon, Wed, Fri
Breakfast
JS Open Ere Idaraya Training
Rest Break
JS3 Alchemy: Antidote Studies
JS3 Collaborative Magic
JS3 Personal Magic
Lunch Break
JS3 Ecology of Life Studies
JS3 Elemental Studies
Rest Break
JS3 Elective - Open/Pending

The bottom of the schedule listed the classes for B-Block, mostly composed of non-magical classes: English, Yoruba, Mathematics, Natural Sciences, Ethics, et cetera. And on the back of the paper, each class was accompanied by supplemental study sessions for Senior Secondary School entrance exams. TJ blew out a long breath. He knew high schools back in the States would have him changing classes more frequently, but he didn't expect to have a dozen different classes in a single term.

"Hey, what elective did the Oracle suggest for you, by the way?" Ayo asked as they found an open bench in the mess hall. The area was mostly filled with younger students who were eager to start term. TJ assumed the older students were getting as much rest as they could until their dorm leaders forced them to eat.

TJ peered over his schedule again, this time taking note of the bottom. "It says 'open.' I thought that meant I just choose for myself."

"Yeah, we get to choose for ourselves, but the Oracle makes her suggestions. She didn't say you should have Eshu studies or something else like that? That Eshu statue you activated was dormant for a long-ass time."

"Nah, it doesn't look like anything was suggested." TJ fiddled with his schedule. That had to be a bad thing, right?

Ayo took a peek over TJ's shoulder. "Weird."

Out the corner of his eye, TJ saw Emeka getting breakfast with a girl of similar height, deep-brown complexion, and familiar mannerisms, though where Emeka was of average build, the girl was curvier. Like TJ and Ayo, they spoke briefly with the cook, Ozolua. TJ thought he overheard something about the two of them being fraternal twins. When Emeka turned around with what TJ assumed was his sister, TJ tried to wave him down. But the boy, just like the night before, acted as though TJ wasn't there at all. And TJ knew for a *fact* they had made eye contact. What had Oracle Ruby said to him to get him so down so quickly?

TJ wanted to swap schedules to see if that would get Emeka talking, but he couldn't ask since the boy chose a bench on the very far end of the open-air mess hall.

"Oof, exam studies this, and exam studies that," Manny's voice came from behind. She forced her way between Ayo and TJ. Her mouth was filled with the fluffy bean cake known as *akara*. "Glad I don't have to worry about my SS entrance exams yet."

"What do you mean?" TJ asked, trying to ignore how good her green apple shampoo smelled. "What's *your* schedule say?"

Manny flipped her schedule slip over and slid it to TJ. There were no periods for study sessions, nothing about pre-exams or anything.

"Wait," TJ said, "I think your bunk leader gave you the wrong schedule. These are all JS2 level classes."

"That's because I'm JS2." Manny deadpanned.

"What!? You got held back?"

"No, yo. I'm thirteen, not fourteen. Did you forget?"

"Ooo," Ayo mocked through a long and exaggerated stream of cooing in TJ's direction.

TJ kicked Ayo under the table. "Shut up, Ayo. Nah, I knew you were thirteen but, like, an old thirteen. Like, you would be fourteen by the start of term."

"Nope, I don't turn fourteen until December."

"So that means we won't have classes together at all?" TJ tried not to sound too whiny about it, but the genuine shock laced in his voice might've been too much.

"Yeah... that part is going to suck." Manny stopped tossing akara in her mouth, trading her chewing for a frown. "I'll only see you — I mean, I'll only see *you guys* during breaks."

"Not exactly true." Ayo threw up a finger. "All the JS kids have Ere Idaraya training together. But yeah, after that... you gonna fly solo. You should be fine though. Umar was telling me you and some other girl were always hangin' around each other. What, did she not get accepted back like Emeka's friend?"

"I don't know," Manny said dismissively, then jabbed her chin to Ayo's lap. "What's that you're hiding over there?"

Ayo looked over both his shoulders and told Manny to hush. He definitely had something tucked between his egg stew and pineapple juice. TJ recalled how he had snuck a bunch of forbidden items into Camp Olosa during the summer. Only then he wasn't able to bring in more than spirit water. What he had now looked like a pocket journal... with a screen.

"It's my dream journal," he explained. "I enchanted it to relay headlines from *Divination Today* since we can't have our phones during the week. I was keeping track of your reporter, but there ain't nothin' poppin' up."

Manny shrugged. "It was in the States, so it might not be big news over here yet."

"Some random dude tries to trap you and Ifedayo Young's little brother in a stairwell? That should be some pretty big-time news. Which means there's a cover-up. What do you think, Teej?"

TJ wasn't sure what to make of it. After all, the UCMP officials seemed to be hush-hush about everything. Even in normal people's news, folks didn't hear about every ol' thing. TJ was sure there was stuff the FBI and CIA did that never made it to American readers—all that secret spy stuff you'd see in action movies.

"I'll ask Elder Adeyemi next time I see her," TJ said. "She knows about the airport and everything and she doesn't seem all that bothered. By the way, she had a bunch of people with her last night—other magical people, mostly diviners though."

"Yeah, they thought you'd probably have another promised child reading like your sister." Ayo took a sip of his juice as two aziza fairies flew behind him with trays of egg stew. "The Oracle Collective goes through all the academies around the world. Don't worry about all that. What you and me need to be focusing on is how we'll pass first term exams."

"Well, that and Olokun." TJ lifted his phone to Ayo, which read:

Eko Atlantic's Doomsday in 22 weeks, 5 days, 23 hours, 5 minutes, and 59 seconds

"That too, that too. Once that Yemoja frosty gemstone thing is squared away, we'll be good. Plus, my cousin's family owes mine a favor. I might get something going with the Eko Atlantic situation. I just need a little time. But first... did *you* read up on fire transformations during break?"

Nerves stirred in TJ's belly. He had tried to read some of the early chapters relating to fire magicks, but it was a sore reminder of the two years of magical instruction he had missed. The concepts brought up were filled with science-y terms like "thermodynamics," which made him glaze over.

When they all finished their breakfast, TJ, Manny, and Ayo headed over to the flat clearing between the great statue of Ogun and the Oshun waterfalls. TJ tried to cherish his last hour with Manny. But it was hard to do through a grueling physical education class with Miss Graves. It also didn't help that it aggravated Ayo's asthma, which apparently only started up after the summer. Worse yet, he didn't have an ordinary type of asthma. Sometimes, when he coughed hard enough, he belched lightning bolts.

"Maybe Shango is giving me a sign?" Ayo shrugged through a

coughing fit as TJ and Manny lapped him near the mist of the waterfall path they jogged on.

TJ had forgotten how much he hated the taxing workouts, which Miss Gravés seemed to have ramped up now that they were at Ifa Academy instead of Camp Olosa. They had to run two miles instead of one, perform a military regime of push-ups, pull-ups, and sit-ups, not to mention all the added weightlifting.

"Yup, Miss Gravés really is a Keeper," Ayo murmured haggardly as he and TJ switched off to spot each other for their bench presses later.

Manny agreed, stretching out the aching muscles in her biceps. "Yeah… she tryna kill us by… exhaustin' us to death."

At the end of class, Miss Gravés went on her spiel about the importance of physical training to enable their spirit-based magic. Hands on her hips, she ended her session by saying, in her strong voice, "And you JS3 students can forget about passing your SS entrance exams if you're *this* out of shape. Don't take these phys-ical training lessons lightly."

Ayo rolled his eyes and murmured to TJ with labored breaths, "What's she… lookin' at… *me* for?"

14

FIGS OF FLAME

THE STUDENTS ALTERNATED ON AN A AND B-BLOCK, A-BLOCK on Mondays, Wednesdays, and Fridays, and B-block on Tuesdays and Thursdays. Throughout that first week, the SS entrance exams became a recurring theme. From JS3 Alchemy: Antidote Studies, where Mrs. Falade said by year's end, all students should've been able to cure bush baby boils under the Orisha Babalu-Aye. To Personal Magic, where Mrs. Ibrahim told them that by Christmas they should have a handle on simple Eshu Illusionary magic with regards to cloaking inanimate objects. And even in Ecology of Life Studies, they were expected to classify all the major differences between the *yumboes* and the aziza.

That last one wasn't so bad. It was just basic Biology class like back home, except it was taught by a creature called a kishi—an incredibly handsome man with a hyena on the back of his head. Worse, as TJ looked up later, it was said that kishi seduced and devoured women, but apparently, Mr. Ikenna was, as he called it, "vegan".

Just like the earlier weeks of Camp Olosa, TJ struggled. Hard.

None of the classes were designed for his type of magic, save for Collaborative Magicks with Mr. Adebisi, which stemmed around ritualist and long-form magic.

"Great work, Mr. Young," Mr. Adebisi said during their

Wednesday session. "Everyone, look how easily the ritual flows through him and bolsters the whole of the group."

In the second half of the first week, after Adebisi sang TJ's praises to the rest of the staff, the other teachers attempted to mold their curriculums a bit more to TJ. They tried their best to translate decades-old methods that had garnered the academy a reputation for "the best marks in Senior Secondary Schools across West Africa" into methods better suited to TJ's unique talents.

Some of the students complained, including Emeka, who most definitely had some issue with TJ. That was why TJ—before meeting Manny and Ayo—avoided interacting with other teenagers. He just couldn't keep up, and friendships always led to some disappointment. But TJ, for the life of him, couldn't figure out what went wrong with Emeka. Perhaps Oracle Ruby told him to stay clear of him to achieve academic success. Heck, TJ's intrusion into the established curriculum of Ifa Academy would've been a clear sign of that. Still, it totally sucked. Emeka seemed like a cool dude.

By the end of the first week, many of the teachers—well, all of them, except Mr. Adebisi—gave up quickly on catering to TJ. The other teachers all said tailoring their *entire* disciplines to *one* student would be a disservice to the majority.

TJ couldn't blame them; it was completely fair. But it still left him floundering to find where he could fit in and thrive. Camp Olosa was more general magic education, so it was a lot easier to get his head around. Ifa Academy was hyper-focused and demanding. Now he understood why they had an acceptance rate lower than Harvard.

None made that more clear than Teacher Omo of Fon, the instructor for elemental studies.

"*True* magic concerns itself with control, the battle against chaos," she announced in her Friday class with a clenched fist shaking in the air. Despite her only being a foot tall and having a very light voice, she sometimes came off as a war general. "If we fail to tame our magic, it will swallow us whole. Nothing illustrates this better than the unstable element of fire. As I've stated before, when end-of-year exams come, you will be required to have complete control of the five classes of fire. On

Wednesday we went over Class-A: control of combustible materials. Today, we move on to flammable liquids—solvents, and the like."

Like always, their class was conducted in the middle of the Ifa Academy forest, where it was free of underwater classrooms and cave dwellings. And unlike most of the other classes that would usually take place in wide rooms with views that looked *out* into the forest, elemental studies took place *in* the forest among the dirt and foliage. Slanted rocks took the place of chairs, while thick canopies took the place of roofs.

Omo of Fon snapped her fingers and clapped her hands in a sequence of the intricate fae magic she employed. Within moments, a bubble of translucent liquid strung between her fingertips. TJ covered his nose from the burn. It was oil.

While in flight, their instructor wiggled her bare toes and clapped the bottom of her feet together. A fire manifested before her on a long stretch of log.

"Today, you will extinguish the flame on this log before it reaches the mountain fig trees alongside us. And you all know my rules."

"If we burn your mountain figs, you'll burn our toes," the class droned.

"Indeed."

TJ and the class were *pretty* sure she was joking—though they had come to know that Omo of Fon had one vice, her overindulgence of figs. Most of their exercises required them saving her grove of fig trees in one fashion or another, whether saving it from drowning in too much water, protecting it from getting pummeled by gales, or in this case... staving off a full-on forest fire.

"Mr. Young." Omo of Fon flew forward, mere inches from TJ's face. The blood and veins under her skin looked like green vines, and her eyes were the size of bulging softballs. "You will be my first example."

"Example?"

"I mean... prospect, of course, of course. Stand up straight and get to that log."

"Now!?"

TJ didn't get an answer. His only response was the fast-moving fire trail going down the log and toward the fig trees. He rushed forward, Teacher Omo's early lessons on his mind.

Class-B fires must be put out using foam, powder, or carbon dioxide extinguishers, he thought as he outstretched his hands. *Or, if the diviner is strong enough, they can diminish the fire's Ashe at its source.*

At Camp Olosa, TJ learned how to dampen one's use of Ashe by way of his abnormal abilities. But as he pushed out his Ashe toward the roaring flame, there was no magic to latch onto, nothing for him to take away. In fact, he couldn't even see the wisps of Ashe that usually floated before him.

"That will not work, Mr. Young," Teacher Omo of Fon said, floating over the line of flame. "Remember, fire magic takes on a life of its own once it separates from its host."

Okay, fine. Manifesting some foam will have to do. TJ rubbed his hands together like he was washing off dirt until a froth bubbled between his palms.

"*Fóọmù, wá sọ̀dọ̀ mi,*" he repeated as he shot out foam clumps from his palms. Each blob sloshed over the log, and the fire smothered under the foam momentarily but quickly rebirthed with double the intensity. TJ simply couldn't generate enough foam in time to extinguish the flames. Anxiety seized up in his arms.

"Psst," Ayo hissed behind TJ. TJ peered over his shoulder where his friend was giving him a signal they had come up with: a finger across the forehead and a point. It meant Ayo would open himself up so TJ could use his Ashe.

"No, no!" Teacher Omo bellowed. "Step back, Mr. Oyelowo. No cheating. This is for Mr. Young to do *alone.*"

"It's not cheating!" TJ protested. Sweat beaded his brow, more from nervousness and concentration than the heat. "That's just how my magic works, Teacher."

"No talk back. The flame is almost at my trees. Hurry, before they burn!"

Ayo gave TJ a sheepish shrug and stepped in line with the other students, who all stood with stiff shoulders and wide eyes. TJ tried to reach out for Ayo's Ashe anyway, but he was too far back and the other students weren't generating any magic of their own either, even passively.

Heart pounding in his ears, TJ whipped back to the flame. Teacher Omo had set *a lot* of firewood next to the trees, like, enough wood to warm a whole-ass village. And the oil she had manifested and slicked on them didn't help slow the fire roiling over it.

TJ tapped deep into his well of Ashe. He took a deep breath and let it out again. From his palms, more clumps of foam belched forth. He concentrated so hard that some even spewed from his mouth, and a salted chemical flavor coated his lips. Gross. But despite the flame retardant generated from three sources, he could not stop the rushing inferno as it raced to the root of the nearest tree.

Panic squeezed at TJ's chest as he ran straight up to the flame so that his foaming hands could put it out more directly.

It was too little, too late.

Despite how light-headed he was, despite how deep he was wading in his Ashe, without anyone to support him, without anyone else *he* could support who was stronger, he couldn't do a thing. Nervous, horror-stricken shakes took his hands as not one, not two, but three fig trees went up in hot-orange flame. The heat that licked at the tip of his nose and warmed his cheeks was like a sting.

"Help! Help me!" TJ cried out.

The whole forest was going to go up in flames. He couldn't do anything about it; he felt completely helpless.

"Tsk, tsk, Mr. Young," Teacher Omo chided from behind. TJ's mouth curled down in confusion. "Even under duress, you cannot produce JS3-level Ashe."

"What? What are you talking about? The trees! Teacher, you need to help me —"

TJ stopped freaking out when he turned and caught sight of the aziza's face. She shook her head, long and slow, until she lifted her hand and snapped her fingers. In an instant, all the fire went out like it was never there before. The only way someone would've known there was a fire at all was because TJ was sweating bullets and his dashiki uniform was drenched in perspiration and foam.

This wasn't just a test, it was a setup.

He didn't have to freak out about burning down half of Ifa Academy's forest. Of course Teacher Omo wouldn't have had the students potentially torching the place. He felt like a fool.

"Let me be *very* clear." Teacher Omo of Fon lowered her voice as though she were only speaking to TJ, but everyone could surely hear her next words. "Come the end-of-year exams, young man, you will not have others to cheat from. If you were like my kind, you'd have to fend for yourself in the forest alone for days. Half the things your sister did, she had to do alone. You will not always have your friends to sap from, Tomori Jomiloju. Learn to utilize your Ashe properly now, or forever be at the mercy of chaos."

Dizziness whirled around TJ's head and black spots dotted the edge of his vision. But none of that compared to the shame Teacher Omo had stabbed him with. Despite not having to go through the same trauma, the other students lined up shared in their trembling chins and rasping breaths.

"Now, who's next?" Teacher Omo asked, then pointed to Emeka. "You. Your turn."

Emeka's chest heaved so violently it looked like some foul creature could burst from it at any second.

"Hey, man, don't trip on Omo of Fon," Ayo said to TJ later when they were leaving class for the final rest break—TJ definitely needed one. "She's just a little extreme. But, you know, in the best way possible."

"That shit with the trees is going to traumatize me, man," TJ replied, only half-joking.

"Yeah, her kind had this big war. The elders say she used to be a lot nicer. Kinda."

TJ's unease with Ifa Academy's curriculum didn't stop at Omo of Fon's classes. His worry also extended to his elective classes, and, by the end of the week, he had attended nine different ones.

Each one was specific to a certain Orisha. The first one TJ tried was Eshu Studies, but despite knowing the Orisha personally, it didn't help him with the illusion magic they learned there unless he was grouped with others. Then there was Oya Studies. Manny tried to explain to him the concept of air-stepping, but the teacher could only explain how to work the magic individually, not how TJ could use it with others. So then TJ tried Shango Studies, where he could leech off Ayo's magic, but again, when split off from a partner, the lightning cages they were making that week simply dwindled.

On the first Saturday of term, TJ found himself buried in his books from morning until late afternoon. He couldn't even *think* of visiting New Ile-Ife to sample some of the treats from the cafes or visit the magical arcade that was hosting a Major League Crossover tournament with a cash prize.

Between their studies and their research on Olokun and the Aqua Realm and Oya and the Sky Realm, he, Manny, and Ayo had made claim to a balcony of the library tree. Their view overlooked the flat three bridges above the winding river. To his left, propped up on another stack of books was *Ailments and Antidotes* by Ekua Olayinka, and to his right—nearly falling off the edge of the balcony—was *Ancient Creatures: The Facts in the Myths* by Adannaya Temitope, and sandwiched between his hands was *Elements in Perfect Balance* by Olivia Bamidele.

Ayo sat on the ledge of the balcony, his feet swinging over the edge as he cleaned his glasses. After he got done, he slammed his copy of *Elements in Perfect Balance* shut, leaned back, and called out to TJ, "Quick, quiz me on elemental weaknesses."

"I'm not even on chapter two, dude," TJ groaned.

"Fine, I'll quiz *you*. What is divine water weak to?"

"Ayo… give 'im a break," Manny said from the side. She was laid back on the balcony, using her big hair as a pillow as usual. "Not everyone can read a book in an afternoon like you."

Ignoring Manny, Ayo said, "Well… TJ should know that divine waters are weak to divine lightning because Shango's fire was too weak for the ocean. Something we should know if we don't come through with Olokun. Bet money that's why Oya wants TJ to find Shango. And you know what kind of weapons Shango rolls with, right?" He deadpanned. "Lightning, guys. Lightning."

"Yeah, yeah," TJ sighed, "but we'd have to find the Sky Realm, Oya, and Shango first."

"Shhh, shhh." Manny sat up straight and cupped her ears. "Y'all hear that?"

TJ stopped reading and listened closely. There was some sort of flapping sound coming closer to them.

Ayo peeked over the edge of the balcony. "Oh shit. Speaking of the elements... Omo of Fon is headed up this way. TJ watch out." He started to chuckle. "She's comin' to burn them toes of yours!"

"Shut up, Ayo." TJ scoffed and stood up to peer over the balcony as well. Sure enough, the aziza teacher was flying straight up to their spot. Was she really coming to burn his toes? Was the ridicule yesterday not enough? Real talk... she did have a wicked look across her brow, and it made TJ uneasy. Granted, she always wore one sharp expression or another.

"Hey, Teacher Omo of Fon!" TJ waved, trying to come off as friendly as possible.

Kill her with kindness, TJ thought.

"Put away that wave, silly boy," the teacher gritted as she flew on level with their balcony.

Okay, so kindness wasn't going to fly with her. TJ did his best to stop his knees from shaking, and he couldn't keep his eyes from the teacher's fingertips—where any number of elemental spells could spring from.

"And don't look at me like I've just put you on the front lines, Mr. Young. Straighten up." TJ did just as she asked without even realizing he was obeying her. "I'm only here to fetch you. Elder Adeyemi wishes to speak with you at the Summoning Stone. Something about some problem with the ocean you're having. I told her you need to master fire before you even *think* of harnessing the ocean, but she insists—"

"Wait. The ocean? She really said that?"

"Did you just interrupt me, boy?" Teacher Omo of Fon's voice was ice, and its chill slithered through TJ's bones. Being frozen by her for real was probably not much different.

He, Ayo, and Manny all exchanged furtive glances before TJ gulped and said, "No, ma'am. Of course not, ma'am."

The aziza held her gaze and let the silence hang heavy in the air. The only thing cutting the quiet she had created was the light fluttering of her wings. They stood there for several minutes before the Teacher finally said, very slowly, "Good. Now follow me. And keep up."

15

THE CONSERVATORS OF MYSTICAL ARTIFACTS

September in Ogun State was like being in a parka in the middle of a desert, and for some reason, you weren't allowed to take the parka off. The weather made TJ's pits sweat, and he wondered if he should stop by his dorm to get a new dashiki uniform. But to do that, he'd need to catch his breath long enough to tell Teacher Omo of Fon, who was flying ahead of him through the forests of Ifa Academy.

Keeping up with a creature who could fly through the trees and brush like a hummingbird was just as difficult as TJ assumed it would be. It was like the aziza had forgotten that TJ didn't have wings as she did, and he told her as much the moment he could.

"Then air-step, young man." She pointed to the branches of a tree next to TJ's cobbled path. "I know you have trouble generating strong enough wind magic to hold your weight. But you see those leaves. Use the natural currents making them flutter, jump on them, and follow along."

And so TJ did—or at least he tried. A few minutes of an impromptu lesson in air-stepping later—which included a lot of falling on TJ's part—and TJ found himself at the statue portals that led to the underground Summoning Stone. Many of the other students had used air-stepping since he had gotten to the academy —usually the older teens who were late for class. TJ had never followed suit because, one, he had no business showing up late to class with his grades the way they were, and, two, he didn't want to embarrass himself.

As he tried his best to keep up with Teacher Omo of Fon, he had gathered a lot of speed along the way. Too much speed. When it was time to come back to the ground where the statue portals waited, he wasn't exactly sure how to stop himself.

To avoid looking like a total wimp, TJ did his best to clamp down the scream that wanted to escape his mouth as he came plummeting down. He flung out his hands, shooting air gusts from his palms, but his magic was too weak for the speed and he couldn't slow his descent.

This is gonna hurt... TJ thought as he clenched his muscles for the impact. But just before he hit the ground, he was caught in a sudden cushion of wind. All around him, the mist of Ashe lifted him above the ground. Even if he didn't have his special vision, the leaves that floated around him would've told him his wind magic had worked.

"I did it!" TJ shouted, his voice cracking with excitement and terror. "Holy s—I mean, holy crud! I did it. Teacher, are you seeing this?"

TJ turned to find Teacher Omo of Fon floating over him, the green veins under her skin matching the canopy above them. Her hands were oscillating near her chest as though she were waxing a car. Ashe wafted off her fingertips, Ashe that directed a path to the wind pillow TJ hovered upon.

"Yes, I am seeing it." Omo of Fon stopped the graceful movement of her hands and TJ fell onto the hard ground. "You didn't think *you* did that, did you?"

TJ couldn't decide if the pain in his chest was a physical one or one generated from wounded pride. Once again, the aziza teacher had saved his butt—and here he thought he'd done it himself. "N-no, no. I knew that was you, Teacher. Um... Thank you."

The aziza pursed her lips, unconvinced. Then she swirled her finger in a pattern above her head. Air currents gathered below TJ and he was set upright once more.

"That was desperate and stupid just to keep up with me," she said with some bite. "Learn how to air-step, Mr. Young. It's a vital skill to have. And it'll be on your SS entrance exams. Now... go on. The Headmistress is waiting."

Always entrance exams with these teachers...

TJ wanted to shake his head, but instead, he bowed and thanked his teacher once more before touching the leg of the Eshu statue before him. A short moment passed, and a portal blossomed into existence between the Gatekeeper's knees. Once again, his Eshu finger tattoo warmed in concert with the magic, glowing softly. TJ stepped through the portal to the cool breath of the underground cavern, a welcome relief to the warm September day outside.

"Ah, there he is!" Elder Adeyemi clapped and smiled. Her outfit of choice that day was a solid blue dress with seashells set at the hems. Atop her head was a big white headscarf. She stood near the large Yemoja statue that led into that weird pool-like chamber. TJ understood why she was wearing the dress...

It was time for them to get Yemoja's gemstone.

Next to the Elder stood three others. The light in the cavern was dim, but TJ could just make out that each of them wore pointed hats and cloaks of deep burgundy. Each cloak was clasped together by golden buttons near the neck. One man sported a long white beard, the other, a short, blonde goatee and a thick mustache that covered the middle of his face. The sole woman had jet black hair all the way down her back.

"Tomori Jomiloju," Elder Adeyemi started. "I'd like to introduce you to the conservators from the Museum of Mystical Artifacts. They are visiting us all the way from the United Kingdom."

Each of them gave TJ a greeting in the form of bows, but the man with the beard and the woman gave each other sidelong glances. TJ didn't like the way they had done that.

"Our fine friends know about our situation," Adeyemi went on. "Myself and the other councilors of the UCMP have requested their help." She gestured to what looked like a floating jewelry box that hovered between herself and their guests. It was open, revealing a jagged shard that pulsated with an arctic blue radiance. The shard rested over a comfy-looking inner lining fluffed like a pillow. "We have found Yemoja's gemstone. Well... at least where it resides."

TJ drew closer to the group to get a better look at the shard. "What do you mean by 'where it resides,' Headmistress?"

The man with the blonde goatee stepped forward. "Your Headmistress here believes the lost gemstone of Yemoja might be hidden in this shard. You see, this fragment here is an ancient doorway, one that is unfinished. A Frost Realm your deity was working to create over two millennia ago."

"With all due respect." The woman with black hair forced a smile that looked entirely too practiced. "Why are we explaining this to a student? Mrs. Adeyemi—"

"*Elder* Adeyemi," she corrected the other woman kindly.

"Apologies, Elder," the woman said bitterly. "We were under the impression we would only be meeting with you about the Sacred Ice Shard. We never said anything about having a student among us—oh!" The woman did a little jump in her robes. "Excuse me, boy; please, do not touch. That shard is older than most of civilization."

TJ did his own little jump away from the shard at her panic. But something had been calling to him, deep and slow. The jagged stone was mostly unbroken, but there was a sliver near the bottom, a tiny opening where the calling drew him in.

"Sorry, ma'am." TJ took another step away and lowered his head. The woman's voice hadn't carried any apparent malice, but TJ could still feel the chastisement. Maybe it was just because everyone's voice seemed to boom within the echo of the Summoning Stone.

"Master Conservators," Elder Adeyemi inclined her head, "The reason we are here is *because* of Tomori Jomiloju. You and your fellows have toiled with the shard for centuries now. I couldn't even find records of the museum having it in its possession; it's been so long. You've not tried to access the Ice Realm in decades. TJ here can assist you. Together we will crack the code which has been so elusive for your organization."

The conservators all shifted their gazes to TJ, who gave them an awkward wave. "I don't know how much they told you," he said. "But I've got, like, special abilities. This wouldn't be the first gateway I've opened... um... where deities and magic are concerned. Sirs. Ma'am."

The goateed man looked upon TJ with curious eyes. His enormous mustache twitched as he said, "Hang on a minute. You're that boy the Seers have been going on about, aren't you? The one from the summer camp in the States?"

"Yup, that's me!" TJ beamed. "Hopefully you've heard nothing but good things." TJ was hoping he wasn't being too playful, but he wanted to make sure he was selling himself. That's what Elder Adeyemi wanted him to do, right?

"The child is our best way forward," Adeyemi cut in gently. "Our interests are aligned with yours. There's no point in allowing the shard to collect more dust."

There was silence as the trio glanced amongst themselves.

The man with the long white beard TJ could only call wizard-like, stuck out a finger and asked, "Would you give us a moment while we confer with one another?"

"Of course." Adeyemi gave them a small curtsy.

TJ watched nervously as the conservators huddled in and spoke with one another in hushed tones. What was the big deal? If that one guy with the goatee had heard about TJ already, surely they knew what he could do. Sure, that shard did look really old and was probably priceless, but Elder Adeyemi would've told them how important it was to keep Olokun happy. And if that meant finding Yemoja's lost jewelry to make *her* happy, then that should've been an easy yes for everyone.

The next moments snailed by as TJ patiently waited for their answers. The only thing to pierce the quiet was the lapping of the water in the pool of Yemoja's chamber. TJ spent most of his time staring at the Sacred Ice Shard and wondering how a whole realm could fit in there or why Yemoja wanted her ice magic back to begin with.

They will not allow you to touch the shard, a familiar voice said gently in TJ's mind. It sounded like Elder Adeyemi.

TJ whipped his head to his headmistress with a questioning look. "Did you say something?"

The group stopped their conversation to look over their shoulders at TJ. Adeyemi waved them off with a kind smile. "Voices carry in this chamber. The boy must've heard one of your echoes. Take your time, please."

The woman narrowed her eyes at that, and the wizard-looking dude raised an eyebrow, but both turned back to their mustached companion.

TJ scratched his head. He was almost certain he had heard Elder Adeyemi in his head.

It is me, Tomori Jomiloju. Don't look so frazzled. They aren't going to allow us to use the stone as we would like. So I'll need you to follow my lead.

TJ stiffened again. It was weird having someone in his head. During the summer, Elder Adeyemi had mentioned she had a talent for telepathy, but she had never used it on him before.

Follow your lead? TJ thought-spoke to the Elder, hoping that would work. *But why didn't you tell them about me?*

Because they wouldn't have come, and they would've kept their little shard locked away in their vaults. TJ stared at Elder Adeyemi, whose face looked perfectly at ease, a neutral smile on her face.

Woah, TJ thought, *so thought-speaking back at you is pretty easy.*

Child, try not to move your lips when you 'thought-speak' back to me. You'll give us away. Actually, don't actively think at me at all. The female conservator can read your active thoughts if she's aiming at you; she's been attempting to press into my mind this entire time. Just… listen to what I have to say and then do it. Do you understand?

TJ was about to think back at Elder Adeyemi, but instead, he just flung a thumbs up at his side.

But before we do this. This will be dangerous, Tomori Jomiloju. I believe if we are to make Olokun happy, it is necessary, but the risk lies on your shoulders alone. Are you sure you want to do this?

TJ wanted to ask how dangerous it could be, but he knew Elder Adeyemi wouldn't put him in any real danger, especially while they were on school grounds. Without thinking about it too long, he gave the Elder another thumbs up.

Good, now listen closely.

16

FROSTY RECEPTION

THE CONSERVATORS DELIBERATED FOR SEVERAL MINUTES MORE, which gave Adeyemi all the time she needed to explain her plan to TJ. He was a bit nervous and hoped that the woman with the black hair couldn't hear beating hearts along with active thoughts. To keep her from reading his mind, TJ kept humming his ABCs on repeat in his head.

"We have come to a majority decision," the wizard-looking guy with the white beard declared.

TJ made particular note of his words "majority decision."

"We will only allow you, Elder Adeyemi, to examine the shard." The woman inclined her pointed hat and her hair fell forward with her. "You *alone.*"

The man with the blonde goatee didn't say a word. TJ would've guessed that he was the one who didn't agree.

Well, goatee guy, TJ thought, *you just went to the top of my favorite people list.* For whatever *that* was worth.

"Very well," Elder Adeyemi said. "As you wish it. Do you mind if I hold the Sacred Shard over the pool for a moment? There's a ritual I'd like to attempt to see if there's anything I can do to awaken the doorway to the Ice Realm."

The conservators glanced at one another. Each of them gave the other a nod of approval. The woman at the center gestured toward the floating box that housed the shard. "We will allow it."

Gingerly, Elder Adeyemi lifted the shard over her veiny palms. And with her signature grace, she glided over to the pool of the Yemoja chamber. The moment she crossed the threshold of the stone pillars into the chamber, the shard lit up in a sharper, brighter blue. The large slabs of stone surrounding them reflected its color, casting off the craggy rock walls and giving light to the Yemoja statue that was overwatching from above. And then... The shard shook in Elder Adeyemi's hand as though a tiny creature was about to hatch from it.

"My word!" the conservator with the blonde goatee said. "Can it actually be?"

It was working!

Now, as Elder Adeyemi explained it to TJ, there was nothing she could do with the shard on her own, but she had to make it *appear* as though something was progressing. Through his Ashe vision, TJ could see her magic at play: The light from the shard hadn't come from the source or some ritual. Adeyemi had just cast a bit of Orunmila's Glow around it to make it seem as such. The shaking, however, was a nice added effect. The Elder hadn't mentioned she'd do that. But it was a perfect segue to what was coming next.

As the shaking continued violently between Adeyemi's fingers, she did her best to grip it to her chest. But as she shifted her hold, the shard slipped through her fingers and *thunked* into the pool below. The ancient artifact fell hard and fast, sinking straight to the bottom.

"The shard!" blurted the female conservator.

"Quickly, before it reaches the bottom," the wizard shouted as he drew a wand from his cloak to summon a strange wisp from its tip. It wasn't like the Ashe TJ often saw. It was a more jagged thing, like streams of symbols flittering through the air. But TJ could see it well enough to understand it was arcane, divineless magic, and it had a hard time pressing through the enchanted spirit water of the pool.

Now it was TJ's turn to play his part in the charade.

"I'll get it, Headmistress!" he called out as though it was his only line in a stage play.

Diving into the pool, dashiki uniform and all, TJ rushed

through the waters, letting its sharp chill wash over him. He couldn't afford to think how cold it was. All he could do was race down to that shard and get a finger on it.

Using water magic to propel him forward, TJ shot for the sliver of ice that was disappearing into the dark depths of the pool. Were it not for its faint glow, TJ might've lost sight of it entirely. What if he *did* lose sight of it? What if he couldn't make it and they lost their chance? Fear tried to force its hold around his thrashing arms, but TJ didn't allow it to stop him. He reached out, and his finger grazed the edge of the shard.

Energy flooded his body, his veins, his very blood. It was like being back at the lagoon at Camp Olosa. The sensations he felt then came racing back to the present: how fast Ol' Sally, the giant alligator, swam to the bottom as she showed him the way to the Aqua Realm. And just like that, before TJ knew it, he was squeezing through a cold, letterbox-crack, vomited out onto a slick, slippery surface.

If he had thought he was cold before, it was nothing in comparison to what he felt then.

All around him was flat ice encircled by a wall of frozen cliffs. It wasn't like he was in Antarctica or some other ice-filled land, however. This felt more like some unfinished level in a video game. The sky wasn't really sky but more a slate splinter, like he was under a block of ice but instead of swimming and freezing in water, he was breathing in fresh chill air. Every so often the ice below, the cliffs all around, and the "sky-ceiling" above sort of glitched out. Ice cracked into itself and reformed in the next moment. The fog that blew off the cliffs had strange, fragmenting colors, like an old 3D movie. And TJ would've sworn the cliffs across from him in the distance were moving. It even looked like faces were carved into them like at Mount Rushmore. Though instead of presidents, they looked like a bunch of monsters.

"*Ujolimo Iromot!*" a strange clipped voice came from behind.

TJ turned to the voice, where he had entered the unfinished Ice Realm and nearly jumped out of his skin. He slipped back on the ice, scrambling away from an enormous, darting eyeball. His heart thundered in his chest, and it took him a long, terrifying minute to recognize the sight before him. He was looking at the same split he had seen in the shard before but from the other side. He was *inside the shard*!

That voice kept saying that strange, slurred phrase, though. *"Ujolimo Iromot! Ujolimo Iromot!"*

TJ reached a hand out to the giant eye, but as his hand pressed against the threshold, he felt resistance. Somehow he knew if he pressed forward with enough force, he'd be sucked back into reality, where there were at least a couple of angry conservators waiting on the other end. Now that he'd made sense of it all in his mind, he realized whose giant eye he was looking at.

"Elder Adeyemi!"

As soon as he cried out, the elder's eye was replaced with a blue one, a blue one with jet black hair just over the brow.

"Nam gnuoy, won thgir ereh kcab teg uoy!" That was the voice of that conservator woman. It had to be. It had that same British accent, it just was... off. Like... like...

They're speaking in reverse!

Something about the barrier, something about the strange place, turned everything on its head. Could they see him and what he was doing within the shard? Would his voice be in reverse on their end, too? TJ cupped his hands and shouted back, "I made it! Where do I find Yemoja's gemstone?"

A whisper came to TJ's ear—as though the frost in the air spoke to him. Then a pull came at his shoulder. He pivoted on his heel and squinted against the bright of the ice blue ahead. But there was something out there in the middle of the ice bed that shone just a little brighter.

A small, uneven ice pyramid stood proud in the distance, and just at its tip, TJ would've bet money that's where Yemoja's gemstone was lodged. It was hard to see from this far though, and as he looked down at the frozen lake, TJ wasn't sure he wanted to risk running on that ice. Then again, he wasn't sure if the same rules applied in this fractured realm. Was there even any real water beneath him at all? Or was it just enchanted ice that couldn't melt or crack?

Where's Ayo to explain these things when I need him?

Behind him, the strange reverse voices called out to him. He couldn't understand much of what they said, but he shouted back again. "I think I have to cross the frozen lake or whatever this is!"

Perhaps he shouted too loudly or perhaps his good ol' nickname of "Lucky Charm" was finally wearing off. But his final words sent a crack through the slit he had come through, and it fissured up and up and up. The strange sky-ceiling splintered and blocks of ice came crashing down right above TJ's head.

He didn't have time for fear. He wasn't even thinking at all as adrenaline forced him out onto the frozen lake and away from the impending avalanche. Feet slipping and sliding, he raced away from the blocks raining from on high. As each piece of the sky-ceiling fell away, the other side revealed more of the real world. TJ could make out Elder Adeyemi's blue dress and the white beard of that wizard-looking dude.

After what felt like a lifetime of running, the avalanche finally stopped behind him, and TJ found himself almost a quarter of the way to his goal.

Well, that was close, he thought.

But then…

A great big roar shook the entire fractured realm.

That cliff with the Mount Rushmore monsters… Yup, they were *actually* monsters. Well, not monsters exactly, more like one very enormous one. A gargantuan ice giant, fused with other ice giants, to make the mother of all ice giants. Its shoulders, back, legs, and arms were all plastered with the grotesque faces of monsters. And it nearly made TJ slip, fall, and crack his head on the ice, just off the back of it simply standing up.

The realm cracked around the creature's enormous bulk. Fractures spidered up the wall behind it, and the sky-ceiling came down again like the hand of a god.

"*Enotsmeg eht! Enotsmeg eht!*" TJ heard Adeyemi's voice call out. He still couldn't quite understand her, but he knew what had to happen next: the gemstone needed to be in his hands, like, yesterday.

TJ was pretty sure he had pissed himself, but that didn't slow him down as he sprinted off to the gemstone, racing the ice giant that seemed to be going for the same thing across the way.

Why am I running toward *the ice giant? Why am I running* toward *the ice giant?*

Freaking out internally every step of the way, TJ sprinted closer to the jagged pyramid housing Yemoja's gemstone. Somehow, running made him feel better. Or maybe exhaustion simply forced him to forget what he was actually doing. There was a freaking ice giant a few hundred feet ahead of him and he was running *toward* it!

As he approached the gemstone, the falling sky closed in on him too, and he had to dodge ice blocks both small and large. Before him, his prism-vision sparked off. Like when he played basketball back at school, he felt where he needed to be intuitively, knew each step he had to take to not get sliced or completely smashed by ice.

But it was one thing to see the path, it was another entirely to follow it.

These were the times when he needed Manny and Ayo. He could already see how he'd direct them to get around this maze of madness. Ayo could have used some of his fire and lightning to break away new paths TJ *saw* but couldn't *take*. Manny could air-step and snag up that gemstone with no issue. It was a terrible feeling to know exactly what needed to be done without being able to physically do it.

And TJ had to do it; Elder Adeyemi was counting on him.

Without his friends, TJ had to take the slow and more cautious path, but that meant losing vital time. By the time he made it to the gemstone, the ice giant was a mere football field away. What was worse, each time the giant got hit with ice blocks, instead of being slowed, it just grew stronger, absorbing the ice into its body to create a new face. TJ didn't have time to think about how utterly screwed he was. He just gulped, grabbed the apple-sized gemstone, and shot his hand out to the ice around him.

Fire spewed from his fingertips, but it wasn't nearly powerful enough to break the enchanted ice, and it certainly wouldn't do a thing to that patchwork ice giant bearing down on him in a rage. He was hoping he could break the ice below the beast, but that was a naïve notion.

Oh shit... I'm gonna die.

"Help!" TJ shouted above to the pieces of reality that were showing through. "I got the gemstone but I need stronger fire! Please, help!"

No answer came.

It sounded like the adults were arguing on the other side and the ice monster was just *feet* away. So TJ closed his eyes, conjured all his strength, and did something desperate and stupid, just as Teacher Omo of Fon had said.

As the ice monster brought down its colossal fist in a hammer punch, TJ summoned wind within his belly and shot it right out through his feet like he had jet packs for shoes. He flew so high in the air he nearly reached the height of the ice giant's face, which tried to bite him out of the air. Putting on another burst of wind speed, TJ dodged away just in time, actually kicking off one of the ice creature's car-sized teeth.

The deadly game pressed on like that, with the ice giant grunting and swiping, and TJ just ducking and diving—and trying not to pee his pants. He took a few cuts here and there, but nothing so major as getting his entire arm cut off, which he realized with great fright could've happened at any time as the ice giant's sharp fist whizzed by his shoulder.

Eventually, TJ's air-stepping came to an end. He couldn't keep it up forever and that meant he went crashing back down to the ice lake.

His thoughts flashed to Teacher Omo of Fon and their trip through the canopies of Ifa Academy. That same terror that had seized TJ when he had fallen then had returned in full force. This time he used the last of his reserves to push wind out beneath him to slow his fall. He had the technique down, rotating his hands like the aziza teacher did, but it was impossible to focus while an ice giant grunted in his ear and kept attacking him mid-air. When TJ's feet made contact with the ice lake, he heard a *pop*, or maybe it was a snap. He couldn't quite tell because he was too busy screaming his head off.

His right ankle swelled with pain.

This is why Manny was the crossover star, *not* him!

Grunting against the agony, TJ lifted to his knees and shot a wind blast behind him to force his body to slide forward—now that his legs were useless. But he was going far too slow. He still had to dodge ice blocks from above, and the ice monster hurled sheets of ice from its body at TJ.

Above, within the cracks between reality and the Ice Realm, strange plumes of fire suspended in the air, as though they were trying to get through an invisible barrier. Was that just like when TJ tried to press his hand through the slit he came in, or when that wizard's spell couldn't get through the pool? Maybe that fire plume needed a push, just like Dad's car. The adults were finally supplying him with some help, but their magic couldn't pass through the realm. But TJ was that "in-between" they all needed to breach the gap.

Diving into his well of Ashe, TJ pulled the fire from the sky-ceiling and brought it down atop the ice giant that pursued him. But the fire didn't just rush down over the giant, it filled the entire realm with reckless abandon, melting everything it touched.

The ice giant let out a pained cry as the frosty surface around it became a lake of boiling water.

Good news for TJ. The bad news... that same melting water was only feet away from him, too.

He needed to find an exit. Anywhere the fire hadn't touched yet. It didn't help that all the fast-melting ice had created great clouds of steam. Two blue eyes, the two dying eyes of the ice giant, widened as the sizzling took it away into the scalding waters.

Sweat dotted TJ's forehead, and it was hard to breathe, but he could just make out the slit he had come in from. He set his hand to the little ice he had left and pushed himself across the sliver he had to get across, straight out and back to safety. As he rushed forward, though, heat baked his bottom and blisters quickly bubbled along his legs.

The pain was like getting fried by every hot iron that existed.

TJ bit his tongue to make the anguish go away, clenched his muscles so he'd have the strength to go on. And then...

He fell onto cold, hard stone.

The bright blue, the white steam that had filled his vision before was replaced with dark gray and shadows. Above him stood the conservators and Elder Adeyemi, all of them with faces of utter shock.

He was back within the Summoning Stone, back within its safety and away from that hellscape of an ice world. TJ's heart pounded in his ears. He hadn't realized until then how totally afraid he had been. It just seemed like his mind and heart were finally catching up.

He winced, feeling every sting that pestered his legs and bottom. But he lifted the arctic blue, shimmering gemstone he still held in his hand, and, through a pained and long sigh, he said, "Please... please, tell me this is Yemoja's gemstone."

17

CAUSE FOR CONCERN

ALL THE ADULTS LOOKED DOWN AT TJ IN UTTER HORROR. OR at least that's what it looked like to him, lying flat on his back on the chamber floor. The Summoning Stone was so dim, it was hard to make out their features. The wizard-looking dude had clenched fists at his side, the woman with the black hair held her hand over her mouth, and the guy with the blonde goatee held the sides of his head, scrunching the brim of his pointy hat.

TJ assumed their terrified expressions were from the way he looked. His pants were mostly burned away, and though he couldn't see his legs properly, he knew they were riddled with blisters that still stung. Blood trickled down his arms and face from cuts he received from that ice monster and he was breathing heavily and haggard.

Yet that's not what any of them were staring at. Their eye lines were tracking somewhere else.

Just to TJ's side along the stone floor, the Sacred Ice Shard that he had just come from lay at the edge of Yemoja's chamber pool. It bubbled and popped, melting from the inside out. It shrunk smaller and smaller until it was nothing but an ice cube, and then… nothing at all, just puddles in the cracks of the floor.

An Ice Shard that was supposedly older than most human civilizations… gone. Just like that.

"Tomori Jomiloju, are you all right?" Elder Adeyemi was at

his side in a flash. A cool sensation brushed over TJ's boils and the stinging pain subsided. "Here, drink this quickly before your boils start festering." She withdrew a vial from her dress, a glass tube with light green liquid that smelled of grapeseed oil. "You never cease to amaze me, young man. You brilliant boy!"

"Brilliant boy!?" The woman conservator was at his side now, too. Her hands glowed a soft green, and the smell of aloe wafted above them as she held her hands above his legs. The woman shook her head and muttered angrily under her breath as she worked to heal TJ. "Over two millennia of existence. Centuries in our care. Reduced to a puddle! What in stars were you thinking sending the boy in like that?"

"Conservator Bennett," the man with the blonde goatee said. "The Headmistress did not mean for this to happen, the boy was just trying to help—"

"She knew damned well what she was doing, Burch. And you're a fool if you believe otherwise," the woman, or rather, Conservator Bennet, replied. She whipped her head to Elder Adeyemi. "Your council will be hearing about this."

The still unnamed wizard-looking dude stepped forward and then kneeled beside TJ. He tapped a heavy, calloused hand on TJ's still-clenched fist. "Let me have a look at that gemstone, little lad."

TJ pulled away from the old man and kept his palm clenched tight around the gemstone. "Gee, I'm doing fine, by the way. Thanks for asking."

"You'll be fine, my boy. Eleanor Bennet here is an excellent healer. As is your Headmistress, I'm sure. You've been very brave. Now let's take a look at what results your courage has yielded us, shall we?" He stretched out his hand again, holding it open for TJ to hand the gemstone over.

"I'm afraid it's not his to give, Conservator." Elder Adeyemi stood, rising to her full height. The Yemoja statue that stood above and behind her seemed to watch over them all, as though backing the Elder up with its glowing blue eyes. "The gemstone was Yoruba-derived, a device of our Orisha, Yemoja, Queen of the Sea. By international magical law, it must remain with us."

The wizard stood back up as well, slower than Adeyemi and

with the long groan of a truly old man. "Legend has it that that shard was created in concert with the deities of the Norse. That ice giant was a *Jötunn*, Elder."

"Well, if the Norse enclave wishes to come and collect the remnant of the shard, I'm happy to keep it safe for them. Or, if you prefer, you can take it back with you yourselves." Elder Adeyemi drew the puddling water up from the ground with a wave of her hand, then poured it into the empty vial from TJ's anti-burn potion. The wizard frowned.

"Listen, Conservator Armstrong," Adeyemi pressed on, "it's our coast under threat. Not the United Kingdom's. You have more than enough protection of your own through the Henge, even if it was. The gemstone stays with us."

Elder Adeyemi was right, but TJ could understand why their guests were as frustrated as they were. They had to answer to someone. If they came back empty-handed, they were certainly going to be in a hotbed of trouble.

"Come now, let's leave the matter on peaceful terms," Adeyemi finished after a prolonged beat.

TJ glanced back down at the Bennet woman, still healing his legs. She had pinched her lips so tightly it didn't look like she had a mouth. TJ was sure she was trying to go over some sort of loophole in her mind.

It was the blonde guy called Burch that eventually answered, breaking the awkward silence with a clearing of his throat. "Of course, well, we can all discuss the issue further once we've checked back in with our councils. How's the boy doing, Bennet?"

"He'll be fine, just some minor scarring. Bedrest and a brew and you'll be back on your feet in no time." She gave a barely-there pat on TJ's shoulder and stood to face Elder Adeyemi. "As I said, you'll be hearing from us."

"You know where to find me, and I believe you know where the exit is as well."

Grunting, Conservator Bennet stepped away. Together, she and the wizard, Armstrong, walked off and out of the Summoning Stone to the path that led back to New Ile-Ife village. Conservator Burch, with his huge blonde mustache, hung behind, his forehead wrinkling in uncertainty. "I'll try to speak to them, Elder Adeyemi. At the very least, I can try to cool things down before we brief our council and get things smoothed out a little in the telling. I'll, ahem, I'll take that as well, shall I?" He gave a nod down to the vial still in Elder Adeyemi's hand.

The Headmistress closed her eyes and bowed her head. "As ever, I am in your debt, Conservator Burch. You should keep up with the others. We don't want to ruffle their feathers further." She held the vial out to him.

Taking another bow, he took it —*carefully*— and left. It wasn't until a distinct *pop* echoed off the dirt walls that Elder Adeyemi turned her attention back on TJ. "Is your mother aware of the situation with Olokun, or of our work to stop him?"

"No, ma'am," TJ answered. Mom would be a good person to share information with at this point, though. After all, she was aligned with Yemoja, and TJ held Yemoja's gemstone between his fingers.

"Good," Adeyemi replied. "Let's keep it that way, shall we? My own heart is still thundering from your latest display of Young family heroism. I don't wish to burden her unnecessarily until we have no other choice."

Despite wanting Mom's help, TJ couldn't help thinking what the Elder said was for the best. Mom freaked out whenever TJ came home with cuts from playing tag with the neighbor kids. If she knew an ice giant nearly made him into Swiss cheese, she might've had a mental breakdown.

After the effects of that green potion smoothed out most of the blisters on TJ's leg, Elder Adeyemi helped him up and led him back to the academy grounds toward the Hospital Tree.

"What was that thing I fought?" TJ asked as they walked through the path of the willows. "What's a Jötunn?"

Adeyemi explained that it was a giant from an old Norse myth. She also confirmed that the rumors the conservators spoke of were true, that Yemoja had worked alongside Norse deities to craft the Frost Realm before the project got cut short by the Great Separation. TJ had more questions, like how that trick with the fire worked at all, or what the laws of magic were in that fractured

Ice Realm, but they had to stop their conversation once Adeyemi handed TJ over to the academy healers.

Later, when Manny and Ayo heard TJ had been sent to the Hospital Tree, TJ was in much better shape, but that didn't stop Manny from looking gravely concerned. "Yemoja's my secondary Orisha alignment. I could've *helped* you!"

Ayo, on the other hand, sucked his teeth and said, "Yeah, man, you should have told us. Fighting an ice giant sounds pretty lit!"

"Can we not talk about anything being 'lit'? Sort of a sore topic at the moment." TJ gestured to his legs, which were wrapped with bandages.

"Heh," Manny let out her first chuckle since she got there. "'*Sore*' topic."

No matter the situation, Manny always found a dad joke in any situation. TJ smiled at that, and almost forgot the dull pain pressing around his entire body.

THE NEXT WEEK IT WAS LIKE NOTHING HAD HAPPENED. WHEN Omo of Fon started to teach them the foundations of ice magic, TJ almost wanted to explain how he took on an ice giant and lived to tell the tale, but Elder Adeyemi had told him he wasn't to mention the ordeal to anyone. Plus, it wouldn't have mattered to a teacher like Omo of Fon, who would've just said something like "Oh, an ice giant? Then show us how we take on such a beast." To which TJ would've had to tell the real truth, confessing that he had fractured his legs and got them burned with crispy boils for his trouble.

Teacher Omo of Fon's words kept pounding in his head, though. When it came to exams, when it came to the *real* world, he wouldn't always have his friends to help.

The little stings on his legs were a *literal* sore reminder.

And because of that painful reminder, that day after class, TJ requested private lessons from a certain aziza.

18

WHAT ARE FRIENDS FOR?

BEING ATTACKED BY A GIANT ICE MONSTER AND GETTING scalded across his entire body was the perfect motivator for TJ's magical education. Teacher Omo of Fon was right. TJ wouldn't always have his friends around and he needed to put the work in where physical conditioning and elementalism were concerned. Sure, he got the gemstone on his own, but it was only because of Elder Adeyemi's fireball that he was still breathing today. He barely got Omo of Fon to give him extra lessons. It wasn't until she proposed training at the crack of dawn—which meant TJ had to wake a whole hour earlier than usual—that she agreed.

The lessons she imparted were invaluable, but they left TJ with almost no free time. Were it not for Collaborative Magicks class, TJ would've thought he'd flunk out of Ifa Academy. His top grades in the class made up for everything else he was well below average in. And thanks to Ayo always helping him with homework, he kept his head above water.

Despite grueling classes, the rest of Ifa Academy was great, almost like being back at camp. On Thursday nights they got to go up to Oracle Rock where they heard patakís—sacred fables—of Orishas while they observed the night sky. TJ had briefly wondered if he could earn extra credit if he told the tale of *The Boy and The Gemstone*, starring him and Yemoja. But he expected Elder Adeyemi wouldn't be very happy with him if he did.

On the weekends, they got to visit New Ile-Ife proper, where Ayo introduced TJ and Manny to the bakery, Sweet Tooth Ruth's, which had the most delicious puff puffs—basically American donut holes but fluffier. They tried to visit Adeola and Mr. Du Bois in the hospital, but no visitors were being permitted. At the academy, there were tons of after-school activities: theater classes where students reenacted the most famous stories of the Orishas, sports teams where students played crossover or enlisted in dueling, and countless clubs for Nollywood films on Friday nights or Enchanted Items Construction on Monday afternoons.

TJ even decided to join one of the clubs: Olokun's Club of the Deep. If he was supposed to gather the praise of the Orisha, that had to be the best place to keep it going, he thought. Acquiring Yemoja's gemstone was all well and good, but he'd still need to make good on his promise to regain Olokun's praise.

He quickly realized, however, that the members of the club were only interested in how to improve their water charms for exams rather than *actually* honoring Olokun properly.

School clubs and lack of praise beside, Elder Adeyemi had made apparent headway with the Yemoja gemstone TJ nearly died to get. She had identified that it was laced with very old, primordial ocean magic. The Elder explained that it was like an old car that needed a bit of a charge before they could use it properly to channel Yemoja's ice magicks.

"So what's this thing supposed to do, exactly?" TJ had asked when they first started charging the gemstone within the pool of Yemoja's chamber.

"As you know, Yemoja is Olokun's wife and partner," Adeyemi had explained. "This particular gem is supposed to help solidify their bond, and that bond, somehow, manifests in ice. I'm hoping this will create the foundation we'll need in the coming weeks for a group ritual I have planned for us both."

"Got it!" TJ had said. "And... that'll appease Olokun, you think?"

Elder Adeyemi didn't look all that convinced, but still, she had said, "It's... a start. A gift to show our appreciation to the Great One."

Outside of class, lessons with Teacher Omo of Fon, and water rituals with Elder Adeyemi, TJ spent most of his time with Manny and Ayo—Manny in particular. Whenever they could squeeze out free time, they always found a way to link up, whether by the flat three-bridges near the winding river, or within the embrace of the whispering trees, or late nights at the mess hall where they enjoyed stuffing their faces.

During one of these late-night escapades of gluttony, near the end of the second week, TJ said, "I still can't get a handle on Teacher Omo's classes. Even with all these extra lessons, I'm getting nowhere with it. When you have her next year, you'll understand. She ain't no joke."

Manny jabbed her knee against TJ's as she dug into her third piece of coconut candy. "Maybe you should do an activity. You know, somethin' light and easy but can still help you with class. Whenever I have trouble, I just play some pickup crossover and I get my wind magic back on point."

"I'm still in search of my crossover, I guess. Maybe that could be basketball, but Ifa doesn't have that here. And even then, I don't see how that would translate to stopping forest fires or ice giants. How's crossover going for you, by the way?"

Manny turned her eyes away to the dark forest spread around them about the mess hall. "It's... not."

"What? They didn't take you after tryouts?"

"Well... I didn't try out."

TJ gave her a look like she needed to explain herself.

"Coach Ali offered me the captain position the first day. She watched my games back at Camp Olosa. She even thinks I could go pro when I get older."

TJ waited for further explanation, but none came. Instead, Manny went for another coconut candy with her head down. There weren't many other students with them, save for the others who enjoyed second and third desserts. Most of the kids there were more interested in their study sessions, though, hidden beneath forests of notes and mountains of books. That's probably where TJ should've been, too, tucked away in some corner of the Library Tree until he fell asleep in a book that would verbally assault him for drooling on its pages.

"You know," TJ started, "my dad wanted me to play in the

NBA. I went to basketball camps every summer since I was seven. But he burnt me out, and the competition was too much at those levels."

Manny sort of jutted her neck out and shook her chin in a cute way. TJ had learned to take the gesture to mean: "Okay, and…"

TJ sighed. "What I'm trying to say is… I understand if you're a little… *afraid* you might not do well. Shooooot, you know *I* know how that be."

Manny gave him a scowl. "I'm *not* afraid."

"Buuut…" TJ egged on.

Manny huffed. "But there is a certain, uh… girl on the team I don't wanna play with."

"Ooo, is there some crossover tea I need to know about? Spill it, please."

"No," Manny said flatly. "And before you ask. No, I do *not* want to talk about it."

There's that Manny shell again, TJ thought. *Just like back at camp.*

Could this girl be one of the reasons she didn't want to come back to Ifa? Maybe. But it was probably best for TJ *not* to bring that fact up.

TJ let a silence settle between them as he watched another set of friends tap out on their fourth serving of dessert.

"Last call for sweets!" Ozolua, the cook, called out, sweat dripping between his lined face. Even at night it was hot.

Far down the table TJ and Manny were at, two boys were playing a game of who could fit more puffs puffs in their mouths, while a trio of girls was flipping coconut candies into each other's mouths with Oya's wind. At the other end, near where the chow line was closing down, Emeka and his girlfriend were getting a last round of meat pies.

Despite TJ and Emeka being dorm mates, they hardly spoke to one another. The kid was still giving him the cold-shoulder, no matter how many times TJ invited him to watch some anime with him before lights out. With everything else going on, he simply didn't have the space in his mind to figure out what was going on there.

Either way, it gave TJ an idea.

"This girl we're not supposed to talk about…"

"TJ…" Manny gritted.

"What's her position on the crossover team?"

Manny gave him a low growl, but she relented through a grunt, "LFD—uh—I mean… Left Flank Defender."

"And what's *your* position?"

Manny's face softened a touch. "Right Forward Attacker…"

"You know what I'm going to say next, right?"

"That we'll hardly ever interact with each other."

TJ smiled, stealing the coconut candy Manny had just reached for and dropping it into his mouth. "Come on, dude. You love that game! You played at camp every day. Wasn't it you who got Camp Olosa to the Summer Finals? I know you're not going to let some left defender scare you off the field."

"Me and her just got beef, that's it. I told you. I'm *not* afraid."

"Then prove it, Martinez."

Manny rolled her eyes, but at least this time she didn't give TJ narrowed eyes or a grumble. "It's already too late. The first match is this weekend, and it's an away game against Benin."

TJ waved the "issue" away and leaned in close. "Here's what you're going to do. And best believe I'm going to make sure you do it. You, me, Ayo, and a few other pickups we can grab, are going to find a nice spot next to the JS team's practice tomorrow. You do what you do. And bet money Coach Ali will see you and come asking for you to join again."

Manny grumbled, "TJ…"

"You're doing it, young lady. And I don't want to hear anything else about it," TJ responded with the tone of a parent.

This time Manny's grumble came out more as a sigh. She leaned into TJ's shoulder with her own, which made TJ tingle. "Thanks, TJ. I guess I better dust off my cleats, then."

"I'll bring the brush." TJ snatched another candy from Manny, but she batted him away with a wind slap. They shared a laugh before TJ went on. "So… Ifa Academy. Besides me being behind in all classes but one… not so bad. I don't know what you could hate about this place—except apparently this left flank defender. Whoever that is."

"Nah, it doesn't suck so much."

"Oh yeah, why's that?"

"I don't know." Manny shrugged, though she was clearly blushing, even under the low crystal light of the mess hall. She chewed at her lip, avoiding TJ's eye contact as she confessed, "I guess... I guess it's 'cause you're here now."

TJ was pretty sure his heart stopped at that moment, and those familiar butterflies he experienced with Manny so often resurfaced once again.

Despite all the signs that Manny might like him back, he never did anything about it. Too nervous. Too cowardly. But perhaps because Manny looked so cute under that crystal-light, or because TJ's belly was full, or maybe because the late, warm September winds enchanted him with uncharacteristic confidence, he said something that caught even *him* off guard.

"Tomorrow morning before we get you on the crossover team..." he began, throat dry as sand. "Mami Wata has a few sisters in the village that swear they have this new vegan dish that tastes *just* like fish stew. Want to check it out?"

"Down!" Manny said immediately. "But... we can't tell Ayo it's vegan. You *know* he'll talk shit. It'll be better if we tell him *after* he eats it."

"Nah, I mean... just..." TJ wished his damn voice didn't quiver so much. "J-just, y-you know, you and me."

"Oh..." Manny mumbled.

TJ's stomach bottomed out. That wasn't the "oh" he was looking for at all. He was so stupid. Manny was just a friend. They were so close because she liked him like... like a brother. And now he'd screwed it all up by practically asking her out on a date. TJ wanted to change the subject, wanted to back step what he had just asked, but his lips failed to form the words. He just stood there with his mouth hanging open like a total moron.

Ugh! Why is she just sitting there chewing her lip; why isn't she saying anything?

"TJ..." she finally got out.

"Don't trip!" TJ blurted. "We could bring Ayo along. I just wanted to give him a break from all the geeky shit we get into and—"

Manny's giggle stopped TJ cold. "TJ! Yeah... I'd love to go

eat fake fish stew with you." The way her dimples caved, the way her eyes softened through her curly bangs, made TJ want to jump straight out of his shoes. "You just caught me off guard, was all."

"So… you're down? Saturday afternoon. For real, for real?" TJ asked, wanting the confirmation for his own sanity. He was a step away from pinching himself.

Manny answered, "For real, for real."

19

LIP BALM & WHITE SHOES

WHEN TJ WOKE THE NEXT DAY, HE COULD'VE SWORN HE'D HAD an incredible dream where he shared a late-night dinner with Manny. More than that, if memory served, he had asked her out on a one-on-one hangout at the Mami Wata Eatery.

And... she'd *actually* agreed to go with him.

It took TJ a whole half hour to realize that that had *actually* happened as he stared up at the craggy ceiling of his dorm.

Without warning, TJ's whole body spasmed in excitement. His legs flailed, his arms wiggled, making his blanket look like a tent full of circus animals had gotten loose.

He stopped the moment he caught Emeka staring at him from the top bunk. The boy was still under his blankets, his eyes slumped with sleepiness. But the scowl that seemed to have become customary from him was unmistakable.

With all the craziness of the first weeks of Ifa Academy, TJ never had the time to settle down and ask what was going on with Emeka. That first day on the bus, the game of *World Cup Crossover* they shared, all of it seemed friendly enough. TJ liked him, and Emeka seemed to like him back. Since that day on the Oracle Rock, though, something had changed.

Feeling as though enough time had passed and Emeka had had enough space, TJ took out a pen and paper and wrote a message. He walked over to Emeka and handed him a note that read:

What did Oracle Ruby say? I'd give you bad luck if you talked to me or something ;-)?

Emeka took the paper, read it, set it down on his bunk, and turned away from TJ.

The hell is his problem?

It took TJ all morning to shake the bad feelings brewing in his gut. He didn't usually care that other kids didn't talk to him throughout childhood, but two entire weeks of the cold shoulder seemed a bit excessive, especially with someone he got on so well with. TJ was still stewing when he and Ayo, along with all the students, visited the carts near the Summoning Stone statues that morning to gather their cellphones for the weekend.

"That Emeka kid," TJ said to Ayo. "Is he shy or something?"

Ayo scoffed. "Shy? Once he gets to signing, he never stops."

"Damn... I must've made him mad or something. Or, actually... I think it's something Oracle Ruby must've said to him. After he saw her, he's been giving me nothing but stink eyes." TJ took a peek ahead in line where Emeka was gathering his phone and having an animated conversation with another girl using YSL.

Yeah, that kid definitely wasn't shy.

"Well, I did hear *some* rumors," Ayo explained. "That friend of his from last year who didn't get in... Word through the grapevine is that he wasn't invited back because a certain TJ Young took his place."

That was a stab to TJ's heart.

No wonder Emeka hated his guts. He would be pissed off too if Manny couldn't attend Ifa Academy because some new student took her place, especially someone like TJ, who was most likely going to flunk out or get held back come year's end.

"Uuugh!" TJ let out. "Why didn't you tell me earlier?"

Ayo threw his hands up, his box-braids jumping up too. "You were so stressed these first few weeks with your classes and the Olokun stuff. I didn't want to pile that on you, too."

TJ sighed again. "You know something... I think I liked it better when you were a little more insensitive."

"Shooot, I can get cold real easy if that's what you want."

TJ rubbed the side of his temples in aggravation. "What should I do?"

"Give him his space, man. But if he starts trippin', I'll check him."

That reminded TJ of something. "How you know Emeka, anyway? You told him to keep his mouth shut back on the bus."

Ayo rubbed the back of his fade nervously. "Oh... that. That ain't nothin'. I just..." He peeked over each of his shoulders, then leaned in close to TJ. "I just had a thing with his twin sister back when we were in JS1."

"Wooord?" TJ's eyebrows hiked up his forehead. "Dude, you never told me you had a girlfriend. I thought you were the player-type."

TJ turned his chin back to the front of the line. That girl who was speaking to Emeka in YSL was the same one TJ saw that first morning. She had to be Emeka's twin sister. TJ could see how Ayo could go for her. Her skin was perfect, she was curvy, deep brown skin, her glasses sat on the bridge of her nose in a cute way, and apparently, she had no issue keeping her voice down despite signing with her hard-of-hearing brother.

"I told you, Emeka!" she exclaimed. "One in eight students never uses history when they get magical jobs. Don't worry about not passing that test."

"Ah, she wasn't my girlfriend," Ayo said. "She doesn't like labels like that. Something about only less than twenty percent of people ending up with their first love and whatnot—she's really into stats. And it was a *long* time ago. We was kids then." Ayo sucked his teeth. "Stop looking at me like that, Teej—and don't laugh. We really was kids."

"Yeah, yeah." TJ chuckled some more. "There's a '*big*' difference between twelve-year-olds and fourteen-year-olds."

"There is!" Ayo's murmur grew louder in his frustration as a pair of SS3 girls in line glanced their way. "You of all people should know, Mr. Growth Spurt. I mean, look at the JS1s over there." He jutted his head at a younger group playing a game of "eye spy with my little eye", except they actually had a magical eye in their hands. One of the kid's answers was Ozolua's beer belly. "You see what I mean? Ugh, why am I explaining myself to you? You don't even have the balls to ask Manny out."

"I'll have you know that I actually..." TJ started to say with a cheeky grin, but Miss Gravés came walking toward them with a stern look.

"Mr. Young, Mr. Oyelowo." She nodded to them both.

"Morning, Miss Gravés," they echoed in answer.

"Miss Gravés!" Umar shouted from the front of the line, jumping up and down with his long thighs and short calves. He had a major case of verbal diarrhea. "Miss Gravés! Did you talk to Coach Ali about me? Did you tell her I should get another chance at the crossover team!? I've got this new diet I'm on that guarantees I'll increase my agility. I just need a week, four moonstones, and a ritual under three high noons—"

"Not right now, Mr. Adebayo!" Miss Gravés shook her head. "Mr. Young, I'll have to ask you to step out of line. You'll get your phone later."

"What? Why?"

"Headmistress Adeyemi would like to see you."

"But... but..." TJ wanted to ask for a raincheck, or even if he could see the Elder later on in the day. He still needed to get ready for his hangout with Manny. But it was *the* Elder who wanted to see him. He couldn't decline an invitation like that.

TJ finally relented and asked, "Will it take long?"

"That'll depend entirely on the Headmistress and whatever it is she wants to discuss with you. Please, follow me, Mr. Young."

With slumped shoulders and a pout, TJ turned to Ayo to give him dab. When they came in for a one-armed hug, Ayo murmured in TJ's ear, "Damn, who's Manny tryna impress?"

TJ whipped his head to the back of the line where Manny had just shown up. She wore white slip-on Vans, ripped baggy jeans, a fitted white t-shirt depicting Storm from X-Men on the front, a purple flannel around her waist, and a dad hat that matched her shoes.

She had... actually dressed up.

Casual for sure. But cute. *Definitely* cute. And when she caught

TJ's eye, she rubbed the inside of her elbow nervously before giving him a wave.

TJ waved back as he murmured to Ayo, "I'll tell you about it later." Then he followed behind Miss Gravés. When he passed by Manny, he explained, "Elder Adeyemi wants to see me. I'll be *right* back. Meet me here at the statues, yeah?"

"Y-yeah, will do." Manny's voice was on the edge of quivering. TJ knew that shaky tone all too well. But usually, it came from him. His stomach did somersaults. There was no way he could ruin their hangout—no, their date. It was definitely a date, right? They never said the words exactly. Though how could it not be when Manny was wearing lip balm and white shoes?

TJ could only hope whatever Elder Adeyemi wanted to talk about would only take a few minutes.

20

THE CAVE BEHIND THE WATERFALL

TJ HAD BEEN THINKING SO MUCH ABOUT MANNY THAT HE hadn't fully considered what awaited him when he met with Elder Adeyemi. Unlike Camp Olosa, where he thought he would get kicked out every other week, he didn't think anything so dire would happen here—not without warning, anyway. But he was still nervous all the same.

The Elder probably had a new idea about how to bring down Olokun. Maybe the gemstone had done what it was supposed to do and Yemoja got her ice magic to work already. Or maybe Elder Adeyemi had figured out a way to get to the Sky Realm. Or maybe she was going to give him a talking-to, since his ability to stop Olokun might've tied directly to how well he did in class.

Following behind Miss Gravés—whose natural speed seemed defaulted to a power walk—TJ took in the new area of Ifa Academy the instructor led them down. Windy avenues of moss and stone paths passing fern-covered statues decorated their path. A fluttering of glittery butterflies glided about a tree face—a tree face set in the image of his sister Dayo.

His eyes watered on cue.

Flowers bedecked where her "hair" should've been, twinkling brown crystals replaced her eyes, and her lips were carved directly from the *iroko* tree. Again, like at the village square at

New Ile-Ife proper, TJ found himself pestered by a scratchy throat.

"When we took in the last of the aziza," Miss Gravés explained, stopping on the patchy path ahead. "They made this for her." TJ turned his face from her as he sniffed up his runny nose. "Elder Adeyemi told me what you were trying to do back at camp—with your sister, I mean. Trying to call her back."

TJ knew what was going on here. Sure, he couldn't be certain that Miss Gravés was truly up to no good, but she was using the same *exact* tactics Mr. Bolawe did back at camp. All she was trying to do was build up a bond. TJ wouldn't have it, extinguishing his sadness and hardening it into skepticism.

Two could play at that game.

"Yeah… and I was pretty wrong on who I was calling." TJ walked the path again before realizing he didn't know where he was going. "So, did you go to Ifa Academy when you were my age?"

Miss Gravés led the way once more with a light chuckle. "No, I studied in the States."

TJ recalled the way Mom referred to diviner academies in the States. As though they were less than—unequal to Ifa Academy. But Miss Gravés seemed to do okay. Then again, she ended up as a counselor at a summer camp. And she'd only now gotten a legit job at an academy *all of a sudden*.

"Oh, that's interesting," TJ went on. "So what made you want to teach here, then?"

"The Headmistress asked me."

"That's cool." TJ tried to sound casual, but his next words were far more direct. "So the Keepers have been pretty quiet lately, haven't they? Nothing major since all that stuff back at camp and the Aqua Realm."

Miss Gravés pursed her lips nonchalantly. "Not that I've heard of. I visited Mr. Du Bois at Babalu-Aye Medical. He's only repeating that 'he's a traitor' phrase twice every few minutes now."

"So, what do you think they're planning? Must be something big if they're keeping things low key."

"Perhaps." Miss Gravés shrugged as they passed a patch of

yellow trumpet flowers—also in the image of Dayo. "I was curious about that myself. Your sister was special, kid, but it surprised me when the Keepers started taking an interest in her."

A shiver raced through TJ. How would Miss Gravés know anything about Dayo and her connection to the Keepers? TJ hadn't even told Elder Adeyemi about what Mr. Bolawe said about her. But Miss Gravés was acting so normal. She wasn't probing for anything. If anyone had been directing the conversation, it was TJ.

TJ chewed on his lip in thought as the landscape ahead of them transformed from flowerbeds to a craggy rock uplifted from the earth like a small hill.

"In through here, Mr. Young." Miss Gravés gestured into the mouth of a cave. Vines and roots wrapped around the rock entrance like wicked, crooked fingers which led into complete darkness. Now TJ was *really* uneasy.

"What's in there?"

"Elder Adeyemi's quarters, of course. What's the matter?"

What's the matter is that you might be a Keeper and there's some sort of dark portal in there that'll lead me straight to your friends, TJ thought, but what he actually said was, "I-I figured Elder Adeyemi would've been up in some big office in one of the tree houses. You know, nice wood paneling, fireplaces... Not a spot where she's chilling with bats."

Miss Gravés chuckled. "You're not gonna find Bruce Wayne in there, kid. Come on, let's go."

"Uh..." TJ tried thinking of an excuse. How far away was everyone else? "I gotta be honest. I'm a little afraid of the dark. Could you go first?"

The teacher gave TJ a questioning grimace. "Sure... Um, are you certain you're okay, Mr. Young?"

"Yeah, yeah, just some childhood trauma involving clowns and dark areas," he lied.

Miss Gravés shrugged and made her way into the cave. TJ peeked over his shoulders twice before following into the chill of the cavern. If anything went south, he'd just sap Miss Gravés' magic and make a run for it. Trouble with that... he never even saw Miss Gravés ever use her active Ashe before. Maybe she'd just grab him with her tree-trunk arms instead.

Like at the entrance hall with the Summoning Stone, the craggy space was well lit, though it was lined with floating crystals of blue and green rather than conventional torches. It was narrower, too. TJ's heart beat a little faster as his mind created worst-case scenarios of Keepers pouncing from the shadows. But the only movement besides him and Miss Gravés were a few bats that twitched between the floating crystals, or the shadows on the Orisha face carvings in the walls that followed their every move. Still, that didn't stop TJ from nervously biting his nails.

Eventually the cavern widened out to a cathedral-sized space that rose at least fifty feet high, where twinkling stalactites pierced down like spears. TJ was utterly floored by the grandiosity of it. Below, at the center of a mossy, vine-covered area was a grand lake that hosted a single tiny island at its middle. Behind the island, a cascading series of waterfalls fed into the cave's basin. Soft blue morning light flooded in from the other end, where the cave opened up again to the backside of a waterfall. The gentle splashing brought calm to TJ's previously mounting nerves, and he barely noticed how far his jaw had dropped.

"Yeah, it gets me every time, too, kid." Miss Gravés smiled. "Welcome to the Headmistress' office."

Her office!? He was about to state his question verbally when he noticed the central island wasn't just an island, but a platform. On that platform, Elder Adeyemi sat behind a stone desk. Wrapped around her were rock-faced bookshelves and masks hanging from jutted crags. In fact, the whole space was full of magical items: Staffs, potion bottles, ceremonial robes and the like —though they all blended in with the space, just like Ifa Academy at large blended in with its environment.

"*Ẹ̀yin òkúta ìsàlẹ̀ odò, mo ke pè yín. Ẹ ma bọ̀ wá sọ́dọ̀ mi,*" Miss Gravés chanted. Several stones uplifted from the bottom of the lake and led a path to Elder Adeyemi's island. This time, Miss Gravés didn't have to ask TJ if he wanted to go first; he was already testing his purchase on the first rocks as he hopped forward.

"Good morning, Mr. Young." Elder Adeyemi interlaced her

fingers and set them in the center of her stone desk. "Thank you for fetching him, Yolanda."

"Of course, Headmistress. Will you need me for anything else?"

"That'll be all. Enjoy your Saturday."

Miss Gravés curtsied, which looked bizarre to TJ's eyes. It was a cultural norm of the Yoruba women to curtsy to their elders, but Miss Gravés, with her big arms, giant thighs, and sweatsuits just didn't seem the type to do such a thing. After Elder Adeyemi officially dismissed the instructor, Miss Gravés pivoted on her heel, hopped along the floating stones, and dipped back into the darkness from which she and TJ had come, leaving TJ alone with Elder Adeyemi.

21

THE WOMAN FOR THE JOB

THE GENTLE THUMPING OF THE WATERFALLS FILLED THE cavernous space of Elder Adeyemi's office as TJ waited for her to speak. At the moment, hills of scrolls fenced her in along her desk. TJ wondered how they stayed dry with all the water in the air. He strained his vision, adjusting to the Ashe of the space, and saw the invisible barrier that surrounded them. It was like being inside a bubble, especially with the light refracting along the Ashe vapors around them. There must've been magical protection around everything to ward off the water and mist.

"So... I noticed your marks are looking a little subpar, young man."

Oh, no, TJ thought.

This *was* about TJ's grades. Maybe he really was going to get some academic probation or something. Without thinking, TJ started biting at his lips.

"You know, your sister shared in that very bad habit."

"What?" TJ pulled his teeth from his bottom lip. "Oh, right..." He hadn't noticed he'd been doing it. Usually when nervous, he rubbed the back of his head like Dad. Lately it had been lip biting. "Sorry, I didn't mean to be rude, Headmistress."

"No offense was taken. It was just a lovely reminder, is all. I do miss her so." The end of her words were laced with a subtle sorrow.

TJ's word's died in his throat a little when he replied, "Yeah, me too."

The waterfalls behind Elder Adeyemi seemed to go more quiet then. Even the glowing flowers, peeking between the stones where dirt and earth had enough room to let them grow, seemed to dim at the mention of his sister's name.

*Damn, did everyone and every*thing *know Dayo like that?*

"By the way, Adeola says hello," Adeyemi said suddenly.

"What!?" TJ nearly jumped. "Is she awake?"

The Elder shook her head. "Unfortunately no. But she has let me into her head a lot more freely. Hopefully, you will get to speak to her soon. Mr. Du Bois as well. Though he's still not taking visitors outside of close friends and family at the moment." She traced a finger along a notepad along her stone desk. "Oroma tells me you're keeping a dream journal?"

"Yes, Headmistress." TJ nodded. "I had a dream about a golden chain rising up through the clouds. Ayo thinks that's our way to the Sky Realm and to Oya."

"A sharp boy, that one is. Please, keep your mind open at night. It's very important." She smiled. "But of course, I did not request your presence to reminisce about Ifedayo, or update you on former Keepers and camp counselors, or even to discuss your dreams. There are two things I wanted to go over. One in the form of our Olokun predicament, and the second in your future magical education."

TJ stopped himself from biting into his lip this time. "Uh… do you mind if we talk about Olokun first?" He was too nervous to find out what his future—or likely lack of one—at Ifa Academy would be.

"I've noticed you've tried to stir up the good word with the student body. You have frequented the Club of the Deep, correct?"

"Yes, but they don't really care about praising Olokun, just passing their entrance exams."

"Yes, the testing we do for upperclassmen can be grueling. But that gemstone we've been nurturing for Olokun's wife this past week has shown a promising face." Adeyemi lifted from her seat, revealing a lavender dress with streaks of gold shimmering down like the stripes of a tiger. There was a wooden chest on her desk which she opened to reveal the smooth, softball-sized gemstone. The stone lay atop a sheet of silk, and pulsated a faint arctic blue.

As Elder Adeyemi stroked the stone's smooth edges, she said, "I believe our next step is clear. Starting next Sunday and each week after, until February's new moon, New Ile-Ife will play host to ongoing Olokun festivals. We are inviting our brothers and sisters from all around to assist us. I've already got the backing of the UCMP for long-form portal travel arrangements. When these festivals commence, I will need you to be in attendance."

"Why?" TJ asked.

Adeyemi simply smiled that gracious smile of hers. "That brings us to part *two* of our arrangement, actually. Mr. Adebisi says he's never seen a student as astute as you with regards to communal magic."

"Yeah, only if I have three or four others around me."

"Well, these festivals will have several more than that for you, if you follow my meaning…"

"Oh! Oh! I get it!" TJ perked up. "You want me to boost the festival?"

"Yes, just as you did when the students called out to Eshu. Though we will need to learn how to… manage your abilities." Elder Adeyemi withdrew from the gemstone. She walked around her desk toward TJ, and for a moment the bright backlight of the open cave and its waterfall threw her into shadow. Somehow, her words held extra weight to them. What did she mean by "manage"? Was his Ashe broken or uncontrollable or something? He never had trouble using too much of it. His main issue was using too little.

"Manage?" TJ asked.

"Why yes. Channeling a few hundred diviners is one thing… but a couple thousand—"

"A couple thousand!?"

"—That will be quite taxing." She cleared her throat, standing tall above TJ, though TJ was catching up to her height. Brushing off dust from TJ's shoulder, Adeyemi continued, "You have heard of Banjoko the Bold, yes?"

TJ vaguely remembered the name from one of the classes he was barely passing. "Some diviner guy who… died, right?"

"Not just died… tore apart. By Ashe itself. We've not seen magic of his scale for quite a few centuries. Well, if your American story about John Henry is to be believed. But back in his day, Ashe was much stronger, and thus, more unstable for mortals. People like Banjoko the Bold, or the Great Ganiru, or Fela the First all met their ends the same way." Adeyemi snapped her fingers and a scroll drifted into her palm. On it, rough sketch lines illustrated a woman whose skin was being pulled apart and put together again like a GIF image. Skin floated away and the only thing that kept her from losing it was the sinew that tried to keep the skin where it was supposed to be. "This is the result of Ashe being overused. Not as much of an issue in our modern world thanks to modern technology, but a fairly common one among prodigies in times of old."

TJ gulped at the scroll. He couldn't keep his eyes from that twisted expression on the woman's face as her skin pulled and repaired, pulled and repaired. It looked *hella* painful. "And… we're gonna make sure I don't end up like Banjoko the Bold or John Henry?"

"Right you are." The Elder snapped her fingers again, and the scroll disappeared. "So, today… today we will test your limits. And to avoid any splitting, you'll need to learn ritualistic preparation."

TJ was about to bite his lip again, but he stopped himself. "Okay, so what are we going to use? Do I get to use a staff? Are my grandma and that Bamidele staff guy bringing my sister's?"

"No, there are still a few months left before they will have run all their tests properly. Today, we will use Yemoja's gemstone. It is activating slowly, but we'll need to jumpstart it if we're to make Olokun happy in time. We'll do that by meditating."

"Oh, okay! How long? Like, an hour?"

"I would expect it would take several more than that, young man. Is there… somewhere you have to be?"

TJ curled his toes, his mind back on Manny waiting for him at the entrance statues with her awesome X-Men t-shirt and that lip balm. But there was no way he could tell Elder Adeyemi that he'd much rather be sampling fake fish stew with Manny than get taught ancient meditation techniques from one of the best diviners in the world.

"No, ma'am," TJ answered. He'd just have to knock out his meditation sooner than later.

How hard could it be?

Elder Adeyemi nodded with approval and paced over to the edge of her island. She flitted her fingers over the cavern lake and water bubbled until a slab of rock peeked from below. A collection of masks with glistening eyes and staffs with shiny crystals were lodged into the side of the stone pillar. All of them were dry, despite being uplifted from the depths of the lake.

The Headmistress examined her magical trophies with a finger to her chin as she said, "For the remainder of the year, each elective period you have will be with me and me alone. Throughout the week, we will sharpen your ritualistic power through preparation, specifically for Yemoja and Olokun, the Great Ocean Orishas."

Finally, the Elder made a selection from her assortment of mystical items, magically calling a silver staff to her hand and whirling it around her body. "And yes, a staff can aid in this. However, we need to first make sure we have a solid foundation before adding such a tool, which can enable a beginner like yourself to grow over reliant." She set the staff back down on her desk, seemingly unsatisfied. "Do you understand?"

Now TJ understood that weight from earlier as he watched Elder Adeyemi pull items from her collection: masks, staffs, ancient robes, amulets. Her shadow against the backdrop of the waterfall had made her look like a specter, but now, with her dress catching the light with little sparkles, TJ couldn't say fear was the right word. It wasn't fear in the same way he'd feel seeing a ghost or a skyscraper-tall Orisha… this fear was the kind a player felt for their coach, what a child would feel for a parent. TJ did *not* want to disappoint his headmistress.

"Yes, ma'am. I think I understand."

Elder Adeyemi clapped her hands together, something that reminded TJ of Mr. Bolawe before he got to teaching. "Then, we shall begin. Follow me."

She turned on her heel, decided on an enchanted tiara with blue crystals, which she placed her head, gently picked up the Yemoja gemstone, and stepped out toward the lake. A floating stone met her foot as it popped up from the water. She pirouetted down, sat, crossed her legs, rested the gemstone in her palm, then beckoned for TJ to follow with her free hand. "Come here with me on the stone, sit, and place your back against mine."

TJ did as requested, testing his balance with a single toe before joining the Elder properly and placing his back to hers in a seated position.

"First, we will match each other's breathing." Adeyemi took in a deep breath. "Once we gather sync for at least five minutes, *unbroken*, then we can begin our exercise in earnest."

The thing about five minutes… it sounded like an easy enough thing to achieve, a very short amount of time. But if you've never sat around for five minutes with no other distraction than the ebb and flow of a waterfall, you wouldn't quite understand the difficulty involved.

What should've taken five minutes, ten at most, took nearly an hour. Adeyemi was militant on their sync; if she or TJ were off by even a millisecond, she would start their time again.

"You must match not only my breathing, but my very essence, child," she explained on their dozenth attempt. TJ was only half-listening, rushing through the exercise with his thoughts on Manny. He even pulled his phone out at one point—and of course, the cave had no signal.

"My breath is the pathway to how I produce Ashe," the Elder went on. "Do you feel it?"

"Uh… yeah, yeah," TJ lied as he tried to hide his phone. They slipped out of sync again.

"You are not being truthful with me. And before you ask, no, I'm not reading your mind. Your vibrations are faltering. What is distracting you?"

TJ blew out of his nose long and slow. If he couldn't conceal it, he had to be honest. "Today… well, I had plans today. With all my schoolwork and this stuff with Olokun and Eko Atlantic, I wanted to just take some time off, you know. Be a teenager."

A silence ballooned between them, and TJ knew he had said the wrong thing.

"Do you believe Olokun is resting now?" Elder Adeyemi asked calmly.

"Um… Probably not."

"Do you believe the Keepers are taking days off?"

"No, ma'am."

"I do not say these things to sound harsh, Tomori Jomiloju. But there is a reality at play here that I need you to take *very* seriously. Not only are the people of Eko Atlantic at risk, but so too are all diviners. A tidal wave the size of Olokun off the coast will uncover our people. Clouded scientists will come looking to do their studies and they'll find that which they should not. They always do."

"Why not wipe everyone's memories?"

"That works on the small scale. Much more difficult when we're talking about thousands of individuals. It *has* worked in the past—mass memory wipes, that is—but there's always a slip. That's why you get conspiracy theories like aliens and the like."

Elder Adeyemi allowed a silence to settle before she went on. Even when she wasn't speaking, TJ could feel the residual presence of her voice. It wasn't Ashe exactly. It was something more than that. Like she spoke each of her words with her very soul.

"Young man, do you know why it is we diviners keep ourselves hidden from the clouded?"

TJ always assumed it was because of persecution and power dynamics. In Magical Ethics class, they always learned about times when magical people groups were exploited or abused throughout history.

"It was not always as it is today," Adeyemi explained. "The concept of us pulling away from the clouded is a somewhat modern notion. That is why you hear clouded folktales speak of mythological beings and creatures so close to our reality. We even ruled in times past. But we have grown much weaker since the Great Ones left us, Orishas and otherwise. And those of us who've made ourselves known to the public have been destroyed.

"You see, we are outnumbered, and over the past century, we have been outgunned. For every diviner or shaman or mage born, there are two-thousand clouded or mundanes or *non magia* born at the same time. If we are revealed, the leaders of the clouded would wage war on us or try to use us as their weapons against one another. And it doesn't help that our magic fails around modern tech, though of course, as you know with Oracle Ruby, there are those who've found loopholes and workarounds.

"So our task is to make sure we keep our world hidden, the same task of the United Council of Magical Peoples at large. To achieve that, we cannot rest. We've only five months more, and those five months will pass quickly.

"Can I put my trust in you, Mr. Young? If the responsibility is too great, I shall arrange for presumably less successful alternatives. But I must be blunt; you are our best shot."

TJ wanted to say no, she couldn't trust in him. He wanted to have the relief that he didn't have to do anything. Let the great diviners of the world do the work. But he knew she was right; he knew he was their best shot. Even though Elder Adeyemi hadn't seen what he did in the Orisha Realm that summer, she knew what power was locked within him.

"Yes, Headmistress. You can put your trust in me."

She took some time to respond, perhaps sensing the truth in TJ's words—no matter how feeble it actually was. Eventually, however, she spoke. "Then, please. Put your mind to rest and focus on the task at hand. Breathe *with* me in… three… two… one…"

TJ took in a breath, letting the earthy fragrances of the cave fully enter his nose. He needed to be one with everything. He needed to be the bats watching them from above. He needed to be those strange glowing flowers giving them light. Most of all, he needed to be Elder Adeyemi.

He and his mentor's sync didn't come right away, but within a half-hour, they were locked in. And as TJ rocked up and down with Adeyemi's back, he could actually feel Ashe connecting them, bringing them as one. His boosting abilities had always felt like this, but never so fierce or steady.

"Now, the next step," Elder Adeyemi murmured, almost in a trance. "We'll need to connect deeply to water to appease Olokun. What I'll do is push a ripple out from the stone we're sitting on.

You will then maintain that ripple and strengthen it so that it reaches the outer edge of the lake. Do you understand me?"

"Yes, ma'am." He peeked over his shoulder to see the Yemoja gemstone still pulsating in her palm.

The Elder whispered, "*Omi, kúrò lọ́dọ̀ mi,*" and the water at the edge of her side of the stone started petering away. TJ started siphoning from Elder Adeyemi to enable his side of the ripple to stretch out, too.

"No," Adeyemi said sharply. "You need to learn to bring your own power into play before you draw on my own, young man. Your specialty may lie elsewhere, but specialities can be as much a crutch as a staff. No student of mine will be so blunted."

TJ's mind hung on the phrase "no student of mine" and a smirk creased his cheek — nearly ruining the sync of his breathing. It hadn't yet sunk in that he was being taught by *the* Simisola Adeyemi. She was his Yoda, Gandalf, and Mr. Miyagi all rolled into one, and TJ was being taught in a way none of the other instructors could teach him, not even Omo of Fon. But, as evidenced by Elder Adeyemi's tough love, his training would be arduous. And something compelled him to rise to the occasion, especially when the Elder just outright told him she was relying on him.

As TJ's mind eased, he used his own Ashe to start the flow of his water ripples. And, once he maintained his own rhythm, he added Adeyemi's Ashe to his own. The waters spread wide around them, blossoming out unnaturally, a ripple that could've only been made by the steady beat of diviners at play.

Without turning his head, TJ could tell the Yemoja gemstone was growing stronger. For one, he could feel it deep in his chest, as though his own heartbeat shared in the beat within the stone. And he could see its arctic blue spilling into the cavern's lake along with the ripples.

Elder Adeyemi said she wasn't reading his mind, but her next words sounded far too familiar for that to be true. "Hmmm. Very good, Mr. Young. Very good. You've calmed your mind. Now, let us continue."

22

WHEN FOMO BECOMES MO

TJ WASN'T SURE HOW MUCH TIME HAD PASSED, TOO FOCUSED on Elder Adeyemi's exercise. At one point, he had asked if they could have lunch, to which Adeyemi replied, "Ashe is all the sustenance we'll need" and they continued on. Eventually, the water ripples finally did reach the edge of the lake, ending their mystical exercise, and the Headmistress dismissed him. TJ thanked the Elder and raced out of her cavern office.

When he rushed through the cave entrance, an orange hue blanketed the trees and foliage around him. Sunset.

Damnit, TJ cursed internally.

TJ figured if he hustled the whole way to the underground entrance hall he could eke out at least an hour with Manny before the sun truly set. But when he air-stepped his way to the Orisha Statues leading into the entrance hall, twilight had fallen and several students were returning from their day out. An elder stood staring at her constellation watch as students filed in.

"Come, children, come. You know sundown is curfew. Hurry, hurry. Miss Kosoko, you and Mr. Ojo need to break it up. Keep your lips to yourselves."

"Sorry, Elder Ogunleye," Tomi, Emeka's girlfriend, replied with a blush. She signed to Emeka that they needed to stop with the kissing. He blushed too when he realized that they had been caught. Emeka and Tomi seemed like the last students to walk through the Summoning Stone portals, both carrying bags from an enchantment shop.

When they passed by TJ, he waved for Emeka's attention and spoke very slowly so his lips could be read. "Hey, man. Sorry about your friend. I didn't know I'd take his spot." But Emeka just gave him a scowl and stomped off. Tomi threw sorrowful eyes over her shoulder, mouthing a "sorry" to TJ.

It wasn't TJ's fault Emeka's friend got kicked out. Well, it was… but he didn't *want* to kick the kid out. Emeka could hate him all he wanted, just… for a reason TJ could *actually* control.

The vacuum sound of a portal disappearing brought TJ's attention around to Elder Ogunleye. Humming a little melody, the Elder clicked her staff against the earth, vanishing portal after portal, one after the other.

"Elder, can I please, please go out for just a few minutes?" TJ asked.

"No, you may not, young man," she continued to hum.

"But I just need to see someone really fast. I made a promise."

"By my count, Miss Kosoko and Mr. Ojo were the last ones in. Whoever you're trying to see isn't out in the village right now."

"But… what?" TJ facepalmed. That's right. Manny would've been over by the crossover field. Well, that's if she took his advice about getting her spot back on the team. "Thank you, Elder Ogunleye. *Ó dàárò!*"

TJ ran straight for the crossover fields, though when he got there it was nearly empty, with no lights. He really hoped he hadn't missed Manny by much. What if the plan didn't go off like it should've? He should have been there for her…

A huddle of older girls crowded around the unique totem-like goalpost for crossover, chatting away as they stretched out their legs. The field was large, with bleachers all around like a long flat soccer field. TJ imagined the sheer noise of the field if all the stands were filled. It must've been quite a spectacle.

"Excuse me!" TJ called out to them. "Was Manny, erm, Manuela out here today. I'm looking for her."

"Oh, yeah! I think I saw her heading over to the JS2 dorms," one girl said.

"Yeah, yeah, she was with that JS3 kid with the braids," said the other.

The third girl stayed very quiet, but TJ didn't pay it much mind. "Thanks, y'all. Um... Go Cranes!"

So TJ tried the JS2 girls' tree house, but Manny wasn't there either. Shame crawled through his body. How long did Manny wait for him, he wondered. Was she disappointed or mad at him?

My phone! TJ thought, facepalming again.

But when he pulled out his phone, it still said he had no service. Not for the first time, he wished the school grounds hadn't blocked phone signals—or maybe it was the mystical fog that surrounded them that hindered signals. This whole thing would've been a lot easier if he could just text Manny. Instead, he was met with that pesky Olokun reminder again:

Eko Atlantic's Doomsday in 20 weeks, 1 day, 13 hours, 18 minutes, and 37 seconds

It wasn't until he gave up and went to the mess hall tucked between the forest that he found her. And—in what was fast becoming a habit of hers—she tackled him in an enormous hug.

"TJ!" she shouted in his ear. "Oh, woah, yo... you're *mad* sweaty."

"Adeyemi worked me hard. Training with that Yemoja gemstone. I'll tell you all about it later. First, you can tell me how well my plan worked to get you on the crossover team." TJ smiled, happy to see Manny as giddy as she was.

"I told her your plan was dumb stupid," Ayo added, coming up to Manny's side with a tray of fish stew, "but it worked like a charm, man. We went up to the fields and—"

Manny smacked her lips. "Hey! *I* made the team. *I* should tell it." She turned back to TJ with a joyful shake of her shoulders, but stopped short, sagging. "I guess I just told him, huh..."

"Shoulda let me tell it." Ayo shook his head.

Manny sighed. "It's just like you said, TJ. We did the pickup game right next to the practice and—"

"We was barely playin' ten minutes before Coach came running over practically beggin'."

Manny smacked Ayo on the arm, nearly making him topple his tray of fish stew. "Damnit, I was still going to tell the story, Ayo."

"Hey, watch out, girl. You 'bout to make me drop my dinner."

"You're just mad because you liked Mami Wata's vegan dish."

"I didn't like that crap."

"Yea huh."

"Nu uh."

Manny took out her phone. "TJ, look at this."

On her phone was a video of Ayo sampling a mami wata fake fish stew. The video was slightly blurry because Manny had her finger over the lens a little, but TJ could still make out the dockside restaurant, with a mami wata lazing over the edge of a dock beaming wide.

"Daaang, this is fire," Ayo said in the video. "What kind of fish is this?"

The mami wata clapped her hands with vigor, making the river water splash onto the dock. "It's not fish at all! You've just had my first vegan stew. I replaced the tilapia in that recipe with tofu."

Ayo's expression completely changed. His lips curled down into a frown that quickly deepened into a full-on grimace.

"Hah! Got 'iiim!" Manny laughed, unseen on the video. "I told you her stew is fire."

"All right, all right, enough of that," the real world Ayo said, cutting the video off. "I didn't want to offend that mami wata. That tofu left a weird aftertaste in my mouth, so now I gotta have the real thing to wash it out."

Despite his friends being as playful as they were with one another, TJ couldn't help but feel like he had really missed out. That was *him* who was supposed to be on that video trying out vegan fish stew. That was *him* who was supposed to be playing with Manny and Ayo in a game of crossover. Instead, he wasted the day away sweating out his t-shirt and stressing over the Olokun festival he needed to prepare for next week. Sometimes, he just wanted to go back to being Ifedayo Young's little brother. The little brother who could mess around and have his weekends off to window shop and throw a ball or two around. Though if that had happened, he never would've met Manny and Ayo to begin with...

"You okay, yo?" Manny asked as they took their seats next to Umar, who seemed to have returned from the village with several muscle-building supplement potions—going by the frothing bottles laid out beside his plate.

"Yeah, I'm good." TJ tried to curl his frown into a faux smirk. "Manny, let's go again tomorrow. You think that mami wata would have any of her 'fish' stew left?"

"Sorry..." She gripped her elbow nervously. "Now that I'm on the team..."

"You've got to go to Benin tomorrow for the away game." TJ sighed, remembering.

"Yo, Manny!" Umar choked as he finished chugging a milky drink that made his face turn purple. "You made the team? Congrats! Can you put a good word in for me with Coach Ali? I —" He coughed and a plume of violet powder filled the air. "I-I." Another cough, another plume. "Gimme a moment!" He rushed off. TJ didn't see it, but he could hear Umar relieving his muscle drink into the forest behind them. Emeka and his girlfriend, who sat on a stone bench near the treeline, covered their noses.

Ayo pinched his nose. "Ain't no one gonna let me enjoy my meal, are they?" Then he lifted his voice toward Umar. "I hope you paid attention in class, Umar! Remember, separate the puke from the leaves by being one with your Ashe!"

Manny sighed, a sick grimace stretched across her own face. Then she frowned when she saw TJ's own turned-down cheeks. He was really hoping to make up their date—or hangout—whatever it was. He'd take anything at this point.

"Yeah... I got an away game. But, hey," she tapped him on the elbow, "rain check for another time?"

"Yeah, yeah. We can do next weekend, or the one after that."

"That's right! Your birthday weekend is in two weeks, right?"

"Yup, yup."

"Oh, shoot, is that right?" Ayo lifted his head from his stew. "Uh... yeah, yeah. I knew that. I—I even planned to throw you a party, man. Over at Eko Atlantic and everything."

TJ rolled his eyes. "Yeah, that's the Ayo I know."

"Ugh… we've got another game against Ghana that weekend," Manny groaned, looking over a sheet of paper she pulled from her pocket. "Back-to-back double-header. I'm so sorry, TJ. I can see if I can get out of it."

TJ sucked his teeth. "And let those Ghanaians take the team down without you there to stop them? Not a chance. Don't trip, we'll figure something out, eventually."

"Yeah, for sure. So what happened with you today, anyway? What kind of training did Adeyemi have you do?"

Ayo chuckled and flicked his spoon in TJ's direction. "I had bets she was gonna have you drop down to JS2 levels."

TJ ignored Ayo but explained the grueling training he went through with Elder Adeyemi. By the time he got done telling them everything, Ayo had finished his stew and Manny had nearly gone through an entire bowl of plantain chips.

"Damn. Just *one* training session," Ayo said. "Did you feel like you were going to split apart like Banjoko the Bold?"

"No… not really," TJ answered. "Then again, it was just me and Elder Adeyemi in her office. Not the thousands of others she said would be in the village next week."

"Plus, Adeyemi wouldn't let TJ explode," Manny added.

Ayo just shrugged. "You never know. There aren't really legit teachers for what TJ's got going on, right? How would she even know if TJ is being pushed too hard?" He dropped his head to the table and lowered his voice. "Just be careful next week, man. I got an uncle who pushed his magic too far. It ain't pretty. You'll end up stuttering like Mr. Du Bois is now in that hospital—and that's *best* case."

"Yeah…" TJ dropped his head too, feeling properly tired for the first time. "But Elder Adeyemi is relying on me."

Manny clapped a hand on TJ's back. "Well, it's like Coach Ali says. There's nothing better than a good night's rest."

It was just like Elder Adeyemi said… Next week would depend on TJ's success. And he'd need a good rest and another week of meditation for it to work out without him splitting into a thousand little magical pieces.

23

SHADOW BETWEEN FRIEND AND FOE

THE NEXT WEEK WENT ON AT A MORE STEADY PACE, WITH TJ waking up at the crack of dawn to get yelled at by Omo of Fon, then zombie-walking to his classes where he fought sleep. At the end of each day, he had a session with Elder Adeyemi, who not only trained him with Yemoja's gemstone but also did a great job packaging everything he learned in one neat little lesson, making up for his lethargic state throughout the day.

By the time Sunday rolled around, TJ felt as prepared as he could be.

The first festival dedicated to Olokun was an overcast day, which TJ took to be a bad omen until Elder Adeyemi told him rain would mean *good* things. Something about water being cleansing and a showcase of Olokun's well-wishes.

The village square of New Ile-Ife was packed with participants from all over the country, of all ages. Most wore traditional Yoruba clothing of aso oke, but there were other West African magical groups there too, like the Igbo with their knitted hats that made TJ feel like he was playing a game of Where's Waldo, or the Ghanaians who wore brightly colored *kente* that made them look like a grouping of rainbows.

Everyone helped to stir the early ritual, some using drums to encourage folks to move, others singing hymns to encourage people to dance. TJ wasn't much of a fan of concerts or events with a lot of people, but he could understand how those older teens and college kids got a kick out of them. The energy was certainly palpable, and it helped him and Adeyemi to enact their ritual.

Sitting back to back near the huge statue head of Oduduwa that stood at the village square's center, TJ and Elder Adeyemi had spent the first few minutes of the festival "gauging the audience" as Adeyemi had put it.

That day, the Elder, for once, wore something plain: a simple white dress. In fact, everyone, except for the visiting magical groups, wore white, almost merging with the gray skies above. They all continued with their hymns and dances and prayers aplenty. None of them knew what they were really doing, though. Adeyemi had only said they were performing general prayer to the sea deity. It was to make sure no one knew they were helping to save Eko Atlantic from impending destruction in only—TJ checked his phone—four months.

TJ had no clue where to start when it was his turn to start boosting the ritual. There were too many people to focus on and draw from. Ashe billowed off them all in wide groupings of fog that TJ couldn't snag within his magical grasp. And anytime he tried to pull from everyone all at once, he could feel the early warning signs of that tearing that Adeyemi had trained him to work against.

Don't become Banjoko the Bold, don't become John Henry, TJ kept telling himself every time he felt so much as goosebumps rise on his skin.

"Remember, Tomori Jomiloju," Elder Adeyemi hummed gently behind him. "Use the crowd like they are the ripples of a lake. Just like we practiced before."

"Yes, ma'am," TJ answered.

He closed his eyes and imagined himself back in Elder Adeyemi's office. Instead of listening to the drums, he pictured them as water droplets from the cave. Instead of hearing the hymns, he heard only Adeyemi's gentle, consistent humming at his back. They were in the center of the crowd, so he focused on the two of them first and foremost. He waited until the Ashe between them was solid and strong, like a rock, robust enough to make any lake ripple. When TJ was satisfied with the roiling energy, he let it drop and spread among the crowd. Then he did it again. Gather, strengthen, release. Gather, strengthen, and release, like a rhythmic drumbeat, long and slow.

The ripples of TJ's Ashe spread over the crowd. Anytime the wave of energy passed over the group of locals wearing white, the Ashe would strengthen even more. So he focused on them to double the output. And eventually, TJ could almost feel the presence of Olokun around him; he could almost see his gargantuan frame towering over them. If something like this wasn't going to please him, he wasn't sure what would.

And this was only one day, the first week of many more rituals to come.

By the time the festival had ended, TJ found himself exhausted, but it was different from the exhaustion he'd experienced after coming out of the Ice Realm. It was a more mental drain, less like he needed to take a nap and more a desire to sit in a zen garden with some peace and quiet. Or maybe he just needed a nice, long bath.

Sure, the festival and ritual weren't as extreme as taking on ice giants, and no one would know what TJ was saving them from, but it was still something to take pride in. TJ glanced up at the mudwall to his side, the same one with Dayo's mural that he saw the first day he arrived. "I think I did a pretty good job today, Sis."

Rain came down as a drizzle, then as a steady, strong beat. TJ still wasn't sure if that was a bad or good sign from the Orishas, but it forced the crowd to disperse, as most of them generated mystical umbrellas to keep themselves dry. A few of the participants approached Elder Adeyemi and TJ to thank them for hosting the event before departing.

"I've not felt Olokun that strong in my spirit for ages," said one Elder.

"Now I understand what my baba means when he talks about the power of the ocean," said another younger student.

"You did good today, Mr. Young," Adeyemi told him once they got done with their last group of thankful festival-goers. "I shall see you for your elective period tomorrow. We should discuss how to get in contact with Eshu once more. You've received no words or signs from him on what may have happened to Oya, no?"

"No, ma'am," TJ answered, looking down at the Eshu symbol stamped on his finger. TJ hadn't worried about it too much. They had made so much progress with Yemoja's gemstone—and now with regaining Olokun's praise. He didn't need to consider everything all at once. But now it was time to focus on bringing Oya into the mix through Eshu's guidance. "And I haven't had any new dreams either, ma'am."

"I see, well, I am sure all is well," Elder Adeyemi said, though there was a shadow of tension behind her expression. Adults always seemed to hide the pressure they felt from teenagers and kids. TJ didn't think it was all that healthy.

Elder Adeyemi cleared her throat and sighed. "Well, we've made at least one step toward success. Have a good rest of your day, Mr. Young."

The rains settled down to a drizzle, and the sky remained a dull gray as Elder Adeyemi made her way back to Ifa Academy's hidden entrance hall cavern, just off the village square's beaten path. TJ watched as she sunk into the earth, then he sat back next to the giant statue head at the village's center. Ayo said he was getting a potion refill for his asthma and would meet up with TJ later, so TJ waited.

"Whatcha need me for when you got a thousand people there," he had said when TJ left that morning.

To pass the time, TJ took out his phone. Manny was away at a crossover game against Benin, but no scores had been posted on the school site yet. There were news reports about strange rain happening in Southern California. It had been going nonstop for a week already. He had even received text messages from his parents telling him not to worry and that the storm was likely to pass over soon.

Dad: Besides. Lord knows we need some rain around here.
Mom: We'll talk to you next week, honey bunny. 🐰

One of the dancers dressed in white came over to sit by TJ's side beneath the statue head. "There were a few reporters snooping around. I took care of them for you."

"Huh?" TJ asked the robed dancer, whose face was covered by a mask.

Ignoring TJ's confusion, the dancer went on. "I wouldn't put too much faith in Adeyemi. She's not all she seems."

"Um, excuse me? Do I know you?" TJ put his phone away and gave the dancer a raised eyebrow.

The dancer lifted his mask to reveal deep-pored skin and a serious face. A face TJ never wanted to see again, with its caring eyes that TJ knew weren't caring at all, a face lined with wisdom, but a wisdom that was twisted by deceit.

Mr. Bolawe. Olugbala. The leader of the Keepers.

TJ shot up from his seat, a fireball already manifesting in his palm. He'd thank Teacher Omo of Fon later for showing him that trick.

"Tsk, tsk, put that away before you hurt yourself, young man," Mr. Bolawe said with eerie calm, putting his mask back on. "I'm here only to talk. But if you make a scene, I can make a bigger one." He nodded to the other side of the square. "My friends have been ordered to ravage the square if things should… take a turn here."

At the corners of the village square, several individuals waved toward him in eerie unison, cloaking themselves in the crowd by playing with children, repairing roofing, and dancing in the drum circle.

"So you're gonna kill more people. Is that all your followers are good at?" TJ questioned, still standing defiantly.

"Do not put words in my mouth, Mr. Young. I said ravage, not murder. Now, please, sit back down and put that fireball away before anyone notices."

"'Ravage,' murder, what's the difference to people like you?" TJ hissed. He shook with anger. "You'd really do that to the square? My sister's mural is right there."

Bolawe stared up at the image of Dayo with a frown. "That mural was made by those who did not know your sister, those who took her true potential for granted. They celebrate her in death, but not in life. I'm not here to argue that, though. So again, I kindly ask you to sit. This does not need to get ugly."

TJ turned back to the few Keepers that revealed themselves in the crowd. He noticed an old woman selling sweets who kept giving him a wicked grin, and a younger man playing an *algaita* for a clapping crowd who winked in TJ's direction. Then someone familiar to TJ, a man with no hair and no eyebrows, swept near a store front and gave him a salute along with a sneer.

That was the same guy who was speaking to Miss Gravés that day in the bus terminal! That parent Ayo said was sort of... off.

Heat boiled in TJ's gut and all the muscles throughout his body clenched. How many more Keepers were among them that he hadn't noticed? Was Miss Gravés hidden under one of those masks or robes, too?

A naïve thought brushed across his mind, a thought that had him thinking he could fight Bolawe off, that he could signal for help. But it wasn't worth the risk. Not with so many children running about and elders enjoying their Sunday afternoon.

So, begrudgingly, he sat. Though he sat as far on the edge of the raised platform as he could, away from Bolawe.

"Very good, Mr. Young." Bolawe, still under his mask, crossed his legs casually. Suddenly, TJ felt himself magnetized on the raised platform he sat on. He looked down. Ashe swirled around him, air currents that would've been invisible to anyone else passing by. Instinctively, TJ let his Ashe swell within his belly as he worked to free himself from Bolawe's magical binds.

There was something odd about the energy swirling around him, however.

He had focused inward, thinking the source of his binds was coming from Bolawe. Even though the man only sat feet away, TJ could see no Ashe falling from him. Maybe TJ was too exhausted, maybe his abilities weren't working correctly because he'd spent all morning expending his magical energies.

"You'll not get out of those binds easily," Bolawe explained. "And I'm not the one holding you, in case you were wondering. My friends are doing that. I'm told you need proximity to heighten and dampen the Ashe of others, yes?"

TJ wondered how he knew that but tried not to let it show on his face. It had to be someone feeding him information... and TJ had an idea of who that could be.

Where was Ayo? They were supposed to meet up already. This wasn't the time for his friend's typical "fashionable tardiness." Who else could TJ use to warn that Keepers were among them? How could he do it without tipping Bolawe off? TJ's mind struggled for answers, but he drew only blanks. It was Ayo who came up with the initial ideas. TJ was just good at executing them.

Wait, what was he talking about? He came up with the idea to get Manny on the crossover team. He took on that ice giant... he couldn't always rely on everyone else! He could get himself out of this; he just needed to focus.

"So, how are your classes going?" Bolawe asked with a nonchalance that made it seem like this was a perfectly normal conversation. Was the man really trying for chit chat? Perhaps *that* is what TJ should do. Distract him long enough with conversation until his slow brain gave him an idea to get free *and* keep everyone in the square safe.

"How did you do it?" TJ asked flatly. "How did you keep your memories?"

Ayo and Manny were still fuzzy on everything that happened in the Aqua Realm. It didn't seem fair that Bolawe kept his memories.

"I didn't. It was Olokun who filled me in, as I'm sure you did with your friends. You should have never agreed to that deal, young man."

"Why do you care? A few skyscrapers tumbling into the ocean should be no skin off your back."

Bolawe sighed, interlacing his fingers and setting them to his right knee. "What is it you *think* you know about us Keepers?"

Bolawe had always been soft spoken. Always pausing before responding as though he was actually listening and taking in what you had to say. The worst part, TJ realized then, was that he actually *did* listen. But he was also a betrayer. A liar. A schemer.

And yet TJ couldn't say he hated him, exactly.

Even so...

"All I need to know is that you're the type of people who would attack a funeral..."

Bolawe nodded slowly. "A necessity under the circumstances."

"I saw what you did to Mr. Du Bois in the Aqua Realm. His voice was all tore up. Face was jacked up too."

"That was self-defense. The man, as you know, is quite stubborn and would not hear me out. I merely reflected what he tried to do to me."

TJ wanted to accuse the Keepers and Bolawe of brainwashing his sister, but something stopped him, that aching feeling that didn't want to hear the truth regarding Dayo. He hadn't seen her in three years... so much could have happened in that time...

No! He couldn't think that way. Bolawe was getting into his head.

For the whole end of the summer, TJ had wondered how much truth had been in Bolawe's words when he said, *"Ifedayo was a Keeper, Tomori. Your sister was one of us. She was our promised child."* The only way TJ could make sense of something like that was if Ifedayo was forced. Perhaps the Keepers said they'd hurt someone close to her, someone like TJ even, if she didn't work with them.

"Considering you don't have any other slander for me," Bolawe said. "I'll assume you know very little of what we Keepers are outside of what's presented to you in *Divination Today* propaganda." Mr. Bolawe drew his hand into the cuffs of his robe. In spite of wanting to do the opposite, TJ tensed, but the man only pulled out a handful of kola nuts. "Would you like some?" TJ answered with a scowl and looked away, but really he was keeping an eye out for Ayo. Any moment now and he'd appear through the crowd from a side street off the square.

"Very well," Bolawe went on. "I'll keep it short, then. I mentioned to you once that I had an unsuccessful career in politics, where I attempted to do it the 'right' way. The fallout of that was the creation of the Keepers. Our only desire is to give power back to diviners, to bring—"

"The Orishas back to the Mortal Realm to empower y'all as they have before."

"Well, I'm glad media outlets have taught you that much, at

least. Yes. If our people still had our true strength, not the weak energy we call 'magic' today, we could have avoided many atrocities, namely The Middle Passage and the colonization of our lands. A fight your sister was quite passionate about."

A brush of wind tickled the back of TJ's neck at the mention of his sister. It was true Dayo was all about fighting against stuff like that. There was never a week with her when she wasn't sharing about some hidden history of their people with TJ. He just couldn't wrap his head around her being a Keeper, and he still had no way of verifying as much. Nothing left over in her room said she was a Keeper. Heck, the journal she left him didn't mention the Keepers at all.

It was all a lie; it had to be.

"Tell me," Bolawe crossed his legs, "have any of your history classes at Ifa told you how our brothers and sisters were taken from their homes? I know for a fact Omo of Fon, your aziza instructor, lived through it."

TJ raised an eyebrow at that. Was that the war Ayo referred to? Had the aziza tried to help back then and paid the price?

"So… what…" TJ gritted. "Are you trying to say you're like Malcolm X or something? 'By any means necessary' and all that?"

TJ couldn't be so sure under the mask, but it sounded like Bolawe let out a light chuckle. "Brother Malcolm is someone who I believe would have seen eye-to-eye with us, especially now." He twisted in his seat to face TJ. "Tomori, Eko Atlantic must be made for us, for *our* prosperity. I know you're already seeing it in your home city. Los Angeles has been 'improving', has it not? And not for the benefit of those who made it what it is. I only want to avoid that happening here as well. Let me help you, TJ. I don't want to see our own dead either."

"Small problem with that, though. I don't trust you. You say everything nice and make everything sound all logical, but you're a liar." It was only a half-truth from TJ's lips. He knew what Bolawe was getting at. He had protected TJ against Olokun's rage. And deep down, TJ knew Bolawe only wanted what was best for diviners. But at what expense? At what cost?

"Today's festival, today's success, was only because of what we

Keepers organized. We need to work together in bringing praise to Olokun."

TJ thought back to those groups of people in the white robes. Were they all Keepers? Did they all help the ritual along because they wanted to see Olokun return as well? Now that TJ surveyed the crowd again, he recognized some of them from before, at the festival. Now they were giving him dark grins and slitted gazes among the villagers. It made him feel rotten inside.

"Yeah, we got the praise part going well. But what about Eko Atlantic itself?" TJ almost wanted to take the words back the moment he said them. It sounded too deferential, too much like he was going along with Bolawe. Perhaps he was, or at least he wanted to. He just didn't want to admit it deep down.

"How's it going with your friend, Mr. Oyelowo? I have connections close to him. I can help with whatever you need. He is hosting a party *in* Lagos if I heard correctly? You will go, won't you? Speak to his father. The man has a significant role within the Eko Atlantic district council."

"And tell him what? To make a big ol' statue in Olokun's honor so he won't drown the bay?"

Mr. Bolawe canted his head before saying, "That might not actually be such a bad start. It would work as well as Yemoja's gemstone, anyway." How in the world did Bolawe know about that? The shock must've been obvious on TJ's face because Bolawe went on to say, "Who do you think helped bring that Ice Shard out of the vault of that museum? I'm sure you saw how hard-nosed those conservators were."

TJ ignored Bolawe's words. He didn't want to give him the satisfaction of knowing he was being helpful. "How do I even know Olokun is happy with what we're doing, anyway? I need a sign we're on the right path with our deal."

"Look to the coast of Lagos. There you'll find a rock face in the ocean in the shape of an open palm. If you can see the tips of its 'fingers,' Olokun has been satisfied that day. If not, and the rock face is washed over, he is less than pleased."

TJ considered the information Bolawe gave to him in earnest. But his face must've been bunched up in a scowl because Bolawe sighed and said, "You don't have to trust me, but please at least heed my advice. And if ever you need to contact me so that you can learn more about what we really are and what your sister was *building* with us, we're always open to teach. I know your instructors are doing a terrible job of instructing you on how to unlock your unique abilities. Their teaching methods are... dated."

"Nah, I'm good. Elder Adeyemi is coaching me fine one-on-one," TJ answered defiantly. He cursed himself, though. He shouldn't have divulged that much to Bolawe. What he should've done was keep his damn mouth shut.

"Ah, so that's how she'll play it. One of her better ideas. She's been lacking in those as of late. But my offer still stands, TJ. We are here for you, as we were for Ifedayo." Bolawe stood up, dusting off his white robes. "When you make your report to Adeyemi about me, tell her I say hello."

In unison, Bolawe and the other hidden Keepers marched off. TJ tried to shoot up from his bench to call out for help, to make it known the Keepers were among them, but the same wind magic that had bound him to the raised platform kept his lips shut tight.

When the magic fell away... the Keepers were gone.

And when Ayo finally showed up from what he called a "light stroll of window-shopping" TJ couldn't even begin to explain what had happened.

24

GATHERING THE MASSES

"DID YOU HEAR ABOUT THAT TJ KID?"

"Yeah, Emeka said he got someone kicked out."

"I heard he's getting private lessons from Elder Adeyemi!"

"What? How? He's bottom of three of my classes!"

That next week back, rumors ran wild around the Ifa Academy grounds. Well, if one could really call them rumors when there was more truth than fiction at play. True, Emeka's friend was kicked out of the academy, but not because TJ "demanded" a place be made for him as an SS1 girl had said during breakfast Monday morning. True, he was getting private lessons from Elder Adeyemi, but not because he "cried about classes being too hard" as a JS2 boy had said during pataki readings Tuesday night.

TJ had never been the most popular kid growing up. He wasn't exactly *un*popular either; he was just kind of… background dressing—a position in teen life he was more than okay with occupying. It was just different when he was *actively* being shunned, especially when it was Emeka that seemed to be campaigning against him.

"I mean… to be real with you," Ayo said that Wednesday morning after Antidotes Studies. "I'd be feelin' some type of way too if I didn't know you and I heard you got special classes with the greatest diviner of our time."

"You mean like this past summer when you were practically going to cut my throat to get to Ifa Academy?"

"Yeah, just like that."

Later that Wednesday, when TJ met with Elder Adeyemi during his open period, she told him not to worry about it. "Teens will be teens. I must say, I do not envy the years you're going through now for their social pressures. Though you should savor being able to eat whatever you like and not having to take naps every few hours. All said, I'll sort the rumors out when I get back."

"Get back?" TJ asked, jerking from his seated position at Adeyemi's back. They had been meditating again on the floating rock in her cool cave pond. TJ had forgotten to bring a sweater, and goosebumps prickled along the fabric of his dashiki uniform.

"Concentrate." Adeyemi warned as they regained sync in their breaths. The surrounding ripples stuttered, then smoothed out again. "I shouldn't be away too long. That business with the storms in Los Angeles is starting to get out of hand. The UCMP suspects there might be something mystical at play, but it could be nothing."

"Yeah, I was talking to my family about it over the weekend. My mom said that the last time it rained this long was the year I was born. There was rain for eight days straight then. But nothing more than that in L.A."

"Yes, but this rainstorm is more consistent. Steady. Eerily so. It's not scattered as it is in natural weather."

They slipped back into a comfortable, thoughtful silence. Unlike conversations with his friends, where TJ often spoke fast to get all his thoughts out before they slipped his mind, when he spoke to Elder Adeyemi, their conversations lasted twice as long. Perhaps it was the Elder's deliberate cadence that guided it and TJ just naturally followed suit. Or maybe it was the gentle lapping of ripples around them that settled him.

"Wait a minute," TJ said suddenly. "Storms on the West Coast... could that be Oya?"

"It may be. That's one of the primary reasons I'm being summoned."

"But Eshu says she's usually stirring up storms on the East Coast around this time."

"Indeed. Which is why we need you to contact Eshu again."

"I've been trying, but I don't know how to connect right now. I thought it'd be enough to do that whole ritual again, like when we came in with the buses, but those school meetings you've been hosting haven't worked." TJ eyed the surrounding waters. The ripples died out the more he focused on them; he was getting flustered. TJ did his best to get them going again before Elder Adeyemi noticed.

"Keep trying this week." Elder Adeyemi held her eyes shut. Good, she didn't notice TJ's stumble. "And if you make contact, reach out to me as soon as you can. You still have that water bowl I gave you, yes?"

TJ frowned. "Yeah. Umar found it the other day, though. Said it must be nice getting special treatment."

"Your connection is slipping," Adeyemi warned, as the ebb of their water circle lost its rhythm once more. "You mustn't worry about the others. For the next few months, your only concern should be the Orishas, not your peers, especially with Olugbala being so bold as to expose himself to you in public. When I'm away, I'll make sure you're watched and protected."

"Yes, Headmistress." TJ forced himself to put everything out of his mind. It was a hard thing to do when he had to deal with cosmic forces and a student body who watched his every move.

"And after today," Adeyemi went on, "I think we've done enough to recharge Yemoja's gemstone. Before those conservators get back with some official order to return the stone to them, I think Yemoja will want her gem back. I'll drop it off to Ol' Sally when I visit Camp Olosa on my way to Los Angeles. She and Olokun should be happy enough with that."

A half-hour passed and Elder Adeyemi dismissed TJ with some literature on meditation stances he should practice while she was away. He scanned it over, then put it in his pocket.

Chilly night air wafted over TJ's face as he left Adeyemi's office that day. Ifa Academy at night was like being at an amusement park with lantern-lit paths and crickets chirping at you all the while. Through the dim path, TJ could make out Manny and

Ayo at the mess hall eating their dinners, Manny with her big hair looking like a halo with the backlight, Ayo with his bright red and white stripes going down his uniform. The moment TJ approached his friends, they dismissed themselves from a conversation they were having with Umar about crossover tryouts and followed TJ to a quiet corner of the mess hall.

"Oya's on the West Coast, you think?" Manny asked after TJ got done recapping them.

Ayo pulled out his dream journal and read a headline. "Yup. Rain in Los Angeles has been steady goin' for a week."

"But Eshu was right," Manny said. "the East Coast is where all the big storms are supposed to be."

Ayo flipped a page in his journal. "Are you sure? Headlines say it's been dry on the East Coast. No storms at all, not in the Caribbean or Louisiana even."

"Oh, shoot!" A horrible thought struck TJ, and it made him stiffen in his seat. "What if it's Olokun? Maybe he's not happy with our progress, so he's taking it out on my home city? I told Adeyemi that rain felt like a bad omen!"

Manny looked over her shoulder to the group of SS2 kids who ate fish stew behind them. Then she lowered her voice. "But didn't you say Bolawe said you're doing good work? And we had Ayo's cousin over at Eko Atlantic check the coastline with that open palm rock face. It was exposed above the sea. We should be good, right?"

"Ugh!" TJ stabbed his fork through his fish, crunching bone. "We need to speak to Eshu right now and figure out what's going on on the other side! I just don't know how to get him to show himself again. How did Oya do it with you?"

Manny shrugged. "No clue. I just know she did it, not *how* she did it. Let's just try again on Friday. We just need to gather more people, is all."

"No one wants to talk to me right now, though." TJ glanced down the table where Emeka and Umar sat together over a plate of jollof rice and a game of *Major League Crossover*. A few times, Emeka would cheer when he scored. TJ tried to catch his eyes and give him a thumbs up, but the kid just frowned every time their gazes met.

Ayo snapped his fingers. "They won't talk to *you*... but they'll want to talk to *her*." He thumbed to Manny.

TJ gave him a look. "Huh?"

"Private lessons with the JS crossover star? Shooooot, you know Umar would eat that up. And half the school tries out for crossover; they'll definitely want the lesson. Even upperclassmen."

"How does that get us a conversation with Eshu?" Manny questioned.

Ayo beamed, pushing his glasses up his nose. "We'll start off the lesson with a prayer to Eshu, of course!"

So, FOR THE NEXT DAY, THEY ALL SPREAD THE WORD ABOUT the star-player Manny Martinez giving out a private session "revealing the secrets of crossover."

Umar signed up almost immediately.

"Yo, Teee Jaaay!" he had shouted on the cobbled path between Ecology of Life and Elemental studies. "I knew you was my guy, my guy. I knew you'd come through and get Manny to help your boy out. Good lookin' out, Teej! Good lookin' out."

TJ could only bring himself to give Umar an awkward laugh.

Umar beamed. "I told Emeka you couldn't be all bad."

And after Umar, there were a few more sign-ups too. But by lunchtime, there wasn't nearly enough for TJ's liking. There were something like two-hundred people when he called Eshu before. Even if they *did* get two-hundred people together, that wasn't a sure thing. Elder Adeyemi had gathered the academy for prayer several times during the first weeks to call Eshu, and they'd had nothing in response. The difference now was that TJ had meditative training, and he spent all week prepping his mind and spirit to facilitate a big ritual for the Gatekeeper.

He hoped that was enough.

"Only twenty sign-ups," TJ said nervously as he, Manny, and Ayo shared lunch together Thursday afternoon. That day it was pepper soup. "Twenty probably won't do it."

"It's the best we can do right now," Manny said, the afternoon light shining through the tips of her naps. "I know you want to figure out what's goin' on, especially with what's happenin' in L.A. right now… but believe in yourself. You been doin' all those yoga poses with Adeyemi and stuff for a reason. We should at least get Eshu to come out for a few seconds. All he needs to do is tell us where Oya is real quick."

TJ bit his lip. "Twenty people is *a lot* different than two-hundred."

"Ah! Don't trip," Ayo waved a dismissive hand as he casually shoveled soup into his mouth. Oh, if only TJ could feel as care-free as Ayo did. "Everyone signs up late, bro. You know how it is."

It was true. The next morning before the tryouts, there were ten more last-minute sign-ups but thirty still wasn't going to cut it. TJ, who of course was freaking all the way out, let that fact be known to Ayo during Ecology Studies.

"This is *not* going to work," TJ gritted as he dissected an *eloko*, a creature he likened to a living tree stump, except the one they were working on had long been dead, according to Mr. Ikenna. Eloko were strange little forest creatures from central Africa, little dwarf-like creatures covered in ferns and bark. Instead of blood, the eloko was filled with sap, and that sour-smelling substance stuck in the air. Thankfully, the classroom had large open windows that led out into the thick forest.

Ayo drew up from the eloko they were working on, wiping the creature's amber sap from his thick leather gloves. "Okay, I have one more idea, but you ain't go'n like it."

"Anything at this point, man."

"The reason you might not be able to call Eshu as easily is because you're not thinking like Eshu. He appreciates a bit of mischief, right? He tests humanity and divinerkind with stuff like that."

TJ went back to cutting out the eloko's stomach, which was supposedly a key ingredient in bush baby boil antidotes. Usually, TJ would be grossed out at something like this, but besides Collaborative Magicks, Ecology was his next best subject and he needed to maintain his "B-" in the class. "So… you're thinking we're supposed to trick the people who sign up?"

"That's part of it." Ayo lowered his voice, dipping in closer to their workstation so the other students around them couldn't hear. "What if you tell everyone who shows up that they'll have a chance at a spot on the crossover team? The one who shows the most talent will be hand-picked and recommended by Manny, the team captain."

TJ shook his head, eyeing the other students, who were hard at work with their dissections. "Manny would never go for it."

Ayo tried snapping his fingers, but the sap on his gloves only made them stick. "Therein lies the real bit of deception. The trick will be on her too. That sort of energy should stir up Eshu."

TJ's stomach bottomed out a little. That was just plain cold. "No way. I can't do that to her. She's doing me a favor as it is."

"Rains in Los Angeles ain't stoppin', bruh. This morning I heard the hail is turning to sleet. And Elder Adeyemi won't be back anytime soon." Ayo shrugged as he extracted the earthy-brown heart from their eloko. "We can try with the thirty we got now and hope for the best. Up to you."

TJ tapped his knife along the workstation in thought. There had to be a better way to manifest Eshu, one that didn't involve him lying to Manny. But Ayo's words had too much logic in them, like always.

"Remember, class, we use *every* part of the eloko," Mr. Ikenna said from his desk near the blackboard. His teeth almost sparkled against his deep-brown, unblemished skin. There was one person TJ knew he couldn't outgrow with a growth spurt, and that was Mr. Ikenna, whose head nearly brushed along the tall ceiling. "Nothing goes to waste here. Make sure your cuts are precise. Each one you make, each piece you remove, is sacred and allows the cycle of life to continue as it always—"

"Ah!" screamed Titilayo, Ayo's ex-girlfriend-not girlfriend. "I thought these things were supposed to be dead!"

Near her workbench, an eloko jumped up on her desk and rang an old rusty bell in its hand. A long trail of sap told of the eloko's path, all the way from the open window from the forest and straight over Titilayo's desk where the little creature was baring its sharp teeth. All the students around the workstation bolted for the corners of the room. Their sudden movement seemed to disturb the lost eloko.

"They're supposed to be attracted to the sap," Ayo explained in TJ's ear. "That's probably a male eloko lookin' for a mate. But... all the ones here are dead. He probably thinks we killed them or something!"

The eloko howled a piercing screech as it vaulted for another table. It didn't seem interested in the bodies all around it, though. Instead, its bellow was directed straight at Mr. Ikenna who had already gotten out of his seat near the blackboard.

"Oh, dear. It looks like this one broke through the barrier," Mr. Ikenna said offhandedly. "Do not fret, students. I'll get it."

TJ threw a glance to the open window and sure enough, he could see the faint markings of a magical barrier of Ashe, only part of it was broken, just where the trail of sap was.

The bones under Mr. Ikenna's long dashiki cracked and snapped as half his body contorted and sprouted a hyena on his back. TJ's own insides felt like they were twisting too. He had never seen something so bizarre. The contortionists on those talent shows had nothing on the odd angles Mr. Ikenna was bending himself in. It didn't seem like the eloko had expected the transformation either, as he turned around and headed for the forests again, ringing his bell the whole way.

Clothes ripped and ruined, Mr. Ikenna, in his twisted hyena form, bounded off into the forest to chase after the eloko. For the next few moments, the students watched and listened as their chase broke through tree branches and cut through vines.

"I told the academy about this!" Titilayo called out as Mr. Ikenna jumped from behind a bush in the distance, with the eloko taking a fanged bite out their teacher's neck. "There have been over twelve accidents in the last three years caused by mystical creatures because of instructor negligence! *Divination Today* placed one in eighty students in avoidable incidents!" Mr. Ikenna was too busy to answer, still wrestling with the forest creature. TJ glanced down at his own eloko and poked it with his knife a few times to make sure it didn't wake.

"Yes, yes, I'm fine, Emeka," Titilayo was saying. TJ looked up to see she was signing along with her verbal responses to her twin. Now that TJ had gotten to know them—well, gotten to know them from afar—he saw the differences between them more easily. Emeka was definitely more reserved, but his sister... his sister always let people know what was on her mind.

"You know... I can see why you like her, Ayo." TJ laughed in his friend's direction.

Ayo covered TJ's mouth, sticking TJ with a load of sour sap. "A little louder for the people in the back. C'mon, bruh. I think *Emeka* could hear you on that one." Despite his lips being glued shut by sap, TJ grinned. It hurt, but it was worth it. "And stop staring at her, TJ," Ayo gritted, keeping his head down. "We're supposed to be figuring out what to do about Eshu, remember? So how about it? We gonna do this crossover deception or what?"

As TJ wiped the sap from his mouth with his own glove, Mr. Ikenna came back with a docile eloko in his hyena mouth. The students cheered and Mr. Ikenna locked the eloko away in an enormous cage.

"I'll set him free after our session is done." Mr. Ikenna transformed into his full human form again. There was a big gash along his neck, but he covered it with a towel covered in a green ointment. "I know this little guy. His kind provides us with their dead at the start of every term. They only live a few years, you know. Wonder how he wandered off from his reservation. Eloko usually keep to themselves in the thickest of the forest."

When Mr. Ikenna told everyone to get back to work, TJ whispered to Ayo, "No one's going to listen to me about crossover tryouts. Or did you forget I'm sort of hated right now?"

"Let me handle it. All I gotta do is tell Umar and he'll spread that shit like that wildfire you let loose in Elemental Studies."

"You had to remind me, didn't you?"

Ayo shrugged coyly. "What are friends for, man?"

25

REFLECTIONS OF A REFLECTION

As always, Ayo was right.

All they had to do was tell Umar that Manny would put the top prospect in tryouts on the team and just about half the school showed up on the crossover field that Friday afternoon. TJ and Ayo had to work double to make sure word didn't get back to Manny, which mostly meant caging her in the Library Tree with important research.

But it was worth it, at least TJ hoped.

He had to count twice, but there were nearly one hundred students on the crossover field. Not as many as that first day, but enough to speak to Eshu for a few moments if Ayo's "theory of deception" was correct.

"Wow, I didn't expect to see this many show up." Manny nodded, sounding impressed. She wore her crossover outfit: cleats, high socks, shorts, knee and elbow pads, and dry-fit shirt. Most of the other students just wore their Ere Idaraya shorts and dashiki tank tops. Umar was decked out in extra pads and even headgear in the green and white colors of the Lagos Cranes. It was so packed with teenagers, some of them even sat atop the totem goalposts, casting tall silhouettes against the dying sun.

"Good call, Ayo." Manny gave him a pat on the back. "Everyone was just last minute."

TJ and Ayo traded sheepish looks.

"Y-yeah... w-we got lucky," TJ stuttered, not quite meeting Manny's eye. He tried to convince himself Manny would forgive him. After all, she knew what all this was for; she knew how he felt about her... right?

"Oh, before I forget." Manny pulled out a hand mirror from her pocket. "This is the enchanted mirror I got off that JS3 exchange student, Fiona. Just a little boost, like we said. When you speak to Eshu, concentrate. You got this, Teej."

"Manny, you're my hero!" Umar shouted. "Just know that I do best as a middleback. My knee on this side doesn't work too good. But you can put me anywhere, too! Whatever you think is best for the team!"

Manny tilted her head in question, and her thick ponytail fell over her shoulder. "What are you talking about?"

TJ waved his hands in the air like a madman and ran between them. "Oh, you know Umar is always talkin' crazy. Don't mind him."

"All right, steppers," Manny began, ignoring Umar's glee. Her tone was large and fierce and TJ almost forgot that Oya was her Orisha and what that entailed. In front of a crowd and in her element, she was a warrior. "You all came here to learn a thing or two about crossover from Ifa Academy's best."

Oh, and cocky? TJ thought, loving the confidence. He had half a mind to let Manny in on the deception. Manny was so awesome; she didn't deserve to be left out of the loop.

Ayo must've known what he was thinking because he shook his head gravely at TJ. "Stay strong, man," he murmured.

"Crossover isn't just a game of fancy air-stepping and flashy dodges. It helps to be strong and fast, sure, but what's more important is your skill and fundamentals. And that's what we'll go over today. You steppers ready?"

The crowd bellowed various affirmations. A few "yes, ma'ams" from a few JS1 students with baby fat still in their cheeks, a handful of "let's gos" from the older kids, and a very loud "hell yeah" from Umar who stood as the crowd's vanguard.

"That's what I like to hear!" Manny exclaimed. "Everyone take a knee as I lead us in a prayer to Eshu." The hard stone that was Manny's face softened as she turned to TJ to smirk at him privately.

Ugh, does she have to wink all cute like that?

TJ did *not* want to do this anymore. It probably wasn't even worth it. Even with Adeyemi's help, they couldn't call Eshu. Now he was lying to Manny. Even if all these kids were here, he couldn't just—

"Hey, man, shouldn't you be doing something right now?" Ayo hissed in his ear.

"I got it, I got it," TJ threw back.

TJ turned away from the field as Ayo stepped forward to join the prayer. One of the meditative poses Elder Adeyemi taught TJ became his focus. It was called the *sebek* pose in the booklet the Headmistress shared with him. He had one leg back, his knee curled into his hip, and his arms to the air.

To ensure he wasn't doing strange poses for nothing, TJ stood at the out-of-bounds line on the field—the threshold between the spectators and the players. The threshold that should have reached out to Eshu's spirit.

Quickly, wisps of Ashe wafted off each student as they followed along with Manny's incantation. And each student actually meant what they said.

"Eshu. First honored opener of the ways," they all said in unison. "Guardian of the crossroads, lord of choice. Guardian of the crossroads, lord of choice…"

TJ knew the students meant their words because they wanted to do well and be on the crossover team badly. Their joined spirit was even thicker than that first day heading into New Ile-Ife. Or perhaps it was because TJ was channeling them more easily, just as he had done with Adeyemi in their sessions and during the festivals.

Soon, much sooner than TJ had expected, Eshu started materializing in the mirror Manny had given him. The mark of Eshu on his finger glowed bright against his forefinger as he gripped the neck of the mirror. The image in the glass started with Eshu's floppy hat, which looked like it floated in the air, until Eshu's face popped into existence with that wide, cheeky grin. Then his pot belly and tunic filled out his body and he was there, ready to talk!

"Eshu! There you are!" TJ shout-whispered.

Like before, Eshu indicated that TJ had to fog the mirror so he could communicate. TJ blew on the mirror a few times, backing it with a bit of heat from his rudimentary fire-breathing magic. Teacher Omo of Fon would've been proud. He kept control of the heat so that it was hot enough to warm the glass, but not too hot to melt it.

The first words from Eshu wrote themselves in the mirror.

Tell your friend Ayo...
... his head's in the right place.
But he forgot one thing about me.

"What do you mean?"

I don't play tricks for the sake of it.
There needs to be a lesson taught.
You could have had me for a half-hour...
... Now you'll only get a handful of minutes.

Ugh! He's right, TJ cursed himself. Now that Eshu reminded him, he did remember that Eshu didn't play tricks on people without a reason. Shoot, the Orisha said as much to him in the Aqua Realm that summer. But TJ didn't have time to get frustrated. He had to be fast with his questions, so he spoke very quickly and quietly.

"Olokun is pissed off. He sent a rainstorm to Los Angeles. Can you speak to him for us? Then I saw Bolawe, who said I was doing good. By the way, I think there are more Keepers in Ifa Academy. Do you know anything about that? Oh, actually, Manny thinks it might be Oya doing the rainstorms. Where is Oya by the way? And—"

Slow down, kid.
You have a few minutes...
... not a few seconds.

Through the fogged mirror, the curls of a chuckle appeared at

Eshu's cheeks. But those dimples were replaced by a serious flat line. TJ couldn't fully tell on the other side of the mirror but it appeared as if Eshu was struggling with his staff, like it were a dog getting away from a leash.

Sorry.
Olosa has not been…
… happy with me…
… But she knows the rules.

Behind him, the prayer ended and Manny was lining students up in drill lines.

"All good," TJ said. "Okay, one question at a time. First, is Olokun mad at me?"

Not at all.
He is happy with your progress…
… and Yemoja thanks you for her gemstone.

Good, TJ thought, *Elder Adeyemi got it to Ol' Sally safely.*

"Great!" TJ sighed with relief. He caught Manny's eye as she shouted at Umar to tighten up his air-stepping technique. TJ gave her a thumbs up. She smiled—which Umar took to mean he was doing a better job—but she yelled at him again to "look sharp." When TJ brought his attention to Eshu again, the image of the Orisha already looked ghostly.

"So what do I have to do to continue making Olokun happy? I know he doesn't like the skyscrapers at Eko Atlantic but I can't just bulldoze buildings. I mean… I *was* joking with Bolawe about making a big-ol' statue or something."

Yes, yes!
Olokun loves stuff like that.
Can you make that happen?

"Ayo might. I'm going to a party he's hosting at Eko Atlantic. His dad is supposed to run things over there. So I was thinking of asking him."

Yes, do that.
Good idea.
It will buy you time…
It will buy us time.

A crossover ball came hurtling toward TJ, exploding in a mud puddle next to him. A trio of kids came rushing after it. Dirt kicked up with each of their footsteps. And all of it got on the mirror. Frantic, TJ wiped it clean with his t-shirt and fogged it up with his breath again.

"What are you doing talking to yourself?" Umar asked as he ran after the kids chasing the ball. "Don't you want to tryout with us too?"

"I'll be there in a minute. I just got this superstition. Gotta talk to my mirror before I go out."

"Oh, yeah? All the pros have superstitions too. Did you know Neda Lafia doesn't wash for a week before a match? And—"

"Umar, get back on D!" Ayo rushed up and pushed the boy along. Then he gestured to the watch at his wrist, then pointed toward TJ and his mirror.

TJ mouthed a "thank you" before turning back to Eshu and saying, "Second question. Keepers in Ifa Academy. Can you check around for that? I think Miss Gravés is mad sus."

I'll keep an eye out for her.

"Thank you. Last question. What's going on with Oya? You said she'd be on the East Coast with her storms but there's nothing. Did she go to the West Coast this year? Is that what all that rain is for in L.A.?"

Oh, yes, yes.
I think she mentioned…
… something about that.

Eshu's staff wiggled out of his hand and he started shouting at it wordlessly. TJ had only met Olosa briefly, but from the little he knew of her in that staff, she was a very testy Orisha.

"So you've been speaking to Oya?" TJ asked, his heart going up a beat. "Did you ask her why she told Manny to go to the Sky Realm to speak to Shango? Oh! And I had a dream about the golden chain. Where is it?"

Mortals cannot reach the golden chain.
Not sure why Oya said that to your friend.

Eshu's image was almost nothing now.
"But you said I'm not like other mortals, right?"
Little squiggly lines appeared on the mirror. None of it making sense in English, let alone any other language.
"Eshu?" TJ asked the mirror. "Eshu!"
No response.
Eshu was gone.
The mirror showed nothing but TJ's own wide eyes and glistening brow with a few skid marks from the mud he hadn't cleaned away properly. At least he got some new information; at least he knew for sure that it was Oya stirring up her storms in Los Angeles. But he wanted to know why! Was she doing some sort of grand ritual to bring back her husband, Shango? If only TJ had another minute for some follow-up questions...
A whistle blared behind TJ. He whipped around to see Manny hustling to the middle of the field where Umar was laid out flat on his back. The boy clutched his knee—his very *bloody* knee.
"Ah! It hurts! It hurts!"
Ayo jogged up to TJ. "Damn... that looks bad. Why am I gettin' a weird case of déjà vu right now?"
TJ turned to look at Ayo. He was right. There was some odd familiarity to the whole situation. What was it? It wasn't like Umar got hurt all the time—despite him getting into all kinds of physical activity, except...
"Oracle Ruby!" TJ exclaimed, and snapped his fingers. "What did she say about Umar... something about staying away from sports or something, yeah?"
Remembrance dawned on Ayo's face. "'Stay away from phys-

ical activity, lest he wanted to be riddled with disappointment and an injury.'"

TJ's chest absolutely caved. He clearly knew what the injury meant, but the disappointment…

TJ barely exchanged a look with Ayo before they both rushed over to Umar.

"Umar! Umar!" TJ shouted. "I'm so sorry, man. Is it hurt bad?"

"Ah, this… this isn't nothing," the boy hissed, trying his darnedest to play it off. He must have realized that if he came off weak, he might not have gotten a spot on the team. Almost all the students surrounded him. Manny held up his knee where Umar winced at the least.

"You should have saw me when I played for the Little Cranes," Umar laughed. "My bone snapped clean off. I probably didn't even break it this time."

"Did someone go get the healer?" TJ asked the crowd. Several students sort of jumped back, others facepalmed. Only a pair of young girls actually ran off to go get help.

"It's okay." Umar shook his head, blood spilling through his fingers. "I know the tryout just started, but I still get a shot at the team, right? I showed heart, didn't I, Manny? The healer will get my leg right by next week."

Manny gave him another curious tilt of her head. "What are you talking about?"

"Whoever does the best gets a spot on the reserve team," Umar said matter-of-factly. Then he pointed to TJ. "That's what he told all of us."

Manny looked between TJ and Umar like she was trying to figure out one of Omo of Fon's thermodynamic equations. "I have no idea what you're talking about."

One of the female students sucked their teeth long and hard. "You see, I told you this was bull." She smacked her friend across the shoulder. "It's just like that kid, Emeka, said. TJ just wanted a laugh."

"Ugh, what an asshole." Her friend shook her head in agreement.

"Wait, no, that's not what—" TJ started, but the truth wouldn't do either.

Everyone started shouting over each other, one demanding a "refund" which Ayo had to remind them wasn't an option because none of them paid anything. Another said they'd report TJ to Elder Adeyemi, but someone else reminded them that TJ was Adeyemi's favorite. The last outcry hurt the most, however. One of the SS1 boys wanted to report Manny to Coach Ali and get her kicked off of the team.

TJ could take all the rest, but not that.

"Everyone, shut up!" he bellowed. Everyone quieted at once, though there were still a few murmurs near the back of the crowd. "This isn't on Manny at all. If you want to get mad at anyone, get mad at me."

"We *are* mad at you!" someone yelled; TJ ignored them.

"I didn't mean for any of you to get hurt."

"Tell that to Umar!"

"This was all a big mistake." He edged his chin directly at Manny and added quietly, "It was all just a mistake, believe me."

"Ugh, let's get out of here," someone in the crowd said. The group started to disperse. Only a few, probably Umar's friends, stayed to make sure he was okay until the healer came to tend to him.

"Didn't Oracle Ruby tell you to stay away from crossover?" the healer said bitterly.

As Umar was carted away with utter hurt in his face, he murmured, "It was supposed to be *my* year, Ruby said... I was supposed to make the team, she said..."

Everyone left at that point, leaving only TJ, Manny, and Ayo in their silence on the empty crossover field. Ayo's eyes ping-ponged between TJ and Manny. He probably wondered who would speak first. A small gust billowed around Manny, making her tied-back hair bounce with it. If TJ hadn't been able to see Ashe in the air, he would've thought it was Manny generating the wind with the cold anger that was surely roiling within her.

It was a long moment—a very long moment—before she croaked, "Did it work? Did you get the info you needed from Eshu."

"Manny, I'm so sorry—" TJ spluttered.

Ayo jumped in. "It was my fault—"

Manny's gaze *bit* into Ayo's dower expression. "I'm talking to Tomori Jomiloju, not to you, Ayodeji."

Ayo threw up his hands and took a step back, clearly wanting none of the heat.

"Answer my question," she venomed at TJ.

TJ cleared his throat twice, thrice before getting out, "Mostly. Yeah. Mostly. Oya's on the West Coast. Olokun is happy for now. It's not everything I wanted to learn, but it's enough."

Manny drew in a long and nearly grunted breath. TJ had mostly only seen her friendly side, the one that cracked up and snorted at dad jokes. He hardly ever saw this muted anger from her. He could almost feel it rolling off her like a kindling inferno. Sure, she had been irritated with him before but nothing like this. And he felt like a papier-mâché under her flame.

Stepping up to TJ, she jabbed a finger into his chest. The full sharpness of her nail dug into his skin under his t-shirt.

"You were so out of pocket for that, TJ," Manny gritted.

"Manny, we can—I can explain—"

"*So* out of pocket. You could've gotten me kicked off the team. Shit, I might not even be on the team tomorrow."

"The team you didn't even want to be on a week ago?" TJ wanted to take it back the moment he said it. He didn't even know why he did it. It just came out. Ayo knew it, too. He bit into his fist, repressing a groan TJ knew he wanted to let out, the instigator he was.

Manny withdrew her finger from TJ's chest, balled a fist, and for a moment, TJ thought she'd use it on his jaw. Instead, she dropped it to her side and, again, in a hushed tone, said, "Don't. Talk. To. Me."

Don't talk to me? Does she mean, like, forever... or for the rest of the night?

Ayo stood stock still, pretending he didn't exist at all.

Before TJ could even *think* of coming up with an answer to that, Manny was already stomping across the field and back to the academy grounds, where she let out a very loud and very raucous scream, gales of wind casting from her mouth. Birds flew from the trees that swayed, and the little eloko from Mr. Ikenna's class scurried from one bush to another—one that was in the opposite direction of Manny.

TJ trembled, and he couldn't understand why at first. He wasn't cold. Then he realized what it was. He was rocked with complete and utter guilt.

26

THE ULTIMATE REMEDY

TJ WOKE UP EARLY TO GO OVER TO THE JS2 GIRLS'
treehouses and apologize to Manny. The fresh morning air almost
shocked the guilt out of him as he tried to practice apologies to
Manny in his head. When he arrived at the foot of their dwellings,
Titilayo and the exchange student Fiona told him she had already
left with the crossover team. TJ felt some relief at that. At least
she could continue playing. It was unlikely Coach Ali would have
cut her best player, but he had still been worried.

"She was quite angry with you," a talking crow croaked on
Fiona's shoulder. "Quite angry indeed." Fiona's stark-red hair
contrasted the crow at her shoulder. TJ was no longer surprised
by it, as Fiona had it with her everywhere she went. According to
Ayo, the crow wasn't a pet but a sort of bodyguard or escort or
something—TJ hadn't asked Fiona directly.

"Shhh, that's rude, *Mhamó*," Fiona said in her Scottish accent.

The crow—or rather, Mhamó—twitched her wings like a
shrug. "Thought the child should know he messed up."

Fiona snapped her fingers to silence her crow with a wind wall,
but her wind magic manifested, spiraled out, and then died midair. TJ
had half a mind to help her with his boosting abilities, but he didn't
want to anger the crow. Fiona had been attending Ifa Academy that
year for a few term to improve her elemental skill, which was lacking.

"Sorry, TJ," she said with a grimace. "My grandma can be a bit forward. Are you going to the party tonight?"

Grandmother!? TJ thought, surprised, but he kept the shock to himself so as not to offend anyone.

TJ almost told Fiona it was his birthday, but she wouldn't care to know. Ayo *said* the party that night was in celebration of TJ but he knew that was all made up to cover Ayo's butt for forgetting TJ's birthday in the first place.

Fiona didn't need to know all that, so instead, he said, "Yeah, I'll be at the party. Can't forget about Nigerian Independence, right? You and Titi are going too, right?"

"I'm trying to convince her to go, but you know how it is with her and," she whispered her next words, "you-know-who."

"I wear glasses, not a hearing aid, Fiona!" Titilayo stomped her foot. "You must be mistaking me for my brother. And I'll have you know that one in five women in Nigeria are dissatisfied in their marriages. Ayo and I are *not* putting labels on our... connection. I will *not* become one of those one in five women."

TJ told them thank you and excused himself. When he was barely ten feet away, they started arguing about Titi and Ayo's relationship, with Fiona's crow of a grandmother screeching, "Fight, fight, fight!"

As TJ headed back to meet up with Ayo, he realized fully that it was his birthday and how hurt Manny must've felt not to wish him a happy one. A sickness crawled in TJ's stomach at the thought of Manny being *that* mad at him. Her look of scorn was plastered to the inside of his mind all last night. He'd have to make it up to her. Maybe he could get something for her in Eko Atlantic. But what kind of gift could you give to a person who felt totally betrayed?

"DON'T LOOK SO DOWN, MAN," AYO SAID A LITTLE WHILE LATER as the tiny Oroma tightened him up with some new box braids in their dorm. Everyone else except TJ and Ayo had left for Independence Day festivities. "After Oroma gets done with me, come over here. I'll hook you. Ain't nothin' better to get a Black man's mood up than a fresh cut."

TJ ran his fingers through his curls and wondered what Ayo would do to him. He liked the way his Afro coiled out of his head; he didn't want to chop it all off. As he waited, he flipped through his sister's old journal, reading her notes on advanced Olokun magic. The complicated ideas of underwater physics made TJ's brain throb several lines into his reading, but he did his best to tough it out. Next time he met with Adeyemi, or did a ritual, he wanted to make sure he was pulling his weight even more, especially when the Elder was counting on him personally.

After a while, Oroma left Ayo with perfectly lined braids with red and white beads at the bottom.

"If you need me for anything else, I'll be near the grove with Mr. Ikenna," Oroma said, with a bit too much honey in her words. Surely she knew Mr. Ikenna didn't mess around as a rule, right? Then again, Oroma probably didn't care.

"Good lookin' out, Oroma. We'll catch you later." Ayo waved as their caretaker left the dorm. "Shooooot," Ayo looked at himself in a hand mirror near his bed, "Oroma need to stop messin' around and open up a spot in the village. No hair comin' out of my braids *and* her fingers are lightning fast. I look damn good." He bit his lip. "Damn good."

"Yeah, I bet Titi will love it," TJ said with light laughter. "You got them Shango beads for good luck, too? Does the red and white invoke some hidden Shango charisma?"

Ayo sucked his teeth and sat his mirror down. "Man, shut your ass up. Come sit over here with your goofy Afro." He grabbed a chair near his work desk and set it in the middle of the empty dorm. TJ complied and set his bottom to the seat, still nervous of what was going to be done with his hair. Ayo swiveled around TJ for a full five minutes while *hmmm-hmmming* to himself, his fingers pressed into his chin. Each time he made a round, his braid beads *clicked* and *clacked* in a rhythm that almost lulled TJ to sleep.

"Uh… should I say something here?" TJ asked when it got too awkward. "Like… tell you what I want, or —"

"Hush, hush," Ayo hissed as he continued his roundabout. "Let me work, let me work."

After another few minutes of humming and turning, Ayo finally said, "A'ight, bet. Here's what I'm going to do for you." He started rummaging through his drawers. "You seem attached to the Fro so we'll leave it on top. But first, I'm going to taper the sides. I think I'll go from zero at the bottom and fade to a three up top. Sound good?"

"What about the top?" TJ asked. "You gonna braid me in one of your man buns?"

"Nah, you ain't got enough swag for that. Imma hook you up with a fohawk though. Gonna be *real* sharp." Ayo finally found a set of clippers in his drawer, which he enchanted to float at his side. "Trust me." From behind him, a barber cape flicked up and over his shoulder. Then it drifted down TJ's body and wrapped around his neck.

"How you know all this?" TJ asked as the first bite of the clippers shaved into the side of his head. He'd be more nervous, but Ayo had top grades with enchantments. "Barbers shops aren't the same in Nigeria as they are in the States."

"YouTube, my man. YouTube. Plus, my baba travels to the States a lot. That's where I learned a bit about barbering."

TJ hadn't gotten many haircuts in his life, despite living in the City of Angels, where that sort of thing was commonplace. But with Dad always sporting a bald head and Mom twisted up in locs, haircuts weren't much of a pastime for the Youngs.

"*You know how much Black folks waste their money on all them haircuts?*" Dad would often complain.

TJ thought the no haircut tradition should change, though. The brush of metal through his coils felt oddly nice, the gentle heat of the clippers was like a massage.

Black snow of hair fell down in clumps at the corner of TJ's eyes, and Ayo cupped TJ's chin to make sure his floating clippers could cut at the right angles. TJ caught a whiff of his cologne and tried to stifle a sneeze.

"You want me to cut your peach fuzz?" Ayo asked. "They say it makes your mustache grow faster. Make you look older."

"Nah, I'm good." TJ wasn't a fan of mustaches. Beards? Yeah. But mustaches on their own? Not so much.

"You sure? There's a grip of older girls that are gonna come through at this party."

"Nah, for real. I'm good."

Ayo rolled his eyes. "You can't get hung up on *one* girl, man. At least tonight you should, you know, have some fun. Get you a li'l honey. At least take your mind off Olokun and the Keepers and the academy and all that." Ayo brushed a hair sponge on top of TJ's head, making TJ's head rock like a bobblehead.

"A'ight, done," Ayo said, then handed TJ his hand mirror.

TJ checked out his cut. It was almost... too perfect. He was bald on the sides but faded near the middle where his hair tapered into his natural Afro. And the top of the Afro itself was cut a little shorter, with defined coils. TJ rubbed the back of his head. There was still hair there, too. He turned his chin to the side to see that he indeed had a full fohawk.

"Yeah, yeah, it's nice. I already know." Ayo smiled behind TJ in the mirror. "Shit, I barely recognize you."

It was true. TJ hardly recognized even himself. But he had to admit it... He looked good. Real good. Like he could be in a movie or something good. Like a girl would actually come up to him rather than the other way around. He almost forgot how bad he felt about... what was he stressing out about again?

"A'ight, a'ight." Ayo took the mirror from him. "Don't get caught up lookin' at yourself like that too much. Now, let's work on what you're going to wear."

27

TOWERS OF EBONY

AYO PICKED AN OUTFIT TJ DIDN'T TOTALLY HATE. A NICE little baby blue button-up, some jeans, and fresh white Air Jordans that were too big for Ayo. The only thing about TJ's outfit that made him uncomfortable was the shoes. They were too clean. As they walked up to the Summoning Statue sign-out table, he walked as flat-footed as he could on the earth path to avoid any dirt implanting itself in the white rubber. TJ didn't know how Ayo was keeping all his stuff clean, from his fresh red and white Mamba Focuses, white jeans, and crisp red shirt.

Then TJ saw the mystical Ashe force field around Ayo's entire body.

"How are you keeping your clothes so neat with your Ashe?" TJ whispered bitterly.

Ayo pointed to himself. "Oh, right! You can *see* my wind wall, can't you? That's basic trainin' in dueling club. You always gotta keep your defenses up. But it also helps keep your clothes clean, too. Takes a lot of energy and concentration though, which is why this line to get out of the academy needs *to go faster!*" He raised his voice to the other kids ahead of them, who were also waiting for their phones. Many of them wore green and white clothing to represent Nigeria's Independence Day.

As TJ and Ayo waited in line for the next Shango statue portal to open up, TJ realized that the haircut and the nice clothes was Ayo's silent way of saying sorry to him about Manny. And TJ was surprised how good that made him feel, that a feeling like that could happen between him and Ayo. He thought he'd only feel that closeness with Manny.

Ayo canted his head at TJ. "You good, bro? Why you lookin' at me like that?"

"Uh... n-nothing, man. Just lost in thought."

"Well, well, well." Miss Gravés, who was manning the sign-out tables near the statue portals, whistled long and stretched. "What are you two young men getting up to this weekend? Is there some concert I don't know about?"

"Nah, Miss G," Ayo said as he signed out and grabbed his phone, "This is just the regular weekend getup. You like TJ's cut, though, huh?"

"I most certainly do. Very handsome, young man."

TJ signed out too, trying his best not to blush. He mumbled a, "Thanks Miss Gravés," and got his phone, which was powered off.

"Well, y'all be safe wherever you're off to. Try not to break too many hearts."

Ayo flung out his arms long and wide. "Us? Heartbreakers? Come on, Miss G."

TJ led Ayo away toward the portal for the underground Summoning Stone. Once they were through their respective portals and in the caverns, he asked, "What were you doin' being all friendly to Miss Gravés back there? You know what I said about her."

"Man, you just buggin'. Miss G's cool." A chime sounded from Ayo's phone. "Oh, and would you look at that." He showed TJ his screen:

Divination Today Breaking: Mysterious week-long rain in Southern California ceases. Still no official word of mystical elements or beings at play.

Third Eye Breaking: Rumor Report - Divine Intervention responsible for flooding in Southwest United States.

"Oh, nice!" TJ said the moment he read both headlines. He powered on his phone, too. "That must've been Eshu. He probably spoke to Oya to make it stop."

The moment TJ and Ayo walked past the Summoning Stone's tall Orisha statues and back out into the village of New Ile-Ife proper, TJ's notifications came in hot as well. *The Eshu Messenger Press*, *Evocation*, and all the other major news outlets were saying the same thing about the rains in Los Angeles.

"Oh, look," Ayo said. "Evo is saying it was some deity named, um... ta.. tla... tlaloc? I don't know, Tláloc-something. Apparently, he was behind it all. Looks like it's not just our Orishas making trouble these days."

"What? But Eshu said—" TJ's phone rang. It was a video call from Mom. Without saying another word, TJ answered it. "Mom?"

"Baby!" She beamed, her palm-tree dreadlocks filling the whole screen. Behind her, the sky was a cloudless blue. "Happy birthday!"

The whole family, Mom, Dad, and Tunde, squeezed their way into the screen and they started singing in unison. *"Happy birthday to ya! Happy birthday to ya! Happy birthday!"*

TJ didn't realize how much he missed them as a warm feeling swelled through his chest and up to his head. They were totally off-key and Tunde was intentionally singing faster than he needed to, but TJ loved it all the same.

"Thanks!" TJ smiled. "How's everything? I was just reading about all the stuff that was going on."

"Everything's fine," Mom said. "The air hasn't been cleaner in Los Angeles in years, but there's loads of water damage."

Tunde jumped to be seen and shouted to be heard. "Mom! Stopped! A whole! Dam! From flooding!"

"Boy, get off your momma's back like that." Dad pulled Tunde off Mom. "How you feelin', son?"

"Good, good."

"Dang, did TJ get a haircut? Look, Dad. Look!" Now Tunde was climbing on Dad's back.

"Lookin' real sharp, young man. Who hooked you up?"

Ayo leaned over TJ's shoulder and waved. "His boy right here. Hey, Mr. and Mrs. Young!"

"Hey, Ayo!" Mom and Dad said together, then Dad went off screen as he tussled with Tunde.

Mom laughed and asked, "How are your classes, honey bunny?"

He grimaced at Mom publicly calling him honey bunny. "Uh... classes... they could be better, to be honest." He would've liked to tell Mom he was freaking out about Olokun, but she'd only worry, and Elder Adeyemi didn't say it was okay to tell her anything yet. Besides, confessing that he wasn't doing so well at school was enough for one phone call.

"Don't worry, you'll figure it out. Elder Adeyemi tells me you have private lessons with her now?" That response took TJ aback. Mom must've been in a *really* good mood for her to be okay with him saying classes were anything less than perfect. "Anyway, let me help get Tunde off your father." She turned her head and raised her voice. "Tunde! Don't you dare trap your father in a wind cage! I don't care how big it is. And I don't care if you're technically in the living room and not the backyard!" Mom glanced back to TJ. "Sorry, Tomori. Let me control this little boy. He thinks he's all that and a bag of potato chips 'cause he helped out with the storms a little bit. Love you. Happy birthday!"

"Thanks, Mom. Love you, too. Bye!"

The moment they hung up, TJ wished they had spoken a little longer. True, the fresh cut and the new threads were making him feel better, but he still felt the weight of everything else piling up on him. Just seeing his family and talking to them did a lot to break some of that up.

"They're always nice to see," Ayo said as he led the way past the Mami Wata Eatery. One of the water spirits tried to give him more tofu, but Ayo declined. "Your brother has a motor-mouth though. Wouldn't stop talking when we were waitin' for you to wake up back at camp."

"Yeah, he's a trip."

TJ and Ayo made their usual round to Babalu-Aye Medical, only to be told that both Adeola and Mr. Du Bois were still not available to see visitors.

"Damn," Ayo said after they left. "Imagine if Manny and I were in the Aqua Realm as long as them? You think we'd be taking this long to recover, too?"

TJ shrugged. He didn't like to think of dark what-ifs like that when it came to his friends.

TJ and Ayo continued walking along the roads of New Ile-Ife toward the village exit, passing by more store shops and open food markets. An aziza was haggling for better prices because none of the shirts sold accounted for wings. Another man with missing teeth and a gray eye held a bunch of amulets over his arm, selling three for one. TJ couldn't help doing double takes at anyone with Olokun robes who looked their way too long. Any of them could've been Keepers. He didn't recognize any from the festival, though. And as the village thinned out, they got fewer looks.

At the end of the last road near the outer wall, TJ and Ayo showed the guards their student IDs and passed through. They walked into a thicket of trees where light could barely press through the canopy high above. It took TJ's eyes a moment to adjust from the bright to the shadows.

"Took you long enough!" a female voice called near a stream flowing by a huge tree trunk. The woman—no, girl—well, teenager, TJ supposed, sat on a rock with an umbrella over her head. She wore a huge sun hat that flopped almost to her shoulders, large, bug-eyed sunglasses, a tank top, and a long skirt wrapped around her thickly toned legs.

"You know it takes time to achieve this perfection." Ayo gestured to himself. "And what you got that big-ass umbrella and hat for?"

She answered in a husky Nigerian tone. "Dark-skinned people have the worst cases of skin cancer because we think we're protected just because—"

"We hardly ever get sunburnt. Yeah, yeah. Titi gave me that spiel before."

"Oh, she hasn't dumped you yet?"

"She can't dump me if we wasn't ever exclusive. She don't use labels; I told you."

The girl sucked her teeth long and stretched. "Yeah, yeah, whatever."

TJ caught himself staring. Clearly, this girl cared about her skin and it showed. It was perfectly unblemished, an even shade of deep, deep brown, not unlike Ayo.

"Excuse my rudeness." Ayo smacked TJ across the chest. "This is my boy, TJ. TJ, this is my *former* sitter *now* tutor, Eniola."

"Former?" She threw up an eyebrow as she stood up, coming barely an inch under TJ's height. Tall for a girl. "Then why did your baba have me come fetch you then, eh?"

Ayo smacked his teeth, answering back with his own Naija cadence, "Because you're family, not because of anything else."

"Family?" TJ asked.

"Ayo's my baby cousin. I helped change a diaper or two of his back when he—"

Ayo threw up his hands. "All right, all right, that's enough—"

"Wait," TJ said, doing math in his head, "you're, like, what? Eighteen? Nineteen? How did you change Ayo's—"

"I said, all right, all right," Ayo cut in.

"Close, I just barely turned seventeen, but I'll be eighteen next year," his cousin cut in harder. "Long story. It's how our family knew I had Ashe to begin with. You see, Ayo took this big ol' s—"

"Come on, come on with that!" Ayo stepped between TJ and his cousin. "We all got places to be. The DJ's supposed to get there early."

"If you hadn't taken so long picking between a coral or maroon shirt, we would be here on time," TJ said.

"You definitely should have gone with coral, cousin. That maroon is doing your ashy elbows no service."

"No one asked your giraffe-lookin' ass," Ayo shot back, rubbing his elbows.

"Don't mind him." TJ leaned in to Eniola. "He's just salty because he's not tall enough to get on the big boy rides."

"Yo, yo, what's with the gang up? Teej, I can jack up that fresh cut real quick if you don't check yourself."

Eniola laughed. "Bring him around more often, Ayo. I like this guy."

Ayo groaned. "Maaan, are we goin' to this party or what?"

"All right, Big Head. *Wá ṣi mi.*" A brass staff—no, a *gold* staff —smacked into Eniola's hand. The peeking sun rays through the canopy glistened over it, twinkling between its sheen. "Hold my wrist." Ayo groaned and took Eniola's arm. "You too, funny guy."

TJ tilted his head in question. "What's going on?"

"Eni's gonna transport us to Eko Atlantic," Ayo explained. "A.K.A. she wants to show off her portal transporting with her new staff. Did you steal that gold from the pyramids you got classes in over in Egypt?"

"Nah, the teachers all like me and hooked me up."

"Oh, so you go to the academy in Egypt, not Ifa?" TJ asked.

"Yeah, but I'm at Heka just so I could swap my old staff for this one before finishing my last year back here at Ifa. Had to come back for Independence Day, though!"

TJ rubbed the back of his head. "Heka?"

"Heka School of Sorcery in Giza," Ayo explained for his cousin.

Eniola beckoned for TJ again. "C'mon, take my wrist. Don't be nervous. I don't bite."

"Don't believe her, Teej. You should see her with a plate of *garri.*"

"You know, I can just leave you here and you can walk the hundred-and-fifty kilometers."

Ayo got real quiet then.

"All right, don't want to make Ayo late," TJ said as he wrapped his hand around Eniola's wrist. It was just as smooth as it looked. Warm, too.

Eniola led them to the stream just beside them. She dipped a toe in and said a prayer to Oshun, the Orisha of Love, Sensuality, and, well... Rivers. At the base of the stream, a whirlpool mani- fested itself with a twinkling glow. Eniola fell into the portal she created, like someone going feet first into a pool, then Ayo, and then TJ. For a moment, TJ thought he was going through the red seas and Eniola was like their Moses. But instead of seeing fish and whales at their side, there were just streaks of blue and green light. Though, for a moment, TJ thought he saw two large glowing eyes, glowing eyes that reminded him of Olokun. Fear seized him when, in a flash, they all stepped out onto a rooftop terrace, completely dry. TJ looked over his shoulder to see a wall fountain of black stone. Then a weight brought TJ's hand down.

Eniola was falling to the marble floor that had manifested below them. Then her knees buckled over a luxury couch.

"Oh, shoot!" TJ blurted. "Are you all right?"

"Yeah, yeah," Eniola sighed. "Just a bit light-headed. Two trips in one day seems to be my limit. Still gotta break in my goldenrod."

"I got her." Ayo pulled his cousin up and led her indoors, just off the rooftop, to a penthouse. "She just needs some juice and a little nap."

"Sorry you had to see me like this," Eniola lulled, looking half asleep. Her huge sun hat nearly fell off her head. "See you around, funny guy."

"Nice to meet you, Eniola," TJ returned.

"You can call me Eni."

"Sure thing... Eni."

"And, Teej," Ayo called out over his shoulder. "Welcome to Eko Atlantic. Oyelowo Ebony Towers."

TJ took proper notice of the rooftop terrace. He was left alone to the artsy, amorphous day couches, propane-powered fire pits, hanging lights strung from rooftop to support poles, and the glass balcony that enclosed it all. So high up, it was a bit nippy. TJ's skin goose bumped, and he rubbed warmth into them, speaking Shango's heat charm to toast his palms. It looked like they were alone on the roof, actually early for once. But that made sense when Ayo was the host.

At the edge of the glass balcony where TJ stood, the whole of Eko Atlantic spread out in all its grandeur. Along the skyline, there were only a few more buildings under construction. The rest were already twinkling as people turned off the lights to office spaces and turned on the lights of their skyscraper homes. Ebony Towers sort of stood as the forerunner to all the rest, just at the edge of Eko Atlantic, like an obsidian guardian against the great ocean.

A terrifying emptiness took TJ's chest and rolled to his stomach. When Olokun came, Ebony Towers would be the first to get hit.

For several long moments, TJ simply stared at the great expanse that was the Atlantic Ocean. Today, the waves were relatively calm. You would never think it could be capable of mass destruction the way it gently ebbed against the sandbanks far below.

Calm waters were not what TJ saw, however.

His vision blurred into a much different image and his ears filled with more than mellow high winds. He saw crashing waves, white-caps smashing into all those buildings and towers and cars below that looked like ants. Heart-wrenching screams, roaring fires, crashing steel and glass against asphalt attacked his ears...

TJ grabbed onto the balcony railing to halt his shaking hands. He hadn't noticed how heavily he had been breathing. He closed his eyes to shut out the violent images. He covered his ears to stop the cries for help.

TJ forced himself back into Elder Adeyemi's cave. He felt the smooth curve of her back. The ripples of her cave pond centered him again. Her lessons muted the anxiety building within. He took three great, heaving breaths. The sickness in his gut didn't go away completely, but at least he could focus semi-normally once more.

The hell was this? Did he just have a panic attack?

When he opened his eyes, his gaze was fixed on an odd shape within the ocean. It was the rock face that looked like an open palm. The same one Ayo's cousin told them about. The same one Bolawe said to watch out for, to know if Olokun was happy with their progress.

It was exposed without a single wave covering it.

Olokun was happy for now, but how long would that last?

How long until TJ's imaginations of mayhem became reality?

His phone buzzed in his pocket and he took it out to read:

Eko Atlantic's Doomsday in 19 weeks, 1 day, 18 hours, 0 minutes, and 0 seconds

28

BAD & BOUJEE

AS NIGHT FELL AND AYO RETURNED FROM HELPING HIS COUSIN, TJ allowed himself to let go of what could be: destruction, drowning, death. He was at this Independence Day party for a reason. One foot in front of the other. One step at a time. So that meant speaking to Ayo's father as soon as he could. But what would TJ even say?

"Hey, Mr. Oyelowo. Could you and your other tower buddies get together and tear down your skyscrapers? Please and thank you!"

"Hey, Mr. O. It'd be *real* nice if you could explain yourself to Olokun."

"Hey, Oyelowo, how'd you like all your people in Eko Atlantic to drown?"

The more he thought about what he'd say, the worse it got. So instead, he busied himself with watching each new guest that came up to the rooftop as the party started. Pretty soon, the whole terrace was full of teenagers, ready for a good time.

Now… TJ knew Ayo was rich. He knew that he was more than regular rich, above the likes of an average pop star, but perhaps below the likes of an Arabian prince.

But seeing it was entirely different from knowing it.

The terrace was already decadent, with all its leather furniture and infinity pools, but the decorations for the party were something else. At one end of the roof was a long stretch of DJ equipment laid out on a stage, where live performers would swap in and out. Some of them TJ even recognized as Afrobeat stars he listened to back in the States.

Which forced a little skip from his toe.

Here's the thing… TJ didn't dance as a rule—unless he was in the privacy of his room back home. But the deep drum beats reverberating from the stereo system, which bordered the rooftop, forced a full-on bop from his head along with the tapping of his feet.

There were green and white lights set up, so bright they matched the stars above. To most, it would've looked like some sort of techno setup, but in actuality, it was in honor of Nigeria's colors and their independence. Occasionally, a light would stream across TJ's face, making him squint.

More than all the fancy technology though… there was, of course, a magical twist. Between the green and white lights, teenagers danced around each other in little wind cycles. And TJ realized the lights strung up weren't filled with bulbs but with adze—vampiric fairies—in little globes. If you got close enough, you could see them playing cards against each other in their little fish-tank-like balls.

"Take a picture, it'll last longer," one of them had said to TJ when he gawked too long.

"And make sure that Ayo boy pays up. We're not keeping these lights on for free," another one told him. "Or else we'll possess his ass. Hehehe!" They had chuckled until TJ finally backed away.

Like the adze, not all the guests were human. TJ would've sworn he saw some half-human, half-animal hybrids, teenagers with giant bird heads, a few aziza flying around, and one particularly short teenager with a hoodie TJ would put money on was the same eloko from Mr. Ikenna's class. Instead of speaking, it just grunted.

TJ had seen magical creatures before, usually when he and his family had to re-register with the magical government, but he hardly ever saw them as a group of teens, and it left him staring at a few of them too long with curious eyes he hoped didn't appear rude.

Ayo and Eniola had said only diviner kids and creatures were allowed that day, no clouded or non-magicals. TJ even watched as Ayo and a few other of his friends who attended other magical schools cloaked the rooftop with enchantments to trap in the sound and lights. Despite them being out in the open air, the music sounded like they were in a little club.

TJ and his family were registered under the Los Angeles branch of the UCMP, which meant that their magic was monitored. Ayo and his friends, who lived in magical communities, didn't have the same regulations and TJ was a bit jealous about how openly they could use their magic.

"You like it, huh?" Ayo tapped TJ's elbow halfway into the party.

"It's uh… a lot," TJ replied loudly over the music.

"Yeah, my party organizers can be a li'l extra. Hey, man, sorry I didn't get you nothin'. I figured the party would be my gift to you, though."

"The party that was never meant to be for my birthday but now suddenly is?"

"Yup."

There wasn't even a birthday cake around. Just a whole lot of underage drinking and boxes on boxes of pizza. TJ rolled his eyes as a half-giant stomped onto the dance floor.

Ayo threw his hands up. "How was I supposed to know you were born on Nigeria's Independence day?"

"Gee, I don't know… ask."

"Oh, so it's like that?" Ayo crossed his arms. "What's my birthday then?"

Crickets.

"Fair point." TJ glanced away from Ayo to avoid the awkward eye contact. A new group of partygoers stumbled onto the rooftop. They looked older, the girls with layers of makeup and the guys with sharp little beards, except the makeup was slapped on with inexperienced hands and the beards were mostly patchy. There weren't any actual adults among them, just teenagers playing as them.

"Let me guess," TJ said. "Your dad doesn't know you're throwing this party?"

"What? Of course not!"

"Damnit, Ayo. Half the reason I'm here is to talk to your dad about Olokun. I think he'd like to know that his towers are in danger. You have told him about Olokun, right?" Ayo ignored the question and swiped a pale-looking drink from a tray held by a hostess. Then he drank it longingly. "Oh my god, Ayo. You haven't told him!?"

"He's... busy. I don't get to see him much."

"Are you serious right now!?"

"What am I supposed to tell him? I can't remember anything from the Aqua Realm. And every time I want to mention Olokun to him, I just get this feeling... like I get all nervous and whatnot?"

"You? Ayo? Nervous!?"

"Get off my case."

TJ made like he could choke Ayo. "Let me speak to your father. I won't get nervous. He has to know."

"Not tonight, TJ! Look around you. Have a good time. We'll talk to my dad tomorrow. Have a drink and stop being a loner in the corner just watching everyone." Ayo tried to pass him a bubbly whatever-it-was, too.

"Nah, I don't drink that stuff, bro."

"Should've guessed you wouldn't," Ayo said snidely before taking a sip. Then he gave TJ a sidelong glance. "Oh, I get it. You don't want to talk to no one because you can't get no one. Not because you're hung up on..." TJ gave him a look that said he needed to shut it. "On you-know-who," Ayo finished cautiously.

TJ thought back to a time when he was battling Olokun alongside Eshu. What had the mischief maker told him then? Flow like Olosa of the lagoon and think like Eshu of mischief? Maybe he needed to stop thinking so hard. Perhaps he only needed to go with the flow of the party and something would show itself. He was where he was supposed to be, at the very least. So he relented, huffing at Ayo. "Fine. If I get one of these girls to get with me, you owe me a birthday cake, on top of the face to face with your dad."

"Deal. But you're not getting anyone here. They're all way out of your league."

"Watch me." TJ stomped off onto the dance floor and tapped the first human girl he saw on her shoulder. She turned around with a little jump, clearly taken off guard.

Looking TJ up and down, and with a very rude tone, she asked, "Do I know you?" and shimmed away with her friends.

Never approach a girl from behind, TJ thought, groaning to himself. *Rule number one. You gotta make sure she knows you're coming. Well, let's try that again…*

He took note of another girl with Afro puffs near the food table. "Wait for her to notice you," TJ murmured to himself. He could hear Ayo snickering behind him and tried to ignore it. "Make eye contact. Then slowly make your way to her."

TJ waited for the eye contact. When the girl with the Afro puffs looked up and caught his gaze with a smile, TJ murmured to himself, "Good. Now walk over there." TJ took his first steps. *Not like that, you idiot. Walk over there with some style. Walk with the beat of the music.*

But that was a mistake.

TJ had no rhythm, and his walk looked more like he had an ache in his knees. The girl scrunched her nose up and pretended she hadn't noticed TJ at all.

"Yo, you never told me you can't dance. I shoulda given you a lesson instead of giving you a cut," Ayo called out with a laugh, then took another sip of his drink.

"Ugh," TJ groaned, "this is stupid."

The next girl that walked by had two bubbly drinks in her hand, clearly making her way to her friends, wherever they were in the sea of teenagers. TJ stepped right in front of her and blurted, "Hey, my name is TJ. Ifedayo Young's little brother. I saved everyone from Olokun this summer and people tell me I'm something between a god or… something. Pretty neat, huh?"

"Huh? What did you say?" she asked loudly over the music.

"Just forget it. Do you need me to help you find your friends?"

"Yes, please."

After asking for a description of her friend group, TJ used his height to point them out. The girl went about her way and TJ turned back to Ayo to say he was officially done. But when he looked over each of his shoulders, he couldn't find Ayo at all. When he finally spotted the boy's side-swept braids and red shirt that glowed with the DJ's lights, TJ called out to him. Ayo didn't seem to hear him, though. TJ was about to call out again when Ayo turned a little, revealing that he was sucking face with Titi.

TJ groaned. *So much for being one of those one in five women, Titi.*

What the hell was TJ doing? He wasn't here for girls; he was here to save the whole stinking tower from becoming fish food. Ayo wasn't going to help, but at least TJ was in his family's tower. Ayo's dad had to be in there somewhere. TJ would just go downstairs, ask some security guard or whoever, and figure it out on his own.

Any job worth doing always had to be done on your own, Mom always said.

29

DAUGHTER OF OSHUN

SHOULDERING THROUGH THE TEENAGERS POPPING THEIR BACKS and flailing their hands, TJ made his way to the elevator just inside the penthouse. The hall inside was tall and wide, like any other luxury space. He passed by large abstract paintings of women holding baskets on their heads. Each of them pointed behind him back to the rooftop passage, but TJ pressed forward to the elevator at the hall's end.

TJ pressed the elevator switch to go down a level. The light that should've blossomed behind the plastic button didn't bloom, though.

TJ pressed it again. Nothing.

"Oh, my bad. Did you forget something?" came a familiar voice from the side. TJ hadn't noticed the hall had opened up as a "T" intersection leading to the restrooms on either end. Each side had a row of oblong chairs, one of which was occupied by Eni, Ayo's cousin. She didn't have her sun hat anymore now that it was nighttime. Her sunglasses were gone too. She had the deepest brown eyes and her straight hair fell to her shoulders.

"Oh, hey, funny guy! Did you need the restroom? They're just down there." She had earbuds on and her phone laid atop her crossed legs.

"No, no, I-I was..." TJ wasn't sure what to say. "I wanted to look around and check out more of the... tower?" It was more a question than a statement.

Eni took her earbuds out, uncrossed her legs, and smiled up at TJ. "What? Why? There's a whole party over there." She nodded back to the terrace.

"Yeah, well..."

"Not your scene?"

"Somethin' like that... yeah."

"Well, I can't let you through. I can only let people come up."

"For real? Why?"

"I'm acting as the security guard of sorts. You know," she dipped her chin low like she was letting TJ in on a secret, "anti-parent security. Like I said, I owed my baby cousin a favor."

TJ collapsed onto the adjacent sofa from Eni. It was just as uncomfortable as it looked. "Let me guess. There's no way I can convince you to let me through, is there?"

"Afraid not."

"So what happens if someone's parent does come up?"

"They all dash their way down the emergency escape like the miscreant teens they are." TJ wasn't sure if she was joking. "So, what you want to go touring the tower for, anyway?"

"Oh, nothing. Just need to save Eko Atlantic from becoming Atlantis." Eni gave him a look. "You know, the ancient under-water city—"

"Yeah, yeah, I know what Atlantis is. Are you being funny again or something? Is there something else going on at the party you don't want to tell me about?"

TJ seized up a bit. "N-nah."

"Come on... we're cool at this point, right? We both made fun of my cousin. You saw me nearly pass out..."

"Nothing, really." TJ needed to get past her, into that elevator, and to Ayo's dad.

Eni stood up. "No, for real. If someone blacked out out there, I gotta—"

"What are you getting into to stave off boredom?" Fine, TJ would have to distract her first.

"Ah, nothing." Eni sat back down and drew her phone closer to her lap.

"C'mon... I thought we were cool at this point, right?" TJ threw back at her.

"Fine." She flipped the screen to show him a game of live basketball, only... it wasn't the NBA.

"Hey!" TJ drew closer to her. "That's the BAL. The Basketball African League, yeah?"

"Yup. My mom's trying to get an arena built out here for a Lagos team. We need one."

"Wait, so you watch-watch? Like, for real, for real? You're not into crossover like everyone else?"

"Crossover is cool too, but there's something about basketball..." Her eyes misted over, but TJ couldn't tell if she was putting on an act or not. So he tested her.

"Favorite player?"

Eni didn't even have to think before she said, "John Stockton."

"Stockton!?" TJ lifted his brows high. "Oh, you're a *legit* basketball fan, then."

"You're not saying that and testing me because I'm a girl, are you?"

TJ let out a light chuckle. "Nah, I'm saying that because your favorite player is John Stockton."

Eni shrugged. "What can I say? I like traditional point guards. And he's *mad* underrated."

"Respect. Respect," TJ replied.

The music from outside buzzed through the couch he sat on. He had stopped eyeing the elevator, too focused on Eni, who quizzed him next. She asked who his favorite team was, to which TJ said the Los Angeles Lakers, to which Eni rolled her eyes at. Then they spoke about how much they hated the t-shirt jerseys from a few years back in the NBA, then about their favorite teams and years of basketball. Their eagerness to speak on their favorite sport had TJ forgetting what he was doing there to begin with. And a fair few times teenagers came up through the elevator without Eni giving them a proper once over. When Eni's game came back on, she offered to share headphones with TJ. He agreed, and they watched together. Eni explained who some of the players were, some of who TJ was only fairly familiar with from the Olympic games.

When the game got to the end of the third quarter, Eni turned to TJ to ask, "So, be real with me. Who's got you all shook out there?"

"Huh? What? Nobody."

"You can't dance or something?"

"No... I mean—yes."

Eni smiled, pulled her earbud out, and hopped to her feet. "Come on then, show me what you all do in California."

TJ gulped. "But, uh, what about your game?"

Eni pulled TJ's own earbud out. "The River Hoopers got the Patriots beat by thirty in the fourth. Come over here and stop acting so shy." She took TJ's hand and pulled him along the middle of the hall, ahead of the elevator, where there was a bit more space.

TJ made his lie about dancing known very quickly. He had two left feet and an internal metronome that needed a tune-up. Eni didn't make fun of him, though. Or at least, she didn't make *too* much fun of him. She was Ayo's cousin, after all, and she was proving just as blunt as her baby cousin could ever be.

"My guy, there's no way you're *this* bad," she would say, chuckling. "You gotta be messin' with me right now."

Eni was patient with him, showing him where he should put his feet and how he should rock his hips. According to her, guys had it easy when it came to dancing in the clubs. All they really had to do was keep the simplest of beats while the girls did most of the work. And, indeed, Eni did do most of the work as she shook her hips and rolled her shoulders around TJ. Despite her being a pretty good teacher, TJ still didn't get it right all the time, at one point pushing into her and making her nearly fall. Before she went down, he grabbed her.

Eni laughed. "Damn, TJ. Maybe this isn't for you."

He couldn't help it. Her laugh was too contagious. So he joined her to the point where he snorted—something he never usually did.

As TJ lifted her back up, she stared up at him with a curious expression. "Okay... okay.. I can see it now."

"What are you talking about?"

"Ayo said you were Ifedayo's little brother. I couldn't really tell at first. But she was tall too, and you both do that thing with your lips when you smile."

What!? She's looking at my lips? TJ thought, but out loud he said, "I didn't realize I did anything with my... uh... mouth." Somehow mouth sounded better than lips to him.

"The way you bite your lip and curl it into a smile with that little snort. It's cute." Heat filled TJ's ears; there was no bashfulness in Eni's words. "Well, cute on you. The haircut, too. Plus, I don't look at girls like that. I mean, I didn't look at your sister like that... not that I'm looking at *you* like that."

Outside, the muted music changed from a dance beat to a slow jam.

"Uh huh, uh huh." TJ rocked behind Eni, her rear end a fraction too close to his jeans in a slow turn. "So, am I doing this right? Keeping the beat, I mean."

"You're doing better, that's for sure." TJ hadn't noticed until then how perky her cheeks were, rosy too. "So, is all your family tall? My agent always said he could've gotten Ifedayo modeling like I do."

"You're a model!?"

"Damn, don't act so surprised, guy."

"No, I didn't mean it like that, it's just..."

Why are you talking to me? TJ thought.

An odd silence fell between them. Not awkward or uncomfortable necessarily, just odd. When silence fell between TJ and Manny it wasn't anything to consider. The pause between him and Eni, however... it made him... nervous, made him want to do things with her he didn't realize he actively wanted to do. Namely leaning in to those full lips and...

No, stop, TJ. Manny's mad, but that doesn't mean going off and...

He didn't know what to think. Plus, it was all in his head. He had just met Eni that day and she could've just been a flirt with her talking about lips and things being cute and whatnot.

Changing the subject! That's what he needed to do.

"So, what's this favor you owed Ayo's family, anyway?"

"My mother's a councilwoman of Eko Atlantic. She needed a

sanction for some infrastructure out front. But it overlapped with Uncle's property and he wouldn't hear it until Ayo convinced him. Boring stuff."

"Wait, so your mother sorts out what does and doesn't get built?"

"Yeah, pretty much."

Flow like Olosa, TJ thought happily. This is exactly where he was supposed to be, exactly where he was meant to end up.

"You think she could build me a statue?" he asked jokingly.

"Heh, what? Ayo said you were pretty low key. Statues don't really suit you."

"Not for me... for Olokun. I'm kind of a big fan and we should, you know, honor the Orishas and all that, right? I mean, Eko Atlantic used to be Olokun's domain, yeah?"

"Slow down there, guy. You have to ask me out first before you meet my mother." There it was again. TJ couldn't tell if Eni was being coy or not. Her next words were plenty clear, though. "I'm free next week. You can take me out then. We'll watch the River Hoopers." She didn't say it as a question, but as a command.

Before TJ could answer, before he could even process what had been asked of him—no, demanded of him—the elevator door opened.

"Shit." Eni took her arms away from TJ's shoulders and twisted to the elevator. She oscillated her hands and a light wisp fell over the hallway in TJ's vision. The elevator door opened wide to a tall woman dressed in a tailored business suit.

"Hello, Mother," Eni choked out.

"Evening... *daughter*," the woman returned cautiously, stilted. Clearly, them saying "Mother" and "daughter" wasn't at all the usual. "I just wanted to take a breather out on the terrace. The celebrations have taken a toll on me."

Eni shifted to one side to block her mother and TJ realized he was cloaked behind an illusion wall. That must've been what the strange Ashe wisp was in front of him. Plus, Eni's mother was looking *through* him rather than *at* him. It was very likely she could only see an empty hallway.

"The contractors told me there's still work being done out

there," Eni said quickly. "They said they were still working on the *west emergency escape* when I spoke to them last. It was the east side they finished the other day."

"Really? This morning it looked fine. Wait a minute..." Eni's mom rubbed her ear. "Eniola, do I hear... do I hear music!?"

"What? Uh... um..." Eni shot a glance over her shoulder straight at TJ. "Emergency escape."

"Huh? What are you talking about?" Eni's mom asked and TJ knew Eni was speaking to him.

"The party is over," she said again. "The emergency escape. Run!"

30

WHEN THE MOON IS BRIGHTEST

TJ TURNED HEEL AND DASHED FOR THE TERRACE. HE HUSTLED through the tall glass doors, cupped his hands, and shouted, "Mom alert! Mom alert! Everyone bail! Emergency exit!"

The music and the cold night air whipping across the rooftop drowned out his voice as the doors behind him closed. But the teenagers closest to him got the message and started making for the fire escapes. The older ones generated portals among the water fountains or fire walls out of thin air. As each of them dived in, the others caught wind of what was going on and chaos erupted.

Tables and chairs flew in the air. One guy got caught in a string of lights, making him look like a green and white Christmas tree. The adze fairies in those light globes threw up angry fists. Another girl tripped over the DJ table, making the music scratch and skip.

TJ scanned the crowd for Ayo but with everyone zig-zagging this way and that he couldn't find his friend. Panic tore through him as he glanced over his shoulder. Eni's mom stomped down the hallway, impeded by her daughter, who tried to stop her. It looked like the artwork lining the wall directed Eni's mom's path—those abstract figures of people pointing straight at the party. Eni attempted to get in front of her mother, shouting something TJ couldn't hear through the glass.

Ignoring her daughter, Eni's mom stretched out a hand and a wind blast shot from her palm, forcing the glass doors to open. TJ bounded to the side, following the crowd to the fire escapes, but there was a huge bottleneck.

"What is going on here?" Eni's mom bellowed. TJ peeked behind again to see her icing teenagers' ankles. One of them was the grassy eloko, who groaned as the hood of his jacket fell off his lumpy head.

"Mom! Mom! Come on, it's not that bad, it's just—" Eni called from behind her mother. The crowd was too thick. TJ couldn't see Eni, only hear her. All there was was the mass of body heat all around him, shoulders brushing against his own or elbows finding his gut. A few times, TJ nearly slipped in a few drinks the other partygoers left behind on the floor.

"Quick, quick, this one is closing," the girl TJ helped with drinks earlier said. She beckoned him near the wall fountain where he, Ayo, and Eni had come through before the party. "Hurry, before she gets you."

She beckoned for TJ one last time before she dipped in and vanished. TJ followed just as the portal was closing. The transportation this time was different. Since he wasn't connected to whoever made it, he was traveling on his own. Flashes of different landscapes washed over his eyes, lamp posts across a highway, cars along a street, a park with a large fountain. Despite feeling dizzy, he jumped and vaulted forward at that one. A park was a better place to land than on a street or highway.

But he jumped too late.

Instead of plopping onto nice, soft grass, he smacked into rock-hard cement. His chin scraped along the asphalt and he felt it open free with blood. He wiped his chin clean with his sleeve, ruining the nice shirt Ayo had given him as he looked around.

He was at a dock somewhere, surrounded by yachts moored at the piers. Thankfully, there was no one around to witness his clumsy ass—except for the winking lights of the luxury boats between a sheet of fog. Still, TJ remained quiet and didn't move for at least a minute until he knew he was alone. As he caught his breath and he touched around his body to check for anything that was broken, the sound of distant cars and buses on the highway rumbled on. A few seagulls called out into the night from the water's edge, and light waves lapped at the piers, too.

As his heart settled into a normal-ish beat, TJ got up and pulled out his phone to call Ayo. His screen was cracked across his camera and down the side like a spider's web. TJ sighed. Mom was going to give him an earful. He could try repairing it but his earth magic wasn't so great, and "glass is the toughest earth magic because its earth at its finest form" Omo of Fon always said during their private lessons. There was still time before the Christmas holiday when he'd see his family again, though. He was sure he could figure out how to fix it before then. Maybe one of the SS2 or SS3 students could help him — so long as they weren't at that fake crossover tryout and hated his guts.

TJ unlocked his phone. He was halfway to calling Ayo when he read a new text he got an hour ago... a text from Manny! It was a voice message which went, "Uh... hey. We beat Benin. So, uh, I feel a *little* better now. So um... Happy birthday!" She put on some fake enthusiasm with that one. Or maybe it just came out stilted because it was awkward. "Did, uh, Oroma give you anything from me today?"

TJ shot his phone to his mouth to reply with his own voice message when he noticed someone familiar across the dock. It was hard to be sure with the dim lamp post lights and the thin veil of fog, but perhaps fifty yards away, the slight orange spill fell over the distinct bulk of Miss Gravés's muscled arms.

TJ's heart dropped.

What was she doing there? Nervous sweat collected at his nape as he surveyed his surroundings. He was all alone, and Miss Gravés was heading his way at her usual power walk speed. Did she see him? He was between two lamp posts within the shadows. But as she came nearer, TJ couldn't afford to figure out if she was searching or coming straight for him. He needed to get somewhere busy. Somewhere safe.

How the heck did she find me? No time to think.

Keeping his phone up to seem casual, he started to reply to Manny's message. He explained what happened at the party and that he was looking for Ayo. As he did, he walked in the opposite direction of Miss Gravés to the boardwalk and, with a quick glance over his shoulder, saw her change direction too. She was definitely following him. The way she snuck behind the yachts… it was clear she was trying to keep a low profile, but that was nearly impossible with her tall height. Unfortunately, the same was true of TJ.

Two large buildings loomed ahead, giving way to a dark split TJ knew he could hide himself in. The fog that was persistent throughout the dock seemed to gather there. As TJ approached the gap, music from what must've been the beach beyond blared from distant speakers. He would've sworn he could hear a woman on a megaphone speaking about the importance of Nigeria's independence, too. His hands shook nervously at his side. He just needed to follow those sounds. That would stop his shaking, that would stop his heart from trying to escape his chest.

"Manny! Miss Gravés on my tail. I'll explain later. If you don't hear from me in the next few minutes, send help. I'm in Eko Atlantic near the docks." Message sent, he put his long legs to use, bolting for the alley and losing himself in the shadows. As soon as he knew he was hidden in the dark, he found himself before a dumpster. He opened it and paused for a moment as the stankiest of stanks attacked his nostrils. But the *squeak-squeak* of Miss Gravés sneakers forced him inside. He tossed himself into the dumpster and closed it after him slowly, plugging his nose against the thick stench. A few moments later, the shuffling of what must've been Miss Graves's shoes came rushing through the alley. TJ held himself tight against the garbage, hoping all the noisy trash bags wouldn't give him away. The music and the megaphone from the beach would surely cover him, right?

Miss Gravés passed right by without even stopping.

She is *a Keeper!* TJ thought with great vindication. He was right all along. Why else would she be sneaking behind him like that? How did she even know where to find him?

TJ had to tell Elder Adeyemi right away. She should've been back from Los Angeles by now, but he didn't have a water bowl to contact her with. Ayo would though… if he made it out of the party okay. TJ hoped he was all right. What if another Keeper was following him too? Maybe there weren't just teenagers at that party.

When TJ was sure the coast was clear, he opened the dumpster gingerly and got out.

Sorry for messing up your shirt and shoes, Ayo. TJ brushed himself free of old fish stew and overripe fruit that made his jeans all kinds of funky.

Out on the beach, the lady with the megaphone continued chanting about freedom, her elevated voice echoing off the alley walls and blocking out all other sounds.

Fog continued to fill the alley, thicker this time. TJ looked up through the tall buildings he was between. High above, the moon shined bright and full despite the encroaching fog. TJ squinted. Something odd was manifesting itself ahead of the moon's light, as though it was being burned like an old film projector.

Then TJ understood it.

It was a fire portal. *Several* fire portals. Three. Four. No, Five! Each of them spiraling into existence and blocking out the moon. And then… people fell from them. People with cream robes and masks with gaping holes for eyes.

The Keepers!

Miss Gravés must've tipped them off!

Adrenaline flooded through TJ, forcing him to run for the boardwalk again, but his path was blocked a few yards ahead by two Keepers wielding staffs of wood. Without thinking, TJ sapped the magic they were already manifesting. He could see in the air that they were trying to freeze him with water magic, but he turned it against them, trapping their ankles in shackles of ice just like Eni's mom did to those teenagers back at the party. The effort took all the air out of TJ's lungs and he became lightheaded. Eni's mom made it look so easy. The magic the Keepers generated was well above what his fellow students could conjure. As they continued to attack with more ice from their staffs, TJ stopped them at their source, capping their staff crystals with their own ice. Again, the effort made him feel empty and his breath left him in a haggard cough. But he put on a strong face.

No need to let them know he was hurting.

"I told you two to use short bursts of Ashe!" commanded a familiar voice from behind. "Do not sustain or the boy will take your magic from you."

TJ pivoted on his heel to find Bolawe and two others at the man's flank.

"You!" TJ narrowed his eyes, too angry to be scared.

"So the boy knows his way around Ashe, does he?" a female to the left croaked. TJ didn't recognize her voice. "Let's see you handle this."

TJ saw her charged lightning swell up her iron staff before she could cast it. But even though he knew what was coming, he could not predict its forked pattern. Despite jerking to one side, one of the bolts clipped his shoulder. Searing hot pain shot through his muscles and he yelped, falling onto his back.

The woman stood over him with her wicked-looking mask, then with an acid cackle, she said, "*Shocking*, isn't it? Too bad you never learned proper defense from that academy."

Ashe stirred within the woman's gut, up her arm, and through her staff. The magic slapped across TJ's mouth, muting the scream starting in his throat. The woman's staff swelled again with lightning.

"Enough, Sister Bisi." Bolawe placed a hand on her staff and lowered it. "I warned you before. Now, hurry. Free those two." The other keepers were still defrosting their staffs and legs. "The UCMP will be on us soon. Brother David, open us another portal. The Oracle will be ready. We need to work fast."

Oracle? Did they mean... no, it couldn't be Ruby.

Bolawe knelt down, conjured some water around his palm, and placed it on TJ's wounded shoulder. The sensation felt nice and healing. "Don't worry, Tomori Jomiloju. We're just going to have a little chat."

31

BLOOD & PAIN

As TJ was forced into a fire portal, he couldn't believe how powerless he felt. It was even harder to believe how fast the fight with the Keepers had gone down. In the movies, fights took minutes, not seconds. One moment he was icing those Keepers at the end of the alley and then the next he was getting shocked with lightning.

Teacher Omo of Fon was right. He was *nothing* without his friends. Even with all his one-on-one lessons with her.

And that reality shook him.

One of the Keepers, the one called Brother David, judging by his low and slow voice, tugged TJ along. "Keep moving, *ọmọ*."

They were on a dark dock that stretched for miles. Shanty homes lined the expanse. A whole slum built atop what looked like a lagoon. A few rowboats with fishermen and whole families slothed by on one of the river avenues. There was even a girl rowing in a wide bucket.

The Keepers didn't even try to hide TJ, and besides a few looks from a few narrowed-eyed children or droopy-eyed drunks, no one cared that a teenager was *clearly* being kidnapped. Or maybe they *did* care, but didn't want to get involved. Or better yet, maybe they thought he was getting reprimanded by his family... a family that wore traditional robes and masks.

The lagoon town was familiar. TJ had seen it in some

YouTube video. Some place called Makoko—a Lagos, Nigeria slum only a few miles from Eko Atlantic's luxury.

TJ wouldn't find help here, and the thought shot fear into his heart. How could he possibly get away? He didn't know this place, let alone how to get away from it. From what he saw, the labyrinth of the lagoon town would be impossible to navigate, anyway. He didn't know how to transport through portals. And worse, absolutely no one knew where he was.

A sharp edge dug into his thigh through his jeans. *My phone!*

The Keepers had been so preoccupied with rushing him out of the alley that they hadn't checked his pockets. He just needed to figure out how to get to it before they wised up. But each of his arms were clenched between the iron holds of the lady who shocked him and the guy who grunted at him to keep moving.

After a few more twists around the shanties, they came to one that was unlit by any hanging lanterns. Now that they stopped, TJ could take in the air unabated. The dark river smelled more like sewage waste than clean water.

Bolawe gave the sheet metal door ahead of them a rhythmic knock that was clearly some code. A moment passed and the same rap came to the door in answer. Bolawe returned with a final signal and the door swung open into a black hole. No one was there. The door opened by itself. Bolawe walked in first.

"In with you." Brother David, with the slow baritone, freed TJ's arm and shoved him in. "You, follow Olugbala."

TJ almost forgot that's how the Keepers referred to Bolawe. Keeping his back to the man, TJ obliged. In front was Bolawe. Behind him were the other four Keepers standing shoulder to shoulder. TJ was boxed in on all sides. The hall they walked through smelled of mildew, packed in further by the small space. They wouldn't be walking for very long. TJ had to act right then and there.

With a casual gait, TJ slipped his phone from his pocket. And with a smoothness learned from years of texting in movie theaters, he slid his screen brightness all the way down. Without looking, he brushed his thumb over where he knew his contacts were at. His hand started to tremble, and TJ bit his tongue to steel some courage. His thumb selected the first contact it could find. Then he slipped his phone back in his pocket just as they moved into a room full of tall cages.

"Hello? Hello?" TJ's phone said in his pocket.

He forgot to mute the caller! With shaking hands, TJ depressed the volume control through his jeans.

"What's that?" the woman who shocked him said. "Who's voice is that?"

"Hello! Hello!" came a voice. Only this time, it didn't come from TJ's pocket. Instead, it came from one of the cages! A pair of bruised and burned hands wrapped around the bars. A face pressed itself between the metal. A face TJ knew: one that was young with a balding hairline up top and a mole over the lip.

The reporter from the airport! Dele! So the UCMP weren't the ones who took him in at the airport; it was the Keepers! No wonder there was nothing on *Evocation* or *Divination Today*.

Brother David banged his brass staff along the bars. "Shut your mouth, ̀olòṣì."

"Hello, hello, Tomori Jomiloju." The young man looked crazed with his blood-shot eyes and bruised cheeks. "Tried to warn you, kid. Be wary of the twins in your life! Obatala told me they'll help you with the golden—"

"He told you to shut up!" The woman tapped her iron staff against the bars and sent two bolts through them. The reporter yelped and sprang back from the bars. A shock of guilt slithered through TJ. The reporter might not have been in his current situation, were it not for him. If TJ had just believed him... but how could he? All those reporters at his house and at the airport weren't exactly the most trustworthy of people.

"Come on, we need to keep moving," Bolawe ordered. He had taken off his mask. His expression was deadpan, apathetic. Were they going to put TJ in one of those cages, too?

As TJ was pushed forward, he glanced over his shoulder to see the reporter winking at him. If TJ could manage it, he would need to apologize to him, then thank him for saving his butt with the phone. And that stuff he said about the twins and Obatala was loud and clear. He just needed to get back to Elder Adeyemi or Oracle Ruby to ask them what all that meant.

A few moments later, the Keepers led TJ into a backroom

filled with the scent of sandalwood incense. It was still dim but a bit brighter than the place with the cages and the hall before that. Rugs with Nigerian designs of orange and red covered sheet-metal flooring. Water buffalo skulls bedecked the dirty walls, each of them gaping at TJ. He turned away from them, his heart climbing into his throat. His eyes fell onto the old man who sat before a divination board at the room's center.

The Elder wore traditional aso oke bottoms, but was bare up top. Instead of a shirt, painted white dots dressed his torso. The dots spotted his arms, his shoulders, up his neck, and around his face. He rocked back and forth, chanting. Cowries clinked between his hands. When he opened his eyes to look at TJ, he revealed a pair of mismatched eyes, in both size and color. One was a normal brown but the other was a milky cataract of a blind man. Yet TJ couldn't help feeling he was being stared at directly. Was that the Oracle they were referring to from before?

At least it wasn't Ruby.

Bolawe kneeled down close to the old man and whispered something to him. Wrinkled lips stretched into the thin line of a smile. Bolawe turned his attention to TJ, then waved a hand to remove the wind gag from TJ's mouth. "You don't need that anymore."

"Why are we in the *Makoko* slums?" TJ asked straight away, disregarding the phlegm in his voice. He needed to make sure whoever was on the call with him knew where he was.

"Oh, you know of this place, then? Then you know more than you let on about the plight of this country. Besides New Ile-Ife, this place houses the majority of the diviner community in Nigeria. For those the UCMP deem… deviant." Was that the reason no one stopped a bunch of robed people from kidnapping a child?

"You know… that's an interesting question to ask, boy," the one called Brother David said. He had pulled off his mask, too. His thick beard and thick dreadlocks sent a shiver through TJ. He recognized the man as the UCMP officer who had taken the reporter away at the airport. He didn't have his British accent anymore, which he must've put on for show back at the airport. "Someone in your position should be asking what we're going to do with *you*. Not where we are." He nodded to the woman. "Sister Bisi."

The woman named Sister Bisi, the one who shocked him, twirled her staff in hand. TJ could see the twirling wind magic in her spell just before he was forced to hang from his ankle. His phone slipped out and clanged against the floor. The phone call he started was still active. On the screen was an image of a smiling Manny with the timestamp of four minutes and thirty-two seconds over her bushy hair.

TJ mouthed an expletive that would've gotten him popped in the mouth by Mom.

Bolawe's eyebrows hiked up his forehead. The big guy with the beard and locs parted his lips in astonishment. And that Bisi woman bared a set of fangs as she lifted her staff overhead and struck TJ's phone with a lightning bolt. His phone slammed harder and harder with each lightning strike the Bisi lady blasted it with, forcing the device to explode in little sparks.

"While I was defrosting these two idiots, you didn't think to check the boy?" she seethed.

Still cool as ever, Brother David replied, "Watch your mouth, Sister Bisi. I was busy crafting an untraceable portal, since *you* wanted to jump the gun and pounce the boy."

Sister Bisi pulled off her mask, revealing light-brown skin. Then, in a flash, she got right up in the man's face. "The good that'll do with the stunt he just pulled."

"Enough," Bolawe commanded gently. "There is no time to argue. We must act." He kneeled before TJ. "Tomori, we only want to do a reading for you. Nothing more."

"Do you really think he'll be receptive?" Sister Bisi snorted.

"Do you make it a habit to question Olugbala?" the big guy shot at her.

Bisi grunted but stepped back and bowed. "Apologies, Olugbala. But his reading will be compromised, will it not?"

"Not if he doesn't want it to be painful." Bolawe stared at TJ, not Bisi, when he said it. "TJ, I do not wish ill on you. If you answer all of the Oracle's questions honestly, I promise this will be over soon."

TJ wanted badly for his hands to stop shaking. He didn't need them knowing he was scared and nervous about whatever it was they were talking about. Obviously, they weren't going to pull out a computer like Ruby. So what was the alternative? Judging by the skulls all over the walls, nothing nice. Manny had enough time to pick up his location, right? She'd get in touch with Ayo or an adult who could get him out of this. But how? He was in the middle of a slum, far away from Lagos or New Ile-Ife.

Oh, please! Whoever is coming, hurry!

Bolawe interlaced his fingers against his chin and gently said, "Come now, Tomori. Just as I said before, it's what your sister would've wanted. She's been giving you signs since you left the Aqua Realm, hasn't she?"

"What do you mean?" TJ was shocked to hear the husk in his voice. What was Bolawe going on about now?

"All those 'habits' you've acquired these past months..."

"... No, that's because of my..." TJ was going to say his growth spurt but stopped himself short. Was Bolawe suggesting that his sister was trying to speak to him this whole time, that all those habits he picked up was just her? And how would Bolawe even know all that stuff at all?

"You see, Oracle Ojo here made a reading that went something like 'quirks will reflect in the child of the in-between.' You were the middle child before Ifedayo's passing, were you not?"

TJ refused to nod.

"At Ifedayo's funeral it was said you two connected," Bolawe went on. "Judging by your face now, I'm guessing that is indeed the case. Am I wrong?"

TJ stared down at his hands, at his chewed nails, just the same way his sister's used to look.

"Do not deny the messages she gives you, Tomori Jomiloju," Bolawe went on. "She is trying to communicate with you from the other side. To tell you what we are doing is the right thing. The Orishas must return to their full strength. Oracle Ojo did readings with her all the time." He placed a hand on the old man's bony shoulder. "Isn't that right, Elder?"

"That's right," the Elder croaked, looking out into the middle of the room. "In this very place, boy. She was our promised child. The one who would bring back the Orishas."

"Just as you brought back Olosa," Bolawe added. "You cannot squander that gift, Tomori. You are meant to continue your sister's work."

TJ swallowed the fear crawling up in his throat. How dare they try to use his sister against him? A sister *they* killed, a sister who couldn't respond or defend herself.

TJ looked Bolawe dead in the eyes and told him where he could shove it. He thought Mom would make an exception for his explicit vocabulary on this one. Just this once.

A shadow fell over Bolawe's face. The already dark room dimmed to a near-black. "Then it'll be blood and pain, I'm afraid. Hold him to the ground."

The Keepers waved their staffs over their heads and each of TJ's limbs were pulled by invisible wind strings. They suspended him in mid-air, his arms splayed out. He tried to reflect their Ashe but they were pulsating the use of their magic, just like Bolawe told them to back in the alley. Terror ramped up within TJ each time he failed to latch on and diminish their holds. Their Ashe just slipped away and came back again in staccato beats. Still, TJ fought bodily against the mystical restraints. He wanted nothing to do with whatever "blood and pain" meant.

"You may not speak the truth to us." Bolawe stood up and looked TJ nose-to-nose. The man's wooden staff snapped into existence in his hand. "But blood never lies. It'll be easier if you stop struggling. For both of us."

TJ gritted against their power, against Bolawe's condescending tone. "Isn't Olokun already coming back? What do you need me or my sister for? Ow!"

Bolawe swiped his staff in the air and TJ's skin split open across his wrist. TJ bit the pain away as Bolawe did the same to himself, and each of them had blood trickling from their wrist. Oscillating his hands, Bolawe commanded TJ's blood to hang in the air. Then the man commanded his blood to do the same. The two clusters joined as one. So much blood spilled from TJ's wrist that it made him woozy.

"Brother David, the cowries, please," Bolawe requested. The large man, still holding TJ in place with his magic, handed Bolawe cowries from his pocket. Bolawe nodded, then covered the cowries in blood. "I've wetted the sacred cowries for you, Elder. Open your palm, please. I am gracing you with them now."

The blind man cupped his hands, received the bloodied shells, and started chanting. A few moments passed and he cast the cowries on the divining board before him. Nothing happened. The room simply filled with a metallic scent, compounded by the fact they were in a metal box. TJ expected some mystical force or some Orisha to manifest in the middle of the shadowed room. The only thing that seemed to change was the tone of the Elder's humming.

"What blood did you give me, Olugbala?"

"The boy's, Elder."

"No, there is something else here."

"Well, I've my blood in there, too. Just like with Ifedayo."

The blind man shook his head and grunted. "That would only work with the promised child. This boy is no promised child of ours. Give me his blood clean."

TJ scrunched his forehead. Why kidnap him to begin with if he didn't even have the right blood?

Bolawe did as commanded, discarding the bloodied cowries and replacing them with new ones with more of TJ's blood. TJ grounded his teeth. Was there really no way out of this situation? He felt violated, and his utter powerlessness made him sick to his stomach.

Once the blind Elder cast the cowries this time, TJ understood why Bolawe said there would be blood… and pain.

A searing burn cut across TJ's open wound. He saw nothing but white and it was as though his throat was being pulled out of his mouth. It took him several moments to realize he was speaking in perfectly fluent Yoruba, but it was an older Yoruba, phrases he didn't quite grasp.

It seemed like the only one who understood him was the Elder.

"Lookouts say Adeyemi and her cohorts just breached the outer lagoon," TJ heard Brother David murmur between jolts of pain. He could barely edge his head to see that David's eyes were stuck behind his head. "Olugbala, we must go soon."

Elder Adeyemi… please… hurry…

Agony shot through TJ in waves and he convulsed against every one of them. Could the Elder get there in time before the Keepers got the information they wanted? TJ didn't know how to slow them down. They hadn't studied blood magic yet at the academy.

"What do you see about the Lost Monarch and his return?" Bolawe asked frantically to the Oracle. "Can he be brought back without the promised child?"

"The boy's blood speaks true, but it reads cloudy." The old man bunched his forehead in concentration. "All I can gather is something about... about a lost gateway—no, lost portal. A lost portal that is at the top of something, something of earth? Earth meeting the top."

"Earth meeting the top? What does that even mean?" Sister Bisi paced the room, spinning her staff in hand to keep TJ from turning her magic against her.

How was the old man gathering all this information off TJ's gibberish? And when would the pain stop? TJ's mental state was near to splitting, like an unready scab being pulled from skin, except around his *whole* body.

"We can work out the meaning later. Adeyemi is in the maze now," David added, his eyes still behind his head. "Olugbala, we must go before she gets a chance to spatially seal the base. I can only do so much against her kind of power."

And how was David coming up with this information? He was in the dark room with the rest of them. How could he know Adeyemi was looking for them?

"She knows we're watching. She's killing my firefenches quickly. I won't have eyes for long."

TJ roared in pain but fought to pay attention. He needed to remember everything he could. Adeyemi killing something? What was going on? Wait, firefenches... TJ remembered them from Mr. Ikenna's Ecology class. Special diviners used them as scouts. Bird scouts. Could this David person see through their eyes like little security cameras?

A lance of hot fire raced through TJ and he closed his eyes, focusing on the voices.

"When twilight smiles down on animal skins and the... in-between, something in-between, I don't know how to translate it," the Oracle continued on, seemingly undisturbed by the commotion around them. "Something about when the in-between feels the falling star, the golden braid will fall."

"But what about the Lost Monarch? What about Olodumare? What about the Great Seal he placed on the Orishas?" Bolawe's voice grew more desperate. "Does Olokun speak the truth when he says he can uncover the promised child?"

"The promised child is unseen! The promised child is unseen!" the Elder cried in reply.

TJ's eyes snapped open as another Keeper in a robe and mask rushed into the room. "She's here. She's breaking all the laws of discretion, skipping straight over the water and wind-stepping over shanties."

Bolawe pulled at the Oracle. "Unseen? Unseen from what!?"

Could the Oracle give them a damn answer already!? TJ's body was near to ripping apart, and his blooded arm was getting really cold...

"Apologies, Olugbala." Brother David pulled at his leader's arm, already generating a fire portal at the back of the room. "Your safety comes before all else."

"The boy!" Bolawe struggled against the much larger man. "Bring the boy!"

"We can't take him. They'll follow if we do. I can't do another traceless portal with an underaged diviner who is registered. Not against Adeyemi."

Bolawe was still grunting for clarity, but his words were snuffed the moment he was tugged into the portal. The other Keepers rushed in, one of them pulling the Oracle along with them.

TJ fell to the ground as their magical bindings came loose. His head hit the hard metal floor, and his vision was dazed as Bisi climbed over him. She was the last one out. Before she stepped into the portal, she flashed a wicked smile of sharp canines. "Study hard, Tomori Jomiloju. Next time we expect a stronger reading than that."

She dipped into the portal, and it closed with a snap. A split second later and a single, concentrated lightning bolt impacted against the corrugated metal wall where the portal had been. Elder Adeyemi came hustling into the room, followed by a dozen men and women dressed in the official uniforms and masks of the UCMP.

"It was... Bolawe," was all TJ could say, splayed along the ground, his ears ringing. "Olugbala... was here."

32

A RUBY IN THE ROUGH

"AND THEN THAT BISI LADY WITH THE FANGS WAS LIKE 'STUDY hard, chump' or something like that before Adeyemi came in with the cavalry." TJ finished his story as he lay back on a hospital cot. After Elder Adeyemi rescued him, she brought TJ straight back to Ifa Academy, to the Healers' Tree, way up in the highest branches. Ayo was the first visitor to be let in once Healer Okoye examined TJ for the 3 "Ps": "poison, possession, and profanation." Thanks to those blisters and boils he got from the Ice Realm, he had created a fast bond with the diminutive older woman—who had apparently tended to Dayo on an almost monthly basis when she attended the academy, according to her. If TJ hadn't bonded with Healer Okoye, she might not have let Ayo in at all, let alone give them privacy.

"Shango's Axe! That's crazy, man!" Ayo sat back in a pillowed basket chair as he chugged his asthma potion. He hiccuped and lightning bolts expelled from his mouth. "Can't believe Miss G set you up like that. But Adeyemi's gonna get all kinds of heat for what she did to get you, though. She exposed herself to a bunch of the clouded. Folks are wildin' about it."

"Dude, keep your voice down," TJ reminded him, wincing at the tight bandage around his wrist. "She's just out in the hall." Adeyemi had stepped outside to debrief the UCMP officials that had followed them to the Hospital Tree; they'd been out there for almost an hour.

The healing chamber was one big circular space. Each window, which looked out into the buzzing night forest, was coupled by a cot set just beneath. It was still dark out, so the orange crystal at TJ's bedside was the only thing lighting the room. The shine of the bright light was making him woozy though, that or he was still getting over the Keepers' blood ritual.

"So, do you think Adeyemi will fire Miss G now?" Ayo asked.

"More like she'll get her UCMP pals to send her to jail, hopefully," TJ grunted to Ayo. "Anyway… your turn. How did you get out?"

"Titi and I made it out thanks to Emeka," he started, lowering his voice this time. "I saw you across the rooftop, but Emeka said there was no time to get you. Yeah, yeah, I know, I know… he's pretty cold. I woulda tried to come for you anyway, but there was so many people runnin' around and all that."

TJ shook his head. "At one point, I thought it was possible to get him to like me, but I think that ship has sailed."

"Anyway, so Emeka and his girl had this older friend who could make wind portals. We hopped in there and wound up at their parent's spot at Pearl Towers. Oh, and by the way," Ayo's rocking chair squeaked as he got up, "my cousin Eni covered for us. Not much we could do for the others who got snagged by her mom, but Eni took the fall. She came up with this story that it was an influencer party and she was just networking and trying to make connections. So now I owe *her* one. That said… when I spoke to her with our water bowl, she had a lot of good things to say about you. What's this about some basketball game she wanted to go to with you… *alone*?"

TJ couldn't decipher what Ayo was feeling. His mouth was between a grimace and a smile. Or maybe he just imagined the expression through the dim light.

"What!?" TJ sat up in his cot, a spike through his chest. "I thought she was just joking around. I mean, at the end she seemed pretty serious, but I couldn't tell if she was just a flirt!"

Ayo sucked his teeth. "She is a flirt! She's a daughter of Oshun, bruh!"

"Oshun? Orisha of Love... makes sense."

In more than one way, TJ thought.

"Anyway, y'all can't go to no game since she's on punishment now. But she said your date with her will be at Jollof & Jubilee next weekend."

"Huh? She can go to... Jollof and—whatever that is—but she can't go to a game?"

Ayo lifted a single shoulder. "That's what she said. I don't know."

That was a bit strange, but TJ had another question. "And what's a Jollof & Jubilee?"

"It's a nice little spot in the village. Upper echelon. Real nice silverware and all that if you get me." Ayo sat back in his chair and scrunched his face. Maybe it was the low-light again, but it seemed as though he were working out a math problem in his head.

"Why are you looking at me like that?" TJ asked.

"I'm over here tryin' to figure out how you're about to pull my cousin. You *stayed* strugglin' on the dance floor."

"I'm trying to figure that out myself, to be honest with you."

"Well... don't go around breaking her heart."

"*Her* heart!?" TJ winced again as he jerked up. "Dude, someone like your cousin is going to break *my* heart."

"I'm talkin' 'bout Manny."

Oh, right...

TJ laid back gingerly. Curly hair, brown eyes, and a pair of dimples filled his mind. That husky laughter filled his ears. "You think she'll be mad?"

"I mean, y'all be vibin' all the time. But she was mad at you, so I think you're in the clear and—"

"Not Manny. Eni! I can't do anything with her when me and Manny..."

"Are just friends. If she even is your friend right now, all things considered."

"Manny's the one who saved me!" TJ raised his voice. Ayo put a finger to his lips and gestured to the door where Adeyemi was at. Lowering his voice, TJ went on. "She got in touch with Adeyemi's people to save my butt. Plus, she sent me a voice message just before I got jumped by the Keepers. Said Oroma was supposed to give me something."

Ayo snapped his fingers and grabbed for something from under his basket chair. "Oh, Shango's Axe! My bad man… Oroma rushed me with this when I got back in. Said she was supposed to give it to you. Manny gave it to her after Oroma braided her hair for her game." Ayo handed TJ a rectangle gift wrap. TJ ripped through it with his good arm to find a thin book titled *Master Any Accent in 24 Hours*. A little card stuck out as a bookmark. TJ pulled it and read the note from Manny:

I expect you to do a perfect New Yorker when I get back. If you make me laugh, then I'll CONSIDER not being mad at you.

TJ smiled at that but quickly frowned when he saw Ayo there. "*Don't* tell Manny about Eni. Please!"

"I ain't sayin' nothin'. But if she ask me directly, I ain't gonna lie."

TJ thought it over before saying, "That's fair."

Silence fell between them. Could Ayo really be trusted? He was a bit of a big mouth. Shoot, could TJ even trust *himself* to keep something like that from Manny? It wouldn't be so bad, so long as he made it clear to Eniola he didn't want to pursue anything. Then Manny would never have to know at all.

Ayo adjusted his glasses and peered at his watch. "And… it's officially no longer your birthday. You had a crazy one, man."

Adeyemi's voice echoed down the hall and through their closed door. "Mrs. Adebayo, please do not listen too closely to the *Messenger Press*. The incident happened well away from the academy. Your children are in no danger." A pause. "I can assure you whatever you heard was embellished. Everyone is safe and accounted for."

Ayo rocked forward close to TJ and murmured, "Parents ain't go'n be too happy. I saw some of the early news on *Divination Today*. It was playin' all over the village when Titi and I got back in with Emeka. No one knows it was you Adeyemi rescued, but they know that a student from Ifa Academy was involved. I wouldn't want to be in Adeyemi's heels right now."

"Mrs. Adebayo, I will have to let you go." Adeyemi's voice sounded from the hall. "A visitor just arrived. I'll put you through to Deputy Headmistress Omo of Fon. She'll give you more information. Thank you, yes. You as well. Have a good evening. *O dabọ.*"

There were a few more whispers and murmurs, followed by the shuffling of footsteps. And then Elder Adeyemi opened the door into the room.

TJ hadn't gotten a real good look at her when she came to the Keeper's shanty, but now he could see her outfit was different from most of her others. It was more utilitarian than audacious, for one. Her heels traded for boots. Her vivid long dress replaced by a navy cloak and trousers with the sharp edges and cuts of the military. Gold buttons lined her cloak from neck to bottom, each sparkling against the single crystal light of the room. Two large men followed behind Adeyemi, and TJ realized why the Headmistress was dressed as she was. She, like the men with her, sported the official UCMP uniform, along with iron masks that completely covered their faces. Last to come in was a much smaller, plump figure dressed in traditional aso oke robes. When the crystal light revealed the figure's face, and before Elder Adeyemi could properly introduce them, TJ exclaimed, "Oracle Ruby!"

Ruby threw up a casual peace sign from under her long cuffs. "What's goin' on, Teej? Sounds like you had yourself a birthday."

"It was absolutely devastating!" Ayo added with a hand to his chest. TJ hadn't even noticed he had climbed out of his chair to bow when Elder Adeyemi came in. He kept forgetting how smooth he could be with the code switches.

"TJ, Ruby is here to help us figure out what was done to you," Elder Adeyemi explained.

"I already told you. I wouldn't tell Bolawe anything, so they took blood off me."

"Yes, but there may be more at play. One cannot simply take blood by itself to divine the future. At least not so quickly."

That woman, Sister Bisi, had said that TJ needed to work hard in school. Is that what the reporter meant, back at the airport? Was TJ's magical education a direct benefit to the

Keepers and whatever they were trying to divine off his blood? TJ had hoped the Keepers at that shanty would've left the reporter behind, but the UCMP officials said the whole place was empty, except for TJ, when they arrived.

Still, all of this could have been avoided if it wasn't for one particular person.

"And what about Miss Gravés?" TJ asked. "Where is she?"

Elder Adeyemi canted her head. "Out giving chase to the Keepers. Why?"

An angry heat simmered through TJ. "I told you she was following me right before I got ambushed."

"Miss Gravés was assigned to protect you tonight, not harm you. Like all the other UCMP officials."

"You mean just like that Brother David guy who grabbed that reporter from the airport? He was supposed to be a UCMP official too, right? It was *you* who said we can't have even the smallest of leaks, remember?"

One of the big guys flanking Elder Adeyemi whispered something in her ear.

"I'll have to excuse myself," Adeyemi announced. "Keepers have been spotted in Old Oyo National Park. Ruby, if you do not mind…"

"I got it from here, Elder." She threw out an exaggerated thumbs up. "TJ and I will fill you in after."

"So what am I? Just a wall?" Ayo asked from across the room.

"Oh, right. This kid, too."

Elder Adeyemi bowed. "We'll return as soon as we can. There are still guards posted outside." She glided out of the room. Her bodyguards, or whoever they were, lumbered behind her, forcing the wooden floors to squeal under their boots.

There was a silent moment between TJ, Ruby, and Ayo before TJ jokingly asked, "Heh, are you going to take blood off me, too?"

Ruby chuckled a little, then sat herself at the edge of TJ's bed with a casual little jump. "Nope. For two reasons. One, it makes for inaccurate magic at the best of times. Two, I'm not very proficient with it, which spells danger. Especially for something as archaic as blood magic used for divination."

"So... what you go'n do then?" Ayo asked.

Ruby leaned back, her thick arms holding her up behind her, her green-tipped dreadlocks falling over her shoulders. "I'm just asking TJ here a few questions. My first one being... who took your reading?"

TJ bit his lip. Elder Adeyemi had asked for a name too, but TJ couldn't recall. He had been too busy freaking out and getting half his blood drained at the time, he couldn't remember *every* little detail. "Uh... They only called him 'oracle' most times. But he was an old dude. One of his eyes was milky. I think he was blind in both, though. They kept directing him everywhere."

"Ah, Elder Ojo. We've been wondering where he ran off to."

"Oh... like Emeka and Titi?" Ayo cut in. "Their last name is Ojo too, yeah?"

"One and the same. Ojo's their great grandfather. Kid wouldn't shut up about it when he went in for his reading, which, to be fair, is somewhat understandable. Ojo's one of the few legits. Present company not-withstanding, of course." Ruby turned to TJ. "So, what did the old geezer read off your blood?"

"He didn't get much," TJ said. "Even *he* was confused about what he was seeing. Something about... a lost portal on top of earth. And then something about some smiling twilight, no, twilight smiling down on animal skins." None of that made sense to TJ, but the next thing the Oracle had said did trigger a familiar brush across the back of his neck. A brush he now knew, if Bolawe was to be believed, was his sister's spirit calling to him. Maintaining his gaze with Ruby so she'd understand the gravity of his next words, TJ continued, "The Oracle said an in-between will feel the falling star, and a golden braid will fall."

"The 'in-between' you say?"

"The Keepers didn't understand it, but I did. The Orishas in the Aqua Realm and this giant alligator back at Camp Olosa kept saying it. *I'm* the 'in-between.' Whatever that means."

Ruby closed her eyes and mouthed something to herself. Then she pulled out her phone and started thumbing away.

"What!? I thought phones don't work on academy grounds?"

Ayo bounded from his corner of the room and peeked over Ruby's shoulder. TJ knew he was probably trying to figure out what trick she used to pull it off.

"*Yours* don't, love."

"But… how did you get around the electric currents conflicting with the Ashe on school grounds."

"Magic."

"Oh, come on! For real though."

Ruby let out a gigantic sigh. "TJ, can you get your friend to stop breathing down my neck while I try to figure this out?"

"Ayo, can you stop breathing down Ruby's neck so she can figure this all out?"

Ayo sucked his teeth sharply. "Fine, fine. I'll go back to being a wall over here." He slumped back in his chair where he sat and crossed his arms. Ruby's fingers flew over her screen. Light from the phone spilled over her face intermittently, revealing the utter concentration on her round face.

"What is it, Ruby?" TJ asked. "What are you figuring out?"

"Wild-Two," she murmured to herself.

"What's that?"

Ruby drew her calves under herself and sat with crossed legs at the foot of TJ's bed. She was turned toward TJ, only inches from his outstretched feet, as she kept biting the inside of her lip in thought. "After our meeting that first day, I had visions about a comet coming near the winter solstice. I did my calculations. Logged it. A few days later, a date came up. December fifteenth. Naturally, I did a little cross-referencing with the OC—Oracle Collective—and Wild-Two popped up." TJ threw up an eyebrow and shrugged in confusion. "It's a comet. Comet Eight-One-P. Also known as Wild-Two. A.K.A. the falling star. *Our* falling star."

TJ shook his head. "I still don't get it."

Ayo shot up from his seat again like he was in class. "Oh! Oh! I do! I get it! A natural phenomenon! TJ, it's like at camp with the full moon, with Olosa. The fallin' star is talkin' 'bout that comet. And the golden braid…" He snapped his fingers, searching for something in his mind. "The golden braid… I just had it on the tip of my tongue."

"You don't think the golden braid could be the golden chain, do you?" TJ asked. "That feels too easy…"

"I don't know, man. What else could it be?"

"That reporter said something about the twins being able to help with it. Maybe you can talk to Titi or Emeka, see what they know about golden chains." TJ turned his focus on Ruby. "So the comet will boost me? I'll be able to summon the chain or something? We can actually speak to…" TJ trailed off, realizing he was divulging too much information.

"Speak to the Orisha, Oya, right?" Ruby smirked. "Best to just assume I know at least as much as Adeyemi does, loves."

Ayo nodded approvingly. "Man, you're *real* good. So is it all the computer stuff or are you using some old-school rituals too?"

"Elder Adeyemi told me." Ruby deadpanned.

"Oh, right, right." Ayo pushed his glasses up his nose. TJ knew he was doing it to cover up his cheeks, which were likely blushing under the low light.

"She tells me everything so I can better serve her." She nudged TJ against the knee with her own. "Her, and you. So… we've got a head start on the Keepers. They don't know the reading I gave you at the start of term. 'The embers are stoked, but the falling star has yet to blaze its trail.' Only you, me, and Elder Adeyemi know about that."

Ayo threw up a finger. "And me!"

"And Manny, of course," TJ added. "Manny is the one who heard and saw Oya in the first place. But," he looked at Ruby, "are you sure we're the only ones who know?"

"Why do you ask, love?"

Elder Adeyemi clearly didn't want to hear it from TJ, but if he could convince Ruby, maybe then his suspicions would be taken seriously.

"Miss Gravés," he said, low and slow to be sure the guard outside didn't eavesdrop. "She *cannot* know what's going on. I tried to tell Elder Adeyemi, but she's not listening to me. Miss Gravés is a Keeper. They're keeping tabs on me, just like Mr. Bolawe was at Camp Olosa. At the Olokun festival, when he came to me, he knew stuff he shouldn't."

"'Do not be alone when the moon is brightest.'" Ruby had her eyes closed as she recited another of her predictions.

TJ snapped his fingers and winced again. This time, he held the bandage at his wrist as he bit away the pain. "The alley I was in… when Miss Gravés was followin' me. There was this big fog in the alley and then BOOM! Mr. Bolawe and the Keepers showed up."

"The shadow between friend and foe is thick," Ruby murmured. "Keep your eyes wide in the fog.'" She turned and winked at Ayo. "Orunmila's stars… You're right, kid. I am real good. So okay… we keep a healthy distance from the drill sergeant for now, then. And as for our Orisha… it seems as though Oya knows something we don't. Something different from your original deal with Olokun. I reckon you follow that path first and foremost, love. And from our readings, it would seem like you have a date with a certain ancient rock at the academy, yes?"

TJ nodded. "December fifteenth. That's our date."

"Ancient rock?" Ayo questioned. "Did I miss somethin'?"

"Animal skins," TJ explained. "The tents at the highest point of Ifa Academy. They're all made of animal skins. That golden braid to the Sky Realm is at the top of Oracle Rock."

33

HARD TIMES, HEARTBREAKER

ADEYEMI DIDN'T RETURN THAT DAY, NOR DID SHE SHOW UP ON Sunday. And when Monday morning rolled around, Oroma informed TJ that Elder Adeyemi could be away for at least a week as she "chased down those dirty dogs" as she had said bitterly. The boy, whose hair she had been braiding at the time, yelped as she pulled his hair too tight.

So TJ walked with Ayo to the mess hall with Adeyemi and her whereabouts on his mind when a rustling came from behind. Immediately he seized up, but he was merely attacked from behind... by a huge hug.

A huge hug from a great mass of dark, bushy hair.

The crushing embrace made it hard to remember what he had ever been worried about with Manny. He coughed out a laugh at the sudden spike of joy, spinning around, with her clutching to his back. On the third turn, he caught sight of Ayo sprawled in a bush behind them and spluttering indignantly. TJ's laugh turned into an outright wheezing fit until he and Manny finally stopped their whirling.

"I tried to sneak out last night," Manny huffed, "but Oroma stopped me. Are you okay? Did the Keepers hurt you bad?" Manny tried to pull TJ up straight from his ungainly lean and patted him gingerly for injuries.

"Hey, we're walkin' over here, we're walkin'!" TJ let out in another chuckle.

Manny cringed as she removed a leaf from one of her Dutch braids. "I see my book needs more time to work its magic. You still suck. The reviews did say it'd take a *full* twenty-four hours, you know…"

"Hey, it's not my fault I got your gift late. Oroma was trying to wine down with Mr. Ikenna. Plus, you know… the whole kidnapping thing."

Ayo coughed from the side. He jabbed at a branch that was clearly trying to wrap itself around his ankle. The familiar whistle of a giggle sounded from the willow. "So y'all really go'n leave me here tangled up in all these vines, huh?"

"'*Leaf*' you there?" TJ joked.

"Hey, hey," Manny poked TJ at his side, "that reminds me. Why do trees hate riddles?"

They both looked at each other, and, at the same time, said, "Because it's too easy to get *stumped.*"

Ayo rolled his eyes, still slapping away the branch that wanted to cuddle with his ankle. "Hah. Hah. Hah. So glad you two made up. Now get over here and help your boy up."

TJ and Manny laughed, then went over to untangle Ayo from the clingy willow. It took a little while and a few kind words from Manny to the tree, but they coaxed him away from the smitten plant. Manny bent down to collect Ayo's glasses, handing them to him with an apologetic smile.

"So," she said as they continued to the mess hall, "after I warned Adeyemi with the water bowl she gave me, I didn't get no kind of update. I read some of *Eshu's Messenger Press* and I figured the stories about the Keepers was about TJ. So… what went down?"

TJ let out a big sigh and explained everything that had happened. First, as they gathered up some pancakes and egg stew, he went over what had occurred at the party—leaving out anything related to Ayo's cousin, Eniola, of course.

Second, once they were done with breakfast and grabbed some *zobo* juice, TJ went over what happened after the party got broken up, how Miss Graves followed him, how the Keepers scooped him up, and how they made him do a blood reading.

And finally, as they started the climb up Oracle Rock, TJ dropped the big bomb about how they'd get to the Sky Realm.

"So... we gotta get to this rock before Christmas break?" Manny asked when TJ finally finished up.

"Yup!" TJ took a swig of zobo juice to wet his mouth. The lengthy explanation had his throat all kinds of dry. He was so happy that Manny was talking to him again, but he wanted to make sure she knew how truly sorry he was for deceiving her. He just didn't know how to bring it up. Would that just make her angry all over again?

Manny brushed her hand along one of the lion hide tents pitched up. "That all checks out. These are the animal skins that your oracle was talking about, right?" She lifted her chin to the gray sky dreamingly. "We're finally going to meet with Oya... I'll get to see her again."

Yeah, no... it was definitely not the time to bring up old wounds. Not when Manny looked like *that*.

"We just have to be sure we're ready." TJ stood at Manny's side, staring up into the clouds as well. "But that's one thing I'm worried about. When we opened that portal to the Aqua Realm, we had Eshu and the full moon to empower us. We won't be able to do this on our own."

"Maybe Eshu can help us again?" Manny shrugged. "Now that we know how to get up there, he can take us *straight* to Oya."

A shiver rolled down TJ, from his chest to his toes. Manny hadn't brought up the Gatekeeper until then, but he knew at some point he'd need to face it.

"This time," TJ said, "we won't leave you in the dark when we call him. We have to be in perfect sync for this to work out."

"Shoooooot, that Eshu ritual didn't even work that well," Ayo chimed in. He dabbed his forehead with a napkin. Pit stains soaked his dashiki uniform. TJ forgot the climb would be harder for him. How was he going to do the whole sky chain if he couldn't even climb up Oracle Rock? "Eshu said 'deception for deception's sake' isn't the way he rolls, so he only stayed around a few minutes."

Manny frowned, staring off into the tops of the tall trees like someone had just punched her in the gut.

"What's the matter?" TJ stepped closer to her, his wrist brushing against her arm. He had half the mind to put his arm around her, but thought better of it.

"I told myself to not let my mind go back to what y'all did to me, to get over it." She scrunched her face, the furrow in her brow deep. "But you really hurt me, TJ."

"I know, I'm sorry."

"I know *why* you did it. I get it, really. But still..."

"I know... I know."

"Just don't do that again to me and we cool," Manny said, more to TJ than Ayo. It was a spike through TJ's heart, but he never intended to do that again. No way.

"Never again. Eshu deception is off the table next time. *Believe* me. I felt horrible the whole time. What we have to do now is get our squad back together and tight if we're going to do this Sky Realm thing."

Ayo swiped TJ's zobo juice and drank the last of it. He let out a satisfied sigh before saying, "This plan with the Sky Realm is all good and all, but we need insurance if we can't find Oya or Shango. And TJ, don't go forgettin' about this weekend. You got that thing on Sunday."

Manny cocked her head to one side. "Oh, right! Another festival with Adeyemi."

TJ stiffened. He couldn't believe he thought Ayo could keep his mouth shut for more than even an hour. At least he hadn't said outright what TJ was doing on Sunday.

"Yeah..." TJ trailed off. "Yeah, I got something with Adeyemi, but I also gotta do this other thing, too."

TJ left a beat of silence and knew he messed up.

Manny spun her hand like TJ needed to go on. "Okay, and..."

"I gotta be at this... meeting," TJ explained. Dates could be considered meetings, right? "Ayo's family keeps track of building stuff in Eko Atlantic. They, uh, might be able to pull off a statue for Olokun."

"Oh! Why didn't you say that? That's great news, isn't it?"

Again, TJ left Manny with a silence he should've filled with some distracting banter or a comment about how nice the flowers grew between the cracks of Oracle Rock even way up here. Instead, he allowed Manny enough time to turn from him to Ayo.

"Ayo... what's TJ not telling me?"

"Uh..." Ayo rubbed the back of his neck. TJ could almost read the words written over his face, an apology etched in the lines carving through his forehead.

What had he told TJ before? If Manny asked directly, he wasn't going to lie?

"What TJ is forgetting to say is that he has to take my family out on a date to win their good graces."

"Take your family out on a date?" Manny crossed her arms. "The hell is that supposed to mean?"

TJ said he'd be honest with Manny. No more deception. No more beating around the bush. He had to come clean. Plus, he needed to save Ayo from getting a headache. Holding in the information he had with the big mouth he possessed was damn near an impossible task. So, with a sigh, TJ confessed that he was taking Ayo's older cousin out on a date.

Manny let out a snort of a laugh. "Hah, that's a good one." TJ didn't quite meet her gaze, and out of the corner of his eye, he could tell her humorous grin had turned into a frown. "Wait... Ayo. He's joking, right?"

TJ was taking too long to respond. Again. He didn't want to lie, either. But as the seconds snailed by, he was giving Manny the response she definitely wasn't looking for.

Tension hung thick in the air.

"I mean, you did see TJ's new cut, right? He's lookin' half-decent," Ayo tried to joke, chuckling a bit. No one was laughing, least of all Manny. "To be honest, I don't know how TJ did it either. He was bombin' mad hard at the party with all the other —"

"Ayo..." TJ gritted.

"What? Manny doesn't have anything to be *jealous* about." Ayo's voice was directed too narrowly in Manny's direction. TJ could *not* believe Ayo took it there.

Very slowly, TJ braved a glance Manny's way. Usually, her

thick hair covered her face, but with it done up in two braids, he could clearly see the beet-red coloring her cheeks. At her side, her thumb kept flicking at her nails. What could she possibly be thinking? She probably hated TJ's guts all over again. Ayo didn't finish what he was saying, but he said plenty enough for her to figure out what TJ was doing at the party.

"That's cool…" she murmured but didn't look at either Ayo or TJ, meaning it wasn't "cool" at all. "That's cool. Yeah, just like you said, Ayo, we'll need some insurance. TJ, good luck with your date. I'm sure everything will work out." Nothing about her tone suggested she meant it, but there wasn't malice behind her words either. It was much worse; it was hurt. Manny started tapping her thigh nervously. "Well, we'll need to gather up materials for when that comet comes. I'll head down to the Library Tree and figure out what robes or masks we're gonna need."

"You don't want us to come with you?" Ayo asked. Manny was already making her way back down the rocky path.

TJ tugged at Ayo's shoulder. "*You* need to be quiet."

"Nah, I'm good," Manny said over her shoulder. "I'll catch y'all at dinner."

TJ waited until she was far enough down the path before he pushed Ayo. The boy was already sitting, but TJ thought it'd be a better look if he were splayed along the ground.

"The hell was that for?" Ayo cried.

"What did you say all that stuff for, dude? Manny's going to think I'm going around with other girls."

Ayo dusted himself off. "Bruh, I did you a favor."

"Yeah? How so?"

"I admit… I fumbled a little at the start, but I totally finessed that shit by the end, though. Now Manny's *really* going to want you. There ain't nothin' more attractive than a guy who's unavailable, *'specially* when you got someone like my cousin lookin' your way. If you woulda let me go on, I was gonna slip it in that she's a model."

This was *not* how TJ wanted this thing to go. He and Manny had just *started* patching things up. It was feeling like old times again; they were fitting together like an old glove again… and it just... fell apart in the space of five minutes. What Ayo was doing was only going to make things worse. How could he not see that?

"Ayo, do me a favor," TJ said coldly.

"What's good?"

"When it comes to relationship stuff, never give me advice again."

FOR THE REST OF THE WEEK, IT FELT LIKE TJ AND MANNY were just acquaintances or business partners, not best friends. They still had breakfast together, like always, but instead of debating about who was the best Spider-Man or if *The Last Airbender* could be considered anime, Manny only seemed interested in talking about how to communicate with Eshu again or if brass or iron masks were better for a Sky Realm ritual.

That Wednesday, they found themselves in the Library Tree where they were going over the properties of comet-imbued rituals. Apparently, outside of full planetary alignments, it was one of the most powerful boosts to Ashe. So much so that staffless magic and rituals without a huge group were viable.

"Why don't we just get Adeyemi to help us?" Ayo asked as he pulled two books from a shelf nearby and placed it in their cart. "She probably knows everything we'll need to do and get."

"Adeyemi is still out chasing Keepers," TJ told him, adding another book to their cart. "She won't be back until later this week, according to Omo of Fon. We're gonna have to handle the Sky Realm stuff on our own. Ruby's got our back though. She even said Adeyemi can't know what we're doing for the stars to align properly, or whatever."

TJ still didn't know what the hell that was supposed to mean, but Ruby seemed adamant about it, and he didn't have much of an option but to trust her.

"I don't know, man," Ayo replied. "It's not like at camp. All this research will be a lot easier if we had an elder helping us. And you're practically on a first-name basis with Adeyemi."

"No. We've been over this. Bolawe knew way too much when we talked. We can't have no more leaks. Adeyemi is fixated on

Miss Gravés and won't listen to me. We'll be fine with just Ruby. Trust me. C'mon, back me up, Manny."

TJ looked up to see Manny rubbing her temples at the end of the row, merely a silhouette against the daylight streaming through the windows of bark.

"Will you two let me concentrate for more than a minute!" she gritted. "We can't screw this up. I have to see Oya again so we can figure out what's going on." She slammed the book she was reading shut. "I'm going to my dorm, where it's *quiet*. I can cram in a little more before my next class."

Neither TJ nor Ayo had the courage to tell Manny that the Library Tree was the quietest place at the academy.

And... for the rest of the week, TJ and Ayo barely saw Manny except for times between classes. And TJ knew what he had to do that Sunday. Despite compromising the ability to get an Olokun statue built, he'd have to make things clear to Eniola.

TJ could *not* date her.

34

JOLLOF & JUBILEE

THAT SECOND WEEK OF OCTOBER SAW AN END TO THE RAIN and the start of the dry season. Though occasionally the mornings were thick with fog, the days grew hot and the students swapped out their full-sleeved dashikis for quarter or short sleeves. By the time Sunday came around, TJ was glad he could put on some shorts instead of his long pants. Then he wondered if shorts were even allowed at the restaurant he was supposed to meet Eni at. When he asked Ayo before he left the dorms, his friend gave him a so-so gesture.

"Sometimes people go in there with t-shirts," he said. "It's just brunch. Don't sweat it." Ayo looked him up and down. "Actually, ditch the cargo. Take this." He wiggled a finger and a pair of shorts from his end table slithered through his drawer, then floated in front of TJ.

"You know damn well I can't fit these, man," TJ said, glancing over a pair of shorts that could fit all of Ifa Academy inside it.

"Put them on. I got you."

With some hesitation, TJ slipped on the shorts, but he had to hold them up so they wouldn't slip off his waist. They were nice, tan-colored, with no cargo pockets, just... a touch too large. Ayo twisted his fingers again, and the shorts shrunk to TJ's waist, just like how Mom shrunk TJ's dashiki uniform back at home. Even the bottom of the shorts lengthened so that it didn't look like TJ was wearing boxers.

"Thanks, man," TJ said.

"Yup, yup. Now get up out of here before you're late."

TJ made his way to the entrance statues, through his Eshu portal, through the Summoning Stone, into the entrance hall cavern, and out of the earth portal in the middle of New Ile-Ife, where he was immediately met with the same bodyguards Elder Adeyemi had with her a week prior. They still wore iron masks that matched the buttons on their military coats. TJ recognized the big eyes, narrow nose, and large lips of the mask. Those features belonged to Ogun, the Orisha of Iron and War.

"Morning, Mr. Young," one of them said, deep and slow. The mask muffled his voice a little, and the only thing distinguishing him was his girth and height.

"Ẹ kàáárọ̀," said the other in Yoruba, just as serious as his partner. He was shorter and thinner. Judging by his voice, he was older, too.

TJ gave them a weak wave and explained that he was meeting with a friend for brunch at the Jollof & Jubilee restaurant or cafe or whatever it was.

"Very well," the English-speaking guard said. "We will escort you."

TJ wasn't sure how he felt about being escorted until flashes of a metal box filled with Keepers sprang to mind, along with the scent of blood, and he decided having two big dudes at his flank was probably an excellent idea.

And so they made their way to the fancy restaurant to meet Eni. Every time they rounded a corner or approached a new storefront, customers and shop owners alike bowed and curtsied to TJ. Well, not TJ, but to the two guards flanking him like two mountain tops. TJ could feel the weight of their power in their lumbering steps, the way their thick iron staffs thumped along the ground as they walked.

There was a reason the men wore Ogun masks. Like the Orisha, they were clearly warriors through and through. TJ could even see Ashe casting off them in waves, like it was always there and ready to be used. Or maybe they just had their latent guards up when they were working, just like Ayo told him he was doing to keep his clothes clean before the party. Whatever the case, TJ felt entirely safe, even when he got his usual stares that he sometimes mistook as secret Keepers spying on him.

But he wasn't so sure it would be cool going on a *date* with them.

When they arrived at what Ayo had described to TJ the previous night as the Beverly Hills of New Ile-Ife, TJ didn't have to wonder why the district was called that. Off a private avenue TJ could have easily missed had he not been looking for it, was a tiny plaza filled with modern, flat buildings, a far cry from the more traditional village. In fact, it felt like a slice of Eko Atlantic had been cut out and placed there with all the glass, wooden paneling, and a crowd of people who carried themselves with a sense of self-importance. The only traditional touch to the square was the tall wooden statues that cleaned storefront windows and swept the streets. They looked very much like the ones that roamed around Camp Olosa.

Ashe floated everywhere. TJ couldn't take it all in. What might have looked like a tech-forward city with electricity streaming throughout, instead there was magic on overload, magic that brought stationary signs to life trying to sell TJ luxury crystals, magic that kept some abstract art piece floating and rotating in the center, magic that enabled weird steampunk-looking chimneys to push out smoke.

When they stopped at Jollof & Jubilee, TJ thought he was at the threshold of a fancy hotel entrance with its big glass double doors lined with gold on the edges. Flanking each door were obsidian statues, and between them was a gilded sign that read "Jollof & Jubilee." The one on the left, a woman with a long flowing dress, poured honey into a pot in the shape of the first "o" in "Jollof". That was Oshun. The one on the right lit a black flame under the second "e" in "Jubilee". That was Shango. Each Orisha statue was on a loop, pouring and lighting, pouring and lighting.

When TJ finally picked his mouth up from off the ground, he walked into the restaurant.

And then his jaw dropped again.

Now, TJ would've never *exactly* called him or his family poor.

Sure, there were a few months here and there where Top Ramen or hotdogs with sandwich bread made the menu two or three times a week, but never more than that. A trip to the lobster joint down the street from his house only ever happened on birthdays or special occasions. But a place where chefs were more concerned with making their food look like art pieces rather than edible food? That was most definitely off the table for the Young family.

And Jollof & Jubilee was *definitely* one of those places where chefs made their food look like art rather than a meal.

The space was filled with moody, subdued lighting. Delicate white cloth with folded napkins on top covered each table. Whoever designed the place had clearly tried to give it a more rustic feel with a few pots and pans hanging as decoration from the high ceiling, though.

"TJ!" came Eni's voice. Initially, TJ couldn't see her between the restaurant's low-light earth tones of orange, brown, and red. But from one of the wicker chairs waved a slightly familiar girl with short hair, like, she-had-a-whole-ass-fade short hair. But the Eni TJ knew had a relatively long style. Had she cut it all off?

"TJ, over here!" she called out again, waving more vigorously this time. This outburst earned a hush and a slap on the wrist from a woman who sat next to her. This woman TJ knew, at least briefly. Eni's mom. Mrs. Afolabi. It was a good thing TJ had been behind Eni's illusion wall back at the party, or else the woman might've given him a slitted stare instead of the smile she was showing him just then.

But wait… what was Mrs. Afolabi doing there? In fact, Eni's *entire* table was filled with people wearing suits or traditional aso oke robes. There was only one seat next to Eni that wasn't filled.

Waving back furtively, TJ forced his face into a smile, but he was almost certain it was coming off more like a scowl. How the heck was he supposed to tell Eni he didn't think it was a good idea for them to date with all those people there? And what the hell were all those people doing there to begin with!?

"We'll be right at the door if you need us, Mr. Young," the English-speaking guard told him. He planted himself to the wall as though he were a statue sentry, not unlike the ones outside.

With his getup and mask, he didn't look too far off. The other guard gave a brief nod and mirrored his partner. The hostess at her booth didn't even question them being there when she asked for TJ's name. When he gave it to her, the woman walked him over to the table... with all those people!

The moment TJ's butt hit the seat, Eni went off. She introduced everyone at the table at a rapid-pace, going between Yoruba and English depending on what would come out faster. Apparently, the majority of their brunch guests were executives, engineers, and politicians. But more than that...

"They're all family," Eni had said and then went off listing how each of them was related to her, from first-cousins, uncles, aunts, grandparents, the whole nine.

"It's so nice to meet you, Tomori Jomiloju," one of them said.

"I've always wanted to meet another Young," said another.

"Orunmila's Stars! He's got Ifedayo's height, doesn't he?" exclaimed a third.

The last one to speak was Eni's mother herself. She looked just like Eniola, just with a few age lines and a slightly shorter neck. "We are all business associates, but we Afolabi like to keep it in the family. I know your mother and the Abimbolas think the same. And our family would love to do anything for yours. We all are in your debt, after all the Hero of Nigeria has done for us."

All of this was *way* too much. TJ had one simple task: get in, let Eni know the bad news, then get out. Now he had to contend with her *entire* extended family on top of that?

"Um, thank you..." TJ took a sip of water from the glass in front of him, then kept to his sipping to buy himself some time. Everyone, literally everyone, stared at him with expectant expressions plastered on their faces. It gave him a bad case of the jitters. When there was no more water left for him to stall with, he placed the cup back down and coughed. Silence blanketed the pristine table of silver goblets and china plates until one of the old guys across the table spoke up.

"So, how did you meet Eniola, Tomori Jomiloju?"

TJ cleared his throat once, twice, then thrice. He wanted to give Eni a sidelong glance, but knew that'd be the wrong play at the moment. They'd know he was trying to come up with a false story. He couldn't tell them the truth either, though, especially when he was at the very party that was broken up by Mrs. Afolabi. His mind raced with too many responses, all of them terrible. So, he stuttered, "I-I w-was... in the village. On Independence day. Well, on my birthday, actually. Eniola was picking Ayo up."

"Oh, right." The Elder turned to Eni. "To take him to that rooftop party that should have never happened."

Eni hid her face with a hand. "No, those were just my friends and personal contacts. Ayo wasn't there. *Bàbá àgbà, mo ti ṣọ fún yín tẹ́lẹ̀.*"

"Oh, yes, yes. That *was* the story, wasn't it? So, TJ, how was your birthday?"

"It was... okay. I... uh... spent time with my ìyá àgbá in the village."

"Oh, did Tiwa get back from her excursion in the Amazon?" An old man leaned into the table, his beady eyes magnified by the thick glasses hanging from his nose. "I thought she was helping Bamidele examine your sister's old staff, no? I should stop by later and say hello. We went to Ifa Academy together in our time, you know?"

"Oh! No, she wasn't here. I had to... um... speak to her on a water phone in the village since she's in the Amazon. Something about bad reception or whatever. That's what I meant."

"Ah, I see. Well, you must have made a great first impression on young Eniola with one mere greeting. She insisted we meet you."

TJ gulped. This was feeling like an interrogation. Not a pleasant morning over brunch.

"Okay, baba, that's enough." Mrs. Afolabi came to the rescue. "Let's eat first before we get into all that. Waiter," she lifted a hand in the air, "we are ready to begin."

Out of nowhere, a waiter appeared at their shoulders—TJ was almost certain he teleported there. He held a brass staff in hand and wore a long dashiki matching the orange and browns of the restaurant interior. "You called for me, Mrs. Afolabi?"

"Yes, we will start with the first course, please."

"It would be my pleasure." The waiter bowed, then lifted his staff in the air. On the table appeared an assortment of brunch salads. In front of TJ was a plate filled with strawberries, blueberries, and nuts covering mixed greens. Oddly, no one ate their salads. Instead, each of them spoke to them.

"No cheese on mine, please," one man said down the table, and the cheese shot up and disappeared.

"Could I have a bit more raspberries, but on the side?" another woman murmured to her plate. Sure enough, the raspberries hopped up and moved to the side of her plate, where more popped into existence.

TJ gawked as Eni nudged his elbow. "You just tell it what you want and it'll appear or disappear on the plate."

"Yeah, yeah, I get it. But... why doesn't Ifa have stuff like this at the mess hall?"

Mrs. Afolabi smiled with the practiced grin of a socialite. "That's because the magic behind it requires a bit of time and finesse, a luxury a mess hall does not have. In fact, we are attempting to apply this magic to restaurants for the clouded via holograms so they can see menu items directly on their plates, but without magic. Obviously, a clouded cook and waiter would have to bring them their food instead of this..."

She leaned into her plate and murmured that she was satisfied with her serving of spinach and blueberries. TJ could *see* how the Ashe mist he always saw disappeared to nothing at all as the food solidified into a real meal.

Eni leaned in and whispered, "My mom works with a lot of industries that convert magic into mundane tech."

Wait, did Mrs. Afolabi and Eni *own* Jollof & Jubilee? TJ couldn't bring himself to ask, so instead, he murmured to his plate, requesting the salad as it was with a glass of orange juice. Then he said, "that'll do, thank you," and the salad solidified into real food.

They all ate and chit-chatted. Everyone else was at ease. This was probably a regular Sunday for them. But TJ felt more than a little uncomfortable, what with all the etiquette he had to keep up with. Several times, Eni had to remind him to keep his elbows off the table, or to place his cup in the exact place he lifted it from, or that he was supposed to keep the rim of his plate clean at all times.

It was like eating with a straitjacket.

And it didn't ease TJ's nerves when, of course, the obligatory mentions of Dayo came up. But he was surprised to find that the usual praise she received from people, especially in Nigeria, didn't come up. Eni's family was not disparaging of his sister, but they *were* recalling embarrassing stories of her... like they actually *knew* her. How did Eni say she knew his sister again?

"And remember when she tried to do the catwalk with little Eniola?" Eni's grandmother said, as main dishes ranging from fancy English muffin tops with over-easy eggs to thin crepes lovingly sprinkled in powdered sugar and marmalade replaced their salads. "Ifedayo didn't have a clue what to do with her neck."

Eni's grandmother stuck her neck out like a chicken and everyone laughed, the kind of laugh that spoke of a memory they all shared. TJ had always seen Dayo as the cool sister, the Hero of Nigeria. It wasn't often that people would say something of her that they might say of TJ.

More stories chimed from every corner of the table, from the time Dayo tried to ask out one of Eni's cousins and couldn't string three words together without stuttering, or how, for the entirety of Junior Secondary School, her Yoruba was abysmal.

It seemed like almost everyone at the table had a story about her. Even Eni, who murmured about how Dayo used to follow her around, even though Eni was a few years younger.

It was like these people were a family he never knew. And for that, TJ became comfortable despite the whole family brunch being sprung on him without notice. And therein might've been the trap... because when the third course—granola parfait—came out, the real questions started in earnest.

"So, Tomori," Mrs. Afolabi said through a bit of Greek yogurt. "Eniola here tells me you have a proposal for us. Something about Olokun?"

35

TONGUE-TIED TRANCE

TJ STIFFENED IN HIS SEAT, MAKING THE WICKER CHAIR HE SAT in creak. Had he really heard that correctly? Did Eniola's mom really just ask about Olokun? Now that TJ finally had the attention of someone who could actively help him in keeping Olokun away, he wasn't so sure how to even start. It didn't help that he felt completely at the mercy of the Afolabi family, caught in their crosshairs.

Eniola egged him on. "Go ahead, TJ. Tell them."

"Well, you see, sirs and ladies," TJ started. *Sirs and ladies? Where am I, a medieval court?* "Well... you might not know this... but I'm a big fan of Olokun, like, he's my favorite."

"Oh, are you aligned with him?" Eni's grandfather asked from across the table.

"Oh, no. But he is, um... quite fascinating. I feel like I really *know* him, ya know?"

"I was hoping to hear something like that from you," Mrs. Afolabi said. "Excuse me, hostess." She lifted her hand. The hostess from the front came over and asked what was needed of her. "A little privacy, please."

"Of course, Mrs. Afolabi." She touched a medallion on her chest, and four portals manifested at the corners of the table. New waiters stepped out from the portals, holding a stool with glass-encased crystals: two smokey black, and the other two dull red.

After setting the stools down, each waiter spoke a hymn and TJ could see the mist of Ashe encasing the entire table within a box. He wasn't sure what it was that was being boxed in until Mrs. Afolabi spoke again.

"So, it's true, then?" she asked in an echoed tone, like her voice was trapped in a small room. The mystical barrier around them must've been locking in all the sounds. "It's true that Olokun will return in February?"

TJ clutched his fork, surprise seizing him in his chair. This meeting was more than just a brunch date, more than a meeting with Eniola's business family. He must've looked absolutely beside himself, because the statues that were his bodyguards shifted in their positions at the restaurant's entrance. TJ scratched the back of his neck and gave his head a tiny shake, and they rested back into their stone stances. Though TJ couldn't see their eyes, he knew they'd be watching.

Elder Adeyemi had made it very clear that no one should know about Olokun under any circumstances, not even TJ's own family. There was no way he could let that be known to a bunch of people he *just* met.

Maybe he could ask "what makes you say that?" or something to that effect.

But TJ's great failing was that he sat there looking shocked. He didn't have to say a word. He all but confirmed Mrs. Afolabi's question through his white-knuckled grip around his fork.

"I knew it!" one of the elders who had shared a story about Dayo croaked. "The oracle I have on retainer said there were tides approaching near the second moon of the new year. I had her cross-referenced with the Grecian oracles. They, too, said potent power would swell from the Great Rift, a power to match Poseidon. They always get into their theatrics, but when Eni started going on about this Young boy and Olokun, I knew something had to be afoot."

"That also lines up with the tip we got from that reporter from *Eshu's Press*," another man added.

"We'll need to inform the others," Eni's grandfather said. "We need to prepare."

More chatter stirred around the table about what they should do and how they should do it. With each new voice, TJ's muscles constricted tighter and tighter until Eni's hand dropped lightly to his thigh. Shock reeled through him at the touch as he looked up to see her mouthing a "sorry."

Had she set him up? Did she actually want him there? Or was he just supposed to come to spill the beans about Olokun to the rest of the magical community? But TJ couldn't think of all that; what had really got him was how Mrs. Afolabi knew when Olokun was coming… down to the month!

"No! Don't tell anyone!" TJ shouted, and his voice echoed back at him from the sound barrier. Everyone stopped talking to turn to him. "Elder Adeyemi said no one could know."

"That woman and her secrets." Eni's grandmother sucked her teeth and waved him away. "She thinks she has to hold the weight of the world on her back, that one. She was just the same when we were kids. Tell us, boy, what has she been doing to halt Olokun from destroying *our* towers?"

TJ didn't know how to reply to that, but he did know that silence was one of the worst ways to go. Where was Manny when he needed her? She could talk their way out of this. Even Ayo could probably do a better job…

"It's okay, TJ," Eni assured him, giving him another gentle squeeze under the table. TJ had got the feeling he was being used by her, but something in the tone of her voice seemed genuine. But was that put on, too? A child of Oshun wasn't just a master of love, but manipulation too, depending on who you asked.

"W-we've been doing festivals," TJ decided to say, "On Sundays in the square. Festivals for Olokun to regain his favor so he won't drown Eko Atlantic."

"He wants to drown the coast!?" exclaimed one of the younger cousins who looked fresh out of Ifa Academy. "How would you know this? Are you a Seer as well? Your sister was aligned with Orunmila too, wasn't she?"

TJ groaned. There was no scenario where the whole truth would work here. TJ couldn't possibly tell them he met Olokun face to face. He was partway to working out a half-truth involving some reading Oracle Ruby gave him when Mrs. Afolabi said, "No, he's no Seer. The boy crossed over. You see, after my daughter came to me with this odd request, I dug a bit deeper where Tomori Jomiloju was concerned. And what did I find? The UCMP is covering up what happened to him at Camp Olosa. And something else very odd came up."

"And... what's that?" Eni's grandfather asked. Even Eni seemed unsure of what was coming next. That gave TJ some relief. She was, at least partially, being ambushed, too.

Mrs. Afolabi lifted a single finger in the air and wagged it in the direction of the back of the rustic restaurant. A moment later, *Manny and Ayo* were escorted from a backroom with dazed looks on their faces. Two wicker chairs were pulled up for them at the far end of the table, opposite TJ.

"What's... going on?" Manny asked as she sat slowly. "I feel kind of... woozy."

"Yeah... me too." Ayo grabbed his head and recognition filled his eyes. "TJ... is that you?"

Manny lifted her head toward TJ, and a questioning quiver came to her eyes.

What in the world is going on? TJ thought.

"What are my friends doing here?" TJ asked, nearly climbing from his seat. "And why are they all... all..." He couldn't find the word. "Like they just got up from a nap or something." Anger boiled under TJ's skin. "Do you people have them under a *potion*?"

"Thank you for joining us." Mrs. Afolabi outstretched her hands, ignoring TJ. "I just wanted to give Mr. Young a little demonstration. I'll start with you, nephew. Please, can you tell me what went on with you, Tomori Jomiloju, and Manuela at the end of the summer? Specifically, what happened at Olosa's lagoon?"

"I don't know what... your... talking..." Ayo tried to get the rest out, but it was like he had something stuck in his throat. "Must be... my asthma."

"Thank you," Mrs. Afolabi said flatly. "And you, Manuela. Can you enlighten us? What went on with Olosa's messenger when she took you under the lagoon?"

"Like I would tell you... any... thing..." Just like Ayo, Manny struggled with something in her throat.

"Classic tellings of a bewitching," Mrs. Afolabi announced to the table as though Ayo and Manny were test rats on a stage or something. "Notably, the tellings of the tongue-tied trance. It's been made taboo for them to speak on anything relating to that event. And something tells me Mr. Young is the only one unaffected, seeing as he has been able to speak on Olokun today. Why is that, young man? And who did the bewitching to stop these two talking about the lagoon?"

"Don't tell her... anything... TJ..." Manny sounded like her tongue had gone numb in her mouth.

The answer seemed obvious to TJ and it might have benefited them all in this situation, in fact.

"Because those who go to the Aqua Realm lose their memories," he said.

"No, no, no, I did my research." Mrs. Afolabi tapped her long fingernail on her glass. "Those who have crossed over and back in the past suffered from memory loss, not utter inability to speak on their experience. Your friends here can't give a straight answer. No truth serum I give them will work, either."

"*Sade Afolabi*, you did *not* give those children a serum, did you?" someone else down the table exclaimed, aghast.

"That's why the orange juice here tastes so weird?" Ayo asked. "Not cool, Auntie."

Okay, the situation had just gone from nerve-wracking to mildly curious to utterly out of whack. Did these people seriously drug his friends?

"Mom, what are you doing?" Eni leaned forward. "You didn't say anything about this. You never said—"

Mrs. Afolabi snapped her fingers and Eni fell silent at once. TJ knew that response. It was the same one Mom gave to Simba... a pet dog. Did this woman truly treat her daughter the same way? Or worse, had she just bewitched her own daughter with the tongue-tied trance?

"How could you just drug them like that?" TJ gritted.

"You mean my *own* nephew?" Mrs. Afolabi gave him a quirked eyebrow and a grimace. "Trust me, what I gave them was within legal limits. My legal team assured me."

"So what are you saying?" TJ asked with heat, edging his eyes to the bodyguards. He might need to summon them at any moment. They had definitely taken notice of the situation; the tall one appeared ready to charge straight over. TJ shook his head again and focused back on Afolabi. "Are you trying to say Elder Adeyemi bewitched them to get all tongue-tied?"

Mrs. Afolabi took a victorious sip of her drink. "Precisely. Glad to see there's something in that head of yours."

Manny's eyes shot almost as wide as Ayo's jaw dropped.

"You spoke with Olokun directly, didn't you, boy." Mrs. Afolabi's words weren't a question, but a statement toward TJ.

A hush covered the table then. Without looking around, TJ felt everyone's eyes on him. Perhaps Mrs. Afolabi could sense his apprehension, because she set her glass down and said, "We are on the same side, Tomori Jomiloju. I'd like to keep Ebony Tower standing and Olokun satiated. You do not have to confess everything to me. Just be forthright with what assistance you need."

If that was true, if she wasn't interested in getting information, just protecting one of her towers, then she was right. She and TJ were aligned with that goal. But she could've gone about this whole thing a different way. Still, he voiced a response. "We need to build a statue. One of Olokun. Preferably in the big center circle of the development where the yachts dock... can you build it? Someone... someone told me it might help."

"Another Orisha?" Mrs. Afolabi asked, and TJ seized up again. "Apologies, I'll stop my prying. Yes, I can have it built. How big?"

"Uh..." TJ thought it over a moment, remembering how tall Olokun had been when he met him. "What's the tallest statue in the world?"

"The Statue of Unity in India," Eni spoke up. Her voice was low, barely above a sigh, and she stared at her hands. Had she even looked up to her cousin or Manny? "The Statue of Unity is over six hundred feet."

"How do you know that?" TJ asked, shifting back in his seat in surprise.

"I looked it up after you asked and I spoke with my mother." TJ thought he understood it then. Eni only knew about the statue. She probably thought this meeting would be about getting it built. The rest of the information was as new to her as it was to TJ.

Looking over the table once more, TJ swallowed long and deep before shifting his attention back to Mrs. Afolabi. "How long would it take to build something like that? That's bigger than the skyscrapers you have now."

"Five years... by mundane means," Eni's grandmother chimed in. "With a... helping hand, if you catch my meaning, perhaps a year, maybe less if we had backing. Backing from the government, I mean."

"And that's where you come in, Mr. Young," Mrs. Afolabi said. Now they were getting down to brass tacks. "We'll need you to speak to Elder Adeyemi for us, vouch for us on her behalf. She doesn't take any of our messages anymore since the passing of your sister."

"And... why wouldn't she take your messages?" This time, TJ eyed the table to all the business suits and watchful gazes.

It was Eni's grandfather who spoke up. "You tell us, Mr. Young. It would seem you have the most contact with her these days."

"That's right." Mrs. Afolabi nodded. "It's not us that need to explain anything. That woman owes you and your friends an explanation here."

The worst part about Afolabi's final words was how much TJ agreed with them. His friends were still struggling to open their mouths and form words properly. Elder Adeyemi had a lot of explaining to do. But how would he even broach a conversation like that with her? And he couldn't even trust Eni's family at all to begin with. What was he supposed to do?

TJ checked his phone under the table. It read:

Eko Atlantic's Doomsday in 14 weeks, 0 days, 14 hours, 37 minutes, and 51 seconds

However he did it, he was *not* looking forward to his next meeting when Elder Adeyemi returned.

36

CLARITY IN THE FOG

It was a strange thing walking out of that restaurant. TJ hadn't realized his breathing had been hitched and caught in his throat until fresh air slapped him across the face.

TJ was going to be in all kinds of trouble with Elder Adeyemi. It was only a matter of time before she found out what he had done, what he had revealed. But she had her own things to explain. How could she bewitch Manny and Ayo? Didn't she trust them?

"I'm so sorry that happened," Eni said, with a hand gripping TJ's shoulder. Her mother allowed her to walk TJ, Manny, and Ayo back to Ifa Academy's entrance. Elder Adeyemi's bodyguards shadowed them a few yards behind. "I knew she wanted to talk, but I didn't know she'd be so…"

"Aggressive about it?" Ayo finished for her. The sun was setting behind him, giving him an orange hue around his big ears. "You coulda told *me* what was goin' on, at least. That was cold."

Ignoring Ayo, Eni leaned in closer and placed her chin on TJ's shoulder. He nearly forgot she was almost as tall as him. "Don't look all grumpy. I mean, I don't blame you if you don't want to see me anymore, but I do… you know… like you. And I want to see you again. If you want."

Out of the corner of his eye, TJ could've sworn he saw

Manny's walk stiffen. Then, without warning, Eni's lips brushed across his cheek, the edge of them sweeping along his peach fuzz and the corner of his upper lip. A series of rolling tingles danced from the kiss and down through TJ's entire body.

Okay, that was not fair.

"Think about it, at least, yeah?" Eni gave him a little smirk, her big brown eyes doe-like, yet unsure. "We still need to go watch the River Hoopers when I'm off punishment."

With that, Manny sped up her pace and pulled away from the group. To anyone else, they might not have noticed. They were entering the village square, which had picked up a bit of foot traffic, so it looked like Manny was just avoiding the crowd. TJ knew what was really up, though.

"Um..." TJ stuttered. "Eni, you're really nice and everything—"

"And TJ would love to go," Ayo finished for him.

"What?" TJ shouted, perhaps a bit too loudly. He just hoped Manny wasn't hearing this. When he peered up to find her, she was already halfway to the Ifa Academy entrance.

How did she get way over there so fast?

"TJ's a little shy," Ayo patted TJ on the back like an old man, "but I'll make sure he doesn't stand you up."

"All right, bet." Eni smiled as they arrived near the sacred earth plot that led to Ifa Academy's entrance hall. "Bye, TJ. See ya, cuz. And seriously, super super sorry for today. That was insanely awkward."

"Imma bowl you later, Eni. That shit was foul, and you know it."

"I know it was! But what was I supposed to do? I said I was sorry! I really didn't know."

TJ and Ayo waved goodbye—TJ more half-heartedly than Ayo. When Eni disappeared around Mami Wata's Eatery, TJ grabbed Ayo around the shoulders. "What did I tell you about helping me with relationship stuff, man!?"

"Bruh, I just did you a favor."

"How? *How!?* I don't *have* to go out with your cousin." TJ peeked over his shoulder and lowered his voice to make sure his bodyguards, who stood out of earshot near a fruit vendor, couldn't hear him. "Her mom's already in with the statue thing."

"Nah, not that. Did you know Manny's got herself a man back in New York already?"

TJ wasn't quite sure he heard Ayo correctly. Manny had never mentioned anyone back in New York outside of her family. How could she possibly be with someone when she was way out here in Nigeria? It didn't add up. Clearly, Ayo had made a mistake.

"Come again, I don't think I heard you right."

Ayo spoke slowly and clearly, exaggerating each word. "Manny's. Got. A. Guy. Back. In. New. York."

Okay, so Ayo wasn't mistaken. But there still could've been something else going on.

"And how are you comin' to this conclusion?"

"Well, Titi and I… met up this morning, you know, and, well… Titi said when Manny picked up her phone that she… saw her texting some guy. Texting kissing face emojis and all that."

TJ shrugged. "That coulda been anything."

"Nah, man. Titi said Manny made sure she saw the screen. And Manny knows Titi and I are sort of a thing right now again so of course that information would get back to me. If you think *I* got a big mouth, man, you should hear Titi."

TJ felt gutted. Utterly gutted. "She never told me about anyone in New York…"

"Like I said, man. I did you a favor. And I'd really like some appreciation here. I'm trying to wingman for you with my cousin. I don't know if you noticed, but I'm not the kind of guy who lets any ol' dude get at my cousin. That's a best-friend-only kind of deal, you feel me? And you're a nice guy. Way better than the other guys she's —"

"Yeah, yeah, thank you." TJ realized he sounded a bit too cavalier. "I mean, seriously, dude. Thanks. There's just been a lot going on. Sorry I haven't really been, you know, like, all there."

"Appreciate it."

TJ shouldered through the last few of the crowd. "What were you and Manny doing at the restaurant, anyway?"

"We were invited!" Ayo explained. "We were doing more

research at The False Prophet to figure out more about staffless magical rituals—by the way, we'll definitely need the twins help on that—and then my aunt showed up and told us there was some food she wanted us to try. It wasn't weird because she has me test out stuff for the restaurant all the time. Uh… by the way, who are those guys following you?"

"I'll explain later." TJ turned to see his bodyguards were catching up, so he raised his voice and said, "Uh… thanks for watching my back today, you two. I appreciate it."

"Adeyemi will return to Ifa Academy tomorrow morning," the taller English-speaking guard said, voice muffled by that iron mask. "Your training will resume then."

"*Mà á rí è láìpé, Tomori Jomiloju,*" said the shorter, Yoruba-speaking guard.

Once TJ and Ayo dropped into their own earth portals and came out the other end to the Summoning Stone, Ayo said, "Man, that's messed up what Elder Adeyemi did to me and Manny. Can't believe she'd think we'd speak on the Realm when she told us not to. Am I really *that* bad at keepin' my mouth shut?"

Thinking on it, TJ could probably let the whole bewitching thing slide when it came to Ayo… But Manny totally would have been fine without.

"So, how are you going to bring up all that stuff about us being bewitched to Adeyemi?"

"Still figuring that out."

TJ WAS STILL FIGURING ALL THAT OUT WHEN HE WALKED INTO Elder Adeyemi's cave office the next morning. The space, which was usually filled with dim light from the cavern's waterfall mouth, was covered in fog. That was odd because October in their part of Nigeria wasn't particularly cold. Perhaps he was too preoccupied with coming up with his intro spiel for Adeyemi because it took him a good long while to properly notice the odd weather.

"*Gee, Elder Adeyemi, did you really bewitch my friends?*"

"Oh, hey, Headmistress. I really do think you should fire Miss Graves, like, yesterday."

Nothing sounded good.

Bad introductions aside, the thick mist did remind TJ of Ruby's warning that the fog would be thick between friend and foe. He just never would have thought Adeyemi a foe. Even now, despite feeling betrayed, he didn't quite feel that. After all, she just broke several magical secrecy laws just to get him away from the Keepers.

TJ skipped along the rocks to Adeyemi's central slab with trepidation. He heard her before he saw her.

"Is there nothing that can be done? It's very important we keep the gatherings going."

"I'm sorry, Headmistress," another voice answered. A woman's voice. British. "But the board is very firm on this, and you've lost favor on the Isles. We'll speak more about this later."

"Very well, Director. I'll be in touch."

At the last words, TJ had skipped enough stones to make out Adeyemi in the fog. Unlike last week, she was back in her usual stylish attire. This particular robe was all blue, with a single lily pad pattern rising from the lower hem. And, of course, it looked like the lily pad was literally floating on water.

TJ didn't think she had a single ordinary dress in her entire wardrobe.

"Is it okay to ask who that was?" TJ questioned. It was a better introduction than the others he had planned, and he was sort of glad he could use it as an excuse. His palms were already getting clammy from the thought of confronting the Headmistress.

"That," Adeyemi sighed, "was the Director of Public Relations from the UCMP."

"Bad news?" TJ tried to keep it casual as he took a stone seat across from her desk.

"All public gatherings in Nigeria and Benin are to be halted until the Keeper threat is squelched." The words seem to add decades to the Elder. Sure, she was old, but she never actually *looked* old. Today, however, her age was showing. "Unfortunately, that means it will be hard to continue our festivals for Olokun, and communications with Eshu via ritual will be nigh on impossible as well. But I was thinking we could discuss what's going on with Eshu, Oya, and the Sky Realm by doing a bit of brainstorming. Before that, though, I owe you an apology."

Crap, that's right. She can read minds!

TJ gulped and his dashiki suddenly weighed like a winter coat —he was so warm. "Um… what about?"

"I failed to ask your forgiveness for putting you in harm's way with those Keepers. I had people watching you, and I should have gotten to you sooner than I did."

"Oh, yeah…" TJ let out a huge internal sigh of relief. "I mean, I get it. It takes time finding a kid in a huge slum like that."

Elder Adeyemi hummed under her lips and gave TJ a flat smile. "So, how was your week? Oracle Ruby tells me the Keepers didn't get much out of you."

"About that…" TJ's dashiki went on heater mode again, but he tried to combat it by going zen. Dad always said it was better to rip a band-aid away quickly, not pull it inch by inch. So he explained everything that happened to him since he last saw Adeyemi—everything except the way to get into the Sky Realm, which he, Ayo, and Ruby had figured out. But his meeting with Mrs. Afolabi… *that* he didn't hold back on. "Is it true you bewitched Manny and Ayo with some tongue-twister curse?"

Elder Adeyemi had been an engaged listener up to that point. After TJ's last words, however, she visibly sighed. Against the stark-white vapor coming in from the falls, she was almost a deep-blue silhouette, a shadow TJ suddenly feared. That same fear he felt that first time he visited her office. Then, in almost the same instance, the space lightened up again, and she corrected him coyly, "You mean the tongue-tied trance." And then, with sharp honesty, she finished, "And yes, I did."

TJ drew back in his stone seat a little. "What? You admit it? Why didn't you tell me? Why didn't you put the trance on me, too?"

"To be frank, I tried." She frowned and steepled her fingers over her desk. TJ wasn't so sure he liked all this honesty from her. It seemed almost callous. "The moment you and your friends came back from the other side, I tried. I was successful when it came to Ayodeji and Manuela. I couldn't let anything slip to the wrong people, of course. We do it at the UCMP often. Teenagers aren't the best at discretion most of the time. But when I tried to place the trance on you, I was... hindered."

"Hindered? Like I have a force field or something? But how come that Bisi lady and everyone else can blast me with magic and hang me from my ankles?"

"The tongue-tied trance requires manipulation of one's ori — one's divine mind. I hadn't mentioned it before, but even reading your ori, your subconscious thoughts, are shrouded." *So she was trying to read my mind.* "I haven't figured it out yet, but your ori is," she jabbed her steepled fingers into her forehead, "what's the word..."

"Different?" That seemed to be a theme for TJ ever since he got in touch with his Ashe. "I still don't see why I couldn't know about Manny and Ayo."

"I didn't want you to keep secrets from your friends. True ones are hard to come by, and they don't deserve to be lied to, not by you."

"Not by anyone." TJ replied, sharper than he expected to be.

"Of course. Had there been another way..." Adeyemi shrugged, as gracefully as she did everything else.

TJ could understand the thinking, barely. After all, he had been keeping things from Manny lately — for worse reasons — and look where that got him. And he knew being outright honest the way Elder Adeyemi was right now wouldn't have done him any better.

Still...

"I don't buy that," TJ decided to say. "You're always giving me the run around with this stuff. You won't even listen to me about Miss Graves. I told you, she's feeding information to Bolawe. There's no way he could know as much about what's going on in the academy without her saying something. And I *told* you she was *following* me."

"I just got done working with Miss Graves, young man. She and I were giving chase to the Keepers all week."

"And did you find any?"

The Headmistress opened her mouth, then closed it. It was the hesitation TJ was looking for. "I know what you're getting at, but Miss Gravés was vetted. I trust her."

"Mr. Bolawe was trusted, too," TJ reminded her with some heat in his tone. "You even said you two were close. You still had no idea that he was Olugbala."

"Tomori Jomiloju, it would be wise for you to change your tone. I've tolerated quite a bit today. I know you've got a lot to handle at the moment, and Olokun's return looms over us both—over us all. But you need to trust me. Let's put the subject of Miss Gravés to bed. What we need to consider now is how to satiate the Lord of the Deep without any public gatherings. Even if I get approval from the UCMP for a statue project of that size... it might not be enough, I'm afraid. There's also been a new development. You recall the rains in Los Angeles?"

TJ nodded. He'd thought Olokun was the one behind that, sending a message or something. But it turned out to be some other deity. Was that not actually the case?

Adeyemi's next words held a heavy weight behind them. "There seems to be something *very* wrong with Oya."

"Wait, what do you mean?" The surrounding fog thickened, as though Oya herself was blowing life into them—that got TJ's attention. He knew better than to ignore a sign like that.

"From what I've investigated over these past weeks, and according to the shaman and the oracles I've spoken to, here, and in the Americas, we all agree. Oya has gone quiet. *Utterly* quiet. After you mentioned Eshu saying Oya wasn't stirring up her usual storms off the Atlantic, I started to wonder. She's been quiet ever since the day young Manuela Martinez had her encounter with the Windweaver in New York."

"But everyone says the Orishas are quiet these days, except for those few sightings. What's different now?" TJ had a very bad feeling about this. If Oya was gone, then why would Eshu say she was going around doing her thing as usual? TJ stared down at the bone-white tattoo on his forefinger. It pulsated lightly.

"The Orishas do not speak to us directly," Adeyemi started, "but there are other ways they communicate with us. All of Oya's usual signs, her storms, the sound of thunder, the whistle through markets. All are quiet. I've only heard of one Orisha going totally silent before. Can you guess which?"

TJ thought long and hard. The images of a giant alligator and a portal through a lagoon spread wide in his mind.

"Olosa," he murmured. "Olosa has been gone."

"And where is Olosa now?"

TJ's chest caved. "In Eshu's staff."

"In the Gatekeeper's staff, indeed. Young Manuela did say Oya mentioned Eshu, did she not?"

"Yeah, but she didn't really hear what she was trying to say about him." What *had* she said about him? TJ tried desperately to remember. Manny had said Oya was saying something like, "Eshu has me…" Oh, no… It was so obvious now. She was warning Manny against Eshu! But why would the Gatekeeper trap Oya in his staff? It wasn't like he had a gripe with her the same way he did with Olosa. Unless…

"Oh, man…" TJ breathed out. "Oh, man, oh, man… He trapped her because she was trying to speak to Manny. Speak to her directly."

"Like I said, we're only brainstorming here. But, TJ, tell me. When you saw Eshu last, did he have his staff with him?"

TJ remembered the staff shaking in Eshu's grip. He opened his mouth to answer her, but something held him back. She had dismissed his worries about Miss Graves so certainly. And even if the drill sergeant *was* innocent, TJ knew the Keepers were getting their information from *somewhere*.

Oracle Ruby *did* say that Elder Adeyemi couldn't know everything for all to play out as needed…

"No… no, I don't think he did," TJ lied. "Not that I can remember. The mirrors we used were foggy."

"Then," Adeyemi rested her back in her seat, "it is paramount we speak to him once more."

But TJ knew that wouldn't happen. That was the real reason they couldn't communicate with Eshu. They knew how to do it; he had done it twice before. What was stopping them now was that Eshu wasn't taking their calls anymore. That was fine, though. Because TJ had a plan to speak to him directly. He and his friends just had to tear a damn golden chain down from the heavens. No big deal.

TJ snorted at the thought and smiled.

It wasn't Adeyemi who had the major explaining to do, after all.

It was Eshu.

37

LOW KEY, HIGH KEY

THE NEXT WEEKS WENT ON WITHOUT EVENT—WHERE ORISHAS and Keepers were concerned. As the last of the rainy season died away with the clearing of the November skies, TJ was surprised that much of his waking hours could be dedicated to *actual* study. And good thing, what with December coming and first term exams right around the corner.

Now he had the time to memorize the ins and outs of the three major laws of thermodynamics, which earned a hint of a smirk from Omo of Fon in Elemental Studies. And in Mr. Ikenna's classes of Ecology, TJ was finally able to answer that the lightning bird, *impundulu*, was classified under the category of vampiric creatures, just like the kishi were. TJ would've sworn his response had earned an encouraging coo from the hyena behind his teacher's head. And then, in Ere Idaraya training, Miss Gravés complimented TJ's ability to lift more than one times his body weight. TJ tried to ignore that last one. She could be friendly all she wanted, she wasn't going to get anything out of him. He needed to be sure he could make it up to the Sky Realm without her knowing, without her telling the Keepers, who were probably talking to Eshu the same way Bolawe was talking to Olokun.

Eshu, as TJ had expected, was entirely quiet despite TJ and Elder Adeyemi's best efforts to open communication with the Gatekeeper. Even the Eshu symbol on his finger hardly glowed.

Elder Adeyemi unraveled bit by bit with each of their meetings. It was a subtle transition, one that went from her outfits lacking a certain glamor, to her wearing mismatched stockings, to her head scarfs having hair poking through. She did a good job keeping face for the rest of the academy, but during her private sessions with TJ after long days, the mounting responsibility of Eshu's silence, Olokun's approach, and the still-missing Keepers, well… her being a *bit* off-step was understandable.

"At the very least," she said one day in her office after another failed attempt at calling Eshu, "I managed to get the UCMP to plant a story about an architectural breakthrough in the clouded engineering community. That Olokun statue in Eko Atlantic might go up just in time for February. So there's that going for us. But I still see no reason why we can't get through to Eshu. I'm aligned with him, for skies' sake."

TJ knew the reason they weren't connecting, but he was still hesitant about telling Adeyemi in fear of any more leaks. Still, Elder Adeyemi was right about Olokun and his statue. Though TJ wasn't allowed to step foot out of New Ile-Ife after his ordeal with the Keepers, Eni sent him updates every weekend, whether through water bowl communication, video calls, or over lunch in person whenever she had time off from her School of Sorcery in Egypt.

"You see this foundation near the statue's feet?" Eni told him one day as they shared a plate of *shuku shuku* —coconut balls—at Sweet Tooth Ruth's. She pointed to a video on her phone with a bunch of construction workers building near the docks. "My mom figured out a way to make it seem mundane to any snooping engineers. Some experimental stuff from the clouded in China. That's how she's selling the story of them building it up so quickly. They're having a bit of trouble with this *Guinness Book of World Records* guy, though."

TJ, who sat shoulder-to-shoulder with Eni among the vivid pastels of the cafe, leaned in and took a closer look at her photo gallery. They already had the bottom of the cement fin in place, which was constructed in the middle of the bay. The base of the fin alone stood fifty feet high. But it was beautiful with little cuts in the concrete in the shape of scales.

"That's pretty dope," TJ said. "At least one thing is going right."

Eni smiled at him, flipping her long faux locs over her shoulder. TJ had quickly realized that she changed her hair often — usually because of a photoshoot on a modeling gig. And, as she told him a week prior, if she liked the way her stylists did her hair, she kept it in. That included her nails, which at that time were long and used to snag a shuku shuku. She lifted it over to TJ's mouth.

TJ bit his lip, rubbed the back of his neck, and glanced around the cafe. The cafe wasn't busy, but it also wasn't very large, with only a dozen small tables which were sparsely filled with New Ile-Ife locals. But in particular, near the front of the cafe were Emeka and his girlfriend, who TJ didn't want seeing him being fed. He wasn't comfortable with all the flirty stuff Eni was into, despite most of their dates — no, hangouts — being in the quietest corners of New Ile-Ife hangout spots.

But TJ still didn't have the heart to outright reject her. Ayo said it wasn't a good idea to break her heart when the new Olokun statue was being built, and besides, TJ *liked* Eniola. Not like-like, well, maybe like-like. It was confusing. She was fun to talk to, she always knew the best places to eat, she knew basketball better than TJ did, and yeah... it helped that she was drop-dead gorgeous.

So, awkwardly, he accepted the treat from Eni's fingers — quickly so that any wandering eyes wouldn't see them...

"You're entirely too cute when you blush." Eni grabbed her own shuku shuku and ate with a giggle.

"There's no way I blush," TJ said, but he could feel the heat rising in his cheeks.

Mr. Adebayo, the cafe owner, came shuffling over to their table with another bowl of shuku shuku in hand. He wore a bright green pastel polo shirt with a pink apron, which matched the outdated wallpaper of the cafe.

"Another one, on the house." The bald man slid the bowl across their table with a smile.

Eni lifted her leather purse and fished for money. "We'll pay, sir. We'll pay."

Mr. Adebayo waved away her enchanted cowries. "No, no, no. Mr. Young and his friends don't pay here."

Ever since TJ had started coming to Sweet Tooth Ruth's, he had always gotten free shuku shuku because, apparently, Mr. Adebayo was very fond of his sister Dayo. But this time, there was more to the bowl of sugary coconut balls. Just beneath the pale lemon-colored bowl, a black-and-white photo peeked out, stark against the bright pink table cloth.

Mr. Adebayo must've noticed where TJ's eyes had traveled to because he said, "I told you I would find it. That was taken maybe six or seven years ago—whenever it was your sister was in JS3." TJ slid the photo from under the bowl to get a better look. "See her in the corner there? That's when we had the reopening after that lightning bird incident that burned the place down." A crowd filled the borders of the photo, all of them eagerly awaiting the opening of the store. And just there in the corner was Dayo, tall as ever, with her arm slung around a much shorter girl, a girl TJ knew, except these days she was a young woman and was still hospitalized a few blocks away: Adeola.

TJ drew a thumb over the photo, as if doing that would allow him to feel his sister's skin.

"She was never too far away from that Adeola girl when she was at school." Mr. Adebayo cleared his throat, sounding proud. "Probably because they were both Americans."

"Thank you, sir." TJ inclined his head, already feeling his voice quivering. He definitely didn't want to get teary-eyed around Eni, or Emeka for that matter, who, at that point, had looked over to TJ's table.

How well could the boy read lips, TJ wondered.

"That's yours to keep, Mr. Young." Mr. Adebayo hooked his thumbs into his apron. "Well then, I'll leave you two to it." He gave them a nod, twisted on his heel, and headed back to his check-out counter.

TJ spent the next several moments staring at the photo, savoring that goofy smile spread across Dayo's face, relishing in the wide, excited mouth Adeola held open. He nearly forgot he was in the cafe at all as he imagined the scene in his hand, the delighted laughter that must have permeated the air, the sweet smells of the bakery filling everyone's noses.

Then TJ's thoughts raced back to that backroom with the Keepers, all that blood, all that talk about Dayo and how she had been their promised child.

Was he doing the right thing with Olokun? Did she really want to bring the Orishas back? The idea of the ancient deities returning didn't seem like such a bad thing on paper. And TJ tried over and over to convince himself that the reason Dayo had been killed by the Keepers was that she didn't want them using the Orishas for their own nefarious reasons. Maybe it *was* up to TJ to continue her work. But how when he wasn't even sure what she was up to?

Without even realizing he was speaking aloud, TJ murmured, "I don't even know who she was as a person, really."

Eni, who waited patiently as TJ looked over the photo, reached out and placed her hand over his. Her skin was warm, inviting, nurturing. "For one, she was kind, TJ. She also cut the crust off her bread before she ate. Her Yoruba was still shit even after becoming the Hero of Nigeria. But most of all, she was a friend. I knew her TJ." He glanced up to meet Eni's deep-brown eyes that seemed to twinkle. "She was at Ifa the same time as me, remember? I didn't have classes with her, of course. By the time I was doing my SS entrance exams, she had already graduated. But she still made time for me. For everyone. She made each person she met feel special, feel seen." TJ knew that all too well. That's how she made him feel whenever they spent time together. "It didn't matter if you knew her for a year or for five minutes. That's just the kind of person she was."

But the last three years, though… TJ's own thoughts trailed off.

"You're the same person she was, too, TJ." Eni grasped his wrist tighter. "Not just the lip biting or how much you love peaches. You got the same kind of vibe she had. Like she's right in there." She nodded to TJ's chest.

Eni didn't know how close to the mark she had gotten.

TJ breathed in deep and slow to save himself from losing it. "Thank you, Eni. For real. You been really nice helping me out and talking like this and stuff."

Eni drew her hand away from his wrist. She tapped the table a few times, opened her mouth, closed it, looked up at TJ, looked away. It was the first time he had seen her appear legit nervous. Then she breathed in deep to ask, softly, "TJ, can I ask you something?"

A shiver cascaded down TJ's entire body. He knew something like this would come at some point. They had been texting each other for a month, every weekend while Eni was on punishment. First, it was just to keep in touch about the construction of the statue, but then Eni would want to talk about the latest basketball game or what she did that week out in Egypt. A short hello always ended up becoming a whole thing. And the worst part... TJ didn't mind at all. Eni was super awesome, but he just couldn't bring himself to take steps forward with her.

To avoid the awkward pause that was brewing between them, TJ said a quick, "Sure."

Eni spoke right away, though just as softly as before. "Why haven't you asked me to be your girl yet?"

Now she was playing with her nails, digging her thumb into her forefinger. Despite her utter confidence, getting a question like that out seemed to have disarmed her completely. TJ knew exactly what she was feeling. *He* was the one usually on the other end. *He* was the one who asked girls out and got turned down, from preschool playgrounds all the way to middle school hallways. He knew how much it hurt to be rejected, how much it took to share your feelings with someone. And after getting to know Eni, he knew she was genuine.

So... TJ just... shrugged. "I don't know."

"Is it because you're nervous?" Eni pointed to herself with wide eyes. "Because I get nervous, too. That's how I know I like... that I... you know..."

"Nah, it's not that."

"It's because of my family, huh?" Eni asked. TJ stayed quiet. "I mean, I get it. And I *swear* I'm not even talking to them right now except for the statue. They put us both in terrible positions. But... I don't know. I thought we had a little vibe goin' on."

TJ shook his head. He just had to be honest. "It's not because of your family, Eni."

"What is it? It's because I'm too forward, right? I-I know I can get loud."

"Nah, nothing like that."

"It's because I talk too much, isn't it? I text too many GIFs, don't I?"

"No, no. I love your GIFs. Your GIF choices are always on point!"

"Then what's wrong with me?"

"Nothing! You're perfect." TJ sat forward to make it clear Eni was getting it wrong. There was nothing wrong with *her*; it was all on TJ. "You're really funny. You crack jokes on Ayo more than I do. You're nice and friendly. Easy to talk to. Very bubbly, you know. And... I mean, look at you." TJ gestured to her stylish outfit and hair. "You're, you know... beautiful. You're—"

TJ couldn't finish the rest of what he was saying because Eni leaned forward and pressed her lips against his own, her very *full* lips, her very *soft* lips. TJ froze in place as though her mouth had some sort of ice charm on them, but she moved to his bottom lip where she sort of "hugged" it with her own lips. She tasted sugary and sweet like the shuku shuku they had shared. She had *definitely* kissed before. And even if TJ had had the mind to kiss her back properly, he wasn't sure he could match the experience she clearly possessed. But as soon as the kiss began, it ended. Actually, TJ wasn't sure how long they had been pressed into each other. Time didn't really seem to exist at that moment.

When they pulled apart, Eni was smiling. "Then ask me out already. I swear my family will be left *completely* out of it. I won't even tell them."

It felt like Eni had put a tongue-tied trance on TJ; he still couldn't find his voice.

"Tomori Jomiloju, will you be my boyfriend?"

TJ couldn't speak; he didn't know what to say. He had never been in this position; he wasn't built for this! So he just sat there, catching flies.

"Just say, 'yes,' okay?" Eni said, nodding her head up and down slowly, deliberately, like she was teaching a baby how to speak.

Holding in a breath like he was underwater, TJ let out the worst three-letter word he could say, "Yes."

38

SECOND BASE

TJ SHOULD HAVE SAID NO.

How hard was that? You open your lips, put your tongue to the roof of your mouth, then you let the sound fly.

No.

That's all he could think about as the next week came and went. It was all he could think about when, of course, it got around the academy: TJ Young was dating *the* Eniola Afolabi. It was all he could think about when Manny gave him those terrible frowns anytime Ayo brought up Eni, in any context, even if it *did* have to do with the Olokun statue or anything completely unrelated to TJ being her... boyfriend.

And instead of being a good... *boyfriend*—it was a difficult word to say even in TJ's own head—TJ had plotted how he would give Eni the bad news that he had been put on the spot and made a mistake. He had written several notes sprawled around his dorm room of what he would say, hidden beneath talking books, between empty potion bottles, and laid out against his private desk. He had even written and deleted several text messages until he decided he had to do it the right way.

Breaking up with Eni had to be done in person, face to face, not through some letter like they were in the fourth grade, or over text like some insensitive jerk.

Eni deserved better than that. He had meant all he said about her. She *was* super dope.

Luckily—or unluckily, rather—for the entire month of November, Eni was booked every weekend, either on a video or photoshoot. And anytime she wasn't booked, she was studying for her own exams out in Egypt. During those times, TJ spent his free periods with Manny and Ayo doing as much research about the Sky Realm as possible. That, or he was with Elder Adeyemi, continuing the festivals for Olokun in the village square. The crowds were much smaller, but with the Keepers quiet, more and more people came out. And reports from the Eko Atlantic towers were that the stone hand in the ocean was never covered by the waves—meaning Olokun was happy with what they were doing.

TJ would take any small victory they could.

It was after one of these festivals that TJ had done his dozenth run-through of Dayo's journal, where he found some ancient theories about something called "essence transfer." The mystical technique thought lost to time among diviners was a method in which a spirit could be transferred through certain objects. Dayo had been looking at other magic users around the world and how they expelled certain poltergeists from unwanted locations, like a spirit in the United Kingdom that liked hiding away in dark closets to scare people with their deepest fears. The equations and theories she jotted down went way over TJ's head, so he passed the information along to Ayo.

"Man, TJ," Ayo had said to him as they studied near the three-bridge crossing. "Your sister was really smart. I guess all the brain cells went to her in the family, huh?"

"Hah, hah," TJ had responded.

"Give me a week with this. I'll come up with something."

And just like that, a few days later, Ayo came up with a collection of ancient rituals that might help them expel Oya from Eshu's staff. The only issue—besides the impossible task of parting Eshu with his staff—was that Oya would need to latch onto a new host, which was a bit of a problem. Oya had mounted Manny for only a few seconds. If she did that indefinitely, Manny's body would have perished. That didn't seem like a great idea, so they put their heads together, and during a mile-run in Miss Graves' class, TJ recalled something Eshu said to him at the end of the summer.

"The Joshua body," TJ coughed through heavy breaths. "Eshu said he got it made for him by Obatala, the Creator Orisha. He's up in the Sky Realm too. Maybe we hit him up first before we confront Eshu. Heck, he might even know the essence transfer stuff."

All of their theorizing would've been a lot easier if they could speak to Eshu directly—and if Eshu was still their ally. But when the start of December came around, TJ wondered if he'd ever see Eshu—or Eni—at all. The weekend before the big Sky Realm mission, TJ still hadn't seen either of them, in spirit or the flesh, respectively. But he did find himself alone with Manny for the first time in a long time. They sat with one another at Mami Wata's Eatery while Ayo was off picking up an Oya mask he had ordered from one of the local village crafters.

TJ kept flipping through his phone, between a new draft of a breakup text and the Eko Atlantic countdown, which now read:

Eko Atlantic's Doomsday in 10 weeks, 0 days, 16 hours, 57 minutes, and 7 seconds

TJ put his phone down, lifting his gaze to the dockside eatery. It was an odd location. Unlike Jollof & Jubilee, which had a more traditional restaurant layout, Mami Wata's was slung off a rickety dock. Instead of housing boats, there were floating tables roped off along chipped wooden poles. In between each of the dock lanes, the half-serpent, half-woman waitresses swam, serving vegan fish stew and refreshing zobo hibiscus.

An assortment of enchanted talismans associated with sky magic were scattered about TJ and Manny's splintered table. TJ had spent the past half-hour trying to activate a sunstone in the middle of his talisman. It had been a challenge because the best way to charge the sunstone was to have sun and it was, unfortunately, overcast that day. But anytime light managed to peek through the clouds, TJ could do his work again.

"Shoot, I should've asked Ayo if he told Titi about next week,"

Manny said as she slammed down a talisman with a moonstone — which was giving her just as much trouble for similar reasons.

"He did tell her," TJ answered. "She's coming to help with the ritual. He didn't tell her *why* though. Ruby will be there, too."

"You think that'll be enough?"

"Hard to say. One more might help."

He and Manny were still on shaky ground, but over the last month, they had upgraded to speaking terms, though that only happened if they were speaking about the Sky Realm. TJ would have preferred it if they could go back to making fun of each other's terrible impressions.

Manny rummaged through their collection of books and scrolls until she found a sheet that was entitled *Ibeji, an Orisha of Two*. "I'll try speaking to Titi about getting Emeka to come."

TJ leaned back in his seat to see Emeka with his friends across the dock studying for exams. "That's... still going to be a long shot. Even Umar is giving me the cold shoulder, and his leg healed weeks ago."

"I wish there was another way. I keep comin' back to this stuff about the twin Orishas and how their power doubles with, you know, twins. According to Ruby's calculations, your boost should be just enough with both of them. Then there's the reporter that outright told you to 'seek the twins.' But hey, I'm all ears if you have any other suggestions."

TJ watched as Emeka signed something to his friends that made them laugh. Over the past couple of months, Emeka definitely seemed like he was in a much better mood. A lot of that probably had to do with TJ keeping his distance, though.

"Fine," TJ sighed. "But he can't know it involves me or he'll bounce before anything pops off. And we gotta keep the numbers low so it doesn't get back to Elder Adeyemi or Miss Graves. I've been training with my ritual boosting in my private lessons *and* with Mr. Adebisi's Collaborative Magicks class. I think I can manage it between you, Ayo, Ruby, Titi, maybe Emeka, and this comet we got going overhead. Do you still have those Ashe calculations from Ruby?"

Manny went through their stacks of research again until she found her phone with one of Ruby's formulas saved. Neither TJ nor Manny could make sense of it, but Ayo had simplified the divine math, star charts, and algorithms within a rudimentary app for them. When they inputted the calculations for Emeka's supplied Ashe to the ritual, it came out to be a little more than enough.

Manny threw her chin to the sky. "What you said about the oracles and Adeyemi is right. Oya has been quiet. My wind magic hasn't been as good. Everyone on my crossover team can't summon wind the same. We lost two crossover games back to back to Ghana." TJ had seen a lot of determination from Manny the past few weeks, that warrior coldness that was often attributed to the Windweaver. "I want Oya back, TJ. We just gotta figure out how to find Obatala's palace so he can explain this essence transfer stuff."

Ayo coming up with a solution to Oya's essence transfer was great, but their research on Obatala himself—and his place of residence—was a touch more difficult. The most they could pull from their books and scrolls were a few stories about Obatala being a drunk and creating disabilities in the world. There were a few mentions of him living in the Sky Realm, but no real details about *where* in the Sky Realm he resided.

TJ tapped his temples as something shiny caught the side of his eye in the river. "Maybe we're not looking in the right place."

"But we've been through the whole library twice." Manny dropped her hands on the table in forfeit. "And the librarians don't have anything useful about Obatala when it comes to his palace."

"Maybe we shouldn't be asking the librarians or looking in these books. Wouldn't it make sense to speak to an ancient spirit? Like say…" TJ lifted his chin to the mami wata who was serving Emeka and his friends some tofu fish. Her scaly tail flickered in the brief sunlight.

"Good thinking." Manny smiled. TJ's stomach fluttered. That was one of the first smiles Manny had given him in a long time. He'd forgotten how disarming those dimples of hers could be.

They waved their hands in the air, making it look like they wanted more food. One of the mami watas swam over with a pot of stew in her hands.

"Hey there, children," she said soothingly. "What can I do for you?"

"Hey there, Mami Wata," Manny started—TJ still wasn't used to calling all the mami wata Mami Wata, but it was a cultural norm for them. "So we have this big final project going on at the academy and we were wondering if you could help us?"

"Of course, little twin! What's your question?" All the mami wata had taken to calling Manny their "little twin" because they all had very big hair like her.

"Obatala's Sky Palace." Manny pointed to the sky. "Do you know anything about that?"

"Hmmm, I'm more familiar with the Orisha's Aqua Realm." She flipped a tail fin from the water as though to remind them she didn't have wings. "I'm not quite equipped for the clouds."

"Our question might be simple," TJ added. "We just want to know what Obatala's palace looks like."

"Oh, I see. Well, that's simple. It's the biggest one. He's very important up there, after all. Like the Yemoja or Olokun of the skies. I've heard they have a bunch of floatin' islands."

"But… nothing more specific than that?"

"Well, I hear that those wretched impundulu like to nest near his neighborhood. You see, the Sky Realm likes to move a lot, so no one's home sticks to one place for very long. But those lightning birds always put themselves close to Obatala. If you find them, then you're in the ballpark."

"Thanks," TJ said.

"Was there anything else you need to know?"

"Actually, there's one more thing." Manny swung her legs around the bench to face the mami wata more fully. "Have you ever heard of spirits being trapped in a… magical object, and maybe how to get something out of that magical object?"

"Like one of them genies and their lamps?"

"Eh, kinda. Something more like a…"

"Like a staff…" TJ finished for her. He was liking this moment with Manny, getting information out of an unsuspecting party. It felt like being back at camp.

Mami Wata continued to stir her pot of stew. "Hmmm, there is an old tale, very old… I'm not sure it works with staffs though.

But to extract a source, it's best done by transferring that energy into a new vessel."

An idea lit in TJ's mind. "You mean if the staff acts like a host, then something else can house that spirit in a transfer?"

"I believe so."

TJ traded a look with Manny before saying with a sidelong glance, "Hypothetically, let's say that energy was being transferred between a staff and, say... a human body? Would that work?"

"That would be extremely dangerous for the human host. You'd surely need an empty husk for something like that to work."

And TJ knew of a certain Orisha who dealt *exactly* in empty husks, or at least he hoped so. When Eshu left Joshua's body that's essentially what he left over.

"Even so, you must remember," Mami Wata added, "You'd need a huge energy source to do somethin' like that. Advanced magic. Collegiate magic. You two can't be more than ten or eleven human years, no?"

"What? I just turned fifteen!" TJ exclaimed.

"And I'll be fourteen soon," Manny chimed in.

"Oh right, I do mix up mortal years quite often. Apologies. This one," Mami Wata pointed to TJ, "is quite tall, isn't he? Anyway, if there is nothing left to ask, I've still got a few orders to get out."

"That was great, big twin." Manny waved goodbye. "Thanks again."

"Anytime. I hope you pass your exams!"

TJ and Manny waited for Mami Wata to swim off to help the next of her customers before returning to their table and scrambling for one of their books about transmutation. Manny, who had been doing most of the rummaging that day, was the first to find it.

"Doctor Pierre," Manny asked the leather-bound cover. "Is there anything in this book about human bodies as hosts for a transmutation ritual?"

"There are several passages in my work," the book answered. "Would you be interested—"

TJ's phone buzzed from somewhere underneath the forest of books.

The book shuddered. "Sorry about that, that tickled a little. As I was saying, would you be interested in the biological or —"

Again, TJ's phone buzzed.

"Okay, that's just irritating. Would one of you pick that up?"

TJ clenched up. "Sorry, sorry, I'll get it." He fished for his phone, finding it under an enchanted bangle and another scroll. The book kept speaking to Manny as TJ checked his the screen.

> *Eni: wish u were here.*
> *Eni: im bored out of my mind at this shoot. so. many. resets. wyd?*

TJ replied quickly.

> *TJ: studying up. first-term exams coming.*
> *Eni: when i get done ill go over notes with you. i passed all those exams ez. i can be a big help* 😌
> *TJ: bet! and thanks! u tryin to meet me in NIL?*

So I can tell you I totally made a mistake and break up with you face to face, TJ thought. His heart started a drumline against the inside of his chest when the three message dots from Eni started to bounce on screen.

> *Eni: cant. im stuck in giza this weekend. what about next saturday?*
> *Eni: wait! wait! im lying. next weekend is no good either. family is going to zanzibar.*
> *Eni: ooo ooo maybe you can come?*
> *TJ: cant. adeyemi wont let me leave NIL until we go home*
> *Eni: ugh! we'll figure something out. maybe i can convince my mom to let me see you in LA during holiday. but i have to actu-ally talk to her first* 😩 *ttyl* 😘 *?*
> *TJ: yea, ttyl*

"So that's going well, then?" Manny asked as she finished

jotting down some notes about biological and metaphysical transformations. How had she known he was texting Eni? "So she's
really your girlfriend now?"

"Erh… yeah, I guess so." TJ tried to speak as little about Eni
around Manny as possible. Over the past few weeks, it felt like he
and Manny were finally *starting* to be normal around each other
again. But whenever Eni came up in any capacity, that all seemed
to shatter. So it was strange Manny was the one bringing her up
at all.

"So…" Manny flipped her hair over her shoulder to get a
better look at TJ. That's when TJ knew she wanted his attention.
"What's it like being with her?"

"Um… you really want to know about that stuff?" This was
not at all what TJ thought she'd ask.

"Yeah… I mean, I get it, she's funny, mad smart, *and* beautiful,
well, gorgeous really, those cheekbones, her lips… I mean, even
I'd…" Manny frowned before shrugging awkwardly. "Look,
c'mon, this is what friends are for, right? Talking about who we're
dating and all that… stuff? I don't know."

Maybe Manny was just trying to be an adult about it? That or
she really had gotten over it? Did TJ even want that?

"Come on. Don't make it weird." Now Manny had her body
fully turned to TJ. She even pushed the books and papers aside,
her leg hooking over the bench they shared.

TJ drew back a little on the bench, looking around to make
sure no one was listening. The place had emptied a bit since he
had last looked. The sun was starting to set, and the overcast sky
appeared more like a dim shadow now. Emeka and his friends
were leaving; one of the elderly couples was turning in too. Once
they all left the dockside, TJ turned back to Manny with a huge
faux sigh. "Fine, I'll play along. Don't tell Ayo, but we've been to
second base."

Manny's neck went through a whole-ass aerobic routine and
her words came out stretched. "Well, *excuuuse* me." She didn't
quite meet TJ's eyes with her next words though. "You know
something. Everyone has a different definition of bases. You're
gonna have to be a bit more detailed about what you mean
here."

"Well, she's older so she's been teaching me stuff. According to her, second base is... well, it's better if I show you."

Manny's head darted around the dock just like TJ had a moment prior. Then she lowered her voice. "What you mean, show me?"

"Apparently, I was doing it all wrong." TJ faked a yawn and interlaced his hands behind his head. "C'mon. What are friends for?"

"Uh... would your *girlfriend* be okay with this?"

"Don't make it weird." TJ dropped his hand, palm up, on the table. "Hold my hand."

Manny parted her lips a little, just a little. Without moving her head, she glanced down at TJ's open palm and then back at TJ. A light giggle escaped her and she did her best to reel it in with a smirk. TJ didn't know how he didn't giggle along with her, but his lips were a steady line and he threw up a single eyebrow in a challenge. Manny rolled her eyes and took his hand, placing her whole palm over his own.

Her hand was soft and her grasp firm. Firm, but not harsh. That warrior energy she had been keeping up the past few weeks seemed to melt away into TJ's palm. Waves of jitters prickled from their handhold, all the way up TJ's arm, down his back, through his legs, and down to his toes.

"Now, you see how you're cupping my whole hand. That's wrong." TJ moved his hand so that his fingers interlaced with Manny's. "*That's* how you're supposed to hold someone's hand."

Where before TJ's whole body was taken by jitters, now it was cascading with a full-on surge of pure, unadulterated awesomeness. It was just like back on the plane when Manny decided to use him as a pillow. It felt right. More than right. Holding her hand like this had no business feeling so good. But it did.

And TJ liked it; better yet, he knew Manny did, too.

Her face was flushed of color, her interlaced fingers held on tighter than she really needed to. TJ wanted so badly to tell her he intended to break it off with Eni the next time they met up, tell her he made a mistake, tell her that Manny was the one he wanted to go "second base" with. And then...

"Bullshit!" Manny drew her hand away from TJ, laughing nervously. "You know damn well that's not no second base."

TJ laughed, too. That was the best way to get out of that corner of a conversation, but he wasn't sure he really wanted to get out of it at all. Besides, they had been talking about *him* for far too long; now it was time to turn the tables.

"So what about this mystery dude from New York you never told me about?" If the topic of Eni had been something pushed to the don't-bring-it-up category, then Manny's boyfriend back in New York was in the abyss of the this-doesn't-exist category.

Manny waved a dismissive hand. "He been askin' me out since we was in pre-school. I just finally gave in. He's actually… kinda cool. We've only been face timing, though."

"Come on, Manny. By this point, I know when you're lying."

"Lying? I *am* going out with him."

TJ let a beat pass so that Manny could correct herself or crack a joke. But she was dead serious. Her skin scrunched into elevens on her forehead and that warrior spirit sprang back out instantly.

"Are you just saying that because of Eni?" TJ asked.

Manny scoffed, "No, why would I say that? What are you tryin' to come at me with?"

"Nothing, it's just weird. Not a single word about this guy and all of a sudden—"

"*I'm* not being weird; *you're* being weird." There it was. It was like the last few minutes hadn't happened at all. Manny crossed her arms and swung her legs back under the table.

"Sorry…" TJ said quietly. "I didn't mean to…"

Manny sucked her teeth. "Nothing to be sorry about." Her tone made it clear there was *definitely* something to be sorry about.

The book Manny still had opened cleared its throat. "So, young lady. Did you still want me to explain metaphysical transmutation… or did you need me to recommend literature on… hand-holding?"

Manny groaned, rolled her eyes, and slammed the book shut, to which the book said a muffled "ouch." Then Manny hurriedly gathered up the research items, scrolls, books, and notepads.

"Where are you going?" TJ asked.

"I think it's better if I do the rest of this alone. I'll let you and Ayo know what I come up with later." Before TJ could stop her, she stomped right by him. A cold wind followed along with her and he expected it was more than just the chilling temperature of the setting sun.

TJ found himself alone at Mami Wata's until near closing, thinking of how he screwed that whole thing up. A terrible emptiness filled him as he played back his conversation with Manny in his head. And when Ayo arrived with a handful of masks associated with Obatala, TJ didn't even respond to him when he excitedly explained how he had got the items for free because he said he was friends with "Ifedayo's little brother". Ayo probed TJ about what was bugging him, and when he said, "it has to do with Manny, doesn't it?" TJ walked off back toward the Ifa Academy dirt patch, through the Summoning Stone, straight to his dorm, and under his blankets.

That night and every night leading up to the Sky Realm mission, TJ dreamed of all sorts of things: Eni showering him with kisses, which led to Manny shunning him. Olokun drowning TJ in a place not unlike the Aqua Realm with its glowing fish and dark pits. But most interesting was a location filled with floating islands, waterfalls falling from their sides. And at the end of every dream, a giant with stark-white skin and iris-less eyes would say to him in a deep and gentle voice, "Hello, Tomori Jomiloju. We will meet each other soon."

39

A BRAID OF GOLD

IFA ACADEMY DESIGNATED THE FOLLOWING WEEK FOR THE first term exams for JS3 students from Monday to Wednesday. To enter into second term, a student had to pass seventy percent of their classes at a rate of a "C+" average. By the Grace of the Orishas, TJ had passed all of them, more than one with flying colors, including Elemental Studies, where he squeaked out a "B+", which earned a curt nod of approval from Teacher Omo of Fon.

By the time Sky Realm Thursday rolled around, TJ was feeling pretty good about himself, save for the whole Manny cold-shoulder situation. The foundation of success for their ritual was that they'd all be in sync, and nothing TJ did that week helped that case. So he just hoped that Manny's general determination to see Oya again would be enough.

Most of Thursday morning was free periods, where TJ and Ayo went over their plans and equipment for any imperfections. By the time they arrived at the top of Oracle Rock in the late afternoon, TJ could recite their ritual backwards and forwards.

The late Thursday sunset over Oracle Rock outlined the thick clouds above with vermillion highlights. The crags of the Rock were only just cooling from a long, hot day. Little bush rats poked their noses out from under rubble and grass roots. TJ was as pleased as them for the cooling rocks as he slipped on his all-white robe over his painted skin.

Manny, Ayo, and Ruby were mostly quiet as they gathered their ritual items and put on their own garb. Classes had ended hours ago, and it was just the four of them up on Oracle Rock now—well, just them and all the animal skin tents that dotted the lofty peak. Each of them had something associated with Obatala or the Sky Realm. TJ was reminded of the summer at the end of Camp Olosa when they were all decked out in oversized masks and robes, ready to summon TJ's sister. Now they were preparing for a much different endeavor, under very different circumstances. Circumstances TJ didn't like one bit.

Manny had barely even looked at him when they met with the others near the oracle tents.

Ruby glanced at her watch, which, like Bolawe's from the summer, depicted the milky way instead of clock hands. TJ still couldn't understand how to tell time from it, but as a star twinkled in and out on the watch face, Ruby said, "Only a few minutes before we'll be able to see Wild-Two in the sky. TJ, you'll be strongest when it reaches its zenith. You said a set of twins were comin' to help, yes?"

TJ turned to Ayo. "Where's Titi and Emeka?"

"Ah, you know Nigerians don't show up on time for anything."

TJ grabbed at Ayo's robes frantically. "This is serious, man."

"Which is why I told Titi to be here at five-thirty instead of six."

"It's six o-five." Manny tapped at her own watch.

Ayo got red in the face. "I-it might not be so bad. If your training with Adeyemi and Omo of Fon is going well, the comet's natural powers should be enough."

TJ shook his head and the beads of his mask clacked together loudly. "We can't leave this to chance, man. Every little bit helps. We were lucky enough to get Titi. No one else in the academy wants anything to do with me."

He twisted to Ruby to get some backing, but she sat hunched over her tablet as she did last-minute calculations. TJ was wise enough not to disturb her. So he let Ayo go, pivoted on his heel, then counted to ten so he wouldn't explode. The counting didn't help but the tall trees of Ifa Academy out in the distance aided in quelling his boiling blood a bit. The trees listed peacefully in the late afternoon wind, with sparkles of golden hour shining on their edges. Their rippling effect brought calm to TJ as he was reminded of the ripples in Elder Adeyemi's cavern office.

"Don't sweat it, Teej." Ayo's tone was genuine, but it only served to irritate TJ. He was tired of Ayo being so cavalier about everything. He wasn't the one who got captured by the Keepers. He wasn't the one who had the responsibility of taking down Olokun. He wasn't the one who was the key to crossover to the Sky Realm. That brief moment of meditation went to complete waste as TJ's nostrils flared.

"No, I should sweat it." TJ rushed Ayo again and grabbed his robes more roughly. "And you should, too, man."

"Nah, nah, I mean, look behind you."

TJ let go of Ayo to see Titi and Emeka climbing the last slope up Oracle Rock with all-white aso oke robes. The moment Emeka caught sight of TJ, he groaned and turned on his heel. Titi grabbed him by the arm and started signing vigorously at him. Emeka's hands shouted back with a reply TJ didn't completely understand, but the meaning was clear: *I'm not doing shit with that guy around.*

TJ brushed past Ayo who murmured a "sorry, I thought Emeka would be cool with you by now."

Jogging, TJ reached the twins to block Emeka's way back down the rock path. He lifted his hands and spoke loud and clear. "I know! I know you hate me! I can't get your friend back into the academy. The reason I probably got accepted to Ifa Academy at all in the first place is because I... I got these... different powers. Different Ashe. What we're doing here is important. If we don't do this ritual, the Keepers are going to bring back Olokun and drown Eko Atlantic. We need to cross over to the Sky Realm to get help from Oya and Shango."

There was a long pause. Ayo coughed awkwardly behind TJ.

"Oh, right..." TJ trailed off. "Titi, can you tell Emeka what I said?"

"*I'm* still trying to process what you just said!" Titi looked to

Ayo in particular. "I thought this was just for a project. You do know that one-hundred percent of people who've crossed over have come back crazy, right? Not ninety-nine-point-nine. One-hundred!"

TJ nearly forgot that Titi kept track of stats like a human CPU. What he didn't expect, though, was the hurt on her face, told through her upturned brows and parted lips. The expression sent a spike through TJ's chest. He had been most worried about Emeka, but Titi could have called off the whole thing, too. It was odd, though. It seemed like she and Ayo had just hooked up every so often. He hadn't thought she cared about him so deeply.

"Well… there's something I didn't tell you." Ayo cracked his knuckles nervously. "There's three diviners in history who have come back okay." He jutted his eyes between TJ and Manny, then he jabbed a thumb toward TJ. "Really, because of this guy."

"So that's how you got into Ifa?" Titi crossed her arms and scrutinized TJ. Emeka mirrored his twin's stance. "You got some special Orisha Realm crossover magic or something?"

"Or something." TJ stared up into the sky. It was still free of any comets. "Could you explain it to Emeka, please?"

Titi sighed, pushing her glasses up her nose. "Do you really have to do this?" Her question was to Ayo, not TJ. "Why can't Elder Adeyemi do it? She's always got those government people around. This isn't kid stuff, Ayodeji."

"Some of those UCMP people might be workin' with the Keepers. We can't let her know on this one. Plus," Ayo grabbed her hand and jutted his head toward Ruby, "we got the best oracle in Ifa helpin' us. Everything will be fine. For real, for real. We've done it before and made it back. I mean, I don't *remember* how we did it. But TJ's my boy. He'll take care of us."

Titi looked wholly unconvinced, and it was Manny who approached with her Obatala mask in both hands. "Last time we crossed over, we were chasin' Keepers and Orishas. This time we're only going to talk."

"*She's* the one chaperoning this whole thing?" Titi eyed Oracle Ruby up and down with utter skepticism. "What are you, like, nineteen? Twenty?"

"Oh, that's quite flattering." Ruby exaggerated a hand to her chest and batted her eyelashes. "I turn twenty-three in the new year, love. And trust me. So long as you and your twin support us tonight, this thing will run smooth as butter over a scone."

"We have to do this, Titi." TJ lowered his voice to give it more gravity. "I know this is coming on fast. But if we don't figure this out, everyone in Eko Atlantic is in danger. Maybe everyone in Lagos."

Titi glanced between them all as though waiting for one of them to jump up and say "just kidding" but each of them held their faces firm. So... she groaned. "Ugh... fine. On it."

Titi and Emeka threw up their hands again with great animation, clearly arguing. It was a lost cause. TJ could tell. Emeka would never help them, and his shoulders slumped for it.

"Come on." TJ spun to Ruby, who glanced between the sky, her tablet, and her watch every few seconds. "Let's get ready. The comet will come at any time now."

As Titi and Emeka continued to argue, the rest of them got ready for the final steps of their ritual. TJ put on his Obatala mask of hanging beads as Ruby explained the process. They would each need to hold each other's hands, then raise them aloft as she led them in an ancient chant to Obatala, which they would need to repeat. It was mostly a request of the Great Deities' grace and guidance down the path of the golden road. As they began, TJ could see Ashe spring from each of their chests and up into the heavens.

"Open to us," they all said softly. "Show us the way. Give us your golden path, Most Gracious One."

Unlike the other chants they had done, which included strong voices and an almost sing-songy presence, now they were almost whispering. Obatala was one of the more reserved Orishas, and TJ could feel it in the magic they stirred. Instead of swelling with great energy, like an adrenaline rush after a good sprint, the sensation was more like the ease of getting a head massage.

TJ's mind went back to all his exercises with Adeyemi over the past few months. They had been working with water, but TJ found it easy to translate the idea of the ripples from a center to the ebb of wind cycling between them. He'd bet anything he had his connection with Manny to thank for that.

He was glad he was right about her determination to see Oya again.

"Well, this is new. I've never felt such power before," Ruby said in awe, her eyes closed and head to the clouds and twinkling stars. "I was only sixty percent sure this could work. Elder Adeyemi was right about you, love."

But TJ didn't share in her confidence. The mystical tether that bonded them was reaching up and up and up, but it was barely approaching the clouds. Even with their enchanted necklaces, bangles, and masks, it wasn't enough. Even with the approaching comet, it wasn't enough. TJ did his best to recall his lessons with Adeyemi, to find the balance in everyone's Ashe and push it out again.

But he just wasn't strong enough to do it.

"Ayo, take my hand!" Titi shouted, running over to them. Ayo and Manny broke hands and let Titi join between them. Emeka still stood away from them with crossed arms. When everyone reconnected again and followed Ruby's renewed chant, the tether bloomed once more between them, this time reaching higher into the sky. The blaze of the comet, millions of miles in space, brushed across TJ's skin like a new summer's day. He harnessed that energy and let it stretch straight up. Their collective tip of energy touched a star high above, and that star split open and widened like an expanding balloon. From its bright depths, a chain fell from its mouth.

A braid of gold.

TJ let out a suppressed breath. His mental fatigue and concentration sent spikes through his head.

"It's working!" Manny called out. "Everyone, concentrate! It's working."

The chain fell and fell and fell, but just as it reached a hundred feet above them, it stopped.

TJ could have screamed.

"What happened?" Ayo gasped. "Did we do something wrong?"

Some sort of resistance tugged at TJ's chest, like the connection between the group and the chain had been blocked. Something was wrong. But he didn't care anymore. The damn chain was right there. They had to get to it.

Wind tickled the back of his neck, making his hairs standup. But instead of brushing from side to side like it usually did, it drifted from his nape and up to the back of his head. The sensation guided his head up to the heavens, to the bottom of the golden chain.

Was that Dayo? What was she trying to say to him?

He realized then, with sudden clarity, what he needed to do.

It didn't matter how dangerous it was.

"Let go of my hands. I gotta go for the chain!"

"What?" Ruby broke her chant, and the chain rose up and away from them, back to the star. "The hell are you on about, love? The plan is to wait for the chain to drop fully."

"It won't. Not without Emeka. No time to explain." TJ let go of everyone's hands, shot his palms down at the ground, and cast wind from them, just like Teacher Omo of Fon had shown him. The propulsion sent him flying high, his robes snapping around him like a superhero's cape. Before anyone could stop him, he was already ten feet in the air, twenty feet, thirty feet. His mask fell from his face; he didn't hear it crash below. And then... he started to fall.

His gut ran up his throat and queasiness dominated his stomach as the stars grew smaller in the sky.

So close! TJ was so close. But that was as high as he could air-step.

"Gotcha!" Ayo said as he caught TJ mid-air, then pushed him along his own set of air-steps. "Your air-steppin' is pretty shit, bruh."

Ayo's efforts only lasted a few moments, though, and they both tumbled downward again.

"And yours ain't much better," Manny called from below as she too pushed the boys along her new, much stronger, set of air-steps.

TJ used Manny's deep ties to the wind to generate more air-steps for them to climb, but each new one he manifested was weaker and weaker. As far up as they were—TJ didn't want to think how far the drop was—it still didn't cut it. The chain slinked up and away faster than they could climb. Teacher Omo of Fon said it was dangerous to air-step so high in the sky, especially for novices that didn't know how to break their falls. And they were about to find out how painful their naivety would cost them.

TJ's skin started to split like dry skin being stretched. Ashe tore through him with searing white pain as he forced out each new air-step, as he desperately tried to hold on to the Ashe of the initial ritual. The chain was *right* there. Just a few feet from his fingertips. He could *see* it, could *feel* its divine heat.

He. Just. Couldn't. Reach. It.

And then, without warning, the chain was falling once more, just for a moment, just an inch, just *enough* for TJ to get his hand around its lowest link. And once its heat raced through his palm, his dwindling Ashe renewed. He didn't have to air-step anymore. Now he just had to hold on for dear life.

"Grab on!" TJ called back to his friends. Ayo grabbed one of TJ's legs and Manny grabbed onto the other. Shockingly, their weight felt like nothing.

"We did it! We did it! Wahooo!" Ayo screamed as they shot through the sky.

Manny was just swearing up a storm that would've put a sailor to shame.

TJ looked down at the Oracle Rock, far, *far* below them. He could still make out three figures down there holding each other's hands. Not two figures. Not just Ruby and Titi. But three.

TJ wished he could sign a "thank you" down to Emeka. But he didn't dare risk the gesture as he watched the trio get smaller and smaller on the ground. TJ couldn't be sure with how far away they were, but it looked like Emeka's jaw had fallen wide open. He didn't know if the boy had done it for him, or because he didn't want to see Manny or Ayo fall down, but TJ appreciated the help either way.

Grabbing each link hand by hand, he lifted himself higher and higher still. Manny and Ayo joined him until, before long, all they knew were clouds, stars, and sweat.

40

WAY UP HIGH

EVERYTHING AROUND TJ WAS WHITE.

Cloud mist was thick in the air and it slicked his palms, making the climb difficult. The farther up he and his friends climbed, the harder it became. TJ's Ashe slipped from his fingers and out of his toes like a leaking pipe. Gym class at his old middle school had nothing in comparison to this golden rope. And with each grunt and strain, the painted dots on his skin smudged away into jagged streaks. He and his friends probably appeared more like zebra than Obatala devotees.

"Okay... maybe I should have.... focused more... in Miss G's class," Ayo cried out from below. TJ glanced down briefly to see his friend's glasses nearly slipping off his nose.

Manny gave Ayo a strained laugh, clearly tired herself. "Oh... if she could... see us... now."

"She'd go straight to Bolawe... and tell him... what we're up to," TJ said bitterly, his last words a fuel against his failing grip. The adrenaline that came with reaching the chain was quickly being replaced with nightmare fuel. Fear dominated his every grip. Would that be the one to make him slip? What about his feet? If one of them didn't hook in properly, he'd lose his balance.

Worst yet, TJ couldn't sense his Ashe at all.

One small mistake meant death, and seemingly no way to brace for his fall. Dread shrouded his mind, and he tried to break it up by focusing on his hand over the other. But anxiety always won out when fatigue reminded him how easily he could lose his grip.

"I might need to... tap out." TJ peeked down at Ayo again to find his friend had stopped climbing altogether. "You two... got this." Ayo looked below him. There was nothing but endless clouds. Stopping was *not* an option. "Actually... I don't think... I will be able to... get down—Holy shit! Where did the rest of the chain go!?"

That seemed to revitalize his friend. Ayo was right; he was the last one on the chain and there was nothing below him but a few golden links beneath his trailing aso oke.

"Everyone, lose your robes!" TJ ordered, already slipping his off.

TJ had wondered if something like this would happen. That the test up the chain would be *this* difficult. That they would truly be tested for their worthiness. When they first read about the Sky Realm, they figured they'd have to go through some sort of hardship, just like when they had to be drowned to get to the Aqua Realm.

But knowing there was a test was one thing, actually making the climb was another.

"Ugh!" Ayo groaned. "I... prefer... drowning. That was... much... faster... than this. And my asthma... is being... a little b—"

Ayo was climbing, but nowhere near fast enough. The golden links were fading out below Ayo's panting form.

"You have to keep up, Ayo! The chain's fading!" TJ had stopped climbing to shout back to him and his muscles screamed with relief. "Here, I'll boost you."

"Bruh... how are you... going to... boost... my biceps?"

"Good point." TJ shook life back into his deadening fingers. "I can't feel my Ashe... at all... can you?"

"Nothin'." Manny shook her head. "Maybe we can... let go and... air-step... the rest of the way."

"No... that'll break the test." TJ took in deep breaths and glanced high above. There didn't seem to be an end to the chain. More clouds swallowed it above.

"Ah!" Ayo cried out as one of his hands slipped. Manny reached down to him to hold on to his wrist, but she lost her grip too and hung from a single arm.

"Manny! Ayo!" TJ shouted. They were going to fall if TJ didn't do anything, but TJ couldn't even begin to think about what he could do to help. He was ready to fall himself.

Panic rushed through his veins as he searched all around for anything that could assist them, but there was nothing but that wicked bright white, those serene clouds that seemed entirely disinterested in the mortals that were all about to fall to their deaths.

Ayo only had three fingers left on his grip, his plump face pinched tightly at the strain. TJ could only think of one thing he could do, but it was *completely* insane, which is why he knew he had to do it.

TJ took in a deep sigh and let go of the chain. His body emptied of all feeling as he fell past Manny and then Ayo. He reached out his hand to grab the last few links of the chain. He barely got his grip around the last one with his right hand, then, after some terrifying, heart-stopping flailing, he got his left hand around it as well.

"What… the hell… was that?" Ayo asked, exasperated.

"Shut up… and put your legs… on my shoulders." TJ clenched his jaw against his friend's weight. "Climb up and… help… Manny."

Ayo regained his balance, placing both his feet on TJ's shoulders. TJ felt his skin start to rip apart. At first, he thought he was losing skin on his palm because of how tightly he gripped the golden links. But the sensation was something else, something entirely different. Despite him feeling nothing of his Ashe, there was a strange mystical energy coursing through his arms and legs as he climbed. Above, Ayo helped Manny get her balance as TJ shook under both of their weight.

"Climb!" TJ shouted at them. The golden links cut into his palms, his limbs shook so violently, and his head grew so light-headed he thought he could pass out. But where blood should have slid from his cracking hands, there was nothing. Instead, his hands glowed a bright, painful light. "Ahhh!"

With TJ's last shout, saliva spilled from his mouth, snot hung from his nose. They had to make it! They had to get up to the Sky Realm. They couldn't fall and break all their bones.

TJ *wouldn't* allow it.

A familiar wind brushed along TJ's neck... and a voice spoke his name.

Before TJ could figure out who the voice belonged to, before he could even catch his breath, all around them a collection of floating islands manifested. Some were connected by long, precarious bridges, others hanging by their lonesome. It was like the islands had broken off from landmasses and risen up with exposed earth and roots underneath each. A few of the islands even had waterfalls falling over the sides of the green tops and down into the clouds. Floating spirits wafted around the islands, too. Were they ghosts? That wind that spoke to him... was that Oya... or was that Dayo?

"Look up! Look up!" Manny shouted. "The chain ends up there. Do you see it?"

TJ didn't want to break his concentration as he climbed. He kept his face looking out to the islands and the floating spirits. In the distance, he could've sworn he saw some lightning birds crackling the sky with shock waves as they flapped their wings. But Ayo said, "Yeah, I see it. Did we do it? Did we make it?"

"I-I can't reach it," Manny strained out.

"What are you saying?" Ayo called after her. "Just grab the edge."

"I can't. It's like some invisible wall is blockin' me."

"I got it!" TJ groaned, finally braving a glance to see something invisible was indeed blocking Manny's hand. "I'm the key, remember?"

"Here, Manny, help me get TJ up there." Ayo's short arms shook as he pulled TJ up the line along with Manny. It was a struggle, but TJ was able to touch the same area Manny did, and, just like that, the barrier above them broke apart.

Elation flared in TJ's chest as he finally met solid ground in the form of his very own floating island, filled with grass, stone, and moss. The golden chain was tied around a totem in the shape of two identical monkeys. Barring their teeth in a static pose, the primates pulled up on the golden braid. The chain snaked through theirs hands, its gilded sheen contrasting vividly against the totem's slate wood.

The air up there was thin, making it very difficult for TJ to catch his breath. Flat on his back, TJ felt Ashe roiling through his body once more and the fatigue he had felt before seemed like a distant memory. He opened his cracked palms to examine the damage he did to them. They weren't bleeding as they should've been. They felt raw and scabbed, but instead of red lines or puss-filled cracks, there was only that bright white that seemed to cool and settle like lava into TJ's palms. The same hue of that Eshu symbol tattooed on his finger. The white streaks left behind were like paint stuck to his skin, like the smudges on his body that used to resemble circles.

With energy renewed thanks to the mystical island, TJ turned to help a grunting Manny, who struggled to lift herself over the edge of the floating cliff. But as soon as her feet made contact with flat ground, she let out a yelp. Covering her face, she continued letting out a long, unbroken bellow.

"What's going on up there?" Ayo called out from below.

TJ, covering his ears with one hand and using the other to lift Ayo, said, "I don't know. Get up here and help me with her."

But as soon as Ayo reached the top, he too covered his face and yelled just as long and loud as Manny. TJ stood there dumb-struck as his friends threw their hands over their faces in horror. Thankfully, their screams weren't indefinite. When Manny ran out of breath in her throat, her face transformed into an expression of daze. A few seconds after that, Ayo looked just as confused. And then...

"Oh, my god..." Manny breathed out. "I remember! I remember everything. The submarine. My cousin. Olokun's palace. The fire snakes! I remember it all!"

"That's great." TJ said, still confused. "But what about all that screaming? Are you okay?"

Ayo rubbed his hand under his glasses and groaned. "The last thing we remember from the Aqua Realm... that's why we screamed. We were hit with that big white light when we were helping Bolawe, remember?"

TJ thought back to the Aqua Realm. They had teamed up to save Bolawe from Adeola—who was trying to roast him with a fire spell. Thinking on it with the benefit of hindsight, TJ should've let her do it. But that's not how it went down. Instead, TJ boosted his friends, Manny in particular, and she blasted Adeola with a huge counter-curse, a bright-white energy that exploded like a dying star. TJ was unaffected by the odd and unique spell, but his friends fell unconscious and didn't wake until they left the Aqua Realm. He had completely forgotten that the last thing they would've remembered from the place was that enormous blazing light.

"Are you two okay?" TJ asked, rubbing his temples.

Ayo looked at TJ like he was nuts. "Are *we* okay? Bruh, you was the one doin' your best Hulk impression underneath us. What was that?"

"I don't know," TJ said, sounding defeated. He sat down and crossed his legs on the island, watching the clouds go by. "Our Ashe was gone on that chain. But... I felt something, heard something that pushed me."

"More 'in-between' Orisha-but-not-Orisha stuff?" Manny asked.

"Knowing me... probably."

"Well... thank you, TJ." Manny walked over and wrapped her arms around him. "Let us know when you're gonna do somethin' stupid first though, okay?"

"Ah, what's the fun in that?" He cracked a smile, more out of awkwardness than anything else. But he was glad he did because Manny treated him with a smirk of her own.

For a long moment, they all sat there to take in their surroundings. They were nothing but specks among the great landmasses around them, among the colossal clouds that swallowed nearly everything, with only pockets of lavender hues peeking through. It was quiet, save for the most gentle of breezes, and the space brought a profound morsel of peace to TJ's spirit.

"All right." TJ clapped his hands together. "Now that we all got our memories back, which way should we go in all this?"

Ayo shuffled cautiously to the island's edge, his hand covering his eyes from the radiant periwinkle sky. "Mami Wata mentioned Obatala has the biggest palace, yeah?"

Manny joined him, squinting into the distance where castles, mansions, and towers peaked through mountains of clouds. "Yeah, but from where we're standing, they *all* look huge."

"That way!" Ayo sounded only halfway sure. "That big ol' island to the left next to the cloud that looks like that hyena on the back of Mr. Ikenna's head."

"Well, that's as good of a guess as we'll get. Let's go." Manny teetered at the edge of the island and looked down.

"Yeah, but how?" TJ asked. "We're kind of stuck."

Manny looked over her shoulder and smiled. She jumped where she stood and a few air-steps manifested beneath her. "We got our Ashe back. It's obvious, isn't it?" She vaulted off the island and out of view. TJ and Ayo gasped and rushed over to see where she fell. When they saw her, she was jogging left and right along the clouds, air-stepping like she was playing a game of crossover.

Ayo whistled. "Sometimes, I forget how much of a badass that girl is. Maybe you chose the wrong one, bruh. I mean, my cousin's dope and everything but—"

"Shut up, man." TJ pushed Ayo off the island.

Ayo laughed the whole way down as he righted himself on a cloud. The cloud sort of caught him in its grasp, as though it were some bounce house, then it shot him back up in the air. Once Ayo figured out the balance, he made his way after Manny, who had really started to catch some air with some of her jumps. She had to be vaulting at least twenty or thirty yards up at a time. She giggled and screamed with excitement and joy, her voice filling the Sky Realm unabated. Ayo was chuckling too with each of his jumps, his loose box braids floating up and down atop his head.

"All right," TJ said to himself. "Let's have some fun."

He stepped off the island. Concentrating on his Ashe, thinking of the Orishas he was there to save, he caught the clouds under his feet and found balance. The first cloud he caught felt almost like a pillowed trampoline. He let his knees dip and spring up, lifting him into the highest jump he had ever experienced, even bigger than the one he did to reach the golden chain, bigger than

Manny's jump even. Then he remembered what Ol' Sally said back at camp. In the Orisha Planes, he was more powerful; Ashe flowed more easily.

Wind smacked against TJ's face so hard, his eyes watered. His heart pounded so fast it could've burst from his chest. Jumping high in the sky was nice, but he could do without those weird butterflies that swarmed him when he started to fall. In the end, though, it was thrilling; it was fun!

Together, TJ and his friends leaped and bounced with the reckless abandon of teenagers. Their laughter together was infectious, each roar of joy fueling the next.

They were having fun. *Real* fun.

TJ couldn't remember the last time all three of them had done that together.

41

DOUBLE TROUBLE, DOUBLE FUN

THE JOY OF AIR-STEPPING THROUGH THE SKY REALM DIDN'T get any less thrilling, but their early search for Obatala's palace was harder than any of them thought it would be.

The first and second palaces they traveled to were completely abandoned. But the third palace they approached, which was the size of a football stadium, had two guards manning the gates.

"Hey there… um, sirs, ma'ams?" TJ asked cautiously. Both guards had the bodies of humans but the heads of falcons, and they sliced TJ with wicked stares. "Um… folks?"

"Ra is not here, mortals," the one on the left said with a voice that trilled. "This is his vacation home, and he's away prepping for the Spring Equinox."

"That's fine." Manny bounced forward from a cloud and onto the island housing Ra's palace. "We aren't looking for any Egyptian gods right now. We're in the market for an Orisha."

"Obatala's his name," Ayo added as he gaped up at the giant leopard heads that were carved into the palace's sandstone facade.

"We only speak to Ra," the guard to the right announced, their voice just as screechy. "Go away."

Like machines in perfect sync, the guards spread their wings from behind their backs and flapped them toward TJ, Manny, and Ayo. The force of the gust from their wings was so harsh, it sent all of them flying head over heels back into the endless clouds.

"Well, that was mad rude," Manny spat when she found balance on another island.

"Okay, that next one way over there has to be Obatala's," Ayo said after doing a full somersault through the air. "It's bigger than the last few we just passed."

"Besides the biggest palace, what else are we going on exactly?" TJ asked with a clenched jaw.

Ayo floated off to the next palace that peeked through the clouds. "Those lighting birds, remember? C'mon, let's get movin'."

The next two they passed were abandoned as well. TJ wondered if all the deities and gods were on vacation or something. But the following two they visited belonged to some sky spirits who Manny thought were squatters. Judging by the star-shaped structures, they were supposed to belong to Orunmila and his court, but instead the towers were filled with fae spirits hosting a party. And the last one they checked, which was round and bulbous like a cloud made of stone, apparently belonged to Oya, but now it was completely empty.

TJ had never seen Manny frown so deeply before.

As they continued their search, they passed by two pegasi who were racing each other through a thunderstorm. At first, TJ was too busy being mesmerized by their shimmering white fur and broad, feather-like wings, until Ayo slapped him on the back to talk to them.

"Um, excuse me!" TJ lifted a finger like he was hitchhiking, then put his hand away when he realized that was the wrong gesture for the moment. "Um, flying horsey things —"

"Pegasi," Manny corrected him with a whisper.

"Oh, right! Had no clue that's the plural for pegasus," TJ murmured back to her, then more loudly he asked, "Do either of you know where Obatala's palace is?"

Oh, yes, one of them thought-spoke. *Obatala is two doors down from Oya, I believe.*

"Are you sure?" TJ glanced back from where they came from. There's no way they would've missed Obatala's palace if it was right next to Oya's. Plus, where were the impundulu Mami Wata said would be nearby?

No, you dimwit, the other pegasus thought-spoke to its companion. *That was last moon. Obatala's island would've floated off near those Ibeji twins out past the Triple Rainbow Road.*

Well, how am I supposed to know that, Ajax? the first pegasus retorted. *Some of us don't spend every waking hour reading star charts.*

Maybe if you spent more time reading the stars, then you'd win a race or two against me.

Say that to my face!

Pfft! If you can catch me! The second pegasus sped off into the storm clouds again and the first one gave chase, leaving TJ and his friends alone and confused once more.

TJ balled a fist. "Ugh, no one here is helpful."

"Wait, what about this over here?" Manny landed on a small island housing a single white tree filled with nesting impundulu. "Look, the lightning birds are here. We have to be close! Wait... what's that over there?" She pointed to the sky in the far distance. Two rays of light, one red, the other blue, shot down from the heavens—two rays of light that were coming straight for them.

"Uh..." Ayo stopped his bouncing. "Are those bad light beams or good light beams?"

TJ just stared, mesmerized by the movement of the lights as they twisted into each other like a double-helix. "Not sure."

The nesting impundulu scattered, each of them flying *away* from the beams of light.

"Then again," TJ said, "my dad always said if you see animals going one way, you follow them without question."

"Yeah, let's get out of here," Ayo agreed.

Manny nodded and they vaulted back the way they came. But something stopped TJ, a whisper in his ear. As he set foot on his first cloud, he bounced in place and turned back around to the blue and red lights shooting his way. There was something odd in how the lights spiraled into each other... like a helix. Not unlike his sister's staff that was still being checked by his grandmother and that Bamidele guy. The spiraling lights... something about them was oddly... friendly. And TJ would've sworn he heard... the laughter of children coming from with each streak of light?

"Hold up," he called out to his friends who were already several yards ahead. "Wait, I think we should stay put."

"What happened to following the impundulu?" Ayo called back.

"Listen," TJ told him. "The lights. They're laughing, I think. No, wait. Can't you hear it? They're singing?"

"Catch some lightning, get the birds!" sang the voices. "Grips a-tightening, hold those herds!"

The child-like voices kept going on like that, on and on, louder and louder as they came closer.

"TJ, get away from there!" Manny shouted. "It could be a trick!"

"Whatever it is or they are... they're riding rainbows for crying out loud! Well, not rainbows exactly, but you know what I mean." TJ sunk into the cloud he stood in as the blue and red lights finally approached the white tree. They slammed into the branches and the ivory leaves exploded.

"I got one, I got one! I win the game!"

"No fair, no fair! That one is lame!"

Two children sprang from the leaves, one wearing a long, red dashiki and headscarf, the other wearing blue. They tussled over an impundulu with a broken wing. Each time they pushed and shoved, a lightning bolt sprang from the bird. It kept going like that until the shock was too much and the children dropped it. But the bird didn't fall into the clouds below as TJ would've thought. Instead, it rode them by skidding across streaks of lightning. Even with a stunted wing, it still found a way to cruise across the clouds.

"You made it go away," said the one in blue, a girl.

The one in red, a boy, returned, "I had it fair and square, that's the way!"

"Wait, wait, is this the one we're meant to seek?" The girl in blue looked dead at TJ.

The boy tilted his head, then nodded. "Oh right, Obatala didn't say the one to find had a beak."

"Obatala just said to meet at the impundulu tree."

"You, boy. Stay there, and don't you dare flee!"

TJ swallowed hard. He probably should have been afraid, but

the last time he feared an Orisha, he lost time catching up to Bolawe and Adeola in the Aqua Realm. And that one turned out to be quite friendly, despite the fact that she sucked the flesh and souls from corpses.

These two felt like a substantial improvement.

"H-Hello…" TJ said nervously. "I'm Tomori Jomiloju Young."

"Stay away from him!" Ayo bounced up to TJ's side to protect him, lightning balls cuffed in his hand.

Manny was just behind Ayo, a small gale backing her. "Don't try anything."

"Well, you called us," said the girl in blue.

"So don't make a fuss," said the boy in red.

They both flew up from the trees to show themselves fully. Their long dashiki were hemmed with cowries and agba drums were slung from each of their shoulders. TJ realized then that they were twins, or perhaps just a brother and a sister. They looked almost identical.

"Huh?" Manny questioned. "What do you mean *we* called *you*?"

"You used the Ashe of the twins," the boy said.

The girl nodded. "Young Titi and Emeka helped you win."

"Who do you think sent the chain of gold?"

"It was us, the twins, the brave and bold!"

"We waited at the top at first."

"But you're climbing's the worst."

"We can't hang around all day."

"Next time climb faster, okay?"

"Hold up." Ayo tilted his head and dismissed the lightning balls in his hands. "Y'all two are the Ibeji, aren't you? The twin Orishas."

"That's right!" The girl in blue beamed. "I go by Kehinde; I'm the first."

"But when we were born, I led the way, because she's the worst."

"Huh?" TJ wrinkled his brow. "I don't get it."

"You really need to pay more attention at the academy, bro." Ayo shook his head. "You don't remember the story of Ibeji, the twin spirits? Kehinde is known as the primary twin because she saw into the world first but kicked out her twin brother so he could see if it was safe. So even though Taiwo was *born* first, he's not actually the first twin."

"Ugh, do not remind me of the horror." The boy, Taiwo, threw his hands in the air, making his chubby cheeks jiggle. "The world started out *so* bright."

The girl, Kehinde, waved a dismissive hand, making her own baby fat wiggle. "Oh, don't whine so much. It turned out all right."

"Can you help us find Obatala and his palace?" Manny asked; the gale she had mustering behind her was gone now. "We need his help to free Oya, and to find Shango."

Kehinde clapped with joy. "Oh, you're looking for Baba and Auntie Oya, too?"

"We'll help you right away, through and through." Taiwo gestured a Yoruba sign that would've translated to "a-ok" in American Sign Language.

"You mortals are going the wrong way."

"Come with us and don't you stray."

The twins flew off in the direction from which TJ, Manny, and Ayo had come. TJ followed behind them first, eager to meet with Obatala.

"We were following him." Manny thumbed to Ayo as she started to follow.

Ayo threw up his hands. "Hey! This is what happens when you get directions from a water spirit instead of one from the sky!"

For the next few moments, they dipped and dived along obscure paths through the clouds, which the Ibeji Orishas explained were hidden to most mortal eyes. But as they brought it up, TJ did realize through his peculiar vision that he could *see* the paths the twins were taking even before they took them. He'd just been too busy having fun bouncing in the sky he hadn't paid attention to them. It was like traveling through different tunnels of cyclones, a subway system used by the other spirits and most of the impundulu. TJ would've sworn he even saw those bickering pegasi in one of the storm clouds they took a shortcut through.

"This mortal here's not like the others," murmured Kehinde ahead of them.

Taiwo whispered back. "Are you sure he's not another brother?"

"Apparently, he's not a mortal or Orisha," Manny explained, indicating that, yes, they could hear them. "He's something different. At least according to this giant alligator back at our camp, and Yewa in the Aqua Realm."

"You really do remember everything?" TJ smiled as they slipped through two floating islands that were covered in thick mist.

Manny nodded back. "So, Kehinde and Taiwo, have you seen Shango around? Oya told me to find him here."

As they followed the twins through more hidden sky paths, the twins explained that Shango had been gone for centuries. And Oya, who they had seen more recently, hadn't been around for— what they called—"a few mortal moons."

"That's because Eshu has Oya trapped in his staff," TJ explained.

The twins stopped their flying right then and there, and TJ almost crashed into their backs. Kehinde and Taiwo got angry, pounding their drums to filter out their frustrations. With each of their thumpings, the clouds around them pushed away against pulsating sound waves.

To calm them down, TJ said, "Maybe we can get Shango to help us when we speak to Obatala."

"Bah, he's long gone," said Kehinde, calming down and continuing her flight path, "fighting a war far away in the stars."

"Nu uh," contested Taiwo, "He ran from Auntie Oya. They quarreled a lot, and it left a few scars."

They entered an especially dense cloud, which immediately soaked all of their clothing and nearly washed away what was left of the white paint they used for the Obatala ritual. The forest of mist was so large, it took them a few minutes to get through. The twins used their drums and told them to follow the sound to not get lost. One of them joked that the impundulu might return to give them a shock.

When the cloud finally started to break up, TJ could just

make out the impressions of a palace. No, not just a palace, a whole fortress. It was impossibly huge, at least four or five times the size of anything TJ and his friends had seen, bigger even than Olokun's in the Aqua Realm. Glistening ivory towers stacked and stacked to a high point so far above, TJ couldn't see where it ended. Perhaps it was because they were still within the thick of the mist, but TJ couldn't even see where the palace started below them.

TJ floated in the clouds in awe. Deep within himself, he could actively feel the weight of the structure. Ashe pulsated off it like a giant heartbeat. This definitely had to be the right place.

"And here we are," said Kehinde, "the palace of the Great Creator."

"Oh no, but look," said Taiwo, "there's that filthy traitor!"

TJ heard the twins before he saw them. But when the cloud finally broke, and he got the full view of the palace, there was a notable feature: A door, the size of a large hill, stretched tall from the base of the largest floating island they had found. And there was a figure who stood before it that TJ hadn't expected to see. A figure with a drooping, long hat, exposed, round belly, and a staff in hand that TJ was all too familiar with.

Perhaps TJ should've expected him to be there. After all, Obatala's palace was a very large place with a humongous gate.

And Eshu *was* the Gatekeeper.

The Orisha of Mischief gave them all a cheeky grin and asked, "Oh, are you here to meet my old friend, too?"

42

DEFENDER OF DOORS

FOR A VERY LONG MOMENT, NO ONE ANSWERED ESHU. TO ANY birds passing by, it might have seemed they were all frozen in place: Manny, Ayo, the Ibeji, and, of course, TJ. The only thing to betray otherwise was the wind rushing through the clothing of all those present.

But there was one individual who was not interested in a staring contest.

"We all know you have Oya in your staff!" Manny clenched her fists. "Let her out!"

The mirth on Eshu's lips changed in a subtle way. It was still upturned in a smile but a new little twitch came to it. His tone, while friendly, was different, too. "Ah, I see then. And who told you that?"

"You did," TJ said coldly. "You said Oya was making those storms in Los Angeles, but she was supposed to be on the East Coast. And all the oracles in the Mortal Realm say she's been missing."

Eshu gave them a light chuckle and shook his head. Then he flicked the crystal in his staff. "That's ridiculous! You kids know Olosa is in the staff, not Oya!"

"Let us see who's in there, then!" Ayo demanded.

The Ibeji Orishas watched everyone back and forth like a tennis match, resting their chins on their drums.

Eshu looked between the children with disappointment. That slight stiffness that had come over him before had gone away, melted into his usual casual presence. He leaned his cheek against his staff in a lackadaisical way, and his voice came out all sing-songy. "I cannot do that, little ones. The deal with Olokun is clear. The boy is to deal with Eko Atlantic before I can release Olosa."

"When is the deal supposed to be done?" TJ found himself clenching his fists, too, his forehead lined with anger. "I've had people praising Olokun and the world's largest statue is being built for him. What else could he want?"

"It's true Olokun is happy with your progress," Eshu replied, "but you and I both know what will satisfy his anger. Praise and statues are but band-aids. Only the complete clearing of Eko Atlantic and the return of that coast to its natural state will do."

"That's not fair!" Now it was Ayo's turn to share in the outrage. "My family has a tower there. You know how much money went into that? Olokun can't just expect —"

"You mortals do *not* make demands of the Orishas." Eshu's voice grew dark. "As somber as it might be, that city must be gone. I've tried these past few moons to negotiate but Olokun has made his demands clear."

Kehinde pounded her drum with force. Its thump reverberated against the palace walls and back out into the Sky Realm, making her blue cloth billow. "The mortal children have a point, Gatekeeper!"

Taiwo pounded his drum, too. His red cloth snapped like a cloak. "Olokun is acting like some grim reaper."

"And you're no better taking Auntie Oya like a thief."

"Who died and decided to make you chief?"

Eshu drew in a heavy breath. TJ had noticed that he didn't quite appear the same as he did at the end of summer. His glowing eyes were somehow faded, shrouded in some odd mist. Maybe he had always looked like that, even when they spoke in those mirrors. They *had* been foggy. What did that change to his eyes mean?

Eshu stood up straight and tall and pinned the twins with his gaze. "It was the Great Monarch himself, Olodumare, who told me to keep the Orishas in line. Any who challenges the Great

Separation will be trapped and jailed. Olosa knew this. Oya, too. Keep this up and I'll have to do the same to the pair of you."

The wind around them whistled deep and long. They were clearly at a deadlock. Eshu knew why they were there, at least that they wanted Oya. They knew why Eshu was there, too—to keep them from getting her.

"Oya! Oya!" Manny shouted. "I'm here. I brought TJ Young. Give us a sign. Tell us—" Manny's chest jerked as though caught on a hook. Her eyes bloomed white and her hair flared out like it was floating underwater. The voice that came out of her mouth afterward was not her own. *"Stop him! Destroy the crystal and free us!"*

Eshu closed his eyes and sighed. "I suppose that's the end of the pleasantries, then." The crystal in Eshu's staff lit up in vivid red. Manny dropped to her knees and her eyes returned to normal.

"Children, get behind us. We'll protect you!" Kehinde lifted her hand over her drum.

Then Taiwo. "We stand with Auntie, two by two, through and through!"

As Eshu brought his staff down, the twins thumped their drums. This time the sounds of their pounding took on an ethereal quality and TJ could *see* the invisible energy cast from it fan out like a rainbow. Eshu's spell and the twin drums clashed in the middle of the air. Everyone was thrown back, even the grand palace doors shook and rattled from the force of the impact.

Manny, who was a natural in the sky, was the first to recover as she vaulted from a cloud bank. Her hands swirled overhead and the clouds swirled with her in mystical concert. She threw her manipulated storm down at Eshu, rain and sleet caking her magic. But as the mini hurricane fell upon Eshu, each droplet and piece of hail transformed into harmless bubbles.

"Good form, young mortal." Eshu beamed. "But your Ashe is child's play."

Ayo, who had fallen onto a nearby sky island off the main one, drew his Ashe into his belly and let it out again in a cage of lightning. Several bolts birthed from him, forking in all directions and then racing straight for Eshu's staff. But when the lightning bolts reached Eshu, they blossomed into fireworks.

"Great control with your forking, child." Eshu rocked back and forth like a boxer. "But you're no Shango or Thor; I've tangled with the best of them."

Eshu raised his staff again in the direction of Manny and Ayo, and again, before his spell could reach them, another soundwave with the bass of a celestial drum halted his assault.

The twins were really saving their necks.

Eshu harumphed and placed a hand on his hip. "Oh, you two are very irritating, aren't you?"

Anxiety clung to TJ like a crab pinching his muscles. He'd forgotten how powerful Orisha magic could be. His friends didn't stand a chance. Not without *his* help.

Kehinde floated high above with her drum. "We'll take that as a compliment from the mischief maker!"

"Now better brace yourself, this one's a quaker!" Taiwo, along with his sister, drummed a beat, fast and strong. It pulsated like a quick heartbeat in waves that forced Eshu back against the palace doors.

"Manny, Ayo, on me!" TJ commanded. "Touch me so your Ashe will be stronger." Manny air-stepped down to TJ, and Ayo launched from his sky island. "Grab my shoulders and funnel through me."

Manny and Ayo grabbed TJ's shoulders and instantly he felt their dual-Ashe at work, the natural connection of Oya and Shango, the Orishas of Thunder and Lightning. Their power coursed through his head and down through his chest like a tornado touching down to earth.

As Manny had done before, TJ reached up and caught the clouds. He roiled them into a thick cumulonimbus formation. And, like Ayo, TJ called the strength of lightning, igniting each cloud with its own storm. Unlike when he was in the Mortal Realm, where he'd need a week-long ritual, a fortnight of training with Omo of Fon, or a few hundred festival-goers, the effort felt almost as easy as breathing. The result of his storm manifested in a gale that worked in concert with the twins' mystical drums and the soundwaves blasted from them to Eshu. The Gatekeeper was already struggling against their combined might, and with the gale added, he was utterly pinned.

There were no bubbles or fireworks this time.

"Can't keep this up for long!" TJ called out, already feeling their power waning.

"Mortals, keep it up. We'll get that staff!" said Kehinde.

"This next little trick will give him a laugh," Taiwo finished.

This time, the music from the Ibeji's drums rang out like streams of laughter dancing to their beat. Eshu was getting completely pummeled by soundwaves, a storm, and now a collection of giggles. It seemed like the Orisha was trying to lift his staff but Oya was putting up a fight, jerking the staff back against the door and locking his wrists at odd angles.

"Now let's calm you down, you second-rate clown."

"It's time for you to put on your bedgown."

The twins' drums morphed from traditional agba drums to steel tongue drums. Their beats came out less like deep base and more like angelic, hypnotic pulses of sounds in the hue of blue and red. The effect made TJ's eyes droop. Were they casting some sort of sound magic that forced sleep?

Eshu, in his struggle, yawned twice. His eyes, too, seemed to grow heavy. He shook his head, fighting against the twin's spell with deep grunts TJ wasn't aware he was capable of.

"O-Okay, playtime is over." Eshu snapped his fingers and the world warped. Floating islands in the sky became a starfield brimming with galaxies and gas clouds. Despite the change of setting, the cry of the storm and the churning of clouds still persisted. The effect made TJ dizzy. He always hated being in those virtual reality rooms back in the Mortal Realm, especially between scene changes. Plus, the nerd he was, he often associated space with no sound at all. So the changing landscape along with the sounds had him off-balance.

"TJ?" Ayo's voice came from the stars. "Where'd you go?"

"Ow, Ayo, that's my elbow!"

"Oh, my bad, Manny! My bad!"

"Over here, guys," TJ called out to his friends. "Follow my voice. Hold onto me so I know where you are."

Manny and Ayo got their hands around his shoulders and

reappeared once more with total shock written on their faces. In the distance, three stars did battle with each other, or at least to TJ's vision it seemed that way, one blue, one red, the other white. The red and blue trails kept circling the white one in the middle. Each of their attacks manifested in a supernova of sound and laughter, but the center star always stayed intact. Instead of a big boom, though, like a nuclear bomb, those supernovas sounded more like wind and a familiar set of giggles.

It was Eshu and the Ibeji he was seeing!

How had they gotten so far away? Was Eshu keeping the twins away from TJ so he couldn't empower them? Without the help of Manny and Ayo's storm, the twins were only matching Eshu, not overpowering him like before.

TJ had never been on the other end of Eshu's illusionary magic. If TJ hadn't had his special vision, he wasn't sure he'd even be able to make out the stars that clashed against each other in the distance. More than that, TJ had never seen Eshu battle with such speed, such nuance. Going against him was scarier than fighting Olokun for one key reason: Eshu was a smart fighter. Where Olokun would've thrown a whole palace at them—or a whole galaxy in this illusion—Eshu's star was bobbing and weaving like a seasoned boxer. The Gatekeeper was doing a great job of getting the twins to separate so he wouldn't get surrounded.

"We gotta help them!" TJ said to his friends. "Can you see those stars in the distance?"

"Like... moving stars?" Ayo asked, holding onto TJ's arm very tightly. "There's just galaxies and stuff."

"Are you seeing something else?" Manny questioned.

TJ nodded. "Just keep holding me. I'll lead the way."

TJ tried to generate another of Manny's and Ayo's storms as they flew. When he called them, the power appeared as gas clouds, and his concentration broke, morphing the clouds into black holes. The magic was distorted and confused within Eshu's damned illusion, obstructing his vision of the fight between the Gatekeeper and the twins.

All right, TJ thought, *if we're gonna do this smart, let's do this smart.*

"Everyone, listen up!" TJ exclaimed. Just like he did when he followed the twins through the Sky Realm, TJ watched for the true paths of magic, the true paths of *Eshu's* magic.

"We can't see each other properly with all these illusions. But I can feel where Eshu is and where he'll be."

The thing TJ hadn't realized up until that point was that the Ibeji twins were little tricksters in their own way, too. Not quite as sharp as Eshu on their own, but together, they at least gave him a run for his money—or rather, a run for his staff. Despite the galaxy illusions cloaking Eshu's movement, the twins separated, they merged, and they were always on the move as they pounded their star drums. And, apparently, they had the gift of a ventriloquist, throwing their voices to counter Eshu's illusions.

The problem was that Eshu was simply better, like he had written the playbook the twins were using.

TJ could be better for them, though. They just needed to slow Eshu down, not outright defeat him. If they could get that staff and then get it to Obatala, this just might work…

Taking in a big breath, TJ channeled his friends' Ashe and pushed it out to where he knew Eshu's star would soar to next. It was like how Dad always told him in football. You have to pass the ball to where your receiver *would be*, not where they were *at the moment*.

"Manny, Ayo," TJ commanded, nodding to the side. "Help me grab that gas cloud there. Now!"

Like with the clouds before, and using Manny and Ayo's Ashe, TJ threw a galaxy storm just big enough to block Eshu's path. The impact that hit the Eshu star created its own supernova, and the Ibeji stars pinned him again with their lullaby magic.

"No! Not that again!" Eshu yawned. "It's not time for a nap!"

The illusion broke and the Sky Realm reappeared in all its brightness. TJ covered his eyes, rubbed them, then saw that Eshu had fallen onto the sky island Ayo had landed on before the illusion. Above him, the twins *tink-tinked* their steel tongue drums, forcing Eshu into the rocky ground. Frustrated, Eshu pounded the island, cracking it with each impact as he fought against the twins' spell. The palace had probably seen better days. The doors and arches were riddled with damage, large dark wounds that cut deep into the ivory walls.

"Damn, TJ," Ayo said through haggard breaths. "I forgot you got big-big power on the Orisha Planes."

"It's not over yet." TJ rolled his shoulders. "We need to get that staff. Manny, are you good for another storm?" There was no answer. In fact, now that TJ was aware of it, Manny wasn't holding his arm anymore. "Manny?" TJ twisted his head left and right but could see nothing. Then Ayo tapped him and pointed up. Manny was air-stepping *up* the palace walls.

"Find the open way, find the open way," she kept saying to herself in a voice that was not entirely her own. "Follow me, children. Follow me!"

TJ cupped his hands around his mouth. "Manny, what are you doing up there? Eshu won't stay down for long. We need to get the staff away from him."

"Uh, TJ." Ayo tapped him again. TJ turned to find Eshu lifting himself up on his sky island. "No time to wait for loopy Manny right now. Gotta just be us two."

Without time to think, TJ nodded, gripped Ayo's shoulder, and felt for the lightning stirring in his friend's chest. When he found a bolt that felt strong enough, he ripped it from its source and flung it out toward Eshu's back. But without Manny's storm to push the lightning along, the bolt died out before it could even reach the Gatekeeper.

And just like that, Eshu was free. Stretching out his arms like wings, Eshu cried out a scream so guttural it nearly blew out TJ's eardrums. The force of the sound was so powerful it blew the twins high into the clouds and TJ and Ayo hard against the palace walls. Even Manny had to clutch onto the edges of a window sill high above.

"Manny, what are you doing!" TJ bellowed. "We need to work *together.* We could've had him just then. Listen to me!"

Manny looked utterly possessed as she continued to air-step the long way up the side of the palace walls, completely ignoring TJ.

"We can't take Eshu down if she doesn't help us." Ayo shielded his eyes against the bright palace walls as he stared up.

"Manny!" TJ called up. "We need you down here!"

"Children, the Mischief Maker cannot be beat." Kehinde spun high above a cloud bank, regaining her balance.

"Get to the door, use your feet!" Taiwo followed behind his sister, pointing to the palace doors.

Heads woozy, TJ and Ayo landed on the palace island, clumsily finding their land legs as they bounded for the grand palace doors. They tugged back on the large handles, but they wouldn't budge. Not even a little. It was Eshu; it was the Gatekeeper. He was probably the only one who could open it, the one who forced it shut.

"Manny, the palace doors! The doors!" TJ called up to her with agitation this time, but she kept checking glass panes with mechanical precision.

"I am the Great Monarch's Messenger! Ibeji, you must heed me." Eshu raised his staff high above the clouds, and this time the crimson light in his staff's crystal was so bright it lit the entire heavens of the Sky Realm in red. "If you do not cease, I have the authority to incarcerate you."

Kehinde and Taiwo didn't listen to Eshu in earnest, instead blowing raspberries at the Gatekeeper in jest.

That did *not* sit right with Eshu.

The twins began to disintegrate into blue and red mist, drawing closer and closer to Eshu's staff as though it were a vacuum, their hues stark against the bright clouds.

"Go, children! Go! We will see you again!" Kehinde shouted, fighting the pull of the staff.

"Run, children! Run! Use your brains!" Taiwo finished.

That was the last they saw of them as the twins disappeared into Eshu's staff.

TJ stared up to where Manny was, but all he could see was her legs jumping into an open window with broken glass. Did Manny do that or had Eshu's divine shout cracked the glass pane?

Ayo shrugged. "I don't know what she's on. But it looks like that's the only option we got."

TJ didn't like it, still thinking they had a chance to stop Eshu, but with the Ibeji gone, they really had no choice. Using more air-steps, TJ scaled the side of the palace just as Eshu turned his attention back to them. He was far enough away that TJ was at least halfway confident they could beat him to the window. Well, maybe thirty percent confident, considering he was an Orisha...

But TJ had elevated power of his own as well.

"TJ, all we had to do was have a little chat!" Eshu lifted his staff, the red crystal in it grew bright again. TJ saw the path of the spell that birthed from it before Eshu could release it.

"Follow close behind me, Ayo," he said. "Copy my moves exactly."

TJ didn't have time to wait for a confirmation, he just had to hope Ayo could keep up. He used his prism vision to follow the safest path up the palace walls as Eshu's spells cracked and banged mere inches from his ears. When the window was in reach, TJ shot out one last air blast from the heels of his feet and dived through like an Olympic gymnast.

He fell into a room so bright it was impossible to see where it began or ended.

43

CHAMBER OF CANDOR

WHITE.

That's all there was in the strange space TJ had entered. Nothing but pure white. No shadows. No nothing. Not even the window they had come through.

Could Eshu follow them? Were they blocked off? TJ didn't see a way the Orisha could follow them when the whole place was one solid color.

TJ glanced down at his feet. There was no context to where he was standing, even though his feet stood on a hard surface. It gave him goosebumps.

An impossibly large voice echoed through the room, gentle but firm. "Mortals, you will not enter my domain without honesty in your heart. You children three must come to terms with one another before you pass into my home."

As the disembodied voice receded into the barren bright, Ayo faded into view at one end of the space, his voice echoing, too. "TJ, is that you over there? What is this?"

TJ cupped his hands and called back, "I don't know. I'm guessing Obatala's entrance hall or something. But in the books we read it's supposed to have lounging cushions and a grand staircase of ivory. I didn't think it'd be *this* bright."

Ayo shook his head. "Nah, this ain't his entrance hall. This is somethin' else. Like some security system since we broke in dishonestly."

"Ayo? Is that you?" Manny's voice came from behind. TJ twisted to see her also walking from a haze line against the endless horizon.

"Manny?" TJ asked. "Are you okay?"

"Yeah, I'm fine. What is this place?"

"You tell me. You're the one that ran us up here instead of following my plan. What the hell was that back there?" TJ hadn't expected his voice to carry such heat within it, but they were so close to getting that staff away from Eshu. If it wasn't for her going off and doing her own thing, the Ibeji wouldn't have been trapped in Eshu's staff like Oya and Olosa. "Why didn't you listen to me?"

"You didn't listen *to me*."

"What are you talking about? I have the power to see where everyone needs to be and boost them. That's, like, the only thing I can contribute to the group."

"Oya was speaking to me directly. She's the one who told me about the open window!"

"What?"

Manny finally got close enough that TJ could see the irritation lined in her face. "Oya. She was speaking to me from the staff."

"Well, why didn't you say that?" TJ threw his hands up in frustration.

Manny shook her hair with her hands. "And when did I have the chance to do that when you kept yelling at me, Tomori Jomiloju, huh!?"

TJ froze awkwardly midway through his retort, then retracted it. "Okay... That's fair. But I would really like it if you stopped with my full name, *Manuela Morayo Martinez*."

Manny growled, face red as she crossed her arms and turned away from him. TJ mirrored her posture as he turned to look in the opposite direction. But there was nothing to look at besides the endless white of the room.

They all stood in silence, their clothes soaked with sweat and cloud mist. Ayo's braids were coming undone, Manny's hair had flattened, and TJ's fohawk was damp with water. But none of them were hurt, at the very least.

"So another really awkward situation for me then, huh?" Ayo said from the side.

"Shut up, Ayo." TJ threw an angry hand his way. "Manny wouldn't be mad at me at all if you hadn't opened your damn mouth back at the academy."

Manny sucked her teeth. "At least he's the only one being *honest.*"

"*Honest!?*" TJ snorted. "His ass is in here like the rest of us. So what is it, Ayo? What are you holding back?"

They both turned to Ayo, but he wasn't there anymore.

"Welcome to my domain, Ayodeji Oyelowo." The grand voice boomed again, as though it emitted from reverberating speakers from the unseen walls.

"Oh, damn. Look at this place!" Ayo yelped from nowhere. "It's huge, just like the book said! Movie screens all around here and everything. Well, not movie screens, more like an ice cave with prism screens. I don't know, y'all will see it." Ayo's voice started to fade out. "Just keep it real with each other. Remember, Obatala appreciates that sort of—"

With Ayo gone, there was an uncomfortable void in the air. It was clear that "coming to terms" and being truthful was not as easy as saying something like "my eyes are brown" or "I peed my pants once when I was seven." The truth TJ and Manny needed to face was a deeper one than that. Ayo always kept it honest with them—too honest sometimes. It wasn't surprising he'd had no trouble escaping the white room.

Manny kneeled down, brushing the floor with her hand as she spoke to herself. "I'm guessin' we gotta get through this weird room 'cause we entered the palace in a dishonest way."

"Manny," TJ murmured.

Manny spoke to herself softly, "But it was the only way to get away from Eshu..."

"Manny," TJ said more firmly.

"What, *TJ?*" She stood up and looked at him straight on. She was only stalling. She and TJ knew what had to happen for them to get out of the situation they were in. It was the one thing they were truly avoiding those past few weeks, heck, the past couple of months. The hard truth neither of them was ready to hear, the same truth that had driven a wedge between them.

"So... what are you keeping from me that I should know?" TJ asked.

"What are *you* keeping from *me* that I should know?"

TJ puffed his chest and let it all out without a second thought. "Well, I feel like our friendship has kind of sucked for a little while, to be honest. And... I think... it's because of Eniola."

"Of course it's about Eniola, TJ! Did it really take you this long to notice?"

"No, I noticed it right away. I just didn't want to bring it up because..." TJ still couldn't bring himself to be *that* candid despite knowing full well that was the way out of the endless room.

"Because... why..." Manny pursed her lips.

"Because you'd look the way you are right now. You'd be all mad and everything."

"Of course I'd be mad because I like you, TJ!"

"I know you like me. We're friends."

"No, idiot. I like-you-like-you."

TJ's heart hollowed out. He had dreamed of this situation happening, imagined a time that Manny would confess something like that to him, or he to her. But the way she said it was almost bitter, not at all sweet as he would've hoped. Worse, he couldn't bring himself to say anything back.

"You're *usually* a good listener," Manny went on. "You act all shy at first, but you're really, I don't know, driven and inspiring. And... I don't know, I get nervous around you sometimes and all that goofy stuff." Her voice got shaky and fast, and she started fanning her eyes. The gesture took TJ aback. He'd never seen Manny so vulnerable before. "And all of this is coming at the same time and getting worse because all those memories flooded back from the Aqua Realm. You really helped me with my cousin and that made me *really* like you more. And then you finally asked me out even though I wanted to ask you first, but I was afraid I'd ruin the friendship. Then Ayo's cousin came into the picture and she's mad cute with her cheekbones and all that and I still got these baby fat cheeks and... Ugh! I'm blabbing now!"

Manny huffed, then sat cross-legged on the ground, away from TJ. She snuggled her head between her knees and let her wet hair cover her face. TJ had no idea how to deal with all that information at once. Just about everything she said was exactly how he felt, too, down to her being an inspiration to him and TJ not wanting to ruin his friendship with her. What he wanted to tell her in reply was that it felt so natural being around her, how holding her hand the other day felt like that was how they were supposed to always be, how her sleeping on his shoulder felt so damn *right*. Instead, like the idiot guy he truly was, he said something else.

"But... your guy in New York. Did you, you know, like... lie about him?"

"No..." Manny answered, her voice muffled by her knees. "He really has been asking me out since kindergarten. I just... finally said yes. Over text. I only did it *because* of you and your..."

"My... what?"

"Ugh, don't make me say the g-word. Makes it feel too real."

TJ sat next to her, touching her shoulder-to-shoulder. "You mean like you and your b-word? Uh... I mean, b-word as in..."

"Yeah, boyfriend, I know. And yeah..."

A brief silence settled between them. Eventually, Manny snuck a peek at TJ. TJ gave her an awkward smirk. She looked away and groaned. Her hand dug into her arm, peeling away some of the paint from the few dots she still had on her arms from the Sky Realm ritual.

"So..." TJ swallowed hard. "You sort of stole my speech." He gave her a nervous laugh. "I was going to say all that stuff about you. That's why I like you, too. How I like that you're honest, a... protector. Like Oya. How you use your hair to hide when you blush. How you make me feel inside. Being with you is just easy. I don't have to think about it. Well, except the last couple of months."

Manny heaved out a heavy breath.

TJ went on, "So... we like each other, then..."

"Wasn't that kind of obvious since the summer?"

"Yeah, I guess it was… but, you know…"

"Yeah, I know."

TJ sighed heavily and found himself stroking Manny's wet hair suddenly. It was awkward and his hand was shaking, but he did it anyway. "Hey, I'm sorry for not being honest about Eniola from the jump."

Manny lifted her head and her cheek slipped into TJ's palm. Her skin was smooth and soft. This time, Manny didn't look away as she said, "I'm sorry for… not saying anything and being cold."

"It's okay. I'm sorry for everything, too."

Another long pause came then as Manny wiped tears away. When she was done, she hardened her face again with the strength of Oya.

"So, what do we do now?" TJ asked.

"Right now, we focus on what we came here to do."

"And then? When we —"

"When we get back safe, when we have the staff and Oya's free, we…" She fought down a smile. "We can talk again. Sounds good?"

"Sounds good," TJ agreed, but the way Manny's cheek had perfectly fit in his hand made him think "sounds good" wasn't exactly right, either. Plus… Manny's face was so close to his. He just had to lean in a few inches and…

The white room around them cracked into a translucent prism. Cleansing energy washed through TJ like cold water drunk on a hot summer's day. Manny's warm cheek cooled as she disappeared, just as Ayo did before them. The floor beneath TJ gave way, but he didn't fall, instead, floating without effort. And high above stood a giant person: hairless, pale, but with a gentle smile. When it spoke, it was as though it was barely whispering.

"Hello, Tomori Jomiloju. It's so nice to finally meet you."

44

LORD OF THE WHITE CLOTH

IT DIDN'T MATTER HOW MANY TIMES TJ INTERACTED WITH THE Great Deities. Reading about an Orisha and meeting one in the flesh—or rather, meeting one in the spirit—was an entirely different thing.

For one, simply being around an Orisha filled TJ with a fullness he couldn't get from a simple meal. It permeated him with a sense of great worth. Second, none of the pataki or lectures or books could describe what it was like to be around such a colossal entity. Sure, Eshu was only marginally bigger than humans. And the Ibeji twins were no larger than small children.

But Obatala was something else entirely, rivaled only by the Orishas in the Aqua Realm.

It suddenly made sense why his palace was so wide and so tall —anything smaller would've never been able to house the gargantuan deity. TJ's entire body was the height of Obatala's eye—Obatala, who had skin so pale it was almost translucent, like faint crystals were hidden under his cheeks. Sparkles danced around Obatala's peerless eyes. The only other shine that matched his skin was the prisms that surrounded them across the room.

TJ was reflected a thousand times in a thousand prisms implanted on the walls that stretched from an endless bottom and all the way to an endless top. Between each prism, other images, images that housed the visions of other people, bordered TJ's reflection, like a first-person shooter, except not many of the prism screens showcased people blasting away zombies or aliens. Most of them were people carrying on ordinary days: listening in class, bored at an office desk, that sort of thing. Others were more bizarre, though, with visions of someone walking through a field of melting clocks or an entire landscape turned upside down.

"These are people's dreams," Ayo explained, appearing at TJ's shoulder. He thumbed up to Obatala above them. "At least that's what Obatala told me."

"Welcome to my dream room." Obatala's gentle but resonant voice rocked through TJ's chest. "I have heard stories of you three. You and your deal with Olokun in particular, Tomori Jomiloju. Tell me, why have you sought me out?"

"Oya sent us," Manny explained. TJ only then realized she was right by his side as well, floating within the prism room. "She told me to get TJ Young to the Sky Realm and to find Shango. But Eshu has Oya trapped in his staff."

Obatala's facial expressions did not change, no twitch of his brow or quirk of his lip, but his eyes brightened slightly. "Trapped in his staff? Are you mistaking Oya for Olosa?"

"No, Lord of the White Cloth." Ayo floated into a prostration. "He sucked in Oya and now he has the Ibeji in his staff as well. He said something about them crossing him, and that he was allowed to because of it."

"Old friend, what are you doing?" Obatala murmured to himself. He raised his giant eyes to the children. "For these past few moons, perhaps more than that, something has been... off about the Gatekeeper, as though his mind has been clouded, disrupted in some way. I will speak to him. He roams my halls now and will probably come to my dream room shortly. He was looking for you mortals, I expect, but you were hidden in my chamber of candor." A shiver went through TJ. He wasn't ready to face Eshu again so soon. "Where Shango is concerned, none of us have seen him for quite some time. I cannot assist you there. And with regards to Oya..."

"There is a theory we've come up with," TJ finished for him. "Back in the Mortal Realm at our academy, we learned that energy can be transferred through a spiritual vessel. Do you think it's possible to free Oya from Eshu's staff if her essence was transferred to another divine item?"

"What kind of item or vessel are you suggesting?"

"A human body," Manny said. She kept fidgeting with her hands, desperation laced within her eyes.

"We had this friend named Joshua last summer who turned out to be Eshu," Ayo explained. "He tricked us into trapping Olosa in a staff."

"Joshua?" Obatala turned from them. He drew close to one of his prisms and tapped it with his giant finger. The image, which had been a POV of someone soaring through the air with flying robots, morphed into the image of Joshua. Only *this* Joshua didn't have any clothes and was floating out of Obatala's dream room with a sluggish wave.

Ayo covered his eyes and said, "Ugh, that was *way* more of him than I wanted to see."

"This wouldn't happen to be your 'Joshua' would it?" Obatala asked.

TJ and Manny nodded, both keeping their eyes distinctly set on the Orisha's face.

Obatala frowned deeply, ignoring Ayo. "He used the body I created for him for such deception?"

"Yeah…" TJ trailed off.

"He said he needed to teach a lesson to a friend. My understanding was he was going to help a mortal."

"He did… sorta," TJ admitted. "He helped me realize a few things. But now he's holding information back, and he's acting weird. We need to speak with Oya. She showed herself to Manny in New York a few months ago."

"Oya *spoke* to you?" Obatala questioned, now hovering directly with Manny's eye line. "Directly?"

Manny nodded again, then explained everything that happened between her and Oya in New York, from the morning when Oya tried to get her attention by blowing over coins in her room, to the reflections Oya showed herself in, and, of course, to all that happened in Times Square.

Obatala processed her story quietly and thoughtfully. The humming in his throat was probably meant to be contemplative, but to the rest of them, it was like a lion was growling low and long. Then he spoke. "Whatever it was Oya wanted you to know, it was very important."

"That's what we figured, too," Manny said. "She seemed desperate. We aren't even sure how she spoke to me when no other Orisha has with anyone else. Well, except TJ with all his 'in-between' stuff and Ayo with his asthma lightning with Shango."

"That is because you crossed over, mortal child. And you and Oya are connected."

"So, can you help us?" Ayo asked.

Obatala took another long while to answer. He seemed to have a habit of waiting before responding—much different from Eshu or the Ibeji Orishas who were rapid fire by comparison. TJ really hoped he'd speed it up, though. Eshu could barge in at any moment.

"It's impossible to trick a trickster out of their toys," Obatala finally said. "You mortals can't get the staff off Eshu, and neither can I. Only Shango's lightning might be powerful enough to destroy it and release the other Orishas."

"So we came all this way for nothing..." Manny's shoulders slumped. TJ felt the disappointment from her words in his gut.

"I was not finished, young one. While yes, I cannot take or destroy the staff, this essence transfer you refer to... It's ancient magic—and I might be rusty with such practices—but it *is* possible. Though what I'll attempt brings no guarantees. You see, Eshu bamboozled me into thinking I drank my way to a recent success. That success being the 'Joshua' body, as you called it. I'm sure you've heard the stories in your realm, but I have had a poor past with palm wine. I might be able to use that against him. However, I'm an awful actor and this ritual you all have presented to me has never been attempted on an Orisha."

"We have to try," TJ said.

Manny nodded in agreement. "We can't let Oya stay trapped."

"It's not going to work..." Ayo sighed. "At least, there's a giant chance it won't. We're askin' the Orisha of Honesty to fool the Will of the Mischief Maker. Ain't gonna happen. No offense."

"None taken, young one. I am aware a career as a thespian is beyond me."

"Maybe he doesn't have to lie, exactly." TJ stroked at his cheek. "Lord Obatala, have you heard of method acting?"

"Oh yes, that actor Leonardo DiCaprio kept dreaming of bears while he was making that one film of his some time ago."

"Just do that!" Manny added. "You just have to *think* you're another person."

"It doesn't matter," Ayo cut in. "Even if we do manage to do the transfer ritual, there's no sure thing it'll even work." He threw a hand out to Obatala. "I believe you said something about it never being attempted?"

"What are you getting at, Ayo," Manny gritted.

"Yeah, man. Being a downer is not what we need right now." TJ peeked over his shoulder, wondering where Eshu would pop up from. Where was the door to a place like this? "We need solutions *only* here, dude."

"I was gettin' to that. I just had to set it up so y'all would be okay with what I'm finna do." TJ didn't like the serious line crossing Ayo's face. Not one bit. "Manny and Oya were connected because she crossed over. The same has been happening between me and Shango. No other Orisha has been able to find him. But I think I can."

Manny drew a hand over her mouth to cover her gasp. "Your asthma attacks?"

"Yeah. It's probably pulling me to Shango. To find him. Like Oya wanted us to. Shango may be the only one who can help us now. Not just with the staff, but with Olokun, too."

"It will likely take a very long time to find Shango, child," Obatala intoned gently. "Your kind do not fare well in this place."

"It's a risk I have to take. Just point me in the last direction you know Shango went and I'll handle the rest."

"The Nine Realms was the last thing he told me before he set off. That's where we go to visit the Norse deities, just as they visit us here in the Orisha Planes. You'll need a lightning tunnel to transfer over. There are a few not far from here."

"Good. Then that's where I'll start."

"Yoooohooo! Obatala, are you here?" Eshu's voice echoed

throughout the dream room. TJ and the others shot glances all around them but saw nothing. TJ's throat went dry as he realized Eshu's voice had come from far, far below.

"Hold that thought," Obatala said. "Let's call that Plan B. Plan A is to play along with me." He waved a hand in the air, and TJ's body locked into place like stone. Wisps of Ashe bound his limbs, and he rose into the air, Manny and Ayo alongside him. They were trapped like flies in a spider's web.

45

METHOD TO THE MADNESS

"OLD FRIEND, IS THAT YOU *WAAAY* UP THERE?" ESHU'S VOICE came again with mirth. "You know, you really need to install these things called 'elevators' the mortals invented. It would save me the time going up all those stairs you have."

Obatala's large shoulders slumped, and he drooped his head a little. "Wha? Wha you say?" His words slurred into one another, sounding very much like an uncle TJ's family never talked about.

"Come again, old friend? I didn't catch that!"

Obatala fell into one side of the room, as though looking for balance against the prism wall. "Was it you who sent these mortals to my room?"

"Ah, I was looking for them. I'll take them off your—" Eshu had gotten close enough to see Obatala's lean. "Oh, old friend, you haven't slipped back into the palm wine, have you?"

Obatala waved Eshu away dismissively, but the motion of his hand was sluggish and unbalanced. "I didn't do no drinkin'."

"You can't even float straight. How many did you have?"

"I did'n do none!" Obatala threw up two fingers and crossed his fingers behind his back. TJ wished he hadn't. Eshu could've seen, and they knew he was only acting. The Orisha didn't need to signal them like that.

Ugh, we're doomed...

"Two? Two dozen, you mean?" Eshu took notice of TJ,

Manny, and Ayo floating there. "Sorry you had to see him like this, kids." He frowned. "He hasn't been this way for a very long time."

TJ quirked an eyebrow. Eshu was being way friendlier than he had been outside. Obatala was right. It was like he was going between two minds. One that TJ knew, and another, more malevolent force.

"Dis is... dis is your fault, Gatekeeper." Obatala threw an accusatory finger in Eshu's direction, which was quite frightening since his entire fingertip was the size of half of Eshu's body. "I woulda been fine were it not for your meddlesome... request. Where is da human body I gave you?"

"Oh, I believe it's been long since relieved by a certain giant alligator back in the Mortal Realm."

"Curses..."

Eshu drifted up to Obatala to place his small hand on the deity's large cheek. "What's bothering you, old friend?"

"I needed to see dat body! All da rest I made... went bad. Spoiled." The Orisha started to weep. "If I could just figure out..." Obatala grunted to himself. "Come, follow me. Imma show you."

Obatala shrunk in size as he pressed his hand into another prism. The wall caved into itself and creaked into a hole that showed a dull room of browns and grays lined with wooden tables. Every few feet, body parts were strewn all over, from a pair of legs slung over threadbare rugs to disembodied arms angled over chipped stools. If TJ didn't know any better, he would've thought he was looking at a department store warehouse where mannequins went to die. Obatala finally got small enough that he could fit through the human-sized hole that led out of the dream room.

"What about the children?" Eshu asked as he peeked into the workshop with a sniff of the stale air. TJ wondered why Eshu hadn't snatched them up and taken them back to Oracle Rock, but it seemed like he had a genuine concern for Obatala once he realized he was "drunk".

"Da children will come, too. Maybe dey will learn somethin'." Obatala flitted his fingers and TJ's chest tugged along behind the

Orisha, like being pulled by a tether. TJ pushed against his restraints and groaned to play along.

"I cain't do dis in my condition," Obatala said as he settled at one of his beat-up workstations. "Lend me dat staff of yours. I show you what I done."

Eshu drew his staff close to his chest like a child with a lollipop. "I'd like to keep my staff if that's okay with you."

"You owe me, Gatekeeper," Obatala said with more clarity than he should've. What was he doing? He was supposed to be method acting like Leonardo DiCaprio! "I've ruined every human body I've made since you left. It's just like all those ages ago."

"You know how sensitive I am about my things."

Obatala seemed to remember himself, pursing his lips, and his slur returned. "I'm not askin' ya to give it to me. Just, uh… hold it high while I go and use its power."

Eshu pressed Obatala with a questioning stare, and TJ knew it was all over. If TJ could pick up the change in Obatala's demeanor, surely the Trickster would too, no matter how much remorse he felt for Obatala.

Escape routes were limited in the workshop. Eshu had all the power with a staff imbued with Olosa, Oya, the Ibeji, and who knows what other Orishas. Could Obatala even fight? For all their luck, he was probably some pacifist.

TJ tried to shift his gaze to his friends but his head was locked in place good by Obatala's spell. They were probably freaking out as much as TJ was.

"Just hold it aloft, you say?" Eshu questioned, then shrugged. TJ's muscles tightened. "Horizontal or vertical?"

Obatala tilted his head to one side.

Eshu prompted again, "What orientation do you want me to hold the staff? Vertical or horizontal?"

The tension in TJ's neck released.

"Ah, yeah… yeah." Obatala cracked his pale knuckles sluggishly, pulled up a stool clumsily, and set his elbows on the nearest table with the heft of a drunk. "Horizontal should do."

"So be it." Eshu slammed the bottom of his staff on the ground, flipped it perpendicular with the floor, and the crystal light bloomed red.

With another wiggle of Obatala's hands, a set of clay-like body parts drifted from the corners of the room to his workstation. First a clump of limbs, then an ash-hued torso, and finally an amorphous blob that could've been a head. One after the other, Obatala set the pieces on an ivory plate, like a Lazy Susan turntable TJ's family used at dinner sometimes. Only this plate was bordered by symbols of doves, elephants, and snails, all animals associated with Obatala.

Watching the deity was like watching a master claymaker at work. His hands moved with deliberate speed, curving and molding the shapeless into the familiar. Long lumps contoured into knees and elbows, the central block curved into the shape of a female's body, and the head clump became more defined with a jaw, cheeks, and mouth.

Was this how humans were originally created, on a turntable like clay pots? Instead of telling children about babies coming from storks, perhaps parents should have been teaching them about ceramics.

As Obatala continued, TJ found it odd that the two Orishas engaged in light chit-chat like ordinary mortal beings, topics like the strange weather in the Sky Realm or how dusty Obatala's workshop had become. In fact, now that TJ had time to take in Obatala's workspace, it was a far cry from the pristine exterior or the prism dream room. This place was far more neglected than the rest of his palace.

"Bring that crystal closer, Gatekeeper," Obatala requested without breaking focus on his work.

Eshu did as he was asked, but leaned his head in close to what Obatala was doing. "So what are you doing, old friend?"

"The last body I made that was a success became autonomous at the behest of the Gatekeeper," Obatala said with a far less drunken slur as he attached the legs to the torso. TJ could see the Ashe fog binding the two together. "My assumption is that I need *your* Ashe to replicate that success."

"Hmmm, I see, I see," Eshu hummed.

A gentle wave rushed through TJ's chest as the head and arms were attached to the body on the table, a familiar wave. Where had he felt that sensation before? An image washed over his vision, something with a large glass pane and airplanes going across it.

Then it hit him.

It was the spirit of Oya!

Doing his best to look out the side of his eye, his blurred vision showed him Manny. She had her eyes closed, concentrating, just as TJ had expected. That sensation he felt was the same one he and Manny had manifested at the airport, the time TJ thought they were calling Bloody Mary. At that time, the connection felt strong; now, it felt tangible, like holding a gift in hand after a long wait.

A long burgundy wisp melted from the crystal in Eshu's staff and dripped into the clay body of slate, which was slowly morphing into a hue of brown. And Eshu was none the wiser.

It was working! The ritual was working!

Eshu glanced around the workshop like he'd heard a whisper and was trying to figure out what had been said. TJ's heart raced. They'd have to work fast. In class, they learned that all Ashe goes through Eshu. But he never knew what that actually meant. If Eshu could stop their Ashe altogether, he would've done it already. Maybe Eshu could only sense it. It was TJ who could actually manipulate it, though he was still a beginner with his unique abilities. Either way, at one point or another, the Gatekeeper would sense Oya's magic billowing all around them, even if he didn't completely recognize the old magic of essence transfer.

Focusing inward, TJ boosted Manny's internal prayer. He tried to make eyes at Ayo by his side but he didn't have to; his friend was already concentrating, just like Manny was.

Eshu pulled the staff away from Obatala and hissed into the crystal head, "What are you trying to do?"

"What's that?" Obatala asked, eyes still narrowed on his work.

"Oh, nothing." Eshu snapped his fingers. "Ah, I almost forgot. Our little project here might take a hot minute. I should take the mortals back to their realm. They tend to go a bit loopy here. There's this one fella named Mr. Du Bois—terrible demeanor, no fun at all—but now he's just stuck saying the same phrase over and over again. Who knows how long that'll last?"

Obatala hushed Eshu with an outstretched hand. "Just a moment more, Gatekeeper. Just a moment more. It's *almost* there."

TJ pinched his eyes shut, thinking back on that prayer to Oya, *As strong as the wind, more fierce than a storm...*

TJ opened his eyes again. Eshu was peeking over his shoulders toward a corner of the room, a corner of the room filled with bodies that were complete and not at all deformed.

Open your arms and protect us from destruction, TJ thought, feeling the power from his friends within, knowing they too were trying just as hard as he was. *Oya, may we live and die to live again.*

"Old friend." Eshu made the slow turn of his head to Obatala. "I thought you said all your creations have been deformed. What are those clay bodies in the corner there, eh?"

The crystal light in Eshu's staff radiated stark red, then a deep wine. That same deep hue darkened the eyes of the empty body Obatala set in the middle of his table.

And then, the body began to cough.

The spell binding TJ and his friends lifted, and they dropped to the wooden slats below.

"Oya?" Manny asked with a croak. "Did it work? Are you there?"

"Oh, Obatala!" Eshu chortled. "You, deceiver, you! And you didn't even have to lie!"

The room filled with white like a flash bomb, then Obatala's voice called out, "There's no time to wait to see if it worked, children! You must flee!"

The bright white of the room opened up to a wall full of shelves. TJ couldn't see Obatala, but the nearby wall fractured like glass, the shards shattering outward to reveal the exterior of the palace.

"Take the body and go!" Obatala bellowed over the wind that rushed into the room from outside. "Now!"

"Ayo, Manny, help me," TJ called as he rushed to where the body should've been. The rest of the room was still white and there was scuffling sounds between Obatala and Eshu.

"Obatala, you crafty, little—" Eshu sent a blast against the wall.

Obatala grunted and an ethereal drone sprang up, where Eshu's blasts must've hit. "Eshu, look within. You are corrupted. You are not the Gatekeeper I know."

Tapping around in the stark white, TJ felt for the body that should've now housed Oya's spirit. Smooth skin brushed across his fingertips and he latched onto what must've been an ankle or a wrist. "Got her! Help me!"

Together, TJ and Manny slung Oya's body over each of their shoulders and jogged to the opening left by Obatala.

"Ayo, lead us off and make sure we have a clear path."

"I can't believe this is going down; I can*not* believe this is going down." Ayo vaulted forward into the clouds, crafting airsteps beneath his feet. TJ and Manny followed close behind with a more clumsy bound. The body Oya was using was heavier than it looked. But TJ barely minded the weight as the open air of the Sky Realm washed over him once more.

"Oya, can you hear me? Can you hear me?" Manny kept asking as they made their way back out to the sky islands. Which way was it to the sky chain?

A blast came from behind. TJ twisted his head over his shoulder, where Eshu shot out of the broken hole in the palace. What happened to Obatala? Did he get sucked into Eshu's staff, too? Did he escape into the depths of his palace? TJ didn't have time to wonder further. They were out in the open and Eshu wasn't far away.

TJ searched left, right, and center for anything that could help. They were going too slow carrying Oya, who still hadn't woken up. What if the ritual hadn't worked correctly?

"Children, children!" Eshu cried out from behind. "Well played, I must admit. But the game is over now."

Then TJ saw it. Just a few yards to their right was a white tree filled with impundulu. "Ayo, you see what I see?"

Ayo, who was glistening with sweat, trying to keep up a clear path for them through the clouds, nodded nervously. "Yeah, on three?"

"One," TJ said.

"Two," Ayo said.

"Three!" Manny finished for them.

Together, they shot out their hands and feeble lines of lightning bolts traveled erratically toward the tree. Their spell impacted against the branches, shocking each one. The lightning birds within scattered in all directions. They flapped their wings with such force that bolts sparked off against every cloud. Eshu was hot on their heels, but he got caught up in the sudden storm with a yelp.

"Quick, inside those dark clouds there." TJ pointed just to their side, and they air-stepped into the shadows of the mist. Luckily, they found a sliver of a broken island they could wait on. They waited with bated breaths in the darkness. All they could do now was listen and wait within the abyss. If they made any sound at all, they'd be caught.

"These damn birds!" Eshu shouted from somewhere outside the clouds. "I'll find you, children! You won't make it to the sky chain! This isn't over!"

What happened to the jovial trickster TJ remembered from the Aqua Realm?

This wasn't going to work. Eshu *fed* on Ashe; he would find them eventually. But TJ had one more card to play. He'd been able to sap magic from other diviners, but he'd never tried it on himself. If they were going to hide from Eshu, he'd need to figure out how to do it.

Digging into himself, he "shut off" his Ashe and the Ashe of his friends. It was easier than he thought. They were all so exhausted and mystically fatigued that cloaking their magic wasn't much of an effort. But would that be enough to evade Eshu's senses?

They waited for what felt like forever. TJ finally felt how hard his heart was pounding against his chest. The stilted breaths of his friends sounded like a shout to his ears, but he convinced himself the winds outside their cloud would cloak them.

Floating in that dark vapor atop that sliver of an island was like floating in an ocean of clouds. It took several terrifying minutes, but eventually, TJ felt some sense of security.

"C'mon," TJ whispered to his friends. "We need to find a proper island to settle on. Another island with cloud cover."

TJ was the first to peek out the top of their hidden cloud.

There was nothing around. No Eshu. No impundulu. Just Obatala's colossal palace poking its head out above the clouds. When TJ felt it was safe enough, he led his friends to a small island surrounded by thick, gray clouds. They settled Oya's still unmoving body along the rocky ground, where a small stream flowed from a thicket and over the edge of the island.

Manny caressed the cheek that should've been Oya's, tears watering from her eyes. "Oya, please say something. Please say something."

"It didn't work," Ayo frowned. "It didn't work…"

TJ finally got a proper look at the body Obatala had constructed. It was a middle-aged woman, dark-skinned, wide nose, and thick lips with a shapely figure. TJ had been freaking out too much to realize she was fully naked.

"No, wait, I think I can try something." TJ reached out and clutched the body's wrist. "Manny, Ayo, touch my shoulder, please."

"What are you gonna do?" Manny asked, her voice shaky.

TJ shrugged. "I'm going to give the body a jump start. Like I do when I boost you guys' magic. It's the only shot we got. But whatever I try *might* attract Eshu to us."

Ayo gave him a defeated shrug. "What other choice do we have?"

Manny's tears fell along the body that didn't move. "We have to try."

TJ nodded and clutched the body's wrist more tightly. Then, out loud this time, they said their prayers. This time, the power felt less like a surge and more of a steady decline, their spirits low.

"C'mon, guys," TJ said. "We gotta do better than that."

Manny and Ayo took in deep breaths, steadied their voices, and came out with more strength. This time, the energy was fuller in TJ's belly as it swelled up to his chest. The experience of all those rituals he helped pull along with Elder Adeyemi fueled the last bit they needed then. They spoke their prayer over and over until their voices were hoarse. When they couldn't speak anymore, they gave up. First, Ayo, who slammed his fist into the ground with shocking force. Then TJ, who fell on his back and let exhaustion take him. Manny kept on longer than any of them but eventually stopped too with a light weep.

TJ's mind festered with everything they could've done differently. It was a bitter feeling that ate away at him. Failure was never a good feeling. What was worse... he had no clue what happened to Obatala.

But then...

Eyes fluttering open, coughing violently, the body croaked, "Too late..."

"Oya?" Manny shot up and crawled over to the woman's body. "Oya!? Oya, say that again!"

TJ and Ayo rushed over to the woman's side, too. TJ didn't want to hope, but he couldn't help but feel his chest lift at the sight of the woman. What had she just said, though? Too late? Too late for what?

"Too late..." the woman took in another deep breath, her hoarse voice breaking. "You are... far too late, young ones. Far... too late."

"What do you mean?" TJ asked. "Too late for what?"

"Eko Atlantic is doomed. They will all drown. They will all die."

46

A SHAFT OF LIGHTNING

So they were doomed...

What did that even mean, exactly?

The woman who had to be Oya looked entirely horror-stricken, almost a bit *too* dramatic in the way she glanced around, as though Olokun could come from the depths of the Aqua Realm all the way up to the heavens, to the sky island they sat on.

"Yeah... we sort of figured we were doomed," TJ said. "That's what we're trying to stop."

"You do not understand." The woman grabbed for TJ, forcing him to backpedal into the stream beside them. "You had to extract me *moons* ago!"

"What are you talking about?" Manny leaned in close, her attention locked on the middle-aged body that housed Oya.

"I told you to bring the TJ boy to the Sky Realm and find Shango, *not* praise Olokun and give him the power he'll need to bring your doom!"

"That's what I tried to do..." Manny's voice cowered under Oya's weight.

TJ backed his friend up by saying, perhaps a bit too defiantly, "We're doing our best here, Oya."

But what were he and his friends supposed to do? They had to do *something* for Olokun. They hadn't known the specifics with Oya or Shango. It wasn't their fault; it was Eshu and his lies!

Ayo, just next to TJ, seized up as Oya turned on TJ with wild eyes, her dark skin stark against the clouds behind her. "Your best? You were supposed to get me out so that we could find Shango and prepare to *fight*. Now we are in a losing battle. You and that Elder Adeyemi have been boosting Olokun all this time. You should have been doing that for Shango and me instead. Tell me, boy, if this is your best, what are you at your worst!?"

TJ's chest cavity caved, and his stomach bottomed out more deeply than any fall through the sky could've done to it. When this all started, they had half a year to figure out how to deal with Olokun. And for four of the six months they had spent it giving Olokun all the power in the world. TJ was such an idiot, and now his idiocy was being made apparent under the scowl of an Orisha —even if an ordinary human face diminished that scowl.

Ayo started to cough violently. He clutched at his chest and fell into the stream just beside them. He coughed and coughed and TJ could've sworn something came up from his stomach, into the stream, and off the endless waterfall that cast from the sky island.

"Ayo, are you okay?" Manny asked as she rushed over to him to pat his back. "Is it your asthma again?"

Ayo pounded on his chest a few times before answering, "Yeah… it's really, really bad right now."

Oya lifted her head to the heavens and her human nose scrunched up. "Shango… Your connection with Shango is calling you, child. Do not ignore the pull. We need my husband now more than ever."

"That's great… and everything…" Ayo groaned, a fist to his chest. "But can this connection pull… a little less hard?"

A crack and pop sounded from above. TJ whipped his head up to find Eshu soaring above them at the apex of a dark cloud. His flowing loincloth drifted in the air peacefully, but TJ knew what destruction could be sprung from the staff Eshu held aloft. With his arms outstretched wide, the Gatekeeper almost appeared as a humanoid star atop a Christmas tree made of mist.

"There you all are," he said with a wry grin. "I thought I sensed some magic this way!"

TJ dropped his foot back and lifted his hands up defensively, ready for one of Eshu's spells or illusions. He barely registered how his breath hitched in his throat.

"Hello there, Oya." Eshu waved casually with his staff. "That form doesn't quite suit you, it's more... kindly mother than warrior. Obatala has done better work."

Oya rose to her feet and shot her hands out at her sides. The dark clouds around them swirled with the makings of an early storm. TJ had thought what he did with Manny and Ayo was big, but the sheer scope of how many clouds she called forth—which stretched as wide as a football field—put their efforts to shame.

"I've evaded you before, Gatekeeper," Oya spoke with bitter malice. "You only captured me before while I was bound, communicating with the girl. And these are *my* skies."

Eshu laughed, his muffin top jiggling with every guffaw. "We'll see, Windweaver. We don't yet know how limited that mortal shell of yours is. Go on. Do your worst."

A twitch came to Oya's eyes. A small one. One that told of doubt. But she bit back that hesitation and roared as she unleashed the clouds at her side, roiling them into cyclones and mini hurricanes. As the windstorm converged on Eshu, however, every streak of air dissipated into nothing more than a gentle puff against his cheeks.

Eshu was right. Oya's human body limited her true Ashe. But TJ could help with that. He hustled to her side to place a hand on her bare shoulder. He was about to funnel his power into her when he noticed Eshu tilting his head to one side in a curious manner. "Um... your friend seems to be barfing lightning," he said. "I don't believe you mortals do that these days, do you?"

TJ turned to where Ayo was still hunched over the island's edge, and sure enough, he was hacking up lightning bolts that sparked and smoked against the stream.

"I feel the connection!" Ayo said through pained breaths. "I... feel... him. I feel... Shango."

Manny, still rubbing Ayo's shoulders at his side, said, "Breath, Ayo. Breath. Let it take you, and breath out!"

"TJ, Oya," Ayo gritted. Now lightning was sparking from his eyes like fractured tears. "Hold... onto me. Now."

Ayo was casting off some sort of familiar Ashe. TJ could feel it, something deep within his chest. Where had he felt that before? It was so familiar... the sensation of travel, the sensation of moving through ethereal space.

It hit him.

It was the same sensation he felt when he passed through the portals at school, the same one he felt when Eni helped them travel from New Ile-Ife to Eko Atlantic.

Ayo was generating a portal... from within himself. But he had no control over what he was doing, it seemed. The Ashe stirring within him was born of something else, something elsewhere...

"Manny!" TJ shouted. "Help me with Oya!" Grabbing Oya around the middle—doing his best to disregard she was still naked—TJ dragged her to Ayo's hunched body. But she wouldn't budge, her feet plastered to the sky island as she stood her ground against Eshu like the warrior she was. "Manny, grab my hand, we'll daisy-chain to Ayo!"

"On it!" Manny grabbed Ayo's wrist, then stretched out her free hand to TJ.

"Oh. No. You. Don't!" Eshu called out from above. But he was too late. Before he could cast a spell, TJ hooked his index finger around Manny's own, and they all shot through a tunnel of lightning. All around him, blue and white streaked about him with the pops and cracks of angry fire. TJ's gut lurched as they catapulted through the bizarre lightning shaft that reminded him of hyperspace from Star Wars. Between the curtain of lightning streaks, there were images of strange landscapes, worlds with several moons, tall glowing mushrooms listing in the air like palm trees, an underwater fortress with a lava moat around it...

Wait!

TJ knew that fortress and that lava moat. It was Olokun's palace in the Aqua Realm.

"What the hell is going on?" Manny asked from nowhere. He had just been holding her finger but didn't realize when they had lost contact. Where was she now? Where was everyone else, for that matter?

"No... idea," Ayo answered haggardly. TJ didn't see him either, just heard his voice. "I think... we're traveling... to

Shango. But it hurts... I can't... control it... My skin feels like... it's ripping apart."

"Do not stop, child." Oya's voice. "You must not break this bond. We are traveling along the ley lines between the mortal and ethereal realms."

TJ shot a glance over his shoulder. He was definitely alone, but the voices sounded like they were just beside him. Was Eshu with them, too? Had they really escaped him? And what had Ayo just said? He felt like he was ripping himself apart? That sounded way too similar to Banjoko the Bold and John Henry for TJ's liking.

Portal transport was advanced magic, something they wouldn't learn until after they got their staffs and well into SS2-level classes. Ayo was being pulled by powerful Ashe he was not ready for. TJ knew that feeling well, knew the pain Ayo was suffering. More than that, as TJ reached out with his own Ashe to find him, his friend's pain became his own, a white-hot rod that spidered through his veins.

"Ayo!" TJ called out, fear clutching around his power. "You have to drop us. We're too mystically heavy for you to pull us along. You have to let us go. You'll die if you don't! You'll get ripped apart!"

"No!" Oya cried. "Sacrifices must be made if we're to reconnect with Shango. The mortal must not break the connection."

"What?" Manny's voice this time. "We can't let our friend die! Nothing's worth that!"

"Ugh, you mortals are so shortsighted. This is the way; this is the cycle."

Ayo's pain coursed through TJ's own, hot and unforgiving, searing through his very blood. What if TJ could take that pain away from his friend? What if he could be the sacrifice? Hell, he might even survive with his abilities and wouldn't be a sacrifice at all.

"Ayo..." TJ gritted. "I know... what you're... going through. You're... not gonna... last... much longer. Let me... take... the power."

A gentle push came to TJ's chest, that familiar sensation when he took in another's Ashe to boost it, but something was blocking him.

"That will not work, mortal," Oya said. "The call is for Shango's child and Shango's child alone. It is his burden to bear."

Ayo's spirit was draining, TJ could feel it, he could *feel* his friend dying. He couldn't let it happen, but he didn't know what else to do. Panic attacked his every motion, clenched around his aching heart. It wasn't supposed to be like this.

"No! Ayo, no!" Manny whimpered. "There has to be something we can do. Anything…"

It was Manny's voice that did it for TJ, what really broke down all composure in his soul as tears stung his eyes.

"Guys…" Ayo said low and soft. "It's okay… I think… I see something… I think…"

A long pause came after that. There was nothing left but the crackling of the lightning tunnel as TJ floated by more bizarre landscapes.

"Ayo…" he called out to nothing. "Ayo? Can you hear me?" Then he shouted, "Ayo! Just let us… go. Let us… go. I'll get everyone back… You… protect yourself!"

The voice TJ heard next sounded less like someone who was just at his side and more like someone who was directly in his head. *"Use… the comet… TJ. Tell… Titi… I'm sorry I couldn't make it back. I'll find Shango… even… even if it kills me."*

And just like that, the connection was gone, like TJ had had his innards ripped straight out of him. He couldn't feel Ayo anymore. The pain was gone, lost to an empty void. Part of TJ wanted it back, no matter how much it hurt. At least it told him Ayo was around and alive.

"TJ…" said Manny's disembodied voice. "TJ, are you there? Ayo, are you okay?"

"He's gone…" TJ answered. "He's gone, Manny."

"No… no, no, no… he can't be."

"I'm not saying he's… he's…" More tears drowned his eyes. "I don't feel him anymore… he said Shango was close, that he could find him."

"Foolish, mortal!" Oya cried out again. "He'll never find

Shango on his own. He'll die for nothing now and he's left us stuck in this portal loop!"

TJ was beginning to not like Oya all that much. He knew the Orishas were amoral to mortal whims and principles, but she was being far too apathetic. She was right about one thing though... they did seem to be stuck. But Ayo told TJ to use the comet. That had to mean something. There must've been something Ayo saw on the other side that would help them through.

TJ took greater care to discern the flashing locations zooming by his vision: a neon forest, a land of ice filled with plumes of fire, rainbow crystals floating in bruised-colored clouds; they all went by too fast. He couldn't spot the comet on the other side, even if he tried. So instead of watching them, TJ *felt* them instead. He closed his eyes and concentrated, searched for the heat that empowered him in what felt a lifetime ago.

And there it was!

At the edge of TJ's powers, like a taste of something you couldn't quite place, TJ sensed the gentle lick of embers. The comet was no longer as powerful as it was before. But there was just enough there to latch onto. TJ grabbed on and held it with all his strength, and in doing so he felt control again, could even feel where Manny and Oya's bodies floated just at his side. With a mental tug, he grabbed onto them as well and imagined the Oracle Rock. In his mind, he painted the image of its uneven surface, the tents with their animal skins scattered all around, even the weeds that grew from the stone surface's cracks. There was more to his picture, though, an image he didn't conjure in his mind: five tiny dots that grew larger and larger atop the surface of the Oracle Rock.

It was like a dream, like TJ was up in a helicopter descending back to Earth. And as he fell and fell without feeling like he was actually falling, he finally recognized the five dots. It was Emeka, Titi, Oracle Ruby, Elder Adyemi, and Miss Graves. Each of them held their hands over their brows, as though shielding themselves from a bright light. But to TJ's vision, there was nothing bright at all. Oracle Rock was shrouded under the dark of night. As he glanced left and right, he saw Manny and Oya were by his side in the flesh, and behind them, where their legs should've been, was a blue-white trail of lightning sparking from dark clouds high above.

They were riding a lightning bolt!

A lightning bolt sparked from the comet!

They were crashing down into Oracle Rock very, very quickly. But TJ was in control, that residual power from the Sky Realm, the Orisha Planes, the comet, still rushing through him. He slowed their descent, his, Manny's, and Oya's, until their feet met solid ground once more.

Just like when he left the Aqua Realm during the summer, all the mortal hurts, all the fatigue, all the everything came flooding back to TJ. He collapsed at Elder Adeyemi and Oracle Ruby's feet. Before his head could smack against the ground, a hand cupped the side of his head. Though dazed, TJ was thankful to whoever had saved him from the concussion. Through blurry vision, he saw Manny at his side, rubbing the temples of her head. Slow realization crossed her face as she stared at her hands and looked around. Then she found TJ's eyes watching her.

"Did we do it?" she asked him. "Did we find Oya?"

TJ didn't know what to think. He knew he should answer her, but he couldn't. All he could do was look ahead of her to the empty space of the rock where their friend should've been. He couldn't answer Manny because one single thought dominated his mind: Ayo, their friend, was gone.

47

THE TROUBLE WITH TRUST

"TJ, did you hear me? Did we find Oya?" Manny groaned to TJ softly.

TJ couldn't understand why she kept coming at him with that question. How could *that* be what she was asking about? She should've been freaking out about why Ayo wasn't with them on Oracle Rock under the dark of night.

Then TJ remembered why Manny would be so confused.

"That's right..." TJ breathed out hoarsely, mostly to himself. "Your memories. You don't remember."

Someone cleared their throat above TJ. He didn't want to focus on the others right now. He had to tell Manny, to explain what happened... But as he stared up at the one who cleared their throat, he realized it was Elder Adeyemi. And just at her shoulder was Oracle Ruby, looking like she was in trouble. Not far behind was Miss Graves, who had a hand over her mouth, and just behind her were the twins, looking just as bashful as Ruby.

"And who might this be?" Elder Adeyemi looked something up and down at TJ's side. "You are not one of my teachers. And where are your clothes, ma'am?"

"No, I am not." Oya stood up to her full height, which only reached to Elder Adeyemi's neck. Someone really needed to find her some clothes. A blanket, at least. "And... clothes? Oh, yes..."

She snapped her fingers and a thick fog wrapped around her chest and groin. "I am Oya, the Matron of Storms and Wind."

It appeared as though the Elder had been shot through with an arrow. Her hand went to her heart, her lips parted, then she prostrated herself on the ground. Even Ruby, so often casual and flippant, lowered to one knee, along with Miss Gravés and the twins. TJ felt a little bad for not following suit. So far, he hadn't shown Oya her deserved respect. All he did was earn her anger. But then, he wasn't all that thrilled with her either, not after she suggested Ayo could be a sacrifice.

"Oya?" Manny threw herself to the ground beside Adeyemi. For her, Oya was still a perfect deity. She didn't recall how the Windweaver had behaved in that shaft of lightning. She didn't remember what Oya had said about their friend. She didn't know. "It is you. We did it! Oh, my... TJ, we did it!"

TJ finally followed suit, joining the others on the floor, but his prostration was half-hearted. He saw Ruby quirk an eyebrow his way out of the corner of his eye.

"You may rise, mortals." Oya's voice was dignified, despite the reedy tone of her human form. "You are Simisola Adeyemi, are you not?"

Elder Adeyemi stayed kneeled but lifted her head. "It is an honor, Windweaver. Indeed! Indeed, I am Headmistress Simisola Adeyemi. Caretaker of these hallowed grounds, known to us as Ifa Academy of Tomorrow's Diviners."

"Oh, yes. Diviners. That is what you call yourselves these days..." Oya stared off as though in reverie. The stars shone brightly, the moon even brighter.

"I-I don't know what to say, Great One. There are so many questions we have for you, so much that needs to..." Adeyemi's gaze drifted over the group. Manny had been jerking her head over her shoulders in search of something. With the amazement of Oya's presence wearing off, she finally looked for their friend. TJ fought back the tears he thought he had left back in that shaft of lightning.

"Wait," Manny said. And TJ stood slowly, holding one arm in the other with a harsh grip. How could he tell her? How could he tell them all? "TJ... where's Ayo?"

TJ EXPLAINED EVERYTHING THEY HAD DONE, THE RITUAL TO summon the sky chain, meeting with the Ibeji Orishas, Eshu, Obatala, freeing Oya... and how Ayo had gone off in search of Shango.

They were back in Elder Adeyemi's cavern office, scrunched up on her central island. Oya, in her human form and fully clothed in aso oke robes, paced the ground back and forth with stomping feet. TJ knew she was still fuming because she couldn't get to Shango and because the "silly mortals" had been empowering Olokun for nearly half a year. Elder Adeyemi, Manny, and Ruby all sat around the Headmistress' stone table, listening to TJ intently. Miss Gravés had been sent off to take Titi and Emeka back to their dorms.

TJ hadn't been to Adeyemi's office at night before. It wasn't all that different with it being a cave and everything, but there were a few floating orbs of light. They hung over the cavern pools to support the lack of light coming in from the backside of the waterfall at the cave's mouth.

Adeyemi held to each of TJ's words as he retold the story, only interrupting for clarification here and there. But it was Manny who was keenest to understand what had happened, nursing her head whenever TJ mentioned something she did in the Sky Realm. TJ assumed she *felt* more than she *remembered*, just as she said before, after coming out of the Aqua Realm. So anytime he mentioned something, he knew some conflicting energy within her mind and body battled with one another.

TJ made sure to leave out the stuff that happened in Obatala's Chamber of Candor, of course. For a brief time, he considered how awkward that conversation with Manny would be... especially with what was said there. He wasn't even sure if he should mention it, with her memories the way they were and the tragedy of Ayo. Would she even believe him? How did you even bring something like that up?

"Hey, so we totally confessed that we're in 'like' with each other in this super crazy honesty room. Wanna grab some tofu stew sometime?"

Hell no.

It took a long while for the Headmistress to speak up as she processed everything told to her. She even seemed to list to one side like a palm tree against hurricane winds, and TJ would've sworn he even saw her wipe away a tear, but he couldn't be sure in the cavern's low-light. What was for certain, however, was the prayer she murmured under her lips, one for Ayo, blessing him with a safe journey. Her words came out strained and stuttered, like she didn't believe in her own words. The distressed lines carved in her face told of a war tearing through her as well, a bottle of emotions she capped with a failing expression of neutrality.

Eventually, very softly, she said, "*Abọ́, wá ṣọ́dọ̀ mi,*" and her water bowl manifested at the center of her desk of stone. She dropped in a phial of spirit water, spoke Miss Gravés' full name — Yolanda Linda Espinoza-Gravés — and the teacher's face appeared in the bowl's perpetual floating waterfall.

TJ didn't have the energy to protest that Adeyemi still trusted her. It's not like it mattered. The Keepers had won. Olokun was going to drown Eko Atlantic and TJ had only helped them do it.

"Is there something wrong, Headmistress?" Miss Gravés asked. TJ could only see the back of her head in the water bowl. "I've just returned Titi and Emeka to their dorms. "

"Nothing wrong, Yolanda. We've just got done here. Could you come fetch Manuela Martinez for me, escort her to her dormitories as well?"

"Right away." Miss Gravés's face drifted from the waterfall, and as soon as she did, the water fell back into the bowl.

"Ruby," Adeyemi said. "Take Oya with you to your tent at Oracle Rock. Speak nothing of her presence here. Make sure she's given water and that she eats something until I come for you. The Windweaver won't be used to our troublesome human necessities."

"Yes, Headmistress." Ruby bowed and started to lead Oya out of the cavern office across the stepping stones. She turned her head back and gave TJ and Manny a chin-up nod as she left.

Oya gave the Oracle a curious tilt of her head. "We are to walk back from where we came? Do you diviners not use portals any longer?"

"Oh, yeah, we do," Ruby said. "It's a bit rude to hop in and out of portals in the middle of someone's private quarters. Plus, the Headmistress blocks any access to other —"

Oya flitted her hands in the air and a wind portal sprouted atop one of the stepping stones. On the other end was the top of Oracle Rock with all its tents of animal skins. "After you, mortal." Oya waved a hand inside.

Ruby waited for Adeyemi's approval. The Elder nodded slowly and said, "Go on through. But, Oracle, while you are tending to Oya, please inform her of our laws of magical discretion. Aside from the general clouded, we cannot let it be known that she is among us, including the other oracles. We know how they like to gossip."

"Don't I know it. Of course, Elder." Ruby bowed again, but the embarrassment coloring her cheeks told of the impossible task she was put up to. Oya had generated a portal within the protected office of the Great Elder Adeyemi. TJ frowned. If the Windweaver wished to do as she pleased, how was Ruby supposed to stop her? With a little shudder, Ruby stepped through the wind portal and Oya followed behind. Then the portal fell into itself and disappeared with a vacuum pop.

"Oracles gossip?" TJ asked Adeyemi.

"Like you wouldn't believe. They like the prestige it can bring from the international community. They're as much rumor mongers as they are foretellers, more often than not. But that is not why I wish them kept in the dark, not wholly anyway. It is true what you said. There is a leak within the academy grounds. But it is not Miss Gravés, as you expected."

TJ's focus sharpened with the Elder's last words; even Manny sat straighter next to him. "How can you know for sure?"

"Because," Adeyemi said, "Oracle Ruby has had a vision that 'the leak springs forth from the youngest of cracks.'" TJ gave Elder Adeyemi a questioning look. "It means one of the *younger* individuals is our spy. A student. Not a teacher."

Guilt melted into TJ's gut, but stubborn resolve replaced it. "But... Miss Gravés... she was talking to that Keeper at school —"

"She was merely catching up with a parent."

"But she was following me after Ayo's party—"

"On my orders, as I told you, Mr. Young."

"But..." TJ knew it was useless to go on. Plus, he had been a prime witness to Oracle Ruby's predictions. She was batting a thousand that year. How could he argue against that? That still left another set of questions, though. "So, who then? Who is it?"

"I am investigating the student body starting tomorrow. Everyone is being monitored closely. The truth will come out in time."

"And what about Ayo?" Manny asked. "What are we going to do about him?"

Elder Adeyemi sighed deeply, steepling her fingers and pressing them into her long nose. "That... we have to leave to the Grace of the Orishas. Oya would tell you the same. The Great Separation keeps us from returning to where the boy may be now. If he's anywhere right now. His... existence is in limbo for the time being." She pinched her eyes shut in guarded pain. "I fear I'll have to have a very difficult conversation with his family..."

"No..." TJ let out softly, then with more strength, "No. We can't just leave him behind. I can get the sky chain back. There might be some of the comet's power we used left over. We could all go together this time. We could—"

"I will not allow more of my students to be put in danger, Mr. Young," Elder Adeyemi spoke firmly. "Or did you forget what happened to Adeola Washington and Xavier Du Bois, who even now are still recovering a mere kilometer from here in Babalu-Aye Medical?"

"That's exactly why we have to go back! They were only in the Aqua Realm for a night. Ayo could be stuck longer. If he doesn't come back soon—"

"He will lose himself, yes." The Elder lifted a quivering hand over her mouth that TJ barely registered was another wiping of her tears. "Tomori Jomiloju. Trust me when I say... if there was a way, I would go myself. But there's nothing we can do now. Ayo is on his own journey now, whether in the flesh or as a spirit now..."

"Come on, Manny, we're goin' back." TJ started for the exit across the floating stones, but he didn't hear any footsteps behind him. TJ turned around to find Manny was still standing there with a frown carved deep on her face.

"She's right, TJ," she said softly. "If what you said is true, we have to let Ayo go on his own path. I don't know what happened, but I feel it." She balled a fist over her heart. "He might be our best hope. From what you told us, it sounds like he knew what he was doing, like he seemed to know... something. That's what you told us... that Ayo 'felt' Shango close."

TJ forced his eyes closed to hide their frustration. "Then I'll go alone. I told Titi I'd bring him back safe. I'm not affected by the crazy brain stuff. I can —"

A set of footfalls stopped TJ's words. Behind him, Miss Gravés appeared at the mouth of the tunnel entrance. She stood akimbo, all official-like with those rock-solid arms of hers.

The woman's words came cautiously. "Is... everything all right in here?"

"No," TJ answered right away.

"Mr. Young." Adeyemi stood up at her desk. "Will you allow me a few minutes before you set off and defy me? You and I both know I cannot stop you from reentering the Orisha Plane, as unlikely as that is right now without the comet to empower you. But there is something I'd like you to hear first."

TJ didn't speak, but he didn't move either, which was likely an improvement in Elder Adeyemi's eyes.

"Yolanda, if you would." Adeyemi inclined her head to Miss Gravés. "Miss Martinez here should be off to bed."

Miss Gravés bowed. "Of course, Headmistress. Manuela, please, come with me."

Manny shook her head, her hair gently jostling over her shoulders. "I want to stay with TJ."

If Elder Adeyemi was annoyed or irritated, it didn't show on her face. She did sigh, however, saying, "Miss Martinez. I assure you what I say to Tomori Jomiloju will aid all of us. But it must be said to him alone. Do you understand me?" She blinked wise eyes in Manny's direction, wise eyes that seem to chip away at Manny's armor. Her shoulder lowered in a forfeit, and she set off with slow steps. As she passed TJ, she put a hand to his elbow and squeezed, murmuring, "Whatever you decide to do, let me know. Okay?"

TJ gave her a short nod and watched as she left with Miss Graves. He didn't turn back to Elder Adeyemi until he couldn't hear the echo of their footfalls against the cave walls. The cavern seemed to darken further as the Elder sat there and watched TJ as though she were observing an animal in the zoo. It went without saying, but her look made TJ greatly uncomfortable, and he was relieved when she finally spoke.

"I know I've made it difficult to trust me, young man. The fault, I must admit, is mostly mine. After Olugbala, after Camp Olosa, it's been hard to know who to trust in this new age we're entering." Elder Adeyemi scratched her eyebrow thoughtfully. "Tell me, Mr. Young, have you ever heard the story called 'The Tortoise who had Trouble with Trust'?" TJ shook his head no. "It's a children's story. Quite short. I'll make it even shorter, if that's all right with you."

"Does the story help us find Ayo again?"

Elder Adeyemi tapped her long fingers against her long desk, her jaw clenched as though she wanted to say something, but thought better of it. Eventually she answered, "It will not, but I hope that sharing the story will lead us down a path that does not lead to another student getting stuck — or worse — in the Planes of the Orishas. One that will highlight our own precarious bridge of trust."

TJ gritted his teeth and took a stone seat opposite Elder Adeyemi. "Okay, I'm ready to listen."

"Very well. You see, there was once a tortoise who lived in a forest. Tortoise liked this forest because it had big trees with big holes where he could hide away from dangers. One day, Fox came and told Tortoise there were safer trees deeper in the forest. Tortoise had known Fox only a short time, but he was grateful to her because she warned against predators by screaming like human women do. So Tortoise, on the advice of Fox, ventured deeper into the forest but could not find any trees with good hidey-holes to shelter himself in. In fact, the deep forest held more dangers than before. When Tortoise returned to his original tree, it was occupied by Fox, who was snuggled up in Tortoise's old home. When Tortoise asked for his hole back, do you know what Fox said in return?"

TJ shrugged, uninterested in a child's story with some moral at the end. What they needed to do was make a plan for finding Ayo and he didn't see how the story would help with that.

"Please, Mr. Young, this will only take a moment. What did Fox say in return?"

Annoyed, TJ answered, "Finder's keepers? Step off, Tortoise, this is my home now. I don't know…"

"You are essentially right. Fox claimed the tree for her own and would not return it to Tortoise. So Tortoise went looking for another tree. But when night came, he was slow and plodding, and the predators of the forest nipped at his exposed limbs. But they couldn't get through Tortoise's shell. With all the other trees full with other prey animals hiding, Tortoise was forced to make his very shell into his hidey-hole. Do you know what happened then?"

TJ did his very best to stop his eyes from rolling. "He stayed in that shell for the rest of his days and never let any other foxes trick him out of his home."

"Right you are. But it was Tortoise's hardheadedness that would eventually cause his own demise."

For the first time, TJ lifted curious brows in Elder Adeyemi's direction. He didn't think a children's story would end in tragedy.

"You see, not long after Tortoise found a new home in his own shell, a great danger came to the forest. First, Fox came to warn Tortoise, but Tortoise wouldn't listen. Then came Rabbit, who was always a friend to Tortoise. Rabbit told him to run away deeper into the forest, but Tortoise had heard that trick before and stayed put. Even other tortoises came to warn Tortoise, but he refused to listen to any of them. His trust was broken, and he felt safe where he was. And he stayed there until a great big machine cut the trees down. One of these trees, Tortoise's old home, came crashing down on our green friend… and Tortoise never saw the light of day again."

The crystal lights surrounding the cavern seemed to wink and peeked down at TJ and Elder Adeyemi, like they were listening to the story, too.

"You know why I'm telling you this story, yes?"

This is the part TJ always hated when it came to adults: answering their very obvious questions. He knew the answer, but he didn't want to say it out loud. He didn't want to say that he was the tortoise, Bolawe and Eshu were the Fox and the other forest animals were Elder Adeyemi. The Elder must've known what he was processing in his mind because she said, "There are no bad answers, Mr. Young. Tell me what you think of the story."

"The story was about me," TJ blurted. "I'm the tortoise who can't trust."

"No, Mr. Young." Elder Adeyemi shook her head so slowly it seemed like it barely moved. "What I'm saying is we are *both* the tortoise. And the machine that cut down the forest is Olokun. There are faults on both our ends. I should have been more forthright about the tongue-tied trance. You should have been more honest about what you had planned for tonight with the comet. I acted this way because of the betrayal I felt between myself and Olugbala. You felt that way because I would not listen to your concerns about Miss Graves. We both refused to communicate so we could stay protected in our shells."

"And now we'll both get crushed by the tree."

"I'd like to think we can both brave peeking out of our shells before that happens, don't you?"

The moment of silence between them was profound and TJ couldn't help hearing the waterfalls around them as crashing waves punching into metal skyscrapers.

48

ON THE MEND

TJ STARED AT AYO'S EMPTY BED FOR WHAT HAD TO BE SEVERAL
hours. Even after the sun rose and the other boys woke up and
went about their day, TJ stared. Even after Emeka came over to
figure out what was going on, TJ stared. Even after the room was
long empty and high-noon light slinked through the room, TJ
stared.

It was one day before the term ended. One day and Ayo
could've been going back home to his family in Lagos.

One. Damn. Day.

TJ had to believe he was okay. If Ayo did find Shango, no,
when he found Shango, he would come back and everything would
be fine. Titi could have her boyfriend-not-boyfriend back. Eni
would have her cousin back.

And TJ and Manny would have their best friend back.

TJ laughed to himself, his light chuckle echoing off the stone
walls of his dorm. To think, just a handful of months ago, he hated
Ayo to the point where he shot a wind blast directly into his chest.
If past TJ would've seen him now, he'd never believe it.

The brief levity of the random laughter loosened the tightness
in TJ's chest, but the unforgiving hold came right back a moment
later, worse than before. Because it was all the bonding he had
done with Ayo, all the teasing, all the adventures they got into that

were in jeopardy. That was truly where his sadness lay. The loss of not only Ayo himself but their unlikely friendship.

Even if Ayo came back, would he come back the same way?

It wasn't until Oroma came over with her head literally sitting within her cupped hands at her waist that TJ stirred in his bedsheets.

"What is it, Oroma?" TJ groaned.

"Is it true that Ayo boy got himself stuck in the Sky Realm?" Her head flopped to one side, her stiff basket braids barely moved.

TJ threw his pillow over his head. Oroma loved gossip, and he wasn't anywhere near in the mood to dish.

"I'll take that as a yes. You know, for a kid who doesn't speak, that Emeka boy sure knows how to spread a story around. Everyone is talking about it. In fact, I haven't seen news spread that fast across the grounds since that time everyone was saying you got that Anderson kid from last year kicked out. Hmmm, no... when your sister was at this school, there was a new rumor every week, and they spread just as fast."

"Go away, Oroma," TJ groaned again. "Please."

"Sure thing, kid." The distinct *squish* of Oroma plopping her head on right pressed through TJ's bedsheets. "Oh, yes. I was supposed to tell you that your Manny friend left this morning."

TJ whipped his covers off his body and threw his pillows to the side. "What? Did she go to the Sky Realm?" Why would she do that? They were supposed to do that together. How would she even manage it on her own? Did she get help from Oya?

"What!?" Oroma gave him bug-eyes. "To the *Sky Realm*? Orunmila's Stars! Heavens no. Her dorm leader escorted her to Babalu-Aye Medical. She's suffering from some strong migraines. Thought I should let you know since I always see you two together, and she gave you that present. Are you two an item? Word through the academy was that you were with that Eniola girl."

TJ rolled his eyes, snagged up some shoes, and a jacket, and bolted out of his dorm. Keeping Omo of Fon's lessons in mind, he air-stepped the whole way from his dorm to the entrance statues, where he picked up his phone at the checkout hut. Then he was through the Summoning Stone, through the enchanted earth to New Ile-Ife—where his bodyguards tailed him and did their best to keep up. He continued through New Ile-Ife, brushing shoulders with the locals and saying his "sorrys" and "*pèlés*," depending on who he bumped into, then headed straight to the reception desk of Babalu-Aye Medical. The woman who sat behind the long, plain white counter gave a little yelp as TJ rushed in. Her headscarf, which was wrapped tall and high, nearly tilted to one side. She righted it atop her head before asking, "Oh dear! You again? What can I do for you, young man? Adeola Washington is still not ready for visitors."

Out of breath, TJ asked, "Manuela Martinez? Is she here? I want to see her."

"Are you next of kin?"

"No."

"Are you a guardian of this young woman?"

"Of course not."

TJ and the receptionist went back and forth about hospital protocols and visitation regulations for several minutes. A few times, TJ turned to his bodyguards for help, but they stood there like the gargoyles they always were. It wasn't until one of the healers recognized TJ as "the Hero of Nigeria's brother" that the receptionist's tone changed and she let TJ right in.

"You should have said you were a Young this whole time, young man!"

Ugh, I should have started with that, TJ thought.

The Healer who recognized TJ said, "Right this way. Miss Martinez just came in an hour ago." He led them down the hall.

The hospital was like any other in the world of the "clouded": sterile walls, a perpetual stench of bleach, and blah-white to color the corridors. The only difference was the patients, who ranged from humans suffering from bush-baby boils to aziza suffering from crusty wing strain to even vampires suffering from rare skin conditions. TJ knew all this because the Healer who escorted them explained it all with enthusiasm. He must've been a junior healer, straight out of university. Much like Umar, he was oddly shaped, though most of his unique features were on his face. A small head fitted with large ears and even larger lips.

"You've scheduled your appointment for your adze antidote, haven't you? Those creatures are masquerading as humans again, and it's quite easy to fall prey to their possession."

"Uh, yeah, I think so," TJ answered as they climbed their way to the second floor, where two ghoulish creatures passed by carrying a gray blob in blankets that TJ assumed was their offspring.

"So! You're not an SS1 student, right?" the zealous healer went on. "You should know how to concoct the elixir of chimes before then. If you end up sourcing your staff from the Congo, it'll be a lifesaver against those nasty eloko out there." The Healer turned to TJ's entourage. "You big fellas, too. You should always have the right potions and draughts with you at all times." He tapped at his waist, rattling a utility belt that could've put Batman's to shame. "I've got myself covered. Can't be too safe these days."

"Yeah, yeah," TJ said offhandedly. He was too busy looking through every door with a sliver of a window to see if Manny was inside. After their fifth door, TJ saw a mass of hair poking out from a medical cot. "Wait, wait, I think that's my friend in there!"

The Healer halted in the middle of the hall. "Oh, my mistake. We *did* just pass her room, didn't we? Sorry, when I get going, I really can get going. My instructors always said I could get a bit chatty. Hey, did I mention there's a sunlit beetle epidemic brewing in Egypt? No one will listen, but so long as you have a moonstone strapped around a—"

"Thank you very much, Healer..." TJ looked for a name tag, mostly to cut another rant off from the guy.

"Healer Zakari!"

"You've been a great help." TJ turned to his bodyguards. "Make sure to put in a good word for this man with one of his boss-healers or whatever, would you?"

"Sure thing, sir," said the taller one through his iron mask.

"*Dájúdájú*," said the second, older one in Yoruba.

Healer Zakari thanked TJ over and over, but before he could get out his dozenth utterance of gratitude, TJ slipped into Manny's room and closed the door behind him.

Manny was alone in the small room, laid across a medical bed with an end table filled with phials of potions of purples and blues that bubbled softly. Afternoon light poured in from the back through the lines of the vertical blinds.

TJ took a seat next to Manny with great care. What were all those potions for? Was her chest moving? Once he realized she was breathing normally, he let her rest and simply watched her. Besides a few beads of sweat along her forehead peeking through her bangs, she looked perfectly ordinary, perfectly at peace. TJ wasn't sure how long he was there before she woke up with a yawn.

TJ smiled. "Are you feeling okay?"

"Much better. This Healer Zakari guy might have overdone it with the diagnosis though. He was saying I might have some disease coming out of Giza."

"The sunlit beetle epidemic?"

"Yeah, that's the one." Manny let out a pained sigh. "Elder Adeyemi explained that I had been through a 'spiritual awakening' or whatever, so the healers hooked me up with some potions to clear my head—basically Advil on magical steroids."

"The Headmistress was here?"

"Yeah, when my dorm leader was taking me out, Elder Adeyemi took over. She's still tryin' to keep everything on the down-low, but she looks mad worried. I think she just got done tellin' Ayo's family what happened."

A buzz came at TJ's hip and he checked his phone. Right on cue, it was a message from Eni.

Eni: OMG! WTH happened? R u ok? Is it true Ayo's stuck in the Sky Realm?

"Let me guess. Eni?" Manny asked.

TJ put his phone away. He'd figure out what to tell Eni later. He also had to remind himself that everything was basically reset a whole day with Manny. With everything going on with regards to Ayo, he hadn't even really thought about how to deal with all that.

"Yeah," he said. "It's her. Looks like whatever Adeyemi told Ayo's family, it got around already."

"Something happened in the Sky Realm, didn't it?" Her question held more than general curiosity. TJ knew it was because the topic of Eni came up.

TJ's stomach fluttered. "W-what do you mean?"

"I mean, I don't feel mad at you anymore, but... I don't know why. What happened?"

"We uh... we uh... had a talk."

"What about?"

"Uh... stuff." Manny made a face. "Good stuff. We're uh... not mad at each other anymore."

Two more buzzes came at TJ's hip. He checked his phone again.

Eni: shit! my mom is on a bowl with Adeyemi right now. She is PO'd!

Eni: text me ASAP.

"You should probably be a good boyfriend and answer those," Manny said.

TJ wanted to come out and tell her everything that happened in that room of truth, but he wasn't sure how she would take it. Plus, in her current state, he didn't want to add to her migraines. It hardly seemed appropriate with everything going on with Ayo and Olokun and everything else. Teenage drama could wait. So, he agreed, "Yeah, you're probably right. I'll be back later, Manny. Glad you're doing better."

Sitting up from his chair, TJ made his way to the door. But before he could grab the knob, a howl of wind came from one side of the room. Manny's blankets rose in the air, and a few loose papers on a desk fluttered. TJ's gaze narrowed to Oya stepping out of a wind portal with two bowls of fish stew in hand. Behind her was the dock of the Mami Wata Eatery.

"Oh," Oya said. "Hello there, Tomori Jomiloju!"

Had she already given Oracle Ruby the slip? TJ had to ask. "Aren't you supposed to be with Ruby at Ifa Academy?" He peeked into the hall nervously to make sure no one had heard her come in.

"Yes, I am," was her answer as she brushed past him and went straight for Manny. She bumped into the chair at Manny's bedside as she went. She would've dropped her stew too if she didn't catch it with wind magic before it hit the ground. "Oof, these damn human eyes. You do know your kind are almost completely blind, right? I'd forgotten."

"Um... Oya," TJ whispered so that his bodyguards outside wouldn't hear him. "What are you doing here?"

"Giving Manuela here the care she needs. You didn't think that Healer Zakari is what brought her migraines down, did you?"

Well, it was nice to see Oya wasn't always in warrior-mode. The caretaker persona was definitely one TJ preferred.

"Go ahead, TJ, it's fine," Manny said as Oya cupped her hand over Manny's forehead, feeding her stew. The motherly figure Oya possessed looked right at home at Manny's side. "We said she's my auntie. Everyone's chill about it."

TJ groaned internally before clenching his fist and turning on his heel. Oya better not get herself caught, least of all by the bodyguards or some Keeper spy snooping around. They were working from way behind as it was. The only advantage they had was that no one knew Oya was in New Ile-Ife.

"Oh, TJ, one more thing!" Manny said just as he reached the door once more. "You came straight over when you heard about me, didn't you?"

"Yeah... How did you know that?"

"Your breath is mad funky, man." Manny scrunched up her nose. "You forgot to brush before you came running, huh?"

"Oh, is that what that smell was?" Oya sniffed the air and mirrored Manny's scrunched nose.

Manny laughed. "Make sure to pop in a mint or two before you see your girl, a'ight?"

Oya furrowed her brow. "Make it a dozen, child."

"All right, all right, I get it." TJ blew into his hand and smelled. He nearly burned the hairs in his nose; his breath smelled so bad. Still, TJ couldn't help but smile as Manny laughed at his expense. At least she was feeling better. That's all that really mattered.

49

THE MANGLED AND THE MAD

TJ PULLED HIS PHONE OUT THE MOMENT HE LEFT MANNY'S room and back into the blah, sterile white of the hospital. In the time it took to leave, Eni had sent a slew of texts and even a phone call that went straight to voicemail.

> TJ: i gotta lot to tell you. im alr tho
> TJ: lets facetime tonight?

Eni's reply came almost instantly.

> Eni: for sure. glad u r ok! 😊 😄

It wasn't lost on TJ that this would be the first time he would get to see Eni face-to-face since their… pairing. Could he actually go through with breaking up with her at a time like this?

TJ's bodyguards stood at attention. The one who spoke English asked, "How is your friend, Mr. Young?"

"She's doing all right. Thanks for asking."

"*Gba okan*," said the other one, smiling. He held out a can of mints.

TJ rolled his eyes and thought, *None of them are going to let me live that down, are they?*

The bodyguard shook his mint can and laughed under his

mask. His partner chuckled, too. TJ took a handful and popped them into his mouth. As he sucked them down to cloak his morning breath, he noticed a figure down the hall he had not seen in quite a while.

Violently, his mind flashed back to a time when he was underwater, floating before a grand staircase that led up to the image of his one-time Ogbon Studies counselor at Camp Olosa. Back then, the figure was held up by two jellyfish; now, the figure was held up by two healers.

"Mr. Du Bois..." TJ said breathlessly.

He made his way down the hall. With each step, Mr. Du Bois's face took greater definition. The man's cheeks were still a bit bloated and bruised, and his lips were still a bit fat and drooping, but he was doing a lot better than when TJ found him in the Aqua Realm. The healers even slicked back his hair the way he liked it. But a short beard covered his usual pencil-thin mustache.

"Mr. Du Bois," TJ said when he approached him. The old man shuffled across the linoleum floor at a snail's pace.

"There you go, Xavier," one of the Healers said. He had green skin with horns. "Just a bit more."

"*Ò jẹ ẹlẹtàn,*" Mr. Du Bois murmured. "*Ò jẹ ẹlẹtàn,*" he repeated.

In Yoruba, he was saying, "he's a traitor." TJ remembered Ayo translating that down in the Aqua Realm. That was in reference to Bolawe, who turned out to be the leader of the Keepers, and Du Bois had shouted the phrase like a broken record. Only now, Mr. Du Bois wasn't saying it on a loop. Now it seemed like he was saying the phrase in place of words as he answered the Healer's questions.

"How does that feel, Xavier?" the other Healer, who looked like a humanoid dragon, asked. "Do you think the Locomotion Elixir did the trick?"

"*Ò jẹ ẹlẹtàn,*" Mr. Du Bois answered, and TJ knew by his tone of voice that he meant "yes."

"E-e-excuse me," TJ stuttered. "My name is Tomori Jomiloju. Tomori Jomiloju Young. I know this man."

Mr. Du Bois met TJ's gaze with knowing eyes. "*Ò jẹ ẹlẹtàn.*"

"Ah," the green-skinned healer said, "he seems to know you as well. How are you two acquainted?"

"He..." TJ's voice trailed off, and his eyes trailed to the floor as well. "He was my counselor at summer camp."

"Hang on a minute." The dragon-looking healer kneeled down to get a better look at TJ. She had a hissing kind of voice, everything coming out like a strained whisper. "Oh, yes. Ifedayo Young's little brother. What are you doing here?"

TJ rubbed the back of his neck. "Just, um... visiting a friend. Why is Mr. Du Bois still repeating the same phrase?"

The healers exchanged frowns, the green one whispered into Mr. Du Bois's ear, then he nodded with an approving smile. Or at least, the closest thing he could do to a smile.

"He may be this way the rest of his life," the green healer said. "It's bad enough he was cursed the way he was. But he was down in the Aqua Realm so long... All said, he's doing a lot better than that Adeola girl, surprisingly."

TJ wondered why Adeola wasn't walking the halls as well. The thought of her being like Mr. Du Bois, with a slack jaw and repeated phrases, filled him with shame.

"What do you mean?" TJ asked. "Adeola isn't better yet?"

The dragon-looking healer shook her head. "She has locked her mind away, seemingly in a permanent state."

Locked her mind away? At the end of camp, and earlier in the term, Elder Adeyemi had said she was able to speak to Adeola's mind, just like she spoke to TJ's mind with those conservators back in Yemoja's chamber.

Biting down on his lip nervously, TJ asked, "Where is her room? I'd like to see her if that's okay."

HAD IT NOT BEEN FOR THE TWO UCMP OFFICIALS WHO WERE with him, TJ might not have gotten into Adeola's room. TJ had sort of thought of his shadows as a bit of a nuisance, but in that moment, they had become a bit more useful.

Adeola's room was way different from Manny's. The walls were still painted with boring hues of white and eggshell, but there were no windows, and one long tube sat in the middle. Well, not a tube exactly, more like a dunk tank filled to the brim with a faint green liquid. In the center of the tank floated Adeola, dressed in what looked like a white one-piece bathing suit. Her eyes pinched together like she was struggling with something, her head twisting every so often. The rest of her looked normal, though—except for the whole floating in green slush part, of course.

"She is still in something like a comatose state," the green-skinned healer said softly. "We healers do not know why. Though some have theories. Namely, your Headmistress at Ifa. She says Adeola's mind must simply not be ready."

TJ stepped forward to get a better look at Adeola in her tube. Tiny bubbles lifted from her nose, drifting slowly in the gelatin-like substance that surrounded her.

"If it's all right with you two," TJ said without turning to look at the healers behind him, "can I be with Adeola alone?"

"Anything for a Young," the dragon-looking healer said. "Your two giants are just outside the door here."

A pair of flats *click-clacked* out of the room, followed by another pair of leathery-padded stomps. TJ waited a full minute before he took steps forward to Adeola's tube. It took him another minute for him to actually touch the glass. The moment his skin pressed against the container, it felt like a force magnetized him there. A bright light emitted from his finger and he realized it was the Eshu symbol pressed to it, reflecting off the glass.

Ashe rushed through his body as he tried to pull his finger away, but it was stuck there. Fear tugged at him momentarily. Was he stuck to the glass for good? Adeola didn't stir, even as TJ grunted and pulled. It was like he touched his tongue to a cold pole. TJ was about to call out for help when he saw something reflecting back at him. It was his own face, but there was something odd about it. The shape was the same, but the features were different: his round ears were more pointed, his big eyes appeared more almond-shaped, and his wide nose had shrunk down, too.

What was going on? What was happening to his face? Again, he was halfway to shouting for help when Adeola's lips started moving, and with that movement came a voice... soft and gentle.

The words weren't intelligible. TJ couldn't even be sure what he was hearing was any language at all. It was more a... feeling, like when a mother calls to her child, when someone familiar calls out your name. Wait. It was the same feeling he got when his sister called his name! TJ's eyes flitted back to his reflection, and he understood. Those features he saw before were his sister! His eyes were her eyes, his nose was her nose, those pointed ears... totally Dayo!

"Dayo! Is that you?" As TJ asked the question, it was like a ghost escaped his body and left him empty. TJ fell to his knees, weakened. His finger had been freed from the glass at last.

Above him, someone was coughing. TJ's heavy and woozy head lulled back and up to find Adeola. She whipped her face free from green gloop with one hand, her other arm slung over the tank's brim. She kept squinting and blinking, but eventually, her eyes adjusted and fixed on TJ, her lips curled in a smirk.

Sluggishly, she lifted her arms. "I told you to wait." Shame washed through TJ. That was true. In their fight in the Aqua Realm, the last thing he had done was blast Adeola with a spell cast from two staffs, square in her chest. As though remembering the pain, Adeola pressed her palm over her torso. "Nice shot, by the way."

"Adeola?"

"That's my name. Don't wear it out, dude."

"How do you have your memories?"

"Well, I'm not an old lady yet, so my memories should be fine. Why do you ask?"

That Ashe TJ felt before leaked out as he stood up. "Well, you were in the Aqua Realm, so you shouldn't remember anything."

Adeola's eyes went foggy. "Hang on. Where am I?" Her voice became more rapid, then immediate. "We have to stop Olugbala! He's working with Eshu! The staff, TJ, the Gatekeeper's staff!"

TJ knees wobbled, and he found balance on the tube. It seemed like Adeola had retained her memories for at least a little while, but how? Was it something TJ did to help her? "That was months ago, Deola. There's a lot to catch you up on. Listen to me closely. You are in Babalu-Aye Medical. You've been in a sort of... coma for a little while. You didn't wake up until I..." Wait, was it Dayo who helped bring her back? "Deola, did you see my sister in that thing you're in? I think she helped me wake you up."

Still floating at the top of the tank, Adeola rubbed her head. "Your sister? No... no... the only one who was speaking to me was... Elder Adeyemi. Oh, I'm remembering now. Adeyemi's been in my head this whole time, updating me. Olokun... Olugbala... They haven't been stopped yet, huh?"

TJ shook his head. "Come on, let's get you out of that thing. I gotta tell the healers you're awake."

50

A SILENT CONFESSION

TJ STARED AT THE TATTOO ON HIS FINGER AS THE HOSPITAL room exploded with activity. The moment he let the healers know Adeola was awake, several specialists rushed in and out to check on her stability, and the hospital contacted all her close relatives to come to the medical center immediately.

After the healers realized Adeola was okay—outside of her expected memory loss—they vanished her tank away and put her up in a nice big bed to rest. TJ barely noticed any of this because he was staring at the mirror implanted on the wall near a faucet. He kept pressing his finger into the mirror, hoping the features on his face would change or he would hear or feel that familiar sensation again. But nothing.

"Healer Zakari," Adeola called from her bed. At that moment, the Healer and a host of other medical students huddled around her bed. "Do you mind if I speak to TJ alone for a bit? It's been a minute since we've been able to chop it up."

Healer Zakari bowed with exaggeration. "Of course, of course, Miss Washington. We'll be just outside. But please call on us if you feel *anything* at all, loss of balance, diminished hearing, fatigue, muscle aches, diarrhea—"

Adeola waved a dismissive hand at the Healer. "You'll be the first to know, dude."

"Oh, so sorry! I really can get going. Apologies." Zakari

bowed. "With me, everyone, these results aren't going to assess themselves."

"Bet you forty cowries he'll diagnose her with bush baby boils," a student in the crowd said to another before the door closed behind them.

The room was left in silence, save for the bubbling cauldron that was sitting on the end table next to Adeola's bed. TJ thought he heard one of the medical students saying it was some sort of experimental memory loss potion that wasn't meant to be drunk but inhaled like a humidifier.

Silence hung in the room a bit longer before Adeola said, "Stop staring at that mirror and tell me what I missed. Adeyemi only said so much."

TJ gave his reflection one last long look, hoping his round ears would sprout into a point or for his eyes to morph into an almond-shape. But when nothing happened, he grabbed a chair, set it next to Adeola, and told her everything that happened since he fought her in the Aqua Realm.

"Bolawe and the Keepers jumped me a little while ago, too. They did this whole ritual thing on me. Some reading with this blind oracle."

"Elder Ojo," Adeola groaned. "Your sister didn't like that guy much."

"Speaking of my sister…" Throughout TJ's retelling he'd beat around the bush, not truly wanting to know the truth about his sister, but he knew it had to be done. It was time to *really* know what was going on. "What happened to her, Deola? Is it really true? You and her really were Keepers—um—*are* Keepers?"

Adeola broke eye contact with TJ to look away at where her healing tank had once stood. She clenched her jaw and TJ would've sworn a tear was trying to crest her eyelids. "Yes, TJ, we were Keepers. *Were.*"

It was the answer TJ was expecting, and he should have been prepared for how it would feel, but it was still horrible to hear. He choked on his anger as he blurted, "Why? Why would you join up with those creeps?"

"You have to understand, TJ," Adeola said very slowly. "We thought they were doing the right thing. They weren't so radical three years ago when we started up with them. Real talk... it seemed like they were the only ones who wanted to make any *real* progress in the magical world."

"What do you mean by... progress?"

Adeola shifted her head back to TJ, biting her lip. "The Orishas. They were the only ones who wanted to bring 'em back. Or at least the only ones makin' active steps to do it. When you start lookin' into our history as diviners, there are so many things we coulda stopped, so many things that coulda been prevented if we had the Orishas' power with us again."

Yep, definitely a Keeper. Adeola was sounding just like Bolawe at that Olokun festival. "But in Ethics class they say we are separated from the clouded because if we ever came into conflict, we would lose. There's too little of us if we expose ourselves."

"Your teachers aren't wrong there. And it wasn't our intention as Keepers to expose ourselves. At least, not until we were ready. If anything, it was the UCMP always being on our case that compromised the whole—" Adeola forced herself to stop. Clearly, some old wounds and forgotten anger were resurfacing. She had renounced the Keepers, but the reason she had joined them to begin with hadn't gone away. "Anyway... that's why me, your sister, and a few others went along with the Keepers. And we did a whole lot of good in those three years before Dayo..." Adeola's voice hitched. "Before Dayo..."

TJ put a hand to Adeola's wrist. "Please, I want to know. I *have* to know. The Keepers are right about one thing. I am connected to Dayo somehow. Her spirit is out there trying to speak to me or something, ever since her funeral. She's even giving me her habits and all that. I hated peaches, but now I can't get enough of them!" He sighed, peering back at the mirror over the faucet again. "And her face was on my reflection before you woke up in that big tube."

Adeola gave TJ a curious look, as though searching for the truth in his words. "Dayo and I didn't know what we was messin' with 'til it was too late. No, that's a lie... *I* didn't know what we was messin' around with until it was too late. Your sister was already steppin' off from the Keepers, but it's hard to make a clean break from people like that. Dayo kept tryin' to convince me it was a bad idea to bring the Orishas back, but she never gave me a straight reason why. So we argued. We argued pretty bad." This time a tear did roll down her cheek.

TJ felt himself wanting to shed a tear, too. He cleared his throat to settle himself before saying, "But... *how* did she die?"

Pain stretched across the lines of Adeola's pinched eyes. Another tear escaped her lids and drifted down her cheek, and she sniffed back a third tear. "Olugbala figured out a way to bring back Olokun, but it required your sister's cooperation. There was this meeting, a small one. It was set up for a ritual that should've gotten us into the Aqua Realm. But Dayo defied the order to help. She said she was close to figuring somethin' out. She was having visions, dark visions that came with the return of the Orishas. But again, she couldn't explain herself properly."

"But... Eshu said there's nothing light or dark about the Orishas inherently. They're supposed to be as amoral as a storm or a tidal wave, right?"

"Dayo said the danger didn't come with the Orishas themselves. It came from somewhere else, something generated from their return. She said she needed more time to figure it out, but the other Keepers weren't about to wait. A week later, they started up the ritual to get to the Aqua Realm. I don't know if it would've even worked, but it spooked Dayo enough. She went to stop them, but I told her to just let it happen. We... argued again. A pretty bad fight. Not just about the ritual. There was a lot said that never should've been, on both sides."

TJ gulped. "So, when Dayo went to face the Keepers, she did it alone?"

Adeola nodded sadly. "Only Olugbala's most inner circle was allowed. A bunch of the worst people I once thought were strong and brave. Only the most radical wanted to crossover. And you can't negotiate with those kinds of people. Dayo walked into her own execution. I'm not even certain who killed her... It could've been any of them, Olugbala included." Adeola clenched her fist and dug it into her sheets. She sniffed again, still holding back that third tear that wanted desperately to fall. "When they found her body, I rushed straight over. They said she put up a fight, but she didn't kill any of the Keepers. And trust me, your sister could've taken down half of that inner circle without breaking a sweat. She was... too good. Too damn good." Her last words came out bitterly, like she blamed Dayo for letting herself get killed.

The hole in TJ's chest opened to an endless pit. It was like experiencing his sister's death all over again. Instead of sorrow billowing in his body, though, rage quickly boiled up. Now he knew for sure the Keepers killed his sister. More than that, he might've been in the presence of her murderers. That Brother David, with the beard and dreadlocks, was trusted by Bolawe. He could've been one of the Keepers who ended Dayo's life. That Sister Bisi with her sharp teeth seemed pretty close to Bolawe, too. She was unhinged enough to cast a deadly curse at Dayo without a second thought.

But one thing didn't track in Adeola's story. TJ opened his mouth, his voice hoarse.

"It couldn't've been Bolawe," TJ said. "He loved my sister like his own daughter. I don't agree with him, and he needs to go down alongside his Keepers, but he, for real, didn't want to see Dayo dead, no matter how much they disagreed."

"You're right about that." Adeola adjusted her bangs from her face, but TJ knew she was wiping away another tear. "It broke Bolawe... your sister's death. I didn't think he'd ever be the same. But when your Ashe manifested in the summer, Bolawe thought he had a second chance with you because you might've somehow connected with Dayo."

"Yeah, he tried mixing my blood with his, but that Oracle said his destiny isn't tied to mine like it was with Dayo."

Adeola hummed under her lips. They were a bit chapped, so TJ fetched her some water the healers had brought in.

"TJ," she said after a sip. "I don't know what it is your sister figured out. I know that prophecy about her being the falling star and the one to bring back the Orishas is a thing, but she didn't want any of that. All I know is that she was *very* serious about keepin' the separation between us and the Orishas. Enough that she was willing to die to stop us. I should've listened to her. I *should* have. Olokun *can't* come back. You have to stop him and the Keepers."

"Yeah... and that's where the whole Sky Realm part of the story comes up."

Adeola jerked up in her ned. "You went to the Sky Realm, too?"

"Yeah... Met up with Eshu again, the Ibeji, Obatala, and..." He wasn't sure he was allowed to tell her about Oya being a few floors down, so he kept his mouth shut. "Oya was there, too. She told us we're doomed. We've been empowering Olokun this whole time instead of her and her husband, Shango."

"Sheeesh," Adeola said. "And Yemoja will be at Olokun's side too with that ice magic you returned to her. She and him are linked as the overseers of the ocean, you know. Husband and wife, too."

"Ugh!" TJ pressed his hand to his forehead. "Don't remind me."

A knock came from behind them. Before either of them could answer, the door squeaked open slowly and the dragon-looking healer popped her head in. "Miss Washington, I told your family you were awake. Your cousins came first. They're here to see you."

"Can you have them wait? I'm still speaking with TJ."

"No, it's okay. You should see your family," TJ said. "I'll wait in the hall and we'll talk more later. Healer, let them in, please."

When TJ got up and turned around, he found himself face-to-face with Titilayo and her twin, Emeka. The trio stared at each other like none of them had seen another human being at all, and the silence between them was palpable.

TJ was the first to burst out with a, "Y'all are Adeola's cousins!?"

Emeka stood shell-shocked, but Titi nodded very slowly, eyes wide and drifting between TJ and Adeola.

"Uh..." Adeola said. "I'm guessing you all know each other, then?"

TJ glanced over his shoulder. "So, we were talking about the Sky Realm, yeah?"

"That was the next part of your story, yes."

TJ thumbed to Titi and Emeka. "I forgot to mention they were involved, too. They're the reasons the Ibeji helped us and…" TJ twisted back to the twins. "I haven't told them what happened yet. So um… I guess… everyone, take a seat. There's more to discuss."

Like with Adeola, TJ recounted the story from the Sky Realm, still leaving out how Oya was actually on the Mortal Realm and a few floors down from them tending to Manny. He explained how helpful the Ibeji were and how Titi and Emeka were vital to the golden chain coming down from the heavens. He spoke of Ayo's bravery in the shaft of lightning, their escape, all of it.

"And then he came by to pay me a visit with a wake-up call," Adeola joked.

The whole time TJ told the story of the Sky Realm, Titi hung on every word so she could translate it into sign language for Emeka, which made the retelling slow going. There were times where she forgot to sign though because she was so into what TJ had to say, and she had her own questions about all the Orishas TJ, Manny, and Ayo had encountered. And, of course, when it came to Ayo disappearing and going off to find Shango, she had the most questions. But TJ felt bad that he couldn't give her any good answers. Emeka, however, barely moved at all, save for his blinking. Just like that entire first term, he kept giving TJ odd looks, only this time the expressions weren't grimaces, but rather, something between confusion and sadness.

"So, Ayo… is he okay though?" Titi asked through a hitched voice. "I don't understand how he just… left like that. Is he alive?"

TJ rubbed his hands together nervously. "I honestly don't know, Titi. And it scares me, too. The moment I know I can get back there, believe me, I'm going back."

"Good, I'm going with you, then."

TJ shook his head so hard and suddenly he rattled his brain. "No! No one can cross over with me anymore. It's too dangerous.

Again, I'm so, so sorry about Ayo. I know how much he meant
—*means*—to you."

"Never apologize for a warrior." Titi puffed out her chest. TJ
never realized how tiny she actually was, but that became
apparent as she flexed up. "That's what Ayo is. A warrior. Just
like Shango. He'll be back. We just have to believe it."

At her side, Emeka started signing something. The gesture
was agitated and TJ wondered what sort of insult would be slung
his way. How could the kid be so bitter after everything that was
going on? It didn't track.

"What do you mean, it doesn't make sense?" Titi asked him.
"Of course TJ would bring Adeola back if he could."

Emeka kept signing like Titi didn't understand.

"What is he signing?" TJ asked.

"He's... he's saying... 'they lied to me. They told me TJ
attacked Adeola and put her in a coma.'"

"Well..." TJ started with a bit of guilt. "Whoever 'they' are is
right. I did technically attack Adeola, but I thought she was the
bad guy. I thought she was a—" He stopped himself short and
gave Adeola a sidelong glance. He didn't want to blow that secret
to her family if they didn't already know, just like TJ didn't want
to blow Dayo's secret to his own.

"What are you talking about, Emeka? It's not your fault," Titi
translated as Emeka went on, still utterly agitated in his hand
movements. "He says that we don't understand. It's his fault all of
this is happening because..." She clapped her hand over her
mouth. "Emeka! No! You didn't!"

"Because what?" TJ asked, pushing himself to the edge of his
seat. "What did he say?"

It was Adeola who answered. "He says he's been feeding
information to the Keepers."

All the air was sucked out of the room. TJ's head went on a
carousel as he reeled in his seat. *Are you kidding me?* He must've
heard incorrectly. There was no way that could be true. But something deep down told him it was. It all started to fall into place.
He already knew the Keepers were strolling around New Ile-Ife.
He could already imagine Bolawe or any of the others
approaching Emeka at Mami Wata's or wherever else. And they

could've given Emeka the perfect story: TJ hurting his family, his cousin. The spy was never a teacher at all, not Miss Gravés or any of the others, just like Elder Adeyemi had said, just like Oracle Ruby had predicted.

It was a student.

And didn't that just fit the Keepers' mode of operation? To recruit impressionable kids who were already a little bit angry, to turn that anger into action for their own gains? That's how they roped in Dayo, how they wrangled Adeola.

Emeka started signing again, this time more sadly. He kept his head down, unable to meet TJ's gaze. Titi was still in too much shock to translate, so Adeola did it for her. "He says, 'I'm sorry, TJ. I was an idiot.' He says after his reading with Oracle Ruby, he thought you were the bad guy. And when he found out I was in the hospital *because* of you, the Keepers approached him. They told him…"

Titi slapped her second hand over the first. "Adeola! You're a Keeper, too!?"

Emeka signed angrily at his twin. TJ understood that one. He was clearly making it known that *he* was not a Keeper. Or, at least, that he didn't consider himself one.

TJ lifted his head, looking for an answer in the blank, white walls, but they gave him nothing. "I don't get it. How did you even spy on us, anyway?" Sure, Emeka was around him a lot. They had classes together. But anytime TJ tried to talk to him outside of school, Emeka would just stomp straight off.

Emeka started signing again, and Adeola translated. "He's explaining that he didn't become hearing impaired until childhood, so he's pretty good at reading lips. Apparently, he spent a lot of time reading yours, TJ, whenever he saw you with your friends."

Of course! The first time they met, Ayo had said the boy could read lips. TJ had even spoken to Emeka slowly and clearly for that very reason on the top of Oracle Rock.

Then Emeka did something TJ wasn't aware he could do. He spoke. Well, sort of spoke. "I'm… sorry… TJ… I'll… make it… up… to… you." His speech was halting and drawn out from the effort of enunciating without sound to help him. "I... promise I... will."

TJ swallowed deeply, trying very hard not to completely lose it against Emeka. If it wasn't for him, Ayo might not be gone. TJ might've been able to find Oya sooner and have empowered her for February. Now everything completely sucked. He didn't know how much worse it could get.

Suddenly, Healer Zakari burst into the room. "Did you hear the news? Did you hear the news?" He waved his hand in the air and said, "*Ṣúṣú, kuro lati mi!*" The wall-mounted TV in the room cut onto breaking news from Divination Today. On screen was Chika Ogunseye just outside the entrance grounds of Ifa Academy. Behind her, a group of UCMP officers with staffs and wands in hand flanked someone between them with mystical restraints over their wrists. Whoever it was wore a killer set of robes with actual flowers that stretched to the sun high above, a set of dazzling robes only one person TJ knew would ever wear...

"Again, this is breaking news from the entrance of Ifa Academy of Tomorrow's Diviners. It was rumored before, but now we have visual confirmation."

Titi waved her hands in the air as well and closed captions appeared on the TV for Emeka's benefit.

"In coordination with the Board of Mystical Education of West Africa and the United Council of Magical Peoples," Chika went on, "Headmistress Simisola Adeyemi has been removed from her position as head of the academy and has been arrested for several charges placed against her, including theft from the Museum of Mystical Artifacts in the United Kingdom, violation against the Code of Concealment in the slums of Makoko, and—this just in—child endangerment and negligence. It seems one of the students at the academy has gone missing. Sources close to Divination Today tell us... Is this right?" Chika pressed a hand to her temple and TJ wondered if someone was feeding information to her telepathically. "Orunmila's Stars! The missing student is none other than the child of real estate mogul Mobolaji Oyelowo, his only son, Ayodeji Oyelowo. Again, *former* Headmistress Simisola Adeyemi is being removed from Ifa Academy and is being charged with—"

TJ outstretched his hand and said, *"Sisu, kuro lati mi."* Ashe flung from his fingertips and pressed into the TV button to turn it off.

TJ was completely and utterly numb. Emeka held his head in his hands, and TJ knew why. There was no way Divination Today couldn't've known about Ayo so soon. Emeka must've let that slip to the Keepers as well. Things were going from bad to worse. A painful lump welled up in TJ's heart and he tried to pound it away by thumping his chest, but he couldn't help the convulsions that were coming. His breathing hitched, and he gasped for air.

Emeka was helping the Keepers. His sister really was a Keeper and no one really knew who killed her. Oya was talking doomsday. Ayo was gone, and now... Elder Adeyemi was being hauled away to jail.

In his pocket, his phone beeped and read a message:

Eko Atlantic's Doomsday in 8 weeks, 2 days, 0 hours, 0 minutes, and 0 seconds

No one could have blamed TJ for grunting and cursing at the top of his lungs.

And that's exactly what he did.

51

FREAKING ALL THE WAY OUT

IT WAS TRUE. ELDER ADEYEMI WAS BEING HELD AT THE NEW Ile-Ife embassy to await trial for her crimes. She was completely stripped of all her titles for the time being. Not only headmistress of Ifa Academy but a whole host of others TJ wasn't even aware she had. They were taking away all her prestige before any judge ever heard her case. It made TJ totally sick, and he wondered if the Keepers were behind her sudden arrest. Most of those accusations had no way of sticking.

It didn't help that he had completely ignored Eniola's texts. But with everything that was happening... the last thing he could think about right now was his girl troubles. He'd talk to Eni later. Not that she made that easy. She kept messaging, asking him to let her in and to talk to her. He knew she was only trying to help, and he appreciated it, but it just made everything harder.

For the entire trip back home for winter break, all TJ could think about was how much everything got screwed up at the worst time and no one person was to blame. He could have pointed fingers at so many people: Elder Adeyemi, Emeka, Adeola, the UCMP, himself...

It had been *days* since he last saw Ayo in the Sky Realm, and each minute, each hour, he was away was another nail in TJ's heart.

Coming back home from school during winter break was

much different than the break TJ had at Camp Olosa. Then, he was utterly defeated, with no motivation to return. Well, he was still utterly defeated, now with Olokun returning to power *because* of his ignorant actions. But at least now he knew he had Manny to fall back on, whereas before, Manny was less than pleased with him over the summer camp break.

Every morning during break, he got a new text from Manny.

Manny: Did u cross reference with Evo? There might be something about Orisha empowerment there.
Manny: my aunt might know a good lawyer for adeyemi.
Manny: well she'd have a top lawyer already wouldnt she?
Manny: oya says "doom" about a dozen times a day (and thats just before breakfast)
Manny: what are we gonna do!? this is insane!

Even Emeka checked in with TJ every other day, mostly to apologize.

Emeka: seriously im so sorry for what i did
Emeka: plz put me to work. whatever you need
Emeka: i have an uncle aligned with olokun. maybe he can help?

For TJ, the two-week holiday break was mostly spent in the small corners of his room, more specifically the four corners of his laptop screen. That first weekend back, when everyone was asleep at night, TJ had spent the entire time studying how to empower Oya and where to find Shango and Ayo. When he got too frustrated with that, he stared at his mirror and pressed his finger into it to call Dayo back again. When he got too flustered with *that*, he went back to research. It was a vicious cycle. And during one of those nights of research—TJ couldn't remember which—Mom came in after he shouted in agitation.

When she saw he was looking up the best offerings for Oya, she smiled. "I'm glad to see you studying so hard. Your teachers said you bumped yourself up a whole letter grade. But, honey bunny, please get some rest. It's Christmas tomorrow!"

TJ did not get any rest.

Despite the usual fervor that went on during Christmas morning, where Tunde got a new graphics card for his gaming PC, Dad received a vintage coaching book to add to his collection, Mom was gifted a beanie that could fit her palm-tree hair, and Simba got a new bone, TJ was sneaking looks at his phone about deities and different dimensions and any updates on Elder Adeyemi's trial.

"Tomori Jomiloju, I thought you said you always wanted those headphones?" Mom jabbed him with a candy cane. "Did your father pick out the wrong color?"

"Hey, don't put that on me," Dad said through a cup of eggnog. He wore a Santa hat that had a white beard attached. "Unless the boy's favorite color changed from blue."

TJ put on a fake smile as he put on his headphones. "Nah, nah, this is great. Thanks, Mom. Thanks, Dad."

TJ was about to put on some music to drown out the rest of Tunde's very loud gift opening when Mom cleared her throat. "So... what's this I hear about you going steady with Eniola Afolabi?"

"Huh? Going steady? Who says that anymore, Mom?" Tunde questioned as he started shoving his hands into his stocking hung over the fireplace that didn't produce any fire.

TJ wished he had played some music sooner, now that nervous heat rose through his ears.

"Woah, woah, woah!" Dad pursed his lips, looking impressed. "My boy's got himself a li'l honey?" He chuckled, then stroked his goatee inquisitively. "Hold up, though. Eniola? Yejide, I thought you said the boy liked that girl from New York."

"Ooo!" Tunde cooed, becoming far less interested in his Christmas stocking and shuffling closer to the family. "TJ, you got *two* girlfriends?"

"I do *not* have two girlfriends." Why couldn't TJ have long dreadlocks like his brother? Then he could hide himself under his hair and shut out all the cheeky grins his family was giving him. "Manny has a boyfriend in New York already."

Mom ran her hand through TJ's curls. "It's that new haircut that's made you a little lady's man, huh?"

"Mom..." TJ gritted.

Dad added, "Or maybe it's that Young family growth spurt you got going on."

"Dad..."

Mom gave him a wet kiss on the cheek. "Awww, don't you worry yourself none. I found out from an old friend who saw you and Eniola in that cafe young folks go to for dates. You know that Dayo had a crush on one of those Afolabi boys. She even took up modeling to impress him."

"I don't want to talk about Eniola..." TJ kept his eyes on the discarded wrappings on the floor. "May I be excused to my room? I got more stuff to study."

"On Christmas day!?" Dad walked over and placed a hand to TJ's forehead. "No fever. Is this the same boy we sent off? That academy got you more studious than those Nigerian kids over there. Aren't you the same boy I had to force to write one-page book reports just last year?"

"Mom?" TJ asked, knowing he'd get nothing from Dad. "Please, can I go?"

Despite the jazzy upbeat music playing from the record player in the corner, TJ felt there was only a dark silence as Mom frowned. A seriousness cut through her eyes. "Of course, honey bunny. Come back down for dinner, and then we'll watch the movie at the cinema, okay?"

"Mom, it's 'movies' not 'cinema'," Tunde mock-chided.

"Oh, hush. Go on TJ, we'll come get you later."

TJ nodded, still feeling the impact of Mom's changed expression. Getting up, he turned heel and headed for his room. When he started to climb the stairs in the foyer he could hear Dad saying, "We got a whole-ass teenager now, don't we?"

"Ooo, Mom. Dad said the a-word."

"Jalen, watch your mouth!"

TJ didn't hear the rest of what was said. He closed his bedroom door, turned on his new headphones, and lost himself in another few hours of mystical research.

❄

Dark storm clouds.

Powerful winds.

Screams.

Those were TJ's dreams every night since he got back. They never changed.

Above him in the storm clouds, huge letters of text and a loud cellphone beeping spread across the skies of Eko Atlantic.

Eko Atlantic's Doomsday in 1 month

Huge crashing waves.

Metal creaking.

Death.

TJ couldn't make the dreams stop. He wanted them to stop.

Eko Atlantic's Doomsday in 1 week

He knew they were visions, just like when he dreamed about the Aqua Realm a day before going, just like he dreamed about the golden chain months before he knew how to get there. If he could just make the dreams stop, maybe none of it would actually happen.

Eko Atlantic's Doomsday in 1 day

All around him, lightning cracked. He bled from his ears. His arms cracked. Ashe pulled him apart just like Banjoko the Bold and John Henry. He couldn't help the city, he could hear all the screams, all the death. He couldn't do a damn thing about it. He could only watch from far, far away.

Eko Atlantic's Doomsday is here!

A small hand shook TJ awake.

"Bro! Hey, bro!" It was Tunde with Simba in his arms. "Mom called you down for dinner. What's up?"

TJ wiped drool from his mouth. His keyboard was covered in it, too. He was dreaming, only dreaming! But he knew what he saw was just around the corner. How could he ever stop it?

"My bad, my bad," he told his brother, "I'm coming."

TJ glanced at his screen, which depicted a collection of articles surrounding theories of where certain missing Orishas could be found. Trying to play it off, he closed his laptop screen slowly.

Tunde didn't buy it. Or at least, TJ thought Tunde didn't buy it. His room was dark, except for the glowing stars on his wall that portrayed the Orishas. But in the faint light, it looked as though Tunde's face was neutral. Eerily neutral.

"The UCMP has been doing a great job covering their tracks," Tunde started, "but the story will break soon."

TJ swallowed hard. "How much do you know?"

"I know that stuff that happened in the slum was all you and the Keepers. There's a bunch on that trial about that Elder Adeyemi, and it's all starting to connect back to you. Stuff is leaking. I didn't tell Mom or else she'd bug out. I know something happened at Ifa Academy with the Sky Realm, too. I'm guessin' that was you and your friends. Now there's rumblings about Olokun coming back and drowning all of West Africa?"

"Nah... Just Eko Atlantic. But bad enough." There was no point lying. TJ was surprised Tunde hadn't said anything up until that point, though.

"You weren't looking so good when you got back, so I didn't want to bother." It was like Tunde had read TJ's thoughts. "But you gotta tell Mom, bro. She's gonna freak when this eventually breaks. Even if it doesn't get to Divination Today, she's gonna hear it from one of her old contacts over there, just how she found out about you and that girlfriend you got."

"Yeah, I hear you. I-I'll do it after Christmas."

Tunde looked as though he was about to put a hand on TJ's shoulder but thought better of it. Generally speaking, the two of them weren't all that touchy-feely with each other. Instead, Tunde sat at the edge of TJ's desk, keeping his voice low as Simba tried licking at TJ's face. "Anything I can do to help? That stuff about your friend Ayo is true then? He's not just missing... he's stuck in the Sky Realm? I've been reading about that place. Anyone who's been up there more than a few days—"

"Goes crazy… yeah." Utter sadness laced TJ's voice, a tone he *never* used around his brother if he could help it.

"Do you… want to talk about it?"

"Not right now, no."

Tunde drummed his fingers on the desk, letting a brief beat settle between them. "Well, it's a good thing Dad chose a comedy this year." He gave TJ a half-hearted grin, which was never returned. TJ wasn't sure he knew how to smile anymore.

TJ's NIGHTMARES CONTINUED ALL THE WAY FROM CHRISTMAS to the New Year. Each one was worse than the last, each one more real than the previous. It got to a point where he looked up ways he could stop himself from sleeping. He found it helped in the short-term to research and pull all-nighters about how he could help Elder Adeyemi, how he could empower Oya, how he could ever stop five-hundred foot tidal waves. But that eventually ended up making everything worse. When he crashed, he crashed *hard*. And when that happened, he fell into a deep-deep sleep where he couldn't escape from his dreams at all. Even when he knew he was dreaming, even when he took control and had lucid dreams, he could do nothing to end them.

It got really bad when TJ stopped eating altogether. It was the night after he went without food for three days that his nightmares were the worst. This time, TJ didn't see everything from afar. Instead, he was smack in the middle, falling between the towers that crashed into the waves, watching as everyone fell with him and drowned. It was this nightmare that blew his cover because after that nightmare he woke screaming his head off. Not just one scream, not something you'd hear at an amusement park because someone went through a loop or down a drop. His scream came from the gut, came straight from the terrors of his mind. Tears caked his face and his throat went raw.

Mom came hustling into his room with her nightgown half off her shoulder. "Baby, what is it? What's wrong?"

It took TJ several moments to realize where he even was. It still felt like there was water in his lungs, in his nose. In fact, his bed was soaked. He glanced down at his hands and there was water still trickling down his fingertips.

"Mom… there's something I have to tell you." TJ's voice was low and hoarse. Mom's face was stone-serious at his tone. TJ knew she hadn't seen him like this since he was a kid, hell, he'd never had nightmares, really. Not like this. When he didn't continue, Mom drew him in for a hug tight enough to crush the air from his lungs.

TJ didn't think he could cry any more than he had, but he did.

52

THE WHOLE TRUTH

TJ LAID EVERYTHING OUT ON THE TABLE FOR MOM. FROM THE Aqua Realm to Elder Adeyemi telling him to keep it quiet, to his whole first term at Ifa, including the Keepers kidnapping him, the Sky Realm. All of it.

Even about Dayo.

That was the hardest part. When TJ revealed that Dayo was a legit Keeper, Mom couldn't stop her head from shaking, and over and over she said, "No, no, no. Not my baby. Not my Dayo. No, no, no."

After TJ got done telling her everything he could think of, they sat there in silence for what felt like an eternity. It would've looked like neither of them was moving if it wasn't for Mom pinching her brow and shaking her head sporadically every few moments. The constellations on TJ's wall outlined her headwrap.

Then, finally, she stood up and said, "Where is it?"

"Um… show you where what is, Mom?"

"That water bowl that woman gave you without my permission." She paced his room, looking through his closet and drawers. Then she dropped to her knees and searched under TJ's bed. "Ahah! Here it is. *Wá ṣì mí.*"

A loud smack sounded as something hard punched into Mom's hand. TJ knew she had summoned the water bowl.

"Honey." Mom lifted her head from under the bed. "I'm going to need the room for a little while. There's apple pie in the fridge and I'm allowing you to play video games in the family room. Do you understand me?"

There was no universe where TJ would say no to that. The fact that Mom was offering that at all meant she was about to put in work on Elder Adeyemi. But how was Mom going to manage that when the former headmistress was, well, in jail? Briefly, TJ thought maybe he should speak to the Headmistress first if Mom really could get in touch. The woman had been getting an earful from parents since the start of term, and TJ was sure she was hearing it from UCMP officers and British conservators, too. TJ had a sneaking suspicion that she'd need a hearing aid after having a talk with Mom. But suggesting that would mean having to suffer Mom's rage himself...

So TJ obliged and shuffled downstairs. And the moment he opened the fridge for the pie, that's when the screaming match started.

"I don't care if this water bowl is in some evidence locker! You and I both know she shouldn't be in there to begin with. You put this bowl in Elder Adeyemi's cell and let me speak to her!" Mom's voice echoed throughout the house. "You can supervise all you want."

TJ cursed himself for not bringing his noise-canceling headphones down with him.

After snagging up a slice of pie, he hurried to the living room to fire up his Playstation, hooked in some gaming headphones— which weren't noise-canceling, but close enough—and tried to drown out Mom's outrage.

"How dare you put my son through all of that!? Or was all you put Ifedayo through not enough? You promised you'd leave my son out of that world. Who do you think you are?"

After his first game of Call of Duty, Tunde was the first to climb downstairs and join TJ. After their second game, Dad came down too and joined them. Each of them put on headphones as Mom continued going off. None of them spoke. Outside of a brief nod of acknowledgment, they didn't look at each other either. The men of the family just played their game in silence until dawn peeked through the living room blinds.

When Mom came downstairs, her nightgown was damp with water. TJ gave her an odd look, wondering how on earth she got wet. She explained by saying, "Tomori Jomiloju, you'll have to stay down here for a few hours. I have an air-drying charm that will be finished around noon. I got a little out of hand and I might have splashed a *few* things here and there. Don't worry, everything will be fine. But…" She turned her chin to Dad. "Jalen, we'll need to get TJ a new laptop."

Tunde peeled off his headphones. "Hey, that's *my* laptop with *my* new graphics card!" He leaned in close to TJ and murmured, "What do they say about the spirit of Yemoja?"

"Never mess with her children," TJ answered, wondering if his room had been made into an aquarium.

THE NEXT DAY, A WATER PORTAL WAS WAITING FOR TJ IN THE living room. The blinds had all been shut to conceal the magic, so TJ could barely make out the rolling, floating waves that flecked off droplets against his cheeks.

Mom stood right next to the portal, dressed in formal aso oke robes, along with two UCMP officers, who donned their typical navy and gold uniforms. TJ wore a formal long-sleeved dashiki, not unlike his school uniform.

After Mom's outrage, government people from the local Los Angeles branch had come knocking at their door a few hours later, the same officers that stood in TJ's living room just then. He and Mom were to be escorted directly to the government building in New Ile-Ife, where TJ had to present all the information he had, from his time in the Aqua Realm last summer to the Sky Realm a couple weeks ago—and all the rest in between. Apparently, all the most important magical people would be there, including the Head King of Yorubaland: Ori Oba Adetuna II.

As TJ stared through the water portal the officers had made, transfixed by the view of the other side, with its marble floor and

THE WHOLE TRUTH 419

stone walls decorated with Yoruba masks, staffs, and crystals, he tried his best to settle his beating heart. On and off for the past twenty-four hours, he had stared at the wide round table that awaited him through the portal. He was going to have to answer a lot of questions from a *lot* of people. People who called the shots around the global magical community. He had been freaking out the past two weeks, and *really* needed their help, but he wasn't so sure he could stand up at a great wide desk meant for people *far* more qualified than he was.

That was Dayo's thing, not his.

The meeting room brought anxious memories of being surrounded by Eniola's family, those... business people in that gourmet restaurant. A chill rushed down TJ's arm, bringing goosebumps that brushed uncomfortably against his constricted long sleeves. There was at least one good thing about today; it meant the last two nights were dominated by nightmares of round tables instead of hordes of drowning Nigerians.

"This portal goes directly to New Ile-Ife?" TJ asked, mostly to stave off more troublesome musings. "Why didn't we use this to go to school?"

"We've been generating the link between your home and New Ile-Ife for the better part of the day," the first officer, a woman with a shaved head, said.

"Not to mention the hours spent mapping and charting a leyline route," the second officer, who had an audacious mustache, added.

TJ gave both of them a look of confusion as they worked their staffs over the water portal.

Mom put a hand on TJ's cheek and said, "Portal travel over three-hundred kilometers is regulated and difficult. Anything in the thousands of kilometers range requires hours of ritual—and talented diviners—on both ends. Complicated stuff."

"Not to mention the potential years long-distance portals can take off your life if you get it wrong, kid," the woman added.

TJ hadn't gotten portal training yet, so he didn't know about any of these rules. He thought what Eni and the older students did was pretty simple after getting a few lessons, just like a driver's test. They had made it seem easy, anyway. He had no idea long-distance travel could be so dangerous that someone could age themselves out of existence if done incorrectly. Did that mean stepping through the portal in his living room would have him growing a beard on the other side?

"Is it safe for us to go through?" TJ asked nervously. "I mean, am I going to age a year or something if we're going from Los Angeles all the way to New Ile-Ife in an instant?"

The mustached man thumbed to himself proudly. "Not with *us* making this portal for you, Mr. Young. We've spent the last two hours testing with apples, making sure the aging effects wouldn't be significant."

"If anything, you'll only age a few hours at this point," the woman added. Then she quirked an eyebrow. "You should know about all this already, shouldn't you? What are you? 11th or 12th grade at Ifa Academy?"

Before TJ could answer, Mom gave his shoulder a tap. "Oh no, he's only JS3 levels—um, 9th grade in the States. He's still a couple of years away from learning the laws of portal traveling."

"Ah, he's tall for his age."

A frown snuck its way onto TJ's mouth and he was glad the light in the room was so dim. He hated when Mom spoke for him. It reminded him of when he started Camp Olosa and she kept telling people his attendance there was "only temporary" in a tone of shame. She never did that with Dayo.

"TJ?" Mom asked, frowning. "Are you okay?"

TJ's phone buzzed against his thigh. He expected to get another reminder about Eko Atlantic's Doomsday, but instead, it was a group text.

Manny: boa sorte, tj!
Titi: I prayed to 50 orishas last night for you. Statistically, that should ensure at least minor success at your meeting today.
Emeka: good luck, tj. we all are rooting for u. dont let those adults scare u.

TJ fixed his face, adjusted his tight collar, and took a deep breath. "Yes, everything is fine."

Everything *wasn't* fine, but he didn't need to have another breakdown in front of Mom again. She didn't need that. Plus, the text from his friends had helped. Before musings of doubt could enter TJ's thoughts, he stepped through the mist and into the room with the round table, hoping above all hopes he could keep his breakfast in his stomach.

53

THE ROUND TABLE

EVERYONE HAD A DIFFERENT STYLE OF CHAIR. THAT WAS THE first thing TJ noticed about the gathering. Dozens of them surrounded the marble round table that magically expanded with each new group that arrived—a mismatched circle of garish furniture alongside plain furniture. Behind each chair was a portal wall of various elemental compositions: water, earth, lightning, air, fire, wood, every type TJ had ever heard of, and more. Set above each was a clock with a sign denoting the different time zones of each seated attendant. Some were digital, some analog; all were as varied as the chairs and portals beneath them. Los Angeles, London, Jerusalem, Tokyo... And more were still joining.

TJ didn't recognize most of the people in attendance. He had expected them to be the known leaders of the largest magical hubs from around the world, but that didn't seem to be the case. He only knew a handful from news headlines. The rest were strangers.

Strangers paying an uncomfortable amount of attention to *him*.

TJ was familiar with the conservators from when he retrieved Yemoja's gemstone. They stood behind the London chair—a carved wooden seat that looked straight out of some medieval castle—and were some of the few in the chamber pointedly *not* looking TJ's way.

With their relative familiarity, that was somehow worse.

Across the table, away from the sour-faced conservators, was Mrs. Afolabi. She sat in a Yoruba figural chair. To her left was her grandfather, to her right, a younger, stocky, middle-aged man with designer glasses TJ didn't recognize. Each of them was dressed in Western business attire. Eniola had texted TJ that her mother would be there, so that came as no surprise.

TJ rubbed his eyes. His attention was drawn to the relaxed figure sitting in the seat beside them, Oracle Ruby. She was wearing clothing TJ had never seen on her before: an emerald cloak that shimmered in the light. Beside her stood two others in identical garb. TJ thought he might have recognized her guests from when that large group of magic people showed up at the tents at Oracle Rock early in his term. Ruby made a face that screamed, "When will they get on with the bloody meeting?", and TJ laughed inwardly.

A few minutes passed as a few others filled out the round table. Council members from Poland, Singapore, and Brazil were among the last to join the gathering. Finally, with only one threshold left unused, the seated members turned to acknowledge their host for the day. Head King Adetuna II, the leader of the diviners in West Africa, stepped through the only mundane entryway of the room: a door of oak surrounded by Yoruba designs. He gave a bow to the table, his huge purple and gold aso oke robes caressing the marble floor, and sat directly across from TJ. The man's skin sagged and wrinkles dominated the whole of his face. From how still he sat in his chair, it looked like he had become one of the statues of old, lining the ceiling dome of the chamber.

Everyone is here. TJ nearly jumped from his chair when the words reverberated in his head. The voice was old but strong. A man's voice. It didn't take TJ long to realize it was the Head King who had spoken. Though his milk-gray eyes were unmoving, the Ashe that wafted off him as he made his statement was apparent. *Please, bring in Simisola Adeyemi.*

Unlike most gathered around the table, TJ only had one person at his shoulder: Mom. But he was allowed one other to accompany him, and he had made sure it would be the woman now entering through the ordinary door. She was almost completely unrecognizable, her elaborate head tie traded for a dome of thinning hair, her usual dazzling robes replaced by a dull-gray jumpsuit. The only thing that remained unchanged was her face, one that held an expression carved proudly, her chin held high. Some at the table broke professional decorum as their whispers chased after Adeyemi's shuffle.

Despite the trust that was shaken between them, TJ couldn't think of who might better advise him in a situation like this.

Guards flanked either side of Elder Adeyemi, and the former Headmistress carried a strange glow as she shuffled along. Her Ashe wasn't shimmering as brightly as it usually did. When TJ asked Mom why that would be, she answered, "The Elder's been given the Clouded Concoction. All those in custody, whether in holding or prison, are given that to suppress their blessings, their magic. For now, Adeyemi is as clouded as your father."

A tightness seized at TJ's stomach as he thought of what it would be like to have his Ashe stripped, to be so naked to the world. He'd had a healthy sample of it throughout his childhood, before his sister's funeral, so it probably wouldn't have been such a shock to him. But Elder Adeyemi had been steeped in Ashe her whole long life. It must've been like going blind in adulthood after a life of sight.

"It is good to see you again, Mr. Young." Elder Adeyemi bowed her head with a smile as she took her place at TJ's shoulder. "We've gone and got ourselves into a bit of a pickle, haven't we?"

A man who had to be over seven feet tall at the Head King's side cleared his throat. An oak staff sprouted in his hand with a snap. He gave it a wave and chimes from the ceiling rang out a light, short melody. Then he let his baritone carry over the room. "All parties are present. May we mark this as the six-thousandth, five-hundred and twenty-eighth congregation of the Magical Security Council. We are now called to order. The provisional agenda for this meeting is letter dated to the second day of the first moon of the year sixty-sixty-three as recognized by the United Council of Magical Peoples..."

He went on like that for a little while, describing that the meeting would be a discussion of the Orisha Olokun and the level of threat he presented to the coast of Lagos, Nigeria. Then everyone present introduced themselves and the magical hubs they represented. Despite his nerves, TJ found himself close to nodding off with the boring introduction. He didn't become properly alert until...

"Mr. Young?" the tall man was asking.

TJ straightened. "Yup! I mean, yes! That's me. Present."

The tall man pursed his lips, his eyes devoid of any kindness. "You wish to present vital information to this committee concerning the Orishas Olokun and Yemoja of the sea, and the Gatekeeper Orisha, Eshu?"

"Mmhm. I mean, that's correct. Yes, sir!" TJ's stomach turned inside out. So many adults were staring at him. And not just adults... leaders from every corner of the whole world. Which meant...

TJ realized for the first time just how many people were there.

Could they all be trusted? One of them could easily be a Keeper! "So... um... before I start... um..." TJ glanced over his shoulder to Mom, who gave him a nod of reassurance, but she had no clue what he was about to ask. "Um... so... is everyone here trustworthy? Is there, like, a truth potion or something we can all take right now?" TJ tried to keep his eyes away from Mrs. Afolabi and her group. He only had the idea *because* of them.

Everyone at the table gave him looks of shock and Mom groaned lightly at his side as though he had done some extreme social faux pas.

"Are you suggesting this council might be compromised?" the tall man sneered, as though TJ's words were a personal offense. TJ wanted to come right out and say that yes, that's exactly what he was suggesting. Mrs. Afolabi wasn't the most clean-cut individual, and there was a woman present who was being tried for crimes. As for the rest of those sitting around the room, TJ didn't know *any* of them.

"Excuse Mr. Young, Chief Bolaji," Elder Adeyemi said calmly. "He meant no offense. Go on, young man. All those present were vetted with methods more powerful than truth serums before the council invited them. All can be trusted."

TJ bit at his lip, then stopped himself immediately. The bad habit reminded him of Dayo, and he wondered how she would summon her courage in a situation like this. Was she watching over him now as he made a fool of himself?

Doing his best not to stare down the fire pits that were the gaze of the tall Chief Bolaji, TJ retold his story from the very beginning, all the way back to where this started at his sister's funeral. There were a few times he stuttered or got caught up on his words, especially when he noticed the aides all around jotting down notes vigorously and hanging on his every word. Halfway through his story, when the faces around the table drew in closer and closer, he realized what all this would mean.

Nothing would be the same.

Everyone would know who TJ Young was. He wouldn't just be known by a handful of campers and counselors at some Louisiana camp. He wouldn't just be known by those who roamed Ifa Academy. If he thought he had it bad with a few reporters in his backyard and on the streets of Los Angeles, he couldn't even imagine what was coming for him in the next months. Maybe even the next few years. Not even Dayo's prowess went much further than Nigeria. But she wasn't dealing with the Orishas and the prospect of their return.

When TJ finished his story, he was allowed a break for water. During that time, officials started chiming in with their opinions about building up hype for Oya, setting up battle trenches near Lagos, and deciding on personnel with a bunch of jargon TJ barely understood from war movies. A general from the Head King's retinue argued that they had to be discreet about how they set up defenses or else Olokun would be tipped off, while a rune mage from Norway pounded her chest and said, "Let him come! Our units will hold the line to the last."

This forced TJ to shake his head, and he spoke up. "No, we can't fight him. We won't even make a dent. None of you have seen Olokun, not even our grandfathers' great grandfathers have. But *I* have. The power he has is… it's nothing compared to even a whole group of our diviners. But… you can use me."

Use you? Head King Adetuna II questioned in TJ's mind, his wrinkles constricting in his forehead. *You are referencing your apti-*

tude for communal magicks? You do know the story of Banjoko the Bold, eh?

TJ nodded. "Same thing that happened to John Henry back in the States. But... I've been training a lot with Elder Adeyemi. All those Olokun festivals were us."

"Mr. Young will be our best chance with regards to a defense," Adeyemi agreed at his side.

An odd bit of movement stirred in the room: papers being fiddled with, men adjusting their collars, and women clearing their throats. TJ didn't understand what the shift meant until one of the conservators from Great Britain, the wizard-looking dude named Armstrong, spoke. "I must ask the committee why Simisola Adeyemi is among us today. Is she not awaiting trial for the death of a student?"

"There has been no *death*," the man next to Mrs. Afolabi retorted with a clenched fist atop the table. It was the first time he'd spoken, and his words came out broken. "He is *lost*, not gone." His family beside him nodded in agreement. TJ still couldn't look them directly in the eye. But then he realized something... the glasses atop that wide nose, the stocky build. Was that... Ayo's dad!?

The guilt that always hid away under the wrinkles of TJ's mind resurfaced. Ayo's dad looked so much like his son, like TJ was looking into his friend's future, a future that was currently in jeopardy.

"With all due respect, Mr. Oyelowo," Conservator Armstrong went on, "the boy has been 'lost' for more than a fortnight. The longest any of your diviners have crossed over in recent memory is a mere few days, no? Even if he were to return, he would not be —" The man cut off at a sudden gesture from the seat next to him. For the first time—and TJ wasn't sure how he had missed her before—TJ noticed the woman sitting in the London chair. He felt a shiver up his spine as he took in her slate-stern features and sharp eyes. Who was she? And why had she silenced the conservator prematurely?

Clearing his throat, Conservator Armstrong finished up. "Your son might not be the same if he does return to us."

TJ thought on the man's words, back to Mr. Du Bois and his

condition. How he kept repeating the same phrase over and over, and he had only been in the Aqua Realm a mere few hours. Then again, he had been cursed. Adeola was fine, so was Bolawe. But TJ couldn't help the fear slicing through his chest as images of Ayo getting attacked by cosmic forces sprang forth, or him returning with permanent brain damage, or...

Suddenly, a hand came to TJ's arm. Mom's hand. "You're shaking, TJ," she said. "Don't worry, Ayodeji will be fine. The Orishas will protect him." But her words, like Mr. Oyelowo's, were laced with doubt.

A short woman beside the Tokyo chair cleared her throat. "We'll do as much as we can with the boy, but regardless, our primary focus must be Eko Atlantic and its inhabitants. To that end, Mr. Young, you mentioned having freed Oya in the Sky Realm, but not where she is now?"

TJ swallowed hard, then stared over his shoulder to his Mom and then to Elder Adeyemi. Conservator Bennet, with her long jet black hair, straightened in her chair, clearly interested. She knew what TJ was capable of from first-hand experience. If he could cross into that Ice Realm he destroyed, then surely speaking and freeing Oya from the Sky Realm wasn't as far-fetched as it should've been.

"I'm glad you asked, General," Adeyemi said gently as she raised her hand to the high ceiling with its hanging lanterns and chimes. Each one ebbed from left to right, propelled by a force invisible to everyone else, but TJ could pick out the working of Ashe. Swirls of energy forced the metallic lanterns to clink together like music, and then clouds burst into reality. Diviners, mages, and sorcerers at every corner of the room manifested staffs, wands, and enchanted daggers in hand. Each of them pointed their weapons to the ceiling.

But how was Elder Adeyemi doing it? Wasn't her magic suppressed?

Through all the motion in the room, TJ saw only the Head King, Ruby, and the other woman from London sitting calmly in their seats. The zealous General from Norway was shouting something.

"A breach!?" the General's tattooed, muscled arms were held

at the ready, her fingers and wrists covered in rings and bracelets that glowed with crystal lights. "Here in the Nigerian Capital City?"

As though in answer, Elder Adeyemi nodded to Oracle Ruby, who, with eyes closed and chin jutted up to the billowing clouds, recited a verse:

> *When the wind spoke, they used to listen.*
> *When the wind spoke, their crowns would glisten.*
> *Now the gusts fall on deaf ears*
> *Gales whip for no one to hear*
> *But She'll cut a path so clear*
> *Listen, 'cause Oya is near...*

With the last of Ruby's melodic words, Oya appeared within the gust of clouds along with two other figures. Oya, still in her kindly human form, wore burgundy wrappings and gold bangles. To her right was a very old man with a bald head and an Afro of a beard covered in gray. He wore robes of green, red, and black like a Pan African flag. To Oya's left floated a short, portly woman who looked an awful lot like...

"Grandma..." TJ breathed out.

With a strong and steady voice, Elder Adeyemi announced, "Let it be known that Oya, the Windweaver, is among us. The second Orisha to grace us with their presence in countless ages. The first to address the United Council of Magical Peoples since the declaration of The Great Separation between Mortals and Deities."

In unison, all the Yoruba diviners present dropped their staffs and prostrated before Oya as she descended on the center of the table with bare feet. The witches, shaman, and alchemists of other pantheons didn't drop to the floor, but they lowered their weapons and dipped their heads in respect—some half-bowing from what looked like awkwardness more than anything else.

"This... this can't be." The Japanese delegate was in a full bow. "No deity has been present among mortals for countless centuries."

Tears in her eyes, the delegate from Singapore added in a stammer. "H-How is this possible?"

"Children of the Mortal Realm," Oya spoke, her voice so resonant it stuck in TJ's chest. "I call upon your strength to lift me up in defense of your coast. Olokun is lost and unbalanced, Eshu even more so. Yemoja allies herself with her husband with newfound frost magic. The battle to come will be a hard one, and the boy, Tomori Jomiloju, will aid me in it." She gestured to Grandma and the other man at her side. "I bring to you Staffmaster Bamidele and his mentor Oluwamakinwa Abimbola, who have completed their work on the staff of the boy's sister."

Grandma pulled a familiar staff from her side: a wooden shaft topped with the head of Orunmila, a green crystal set beneath it with a double-helix in the middle that eventually narrowed to a point. Turning and kneeling, Grandma offered the staff to TJ with a smile. *"Hello, grandson,"* she said in Yoruba. *"It's good to see you after all this time."*

"Good to see you too, Ìyá àgbà." TJ gave her a grin as well.

The German delegate, a round-faced man with a strong jaw, frowned. "I do not see how this assists the situation. Does the staff have special qualities of some sort that the committee is not aware of?"

Elder Adeyemi leaned in close to TJ's shoulder to murmur, "Remember at your sister's funeral when I said you had *connected* after making contact with her body?" TJ nodded, eyeing the German and his group, who waited impatiently for an answer. "Haven't you said these past few months you've acquired new habits... habits that have reminded you of Dayo? The Keepers said she was trying to communicate with you, and they seemed to be right."

"I saw her face in Adeola's tube at the hospital, too."

"But she's having trouble communicating. And you may be our only conduit to her, and possibly her power. Perhaps not our 'promised child', but our 'lost child' instead."

"So what should I do to convince them I have enough power?"

"Do not ask me, young man. Ask your sister."

The implications of that statement sent a rolling energy

through TJ. And of course, the concentration of that energy was a gentle touch at the back of his neck.

TJ closed his eyes.

Ever since TJ had been blessed with Ashe, it had been difficult to call upon it without the help of others or while in the Orisha Planes, but at that moment, as he closed his eyes and thought of Dayo, the sensation of her staff was like a thousand voices pressing into his very soul. The Ashe emitting from the staff enveloped him totally and utterly. TJ didn't have to shout, he didn't have to strain.

All it took was a whisper.

"Dayo."

TJ opened his eyes to find the entire room bathed in a green light: the round table, the mismatched chairs, even the members of the committee. As soon as TJ's gaze leveled with the crystal in the staff, it shot toward him and hovered a mere inch from his nose. Green Orunmila crystals worn by members of the council lit up as well. Enchanted bangles wrapped around arms lifted in the air, making some of the battlemages look like they were being strung like puppets. Cloaks hemmed with white Orunmila gems glowed and fluttered as though reaching out toward TJ. Everyone in the room quivered under the display of power.

Everyone, except two.

Elder Adeyemi rested comfortably in her seat with knowing eyes; TJ sat with a straight back, rigid and alert. All he could do was smile. All those months wondering and now he knew for sure... his sister's spirit was truly with him, somewhere out there.

"Orunmila's Stars!" Mom cried out with tears in her eyes, her hand shaking uncontrollably over her mouth. "Ifedayo! My baby!"

Grandma ambled from the center of the table to embrace Mom with a mother's hug.

The Staffmaster, Bamidele, took lumbering steps from the center of the table and approached TJ's side. "The connection between Mr. Young and Ifedayo is strong. True, he is untrained and far, far too young for this kind of burden, but considering his special abilities and what we have all just borne witness to... he's our best shot." TJ didn't know the man, but he liked the way he instilled total confidence in him. What had Grandma told him during all those months they spent together in the Amazon?

"With Oya and Mr. Young working in concert," Elder Adeyemi gestured between the two of them, "we should be able to... mitigate any damage done to Eko Atlantic."

"Mitigate?" Mrs. Afolabi asked. Her family's towers were right on the coastline.

"We are no match for what will come," Oya said. 'The Gate-keeper is empowered through those still trapped in his staff, particularly Olosa, who will bolster the waters of Olokun. And Yemoja, who now has ice magicks."

"Ice magicks she should never have had," Conservator Bennet muttered bitterly, flipping her long hair over her shoulder.

Oya didn't seem to hear her, continuing on, "And while we do not know for certain, Obatala could be captured as well. Whether he was or not isn't as significant as the rest, as his blessings relate to creation only, not to destruction."

For the first time, the delegate in the Chinese chair spoke up. "With all due respect, Great One. That sounds to me like six against one. And our one is you yourself, limited in a human body and bolstered by an untested boy. Is there truly no more we can do?"

"When the time comes, I will ascend back to the Orisha Planes to fully empower my storms and meet Olokun's attack. At that point, the boy will be... as he likes to call it... my battery."

The Indonesian delegate cleared his throat. "Why can't you ascend now? You might be able to rally other Orishas against Olokun and his allies."

"I might. But there is the problem of Eshu. I may be captured by him once again. I've evaded him in times past, but now, with the power he possesses, I'd be apprehended almost immediately. We cannot risk that until we are ready. The boy will help boost me for these next two months and on February's new moon. All said, I do not favor our chances. Eko Atlantic will likely fall."

"But our battlemages—" interjected one General.

"Are but flies to Olokun."

The lady from the London portal sighed. "We can sit around and mope at how this is an impossible threat as much as we want, it's not going to go away. We must simply start solving it the best way we can."

The rest of the council started to argue about how they could fight. Someone even said how Eko Atlantic might have to be a loss they accept, which earned some choice words from Mrs. Afolabi and Mr. Oyelowo. For the most part, the group argued by taking turns in a "civil" debate, but each response was an uptick of tension. TJ tried to funnel out the discussion and arguments of the best strategies for defense. But just as the conversation was beginning to circle itself, an idea occurred to him.

He raised his hand like he was in a classroom. One of the aides to the Russian seat was talking at the time and gave TJ a wild look under bushy brows.

"Um…" TJ trailed off. "If we can't for sure stop Olokun, why don't we… like, evacuate everyone?"

Oya was the one to answer. "If Olokun detects such a deception, your deal will be broken and he will attack sooner than later. Immediately, I would say."

"The Keepers will see to it," Oracle Ruby agreed. "I don't need my third eye to predict that. They'll go running to tell the Lord of the Deep the moment a mass evacuation starts up."

"And what of the rest of the coast?" the Polish General asked. "How much power does this Olokun have? How do we know he'll only stop at Eko Atlantic, Great Windweaver?"

"Because an Orisha keeps their word." Oya was firm in her response. "He won't do anything after taking Eko Atlantic down, not in the short term, not on the back of this deal. Besides, his power may only be enough for that. Six moons of praise was very specific. He knows his time will be limited to enable a drowning of that size. And now he only has four moons of empowerment."

Oh great, that's at least one piece of good news.

"Chief Bolaji, remind me," Oya went on. "How many diviners are registered in Eko Atlantic?"

The Chief turned to the aide at the Head King's left, who pulled a sheet of paper from thin air as she mumbled to herself. Pushing her glasses up her nose, she said, "Just under five-hundred individuals. Two-hundred thirty-eight singles and forty-two families."

"Well," Mrs. Afolabi said, "Clearly we should prioritize our diviners and then the others first. A low-profile evacuation of five hundred people is extremely viable."

"How many clouded are married to diviners in Lagos?" the French delegate, a woman dressed in layered silks, asked. "Will family transport tip the Keepers or Olokun off?"

"There are only a dozen families with non-magical ties that would need to be moved. Shouldn't be an issue."

And Olokun will manifest as a tidal wave we can explain away to the clouded press... the Head King added in everyone's head.

"Wait, wait, wait," TJ blurted. "What about all the rest? What about the clouded?"

"We are very few in the world, Tomori Jomiloju," Mrs. Afolabi said. "I'm not saying the clouded do not matter, but we do need to focus on diviners first."

There was a silence that filled the room at that. TJ looked around the table. He wasn't the only one that seemed disgusted at the thought, but no one was saying anything either.

"Ruby?" TJ whipped his head to her. "You can't let this happen. Can't you tell the military people what will happen in the future to better defend? Elder Adeyemi, we can't let all those people drown!"

"Why is the child still among us?" Conservator Bennet questioned. "He has given us his report, and we have seen his power. He impedes vital groundwork. Same with Adeyemi. She should be back in her cell. She's given us enough of a report."

"Let's at least hear the boy out," said her blond cohort, Conservator Burch, the only one that was friendly to TJ during the Ice Realm debacle. "What would you have us do, young man?"

At first, TJ was grateful for the man giving him a platform, but as he stumbled through half-baked solutions ranging from portal transfers for thousands of people, which was apparently impossible to achieve, to illusions that could fake Eko Atlantic's destruction, which Oya noted would be immediately sussed out by Eshu, TJ wondered if he was actually set up to look like a dummy. When he saw Conservator Burch's face redden with each of his seemingly juvenile fixes, he knew it wasn't a setup at all, and the Conservator was likely suffering from a compounded mixture of first-hand *and* second-hand embarrassment.

With a pitying sideways frown beneath his large beard and curled mustache, Burch's colleague, Armstrong, interjected, "Leave this to the adults, lad."

"Okay, okay, I'm not great at coming up with plans in a meeting full of people, but I'm pretty good at working on the fly."

The Brazilian representative scoffed. "You're not *honestly* suggesting we work from no plan at all, are you?"

TJ's face went hot. It would've been better if he kept his mouth shut.

Conservator Bennet scratched at the back of her black hair, frowning. "Remind us, Mr. Young. It was 'working on the fly' that led to your friend's demise, was it not? If it weren't for you, he'd still be alive, yes?"

A dragon roared within TJ's belly. How could that woman say something like that with such cold bluntness? TJ was embarrassing himself all by himself. Did she really need to add salt to the wound? Before TJ could make an outburst that would've landed him in a cell right next to Adeyemi, it was Mom who stepped forward.

"How *dare* you!" Her voice was a storm. Water wrapped around her right hand as she slammed it against the table. Ice spidered from her fist all the way to the center of the marble table, cracking with each new crystal fissure.

"I was merely speaking on facts presented by your very son," Conservator Bennet said matter-of-factly, but with a hint of condescension. "No need to raise your voice."

"Don't speak to me like I'm a child!"

At the same time, Mr. Oyelowo, breathing heavily, sparks of lightning flecking off his shoulders in a cage of rumbling thunder, said, "I already told you, conservators. Don't you dare curse my son's name. He is alive!"

Mom left TJ's shoulder and rounded the table toward the conservator group. "Say what you said about my son to my face again, *oloṣi*."

Mr. Oyelowo was moving, too, marching around the table

across from her. The scent of burnt ozone followed in his wake as his lightning flung from him like a wicked cape.

Mom and Mr. Oyelowo weren't seriously going to throw hands with the conservators, were they?

Mrs. Young, Mr. Oyelowo, take your positions back at your hosts' seats, the Head King commanded with the subtle anxiety of someone who knew things were about to get out of hand. *Guards.*

From the shadows of the room, guards in sharp navies stood between Mom and the conservators. Mom pushed against them, shouting, "What? The oloṣi can't muster the courage to speak to me head-on?"

Mr. Oyelowo was cursing in Yoruba as he struggled against his own trio of officers. Neither parent was showing any signs of settling down. Nothing would stop Mom or Ayo's dad short of, well, an Orisha.

And that's exactly what happened.

Oya snapped a finger and impenetrable wind walls *thunked* between the struggling parties. "No wonder your world is in such a sorry state, mortals."

The Head King, who was purple in the face, lifted a shaking finger and thought-spoke. *Guards, remove the Youngs and Oyelowos from the chamber. Now!*

54

GET BY WITH A LITTLE HELP

TJ WOULD LATER LEARN THAT, THOUGH SHE WAS WELL WITHIN her rights to do so, Conservator Bennet did not charge Mom or Mr. Oyelowo with attempted assault. Once the Youngs and the Oyelowos were all led out into the lobby of the New Ile-Ife embassy, Elder Adeyemi had said the woman was simply grateful all her limbs were still intact. Mom swore she had only meant to freeze the woman, not harm her. But Mr. Oyelowo had been shouting about fully intending to cook and fry the Conservator, which Mrs. Afolabi insisted he meant in jest to the guards throwing them out. Since TJ was already in New Ile-Ife, he was sent to Ifa Academy to wait for the rest of the students to arrive for the upcoming term.

Second term at Ifa Academy started with none of the students knowing what was to come in a short month and a half. The SS1 students who had returned with their staffs from forests and blacksmiths had no idea that Eshu had a staff more powerful than anything they could come up with. The Juniors who came back excited to learn more water charms were completely unaware of a deity coming to sling a tidal wave at the coast. And the teachers... all they were concerned with—as always—were assessment exams.

None of them knew or cared about all the people who were going to die simply because they weren't magical. What if Dad never married Mom? What if some angry cosmic force drowned Los Angeles and a wifeless version of Dad had to just sit and take it? Neither Dad nor any of the rest of the clouded deserved to die like that.

TJ was angry; he couldn't focus. He couldn't think about what antidote cured fairy bites when his daydreams were filled with broken buildings. He couldn't spend time in study hall with screams assaulting his mind every day. Even the mess hall food hit different. He just found himself tasting salt on his lips like he was drowning in the sea, despite eating bland raw carrots or sweet pastries.

Whenever he got the chance, he traveled to Eko Atlantic on nights and weekends under the guise of prep work with Oya and Manny. Well, not a complete guise. He did go with them—under the supervision of Staffmaster Bamidele. He just took extended breaks during their boosting sessions. Twenty minutes here, thirty minutes there, all spent knocking on doors and coming up with excuses for why people should leave their homes during February's new moon. All of his interactions ended with either having doors slammed in his face, or simply being told to go away. Some of the condo owners and apartment renters even thought he was trying to case their homes and rob them later—which he learned when one called the police on him, leading to TJ not being allowed to reenter Pearl Towers that day.

When he tried to return the next day, the security guards forcibly escorted him out of Pearl Towers plaza. The commotion earned a few dozen looks from the business people having lunch or outdoor meetings near the marina. Avoiding their eye contact, TJ dusted himself off and took steps away to another tower when a young woman bumped into him. He didn't get a good look at her, and he noticed she dropped a piece of paper on the ground.

"Excuse me!" TJ called after her, but she was already lost in the crowd of business people walking in and out of Eko Atlantic skyscrapers. "Excuse me! You dropped something."

A heat prickled at TJ's fingertips and the paper fell from his hand. It unfurled itself in the pencil sketch image of a familiar face: Bolawe's face. Gray strokes carved the same deep pores the man had in real life, and squiggly dark lines coiled the same way the real man's nappy hair did. Bolawe's sketch face shook his head and spoke six simple words, "Stop doing what you are doing." And then, without warning, the paper shredded itself. Its pieces drifted away in the wind, between the busy legs of the business people walking about the plaza.

TJ watched the crowd around him with fresh eyes. He had figured the Keepers would be keeping tabs on him, and he knew going door-to-door was probably a stupid idea, but it was the only one he had. He was desperate.

So, despite the warning, he pressed on.

It was in his second week, during a particularly long break from his ritual channeling, when Manny found him in the halls of Azuri Towers. TJ stood overlooking the nearly complete Olokun statue in the middle of the marina, watching her approach from the corner of his eye.

"So how long were you going to wait before you asked for some help, huh?" Manny said from the end of the hall leading to the balcony.

"What are you talking about?"

"Sneaking off during our breaks with Oya, coming back late after lunches… What you gettin' into?"

"I'm not gettin' into nothin'."

"Hey, I might've only known you since the summer, but you know I can tell when you're lyin', right?"

TJ sighed, hanging his head over the balcony. "I don't want to get you involved. Enough of my friends have suffered for me."

"Too late. I'm already involved. Or did you forget the session we just had with a freakin' Orisha… *on Earth?*"

"Even if you did help… it wouldn't be enough." TJ flung a hand toward all the skyscrapers towering around them as an ocean breeze passed over their faces. "There's one month left. Two-hundred-fifty thousand people are going to die, and I can't do a damn thing about it."

"You have more than one friend, yo."

"Who? The only other person who really knows what's going

on is Ayo. And he's..." TJ clenched his jaw and snorted. "Forget about it. Let's go find Oya so we can keep boosting her up for no reason because there's no way she'll be able to fight Olokun."

Manny tugged on TJ's arm before he could leave the building. "TJ... Don't give up now. What about Titi and Emeka? They helped with the sky chain. Emeka stopped badmouthin' you, so Umar and some of the others might come through, too. I could hit up some of my teammates. And well... what about Eniola? She's got connections. Can she help, too?"

TJ had been trying to forget Eni. He'd finally responded to her texts and calls but only with one-line replies, or a series of "yeahs" and "okays".

"I can't..." TJ said.

Manny lifted her hand and said, "*Afẹfẹ, wà ṣi mi.*"

Wind billowed from her fingertips and blasted straight into TJ's chest. He fell back into the balcony's glass half-wall, pinned by Manny's magic. Then the smooth surface of his phone slid up his thigh until it squeezed through his pocket, up in the air, and straight to Manny's hand. Before TJ could use his Ashe to stop Manny's mystical winds, she was already lifting his phone to her mouth to say, "Siri, call Eniola Afolabi."

TJ might've had the chance to take the phone from her, but Eni, like she always did, answered on the first ring.

"Hey, Eniola. It's me, Manny. TJ's friend." Eni's muffled tones sounded from the other end of the line. "Yeah, yeah, TJ's fine. He's just... *airing* out right now. Hey, listen. What are you doin' tomorrow? We should... hang out, kick it."

THE NEXT DAY TJ FOUND HIMSELF OUT IN FRONT OF AN EKO Atlantic cafe with Eniola, though he had barely noticed she was there. Her voice was a gentle hum somewhere off to the side. Deep in the recesses of TJ's mind, he knew she was going over the speech she had come up with, but TJ was too busy staring into the tall and wide windows of the bright cafe, filled to near capacity by a grouping of Ifa Academy students.

"TJ, are you listening to me?" Eni said, shielding her eyes from the high noon sun. It would've been incredibly hot that day were it not for the ocean breeze mere yards away from them. "Do I have to go over the talking points again? Did you want me to repeat what we'll say about the towers? Did I go through it all too fast?"

Eni was loads of help but she was also a bit too much energy for TJ's social palette. She always needed reassurance and was always checking in, and at that moment she was only making the nerves building up in TJ even worse. Subtle shakes stirred in TJ's belly, a sensation he wished wasn't so familiar to him the past few weeks. The vibrations started small, but quickly built and built as he thought of everything that could go wrong in that cafe. He already failed Ayo, he felt responsible for leaving most of Eko Atlantic's residents vulnerable, and he was faced with even more public speaking, which he had already screwed up with at that round table.

"Are you okay, boo?" Eni rocked TJ's shoulder to turn him around. TJ faced her to find her expression had changed. Unblemished deep brown skin had paled, and purple dominated the shadows under her eyes… like she was drowning. And her clothes were soaked through. Without realizing it was coming, a short yelp punched through TJ's lips.

"Oh my goodness." Eni took both of TJ's shoulders in her hands. "Is it something I said? TJ, are you okay?"

The ding of the cafe entrance rang out, followed by quick footsteps, and a familiar voice. "Eni, give me some space, please," Manny said with sweat glistening her brow. "TJ's about to have another panic attack."

"*Another* panic attack?" Eni covered her mouth with her hand as she stepped out of the way.

Manny's presence shook the image of a drenched Eni from TJ's vision. How had Manny known TJ was about to freak out? She should've been attending to the students in the cafe. Had TJ really looked so horrible from the other side of the window to warrant her concern?

Get a grip on yourself, TJ…

Manny placed her hands on TJ's hot cheeks, staring him dead

in the eye. "TJ, remember Oya's winds, just like we talked about. Like a gentle breeze…"

TJ heard the words, he knew he was supposed to repeat the next phrase, but nothing was coming out. His mouth wasn't working.

Manny gave him a swift slap to one of his cheeks. "TJ, come back to the present. Stay here. Oya's wind… like a gentle breeze…"

Throat dry, TJ croaked, "… Oya, lift me from my knees."

"And where will she lead you? What will her winds do?"

TJ gulped before saying, "Oya's winds will clear the path, all those who oppose will fear her wrath."

"Good, good." Manny breathed in long and deep, and TJ found himself mirroring her. In and out. Up and down. "Now come back to me. Look into my eyes. Feel my hands."

Waves of embarrassment rolled through TJ as he quelled his ever-beating heart. He hated how vulnerable he was, how out of control of his nerves he was. Now that he was settling back down and his heart stopped thrumming through his ears, he felt ridiculous. But he almost forgot about his shame entirely, thanks to Manny's big brown eyes under her coily bangs, those subtle dimples that caved in her cheeks. TJ wondered if it was their Oya prayers that improved his breathing, or Manny herself. Probably both. Though mostly due to Manny.

Was Manny thinking the same thing, TJ wondered.

For a moment they were back in that endless white room. Before, it was TJ who held her cheek in his hand. Now it was Manny who returned the gesture. The energy between them was both electric and tranquil all at the same time. There was no way the feeling ran one way.

Eni cleared her throat; TJ and Manny both jumped like they were caught doing something wrong. "Well…" Eni said, "that was… *very* effective. You've gotta teach me that one, Manny."

Manny blushed as she tucked her hair behind her ear. "Yeah, yeah… sorry, let me get back in there and get the drinks ready."

"We'll go in with you." Eni eyed her with an odd expression — TJ couldn't quite place what it meant. "I've drilled in the plan enough times for TJ. It's now or never."

Manny nodded and led the way into the cafe, where the twins, Titi and Emeka, Umar, half the JS crossover team, and a smattering of Ifa Academy students, from the baby faces of the JS1s to the peach fuzzes and makeups of the SS3s all waited.

"Yo, Teee Jaaay!" Umar said, waving his hands among the bright and spacious cafe. "So it turns out Oracle Ruby was right. I *did* make the crossover team! As an assistant to Coach Ali! She even uses some of my plays in the game!"

"We wouldn't have beaten Togo if it wasn't for Umar," Manny agreed, carrying a tray of coffee for everyone.

The cafe Eni suggested was just as luxurious as anything else in Eko Atlantic, with ceiling-high windows that overlooked the Atlantic Ocean and a view of the Olokun statue that overlooked the city itself. The whole place had a theme of cream and beige, and several of the baristas had given disgusted looks at Umar, who came in with grass-stained jeans and a sweaty shirt. TJ was about to chide Umar for putting his crossed legs up on the summer white couch with his dirty sneakers on, when Eni served him some coffee.

"Don't worry, no one will say anything," she said with a smile to Umar. "My family owns this spot. I'll clean up after we're done here. I need to work on my housekeeping charms anyway. Oh, that reminds me." She called for a barista and whispered something in her ear. Moments later, three more cafe workers came out to place stools at each corner of the private room that they had at the back of the cafe. Each stool held glass-encased crystals: two smokey black and the other two dull red. Sound dampeners. Just like back at Eni's restaurant in New Ilfe-Ife.

"Say what you want about my mother," Eni murmured to TJ as the cafe workers gave them privacy. "But when she has a good idea, she has a good idea." She cleared her throat and turned to the group. When everyone settled down, her voice echoed in their soundproof box. "Thank you everyone for coming out. TJ and Manny invited you today because they feel you can be trusted with what we're about to ask you. Because the adults who call themselves our leaders are going to allow a great tragedy to destroy this city my family helped build. What they'll ask today will be very important, and we all have to ensure complete and utter secrecy. So, if you want to stay, you'll have to drink the coffee that we've served you. It's laced with a tongue-tied tonic so that if any of us speaks on what's discussed today with *anyone* outside this circle, in any manner, we'll only choke on our words a bit."

"Oh shoot, I already drank mine!" Umar blushed with a little burp.

"Well, that means you're in then," Manny said, shaking her head. "But if anyone else wants to leave, now's the time."

TJ had expected a few of the students to leave right away. There were some whispers in the back and furtive looks passed between friends. But eventually, they all nodded and drank from their coffee until there weren't any drops left.

"The tonic will not be indefinite," Eni announced as she took her own sip of coffee. "It'll only last a fortnight, which will be enough time for what we're about to do."

"And what are we doing exactly?" one of the SS3 boys, who looked like a full-grown man, questioned.

TJ stood up, cleared his throat, and examined each face that stared up at him. He didn't want to have to put everyone through it. Some of the kids were barely out of elementary school. But Eni's plan was solid. No one would be in any real danger. When Olokun came, they'd all be far away from Eko Atlantic if everything went right. Still, that didn't help calm his beating heart. He hated making speeches in front of more than just a handful of his friends.

"Hello, everyone. Thank you for coming. Most of you know me, but for those who don't, my name is Tomori Jomiloju Young."

TJ went on to explain the predicament Eko Atlantic was in, the decision of the UCMP, and the hundreds of thousands of lives that would be lost. The steadiness in his tone shocked even himself. His voice didn't crack once and he held eye contact with the whole of the group, speaking to one side of the room and then the next. Unlike class, no one spoke out of turn, even if they had questions, everyone listened intently and waited to be called on.

"So, how are we going to help?" a Junior girl who still had a few baby teeth asked quietly once TJ had finished. "I can't fight some big ol' Orisha."

"You won't have to," TJ assured her. "None of us have to. All we have to do is get as many people away from here when February's new moon comes as possible. That gives us a few weeks to do the best we can."

TJ peeked at his phone on the table, which read:

Eko Atlantic's Doomsday in 4 weeks, 1 day, 12 hours, 8 minutes, and 33 seconds

"This is what we're going to do," Eni began. "We can't tip off Olokun or the Keepers. If we go door-to-door telling folks to leave on a specific day, that'll get us in trouble." She gave TJ a sideways glance that sent embarrassing heat through his ears. "So instead, I came up with the idea of a mandatory drill. Terrorism practice. Natural disaster run-through. That sort of thing."

"In fact," Manny added, "for each building, we have to make it a different reason so it doesn't get tied back to us. And we have to say the evacuations will be at random so that when we're ready..."

"... we all portal-travel to strategic fire alarms... and pull," Eniola finished for her. They shared in furtive nods.

For a brief moment, Ayo's voice pressed into TJ's mind. A repeat of the comment his friend once made about choosing the wrong girl between Eni and Manny. Maybe he was right? Eni *was* crazy awesome. But TJ knew that already. That was never the issue he had with her. Either way, the thought sent guilt flooding through his veins and his mind went back to all her texts he hadn't properly answered.

"Why don't we just tell this plan of yours to the UCMP?" one of the older students asked.

"Because they'll just shut us down," TJ answered, "just like they did to me during the meeting. And that means hundreds of thousands of people dead."

"We don't want hundreds of thousands of people dead," Manny repeated for effect.

Another older student waved their coffee cup in hand. "What about the people who just ignore fire alarms?"

TJ took the stage on that one. "That's what these next weeks are about. We'll be acting like volunteers. Children of the local fire brigade, informing people of the dangers of not listening to them for these *particular* drills. They'll ignore us at first, but if we post up enough fliers about hazards and fines, and really get into people's ears about it, that stuff will be in the back of their minds without them realizing it. It's not perfect, but it's all we can do."

There were a few more questions after that, but the group was feeling a lot better about the task, stiff shoulders and tight necks loosened a little, more closely resembling the casual nonchalance of typical teens.

"Well!" Eni clapped her hands. "Let's get started then, eh?"

55

EVACUATION ON THE DL

As all the students went out to make their rounds over the last week of January, TJ found himself grouped with Manny, the twins, and Eni for most of the time.

It was like he and Emeka had picked up right where they left off that first day at Ifa Academy. Emeka even started teaching TJ some sign language. But their conversations always circled back to geek references and debating who would win in a fight.

"All right, all right," TJ said at one point. "What about Master Chief versus Commander Shepard?"

Emeka typed a response and showed it to TJ. It read:

Emeka: love me some mass effect but its gotta go to master chief

"What?" TJ responded. "Even a Shepard using biotics as an Adept class?"

Emeka: biotics have NOTHING on the chief!

"Um…" Eni stepped between them as they boarded an elevator to their next floor. "Biotics? Master what?"

It was Manny who answered. "Nerd talk. Two sci-fi super

soldiers duking it out. And sorry, Teej, it's got to be Master Chief."

"I can't believe you just said that! I thought we were friends!"

"Well... which one is cuter?" Eni asked, pressing the elevator button for the thirty-first floor.

TJ snapped his fingers to Eni. "Shepard, by a long shot! Well, sort of by default. Master Chief never shows his face—probably for a reason." He chuckled as the elevator lifted.

"Oh, you got me there!" Manny conceded. "I swear I made *the* hottest FemShep though!"

"FemShep?" Titi asked from the rear.

"Female Shepard," TJ explained. "You can be a guy or girl in the game."

Titi and Eni shared looks of utter confusion. TJ hadn't noticed when they left the elevator that it was mostly he, Emeka, and Manny talking, with Eni and Titi on the outs. It was hard for TJ to notice anything when he spoke a mile a minute like that. His spirits lifted for the first time since he and his friends were bouncing around the Sky Realm. He didn't think he could feel so good. Even when they dealt with disgruntled people, like the grumpy old woman from the Azuri Towers, TJ didn't mind it.

"I don't care about any fire alarms," she'd told them late that afternoon. She wore a large yellow headwrap hat-thing that looked like a sunflower plastered on the side of her head.

Doing his best to keep up a friendly smile, TJ said, "Elder, all we are saying is when the alarms go off in the next few days or weeks, you have to get to a staircase."

"Staircase!?" She grimaced at TJ like he had let one loose. "On the forty-fifth floor? Child, you know damn well my knees can't get down all them stairs."

"She's got a point," Titi whispered in TJ's ear.

TJ mumbled back. "We don't have anyone else who can get her through a portal unless we start asking kids from other schools."

"How about Oracle Ruby?" Manny asked in TJ's other ear.

"Oh, right! We haven't asked her yet. She'll keep the secret."

"How long are you children going to keep at my door with all that mumbling?" the old lady grouched. *"Omo Ghetto: The Saga* is about to come on."

"Oh, I love that one!" TJ faked interest. "What's your favorite part?"

"I don't know. I keep missing parts because children this week keep knocking on my door." Her slitted gaze was enough of a signal for TJ to stop the friendly act.

"Well, we don't want to keep you," Manny cut in. "You just remember, when you hear those alarms, you'll leave your apartment, yes?"

"Fine." The woman slammed the door in their face.

OVER THE FIRST TWO WEEKS OF FEBRUARY, ENI'S PLAN worked better than any of them could have hoped. More than a few times, they knocked on doors with people already saying, "Yes, yes, fire drill any day now. Fines if we don't comply. We already know."

The week before Olokun's arrival, TJ was confident they had notified at least the skyscrapers closest to the coastline, eighteen in total. And as Eni pointed out that afternoon, after they got done with their rounds, "The coastline towers might be enough. If they all start evacuating, the rest of the inland towers will follow as well."

"I don't know," Umar said, his voice echoing from the stairwell they were in. "We don't know how fast it's all gonna go down when everything hits the fan."

"Hey." Manny smacked him across the shoulder. "How about a li'l more optimism when a plan's going smoothly, huh?"

Titi, who had been having trouble following up several flights of stairs, grumbled, "Not so fast, you guys. I'm still getting my legs back."

"What happened with you?" Eni asked.

"Acting Headmistress Omo of Fon has us doing morning drills with ice blocks." Titi rubbed warmth into her legs. "We had to burn them away before we could go to lunch. TJ thinks she's preparing us for Yemoja."

TJ punched the palm of his hand and squinted, emulating the aziza. "'You have to allow me to break you to build you back up. Or else chaos will rule you!'" He laughed and rolled his eyes. "At least, that's how she says it in our one-on-ones."

"'Yeah, chaos will be all of our dooms!'" Eni did her own imitation of the aziza but she didn't quite get it.

"Nah, not like that," TJ told her. "You gotta hunch over and get real mean when you talk."

Eni arched her back, making her long neck hook to the hallway floor. "Chaos! Lack of magical control is chaos!" She sounded more like a gremlin than a militant fae creature.

Before they reached the elevator to leave the towers, Manny stepped up to help Eni. "Like this, girl." She flexed, contorted her face into a scowl, and said, "'True magic concerns itself with control, the battle against chaos!'" Despite only knowing Omo of Fon since she took over headmistress duties from Elder Adeyemi the past few weeks, Manny *completely* nailed the aziza's demeanor and cadence.

As the elevator opened, Emeka laughed, turning his phone over to TJ, which read:

> Emeka: i cant even hear her and i kno that was a good
> impression 😂

It wasn't lost on TJ how much Manny had improved with her impression game. And to think just before they left for Ifa Academy at the start of the year, she said she'd never do one. She had gotten better at cheering TJ up by being extra funny, and it worked.

And TJ wasn't the only one to notice.

"You all go on ahead," Eni said. "We'll meet you at the cafe later. I've gotta tell TJ something."

"Ooo," Titi said, making eyes at the couple. "We get it, we get it, we're going."

Emeka gave TJ a wink and a pat on the shoulder. The faintest of frowns crossed Manny's lips, but she sandwiched it into a forced smile before waving goodbye to TJ just before the elevator doors closed.

Eni peeked over her shoulder down the empty hallway. One end looked out to a large window that displayed the statue of Olokun—the deity's elbow, TJ thought. The other end was dim beneath the late afternoon light peeking through its opposite window. They were alone. Eni set her hand to a wall fountain just near the elevator and generated a water portal. Her portal led to the rooftop of Ebony Towers, where they had first properly met at that party. What were they going there for? Eni had an odd look on her face. Did she want to... have some alone time? Titi and Emeka seemed to think so. Manny, too. Since they started up with their warnings across Eko Atlantic, he and Eni had shared in a few hand holds and kisses that she'd initiated, but not much else.

"So, what's up?" TJ asked.

"After you." Eni gestured a hand into her portal. "We need to talk."

THE WIND ATOP EBONY TOWERS WAS GENTLE AND SERENE, drifting through Eni's straight bob cut like little fairies were lifting up her hair. The dying afternoon light highlighted the edges of her dark brown skin in a golden glow. It was a splendid moment for some romance, what with the beautiful girl before TJ, the expensive outdoor couches laid out around them, and a view overwatching an ocean perfectly at peace.

Perfect except for the searching expression on Eni's face.

"TJ, is there something you want to tell me?"

"What?" TJ jerked back, knowing that tone meant he was in trouble. "Uh... no." Eni's frown deepened. "I mean, yeah! You changed your hair, right?" *Girls always want you to notice when they changed their hair, right?* "I like it!"

"No, TJ. I'm talking about you and Manny."

An anvil *thunked* to the bottom of TJ's stomach, nearly making his knees buckle. "Oh..."

"You barely answer my texts. You hold my hand loose when she's around. And you kiss me like I'm your grandmother."

TJ rushed forward and grabbed for Eni's elbows. He'd never seen her so down before. "Nah, nah, it's not like that. It's just been so crazy with everything going on. The towers, stopping Olokun, making sure Oya stops sniffing every perfume shop we pass so no one asks questions if she's a human or — "

"Titi told me about you and Manny." Eni didn't shake away from TJ, perhaps happy for the slight intimacy he was showing her, but her words were firm, challenging.

TJ lowered his voice. "There is no 'me and Manny.'"

"Oh yeah? No giggling in the mess hall. Always having dinner with her? Walks along the three bridges at Ifa Academy?"

"That was before I met you, Eni."

"Then Emeka is lying when he told me you two were holding hands at that dock cafe?"

"Are you talking to that whole family now?"

Finally, Eni shook herself free from TJ's grasp and pointed a finger at his chest. "Don't change the subject, Tomori Jomiloju."

What was it with girls saying my full name like that? TJ thought. Then again, he knew he deserved it. This conversation was *long* overdue.

Eni turned away from TJ and looked out toward the ocean, leaning her elbows over the glass balcony.

"Why?" she asked, not turning to TJ.

"Why what?"

"Why are you with me?"

Now there was a question TJ had pondered but hadn't allowed himself enough time to fully consider. Why was it so difficult for him to be honest with Eni? She'd probably had more relationships than TJ would ever have in his life. She probably had to break up with a bunch of people. So why couldn't TJ bring himself to do the same?

It was the same reason he couldn't tell her no to begin with; he had no backbone.

After a long moment of nothing but the winds filling the silence, Eni swallowed heavily and stepped away. She cleared her throat quickly and glanced down at the space between them. "Okay. Well then, you need to break up with me." She angled her body to TJ, one arm still leaning against the balcony. "You've never broken up with anyone before, have you?" She sighed, looking TJ up and down. And, not for the first time, but somehow more significant now than ever before, TJ felt the impact of their age gap. Eni was scrutinizing him like he were a child, her tone taking on the quality of a parent. "I get you can like two people at the same time, but I know... you *really* like Manny." She thumbed over her shoulder to the Atlantic Ocean behind her. "If all this goes to shit, you should tell her how you feel. You *both* should."

Funny enough, they already had up in the Sky Realm. TJ just had to say it all over again. When the time was right. At that moment though, the time was right for TJ to say the words he should have said months ago.

"Eniola..." TJ stopped himself with half a mind to close his eyes, to look away. But Eni deserved a straight answer and a straight look. "Eniola, I'm breaking up with you."

Despite Eni practically forcing the words from TJ's mouth, a shadow of sadness cloaked her face just then. Did she think she still had a chance? That TJ might've stood his ground and win her affections back? Did she expect him to fight back instead of giving her the cold, hard truth so quickly after being faced with the decision? TJ couldn't be sure, even after Eni walked from the balcony to one of the heaters to say, "Well, your delivery needs work Mr. Blunt-as-all-Hell, but good enough. Remind me to teach you the compliment sandwich next time."

"Thanks, Eni. I don't deserve you." TJ said it to her back as she lit her fingers with fire, crouched down, and turned on the tall-abstract-looking heater.

When had it gotten so cold? And was it getting dark already?

"No, you do not," Eni said, her back still turned. She put on a faux snootiness with her voice, turning. "Hence, the reason you'll never—" Her mouth fell open, long and slow; her eyes expanded, all in slow motion. Her gaze was fixed on something out in the distance, something in the direction of the ocean breeze reaching all the way up to the roof.

TJ didn't have to turn and look to know what she was seeing.

But he turned anyway.

What he saw made his stomach hitch. What he saw forced a terrible wave of horror to seize his entire body. What he saw shouldn't have been possible on planet Earth.

But anything was possible when you were dealing with the Orishas.

And just then, a five-hundred-foot tidal wave hung in the air, smothering the horizon, and forcing the sky over Eko Atlantic into early darkness.

56

THE WINDWEAVER'S STORM

TJ RUSHED TO ENI, TACKLING HER INTO THE CUSHIONS OF THE nearest outdoor sofa sets. As they fell into the throw pillows, TJ shouted, "*Afẹfẹ, wà ji mi,*" and a cage of wind protected them. TJ wasn't so sure it would hold up to a tidal wave, but it was all he could do.

After a long moment, where TJ expected to feel mist overhead or the shaking of the tower beneath them, nothing happened. Heart racing a murderous beat, TJ found the morsel of courage that allowed him to peek his head over the sofa and railing.

The tidal wave was still there, but it hadn't moved.

It was a bizarre sight just hanging there like an aqua specter. How fast had the waves retreated from the shore to lift in the air like that? There were at least a hundred yards between where the shoreline had been to where it rested now. Bits of seaweed stuck to wet rocks. TJ had expected to see flopping fish atop moist stones as well, but they all seemed to be drawn back by Olokun within his wave. In fact, he would've sworn he saw a thousand glowering eyes behind the curtain of hanging water.

Those past few weeks, TJ had had an unhealthy hobby of watching tidal wave videos online. None of those Top Ten disaster videos had anything on the height of the wave before them. Far below, TJ could already see people gathering to witness the phenomena before them. None of them could know what was coming. Or perhaps they should have but were in too much awe to move.

TJ fumbled for his phone and read his countdown app:

Eko Atlantic's Doomsday in 0 weeks, 6 days, 2 hours, 26 minutes, and 3 seconds

Lifting his hand over his brow, TJ stared up at the moon, which smiled at him with a sideways sliver of a grin. It definitely was not a new moon.

"TJ…" Eni's voice quivered. "Is that… is that really?"

"Yeah, that's Olokun." TJ flipped to his favorite's list on his phone and called Manny. "Hey, it's me. Are you by a window?"

"Yeah, just down the hall. We convinced this old man that fire alarms aren't a hoax made up by the government. Why? What's…. Oh my… TJ, what the hell is that!?"

"Olokun. But he's not attacking for some reason. Listen, I'm with Eni at the top of Ebony Towers. We need to get everyone to pull alarms now!"

Manny's voice came over the line with fear. "I-I thought the new moon was next week?"

"No time to wonder the why. Just get those alarms on and meet us at the beach. The SS2 and SS3 students can get portals there."

"On it. Stay safe, TJ."

"You too." He hung up the phone to find the tidal wave still hanging and Eni still staring.

"Eni!" TJ shouted to break her from her reverie. "We need to focus. Where's the alarm nearest here?"

With a shaky hand, Eni pointed to a red box lodged into the wall leading back to the penthouse. Above it read the letters "fire alarm."

"*Afẹfẹ, wà ṣi mi,*" TJ said, and the fire alarm latch came down with a screeching wail. Still, Eni stood at the balcony's edge, quivering. TJ didn't know why but in moments where he should've been scared shitless, he put on a brave face for everyone else, *especially* when they were breaking down.

"Eniola!" TJ grabbed her shoulders, spun her away from the ocean monstrosity, and locked eyes with her. "We have to get down to that beach and get those people away from Olokun's wave. He won't stay put like that for long. I need you to make us a portal to the beach—"

"B-but that means we h-have to come out right n-next to that wave!" Eni's chin trembled as she spoke in a stutter.

"I just need a ride down. After that, you'll need to travel to New Ile-Ife and warn someone. Anyone. You've only used short-distance portals, so you should still have the energy. Can you do that?"

Eni's eyes flitted between TJ and the wave behind them erratically.

"Eniola!"

Chin still quivering, Eni nodded. She got up on shaky knees and ambled over to the wall fountain near the balcony. Placing a hand to the slick surface, she summoned her staff, failed to manifest a portal a few times before she got it right, and led them through. In a flash, they were on the beach, their feet sinking into the wet sands around them, and a colossal wave just above.

Eni's shaking grew worse as she stared up at it. Then she turned to TJ with wild eyes. "I know we broke up, but," Eni kissed TJ on the cheek, "just in case this is the last time I see you."

"Uh... thanks." TJ blushed. "Now, go! Get to the embassy."

Eni gave him a curt nod and disappeared into another portal she manifested.

"Everyone get back!" TJ waved his hands wildly at the idiots with their phones snapping photos and taking videos mere yards from the wall of ocean. "Get back! Get back!"

A faint whisper buzzed in TJ's ear, a familiar wind crossed the back of his neck. He turned back to the huge wave, his sneakers sinking into the wet sands covered in seaweed. "Dayo? Is that you?"

Ashe rushed behind the wave, faint but bright at the same time. TJ stretched his hand out to the water. When he touched it, he heard a voice loud and clear in his head.

But the voice did not belong to Dayo.

Tomori Jomiloju Young, you have broken our sacred agreement. That was the voice of Olokun, a voice TJ hadn't heard for nearly half a year. He had forgotten how deep and androgynous the voice had been. *Did you think the Lord of the Deep would not know what you were doing? Do you admit to a forfeit of our contract?*

"I did everything I could!" TJ shouted at the wave as it swallowed his wrist with a chill. "I couldn't let everyone get drowned!"

Do you admit to a forfeit of our pantheon's parley? Again, Olokun's voice sent shivers through TJ's body—that or the cold water around his arm.

"We never said anything about moving the clouded out of Eko Atlantic. I built up your praise. That's why your wave is so big now, isn't it?"

Eko Atlantic should be gone by now. The marine life that resided here must be restored for balance to be maintained.

"We still have a week!"

Do not deceive me, mortal. You have no intention of bringing down those towers. Instead, you mean to mock me by forcing myself against an empty city.

TJ couldn't have just been imagining it. The frost from Olokun's words wasn't just sending metaphorical chills through him. Coldness was *actually* stretching from his wrist and up his arm with ice crystals embedding themselves into his skin.

Olokun was trapping him!

No, it wasn't Olokun. Frost magic wasn't his thing. But he had a wife who had recently reacquired that particular school of magic. Courtesy of TJ.

Yemoja.

You will not make a fool of my partner, the Lord of the Deep, any longer. This voice was a woman's, with the tone of a chiding mother. *You will stand there and watch what you have wrought, young mortal.*

Our parley is broken, Olokun finished as ice creeped up TJ's shoulder. *Good bye, Tomori Jomiloji Young.*

"No, no, wait, wait, wait!" TJ shouted, his heart pounding so fast he thought the sheer force of it could help him break the frosty hold. The wave began to rise higher. Nothing could be done, though. He tried to light a flame in his fist by saying, "*iná, wá ṣi mi*," but his feeble Ashe was nothing compared to Yemoja's frost. Panic enveloping his every muscle, TJ turned back to the crowd behind him. "Back! Everyone get back! You have to run, you have to!"

Could they even hear him so far away with the rushing waters climbing higher and higher on the wave? Ice spread over TJ's mouth and his words muffled under cold blocks of water. TJ would have shivered but his whole body had already been covered in a mini-glacier. Just as Yemoja said, he would have to stand and watch as the giant wave receded, revved up, and then pushed forward with the force of a thousand battleships ready to ram the first towers.

Ebony Towers.

TJ cried out against his helmet of ice. Those people needed to get back. There was no way they'd survive the tidal wave coming for them. They wouldn't just be hit, they'd be *crushed*.

TJ generated fire from within his belly, desperately clinging to every lesson from Teacher Omo of Fon, every lesson from Elder Adeyemi. His ice cage started to crack in hairlines, but nowhere near fast enough to save those people. They would die, and there was nothing TJ could do.

As the tip of the enormous wave crested and then fell, a shadow loomed large and great above them all. The people with their phones started to run but there was nowhere for them to go. Some of them knew that, standing there with hands outstretched, others in prayer or full prostration. Many curled up and cowered before the great power above them.

And then…

Howling wind punched into the center of the wave like a giant ram buckling the side of a liquid mountain. The impact shook the sloshy sands beneath TJ's ice boots. And though his ice cage made everything sound muffled, the blow of wind thumped deep in his chest. The wave high above was just a collection of water, but to TJ, in that moment, it looked like a heavyweight boxer caught completely off guard by a haymaker. It tumbled back into itself, back into the endless expanse of ocean.

At the beach stood a line of figures, some tiny with wings,

many with robes of aso oke, others in simple street clothes. Most of them held staffs above their heads, but one, who stood as vanguard to the group, merely held a pair of hands up to the sky. The figure had the shape of a woman, and considering the epic wind punch Olokun just took to the metaphorical chin, that woman had to be Oya.

They were safe. For now.

TJ wished he could turn his head to see the ocean behind him —surely Olokun and Yemoja were stirring up a second wave to fling their way—but his face was locked in place. The winged figures flew over in his direction. As they came closer, TJ could make out that they were aziza through the foggy ice helmet. Quickly, they all set their hands to his limbs, flaring their palms with flames. As TJ's frosty cage melted, he could start hearing their tiny voices more clearly.

"He won't make it, Omo of Fon!"

"Another wave is coming!"

"He'll make it! He'll make it!" This voice was familiar, this voice was Teacher Omo of Fon's. The ice melted away enough for TJ to make out green veins under the aziza's skin. "Tomori Jomiloju, if you can hear me, I'm giving you permission to cheat. Boost your Ashe, boy! Use our magic! Hurry!"

Right! TJ thought as he sunk into the familiar well of Ashe he had improved on all year with Elder Adeyemi. Rapidly, his energy filled the aziza all around him. The building heat coursing through their veins became his own and he cycled the energy from within and out again. His ice cage melted away in moments, leaving his t-shirt and jeans soaked and heavy. Before he could wipe himself of excess water, he was pulled into the air by the fairies and they rushed for the group at the beach.

TJ had read of aziza strength, but he didn't know they could lift full-on teenage boys. He didn't have much time to be in awe though. A great shadow passed over them. Wind slapped his face as he flipped his head over his shoulder. His vision was met with yet another skyscraper-tall tidal wave.

"Hurry! Hurry!" one of the aziza shouted.

Drops of water fell on TJ's back and he knew they were

directly under the wave. His muscles seized up, ready for the impact.

"Just get to the line, warriors!" Omo of Fon bellowed, her softball-sized eyes bulging. "Get. To. The. Line!"

But water drenched TJ's back, hitting so hard it made the aziza drop him. His heart convulsed in his chest. Were it not for their forward momentum, they might've been drowned in the torrent of water. Instead, they fell forward into a box of wind surrounding Oya and her band of diviners and magicians who had saved TJ before. Above them, water fell around the wind box and swept straight for the first towers of Eko Atlantic.

They were safe. But the buildings wouldn't be.

A boom shook above and behind the group, followed by shattered glass and screaming. It was his nightmare come to life.

"TJ! TJ!" Manny rushed down to where TJ had fallen in the sands. "Oya is weakening. That first blow took mad energy out of her."

The water rushed over their wind box again, this time flooding back into the deep ocean, revving for another strike. It was like Olokun and Yemoja were hammering nails.

"It's Yemoja's ice that's the worst part of all this," came the voice of Miss Gravés off to the side. "And look, she's weakening the base of the towers with her frost."

"When they attack again, we'll need to be ready!" TJ stood up with the help of Manny. "Oya, how are you feeling?"

"I will break this body soon." Oya's knees sunk deep into the sands. It was true, cracks spidered up her arms just like the stories of the diviners of old. "It's time, young mortal. Just like we practiced. Quickly, before Olokun and Yemoja return."

In the distance, waves gathered into themselves, building dozens of feet in height by the second.

"Everyone, gather around." TJ found a rock and stood on it, Manny right at his heels. "Find the person closest to you and hold their hand. We're going to do the sacred poem of Oya."

Now that TJ was a bit settled, he recognized the collection of faces, none of them worried, all of them ready to fight: from Ozolua the cook, Oroma with her braided hair, his two bodyguards ready with Ogun masks, Oracle Ruby in fitted robes, to

Mr. Ikenna in his hyena form, and a bunch of soldiers from the UCMP. Adults weren't the only ones there, either. Students from Ifa spread all around from Titi and Emeka, Umar, Fiona with the red hair, and more. Each face, every pair of eyes was on TJ, and for once, nerves didn't immobilize him.

"Don't worry if you don't know it!" TJ continued loudly. "On the second or third go around, just chime in. Anything helps. We need to give Oya the strength to defend the towers as people evacuate."

"Quickly... mortals..." Oya said through haggard breaths, pointing to the gathering wave that was now as tall as two stacked cruise ships.

"When the wind spoke, they used to listen," Manny started, strong and firm.

"When the wind spoke, their crowns would glisten," TJ chimed in with her.

Then more started to chant along with them.

Now the gusts fall on deaf ears
Gales whip for no one to hear
But She'll cut a path so clear
Listen, 'cause Oya is near...

"Again!" Manny shouted as the wave stood five-hundred feet against the setting sun.

When the wind spoke, they used to listen.
When the wind spoke, their crowns would glisten.

Oya spread her hands wide, her chin jutted up to the heavens. TJ concentrated, transferring everyone's energy and focusing it into Oya's.

Now the gusts fall on deaf ears.
Gales whip for no one to hear.

A cyclone stirred around Oya's body, and just like Eshu last summer, her divine spirit lifted from her human form like smoke lifting from an extinguished fire.

But She'll cut a path so clear.
Listen, 'cause Oya is near...

"Again!" TJ was the one to shout this time as the wave reached its apex at nearly seven hundred feet.

Again, the group chanted at the top of their lungs, and TJ guided them like the rippling waters of Elder Adeyemi's cavern pool, each bit of energy cascading into the next, making the collective stronger.

"Listen!" Manny bellowed at TJ's side with her hands raised; TJ raised his hands, too. "Listen! 'Cause Oya is near!"

As the wave came down on them all, Oya ripped away from her human body. To anyone else, they would have seen nothing more than a body slumping into the sands. To TJ, however, a bright spread of brilliant light filled the beach, and from its radiance, Oya's true form sprang out as a ferocious storm. A terrible storm that wielded a machete in one hand, and a whip in the other. An awesome storm that crackled with lightning and rumbled with thunder.

It was as though time had slowed to a snail's pace for TJ as he marveled at the sight before him. Oya's true form was large, but Olokun and Yemoja's was larger. And through his Ashe vision, TJ could see husband and wife manifest as bright eyes within the horrifying wave.

And then... sea and sky met.

They gathered in a clash so powerful, the windows that had not yet been shattered in the towers flew into pieces along the beach. Everyone fell down to the sands as the ocean literally fought with the clouds.

A wrinkled hand came to TJ's shoulder, lifting him up back to his feet. "Great work, Mr. Young." It was Elder Adeyemi, still in her drab jail outfit. TJ was still in too much shock and his ears rang too loud for him to smile up at her. "Oya's bought us some time, but we still need to get the rest of the clouded out. Can I count on you?"

"Yes, of course, Elder."

"Good." She withdrew a wooden staff with a green crystal lodged at its head, a double helix at its middle, and a fine point at its end: Dayo's staff. His sister's staff. "You're not old enough yet, but I trust you'll put this to good use."

57

EVACUATION ON THE TURN-UP

THE MOMENT TJ GRIPPED HIS SISTER'S STAFF, ASHE BLOOMED through him, filling him with calming energy. The familiar brush on the back of his neck tickled him once more, and he finally understood why it meant Dayo was overwatching him. She had always rubbed the back of his neck whenever she saw him, whether right before hugging him, whenever he made a joke that made her laugh, or just when they were walking side by side. It was her support of him, just as she supported him now, just as her energy filled his veins.

And he would need everything she could give him.

Because at the same moment TJ had his epiphany, Olokun and Yemoja's wave slammed through Oya's cloud and struck Ebony Towers right in its center. The skyscraper bucked, but it didn't give, and TJ saw a ripple of Ashe where the impact occurred. Was it being protected mystically by some additional enchantment?

The towers behind Ebony weren't as lucky.

The six nearest to the obsidian high-rises fell over like dominos. They were completely naked to the force of the colossal waves from the gods. Six towers. Thousands of people. Gone just like that. TJ couldn't fathom it.

As his hands shook, as his legs quivered, he couldn't grasp the concept of the utter loss that had just occurred. Why was Ebony still standing and the others were not? Did the UCMP give it extra protection just because the Afolabi's owned it? Because it was a skyscraper owned by a diviner family?

Lip quivering, TJ watched as the surf receded from the fallen skyscrapers and spread around Ebony Towers where they left behind ice crystals that crackled at the base with loud pops.

"Ebony Towers won't take much more of that," Elder Adeyemi bellowed. If she was devastated by the loss of life that had just transpired, she didn't let it show on her face. She stared up at the damage and falling glass that fell onto the beach from Ebony Towers. Thankfully, the wind cage generated by the battlemages protected them from the fallout. A dozen or so of them stood in perfect formation, maintaining the walls of gusts with utter concentration lined in their foreheads. TJ recognized one of them from the round table meeting, a big guy who had pulled Mom away from that conservator. He had a tattoo over his face, a tattoo that glowed with each use of his magic.

"There's still people in there." TJ gripped Dayo's staff tightly. All those people in the other towers were lost, but the clouded still in the Ebony Towers could still be saved.

Manny came to his side with tears in her eyes, gawking above. "We gotta get them out."

"And we will. But first, let us fortify and save our own position." Elder Adeyemi turned to the lineup of diviners still throwing up windshields against the ocean. Oya's storm was already waning up above. "Mr. Sani, Mr. Ali, shadow TJ. Never leave his side unless you must."

The pair of bodyguards that had been joined to TJ's hip all year stood at attention, their enchanted armor rattling with their salutes.

"Of course, ma'am," said the first.

"*Lẹ́sẹ̀kẹ̀sẹ̀, ìyá,*" answered the second.

Everyone else! Adeyemi bellowed to the group, speaking directly to everyone's mind. *We must hold the line. Give the diviners time to get those clouded out of those towers.* The group returned their affirmation with a war cry that echoed within their wind cage. *Funnel through TJ Young. He will empower—*

A deluge pierced through the swirling wind with a strange

sonic boom, slicing through it like it was nothing but paper. Battlemages covered their ears. They shouted and grunted as the water roared and crashed. TJ barely had time to think when he instinctively grabbed for Manny's arm and pulled her away from the worst of it. But it was Manny who saved him, not the other way around. As the wave tore its way through the ranks of the battlemages, Manny pushed them away with wind magic, putting them a safe distance from a second wave that cascaded after the first. Through the chaos, the big guy with the glowing tattoos on his face was pulled under the water bodily. It wasn't just a powerful rip current that took him; TJ saw the Ashe that grabbed the battlemage and pulled him under like a giant hand of death.

A stiff chill squeezed at TJ's chest. He knew he'd never see that battlemage again.

"Help!" a voice sounded from above, from within the towers. "Help me!"

TJ turned his head up to the Ebony Towers, which were already leaning too far to one side. He took steps toward it when Manny grabbed him by his shoulder. "We need to stay on the beach for the battlemages."

"They're soldiers." TJ nodded to the beach where the battlemages were already generating another wind wall with double layering, Elder Adeyemi at the helm, shouting orders. "But the people up there need us. They have no idea what's going on."

Manny stared up at the towers and back at the beach. Then she nodded her agreement. Two whirlpools of sand stirred just behind her, churning like a mix of flour until TJ's bodyguards shot out from both of them.

That was definitely one way to keep safe from the wave.

TJ pointed a hand upward. "People need us up there!"

"But what about the beach?" the bigger guard asked. "You're too important to be left to a search and rescue."

"That's all this is at this point!" TJ retorted, tired of adults letting people die. "I'm going to help those people *with* or *without* your help." The hurt in his eyes must've been evident, because the guards looked to one another under their masks. TJ didn't care if they told him no. He wasn't letting thousands more die.

The second guard said something in Yoruba TJ didn't quite

understand. Then the first one translated. "Well... Adeyemi's orders were to shadow you. Nothing else."

"So you're gonna help us?" Manny asked as another tidal wave built up deep in the ocean.

"We'll follow your lead, young ones."

Taking a deep breath, TJ stirred the Ashe of wind in his belly. "We need to get up the towers where the screaming is coming from. Generate some of Oya's wind, and I'll funnel." Manny started first, turning wind magic within her. The guards did the same. TJ took their power, recycled it through his sister's staff, then shot up the side of the building using air-steps. The grouping of everyone's magic, along with the staff, made the effort a simple thing. With each vault, TJ used the power of Manny and the bodyguards at his side, oscillating between his own staff power and their own in pulsing beats.

Left, right, left, right.

"Just up there!" TJ pointed to a cracked window. "Can one of you break the rest of that out?"

The bigger of the two bodyguards raced forward with his iron staff in hand. Whirling around like a cyclone, he catapulted from an air-step and torpedoed straight into the side of the building. At first it looked like he was smashing through staff-first, but the moment his staff tip touched the glass, the window shattered into harmless sand.

TJ followed into a luxurious hallway filled with broken statuettes and paintings hanging crookedly from the walls.

"*Ràn mí lọ́wọ́... Ràn mí lọ́wọ́...*" an old man croaked as he waddled down the hallway with crutches and blood coming down from a large cut on forehead. His left arm was completely missing.

"Help! Help!" another younger woman said near a half-open door further down. "My leg! I can't feel my leg!"

"You two go for her," the bigger bodyguard commanded TJ and Manny. "We'll get the Elder here."

TJ and Manny nodded, rushing to the far end of the hallway to pick up the young woman whose bone had poked through her business pants. There was no time to be rattled by the gruesome sight. They slung her over their shoulders and pushed through to the other side of the hall that faced the dark marina with Olokun's giant statue.

"I don't know how to make the glass into sand like your bodyguard did," Manny said with panic.

"Uh, uh..." TJ racked his brain for a spell that would work. "Just smash it!"

Together, with the help of TJ's staff, they blasted the window out into pieces with wind magic, but it wasn't nearly as clean as what the bodyguard had done. Still, they didn't have time to get fussy about their shoddy spell work or the edges of protruding glass.

"All right!" TJ shouted. "Jump!"

They plummeted out of the window and back down to the ground, acting like a parachute for the wounded woman with their wind blasts—something TJ finally figured out thanks to Teacher Omo of Fon. He definitely needed to gift her a basket of figs if they made it out of this horror alive. When they touched the ground, UCMP officials took over, making portals and taking the wounded away.

The whole marina was filled with the pops of fire portals, the swishing of water gateways. From above, TJ imagined a half drowned marina with flashing lights and colors sparking off with each new magical person that joined in. Word must've gotten out quick, because the entire marina was filled with diviners ready to help. But that meant complete and total exposure to the clouded. How would the UCMP ever hope to cover something up like this at such a scale?

Another portal flashed near a yacht that was splayed and split over a statue. Out from it came Eni and a bunch of Ifa Academy students, including Emeka, Titi, and Umar.

"What are you doing here?" TJ asked. "I thought you were warning the embassy?"

"They already knew what was going on," Eni jogged over with her group, "even said some of the towers have extra protection. I went to Ifa Academy to get some help from the teachers and some of the older students. We're spreading out to get as many clouded out through portals. Glad to see you're okay."

"You too." TJ tried for a smile, but it didn't feel right.

"Eniola!" called one of the teachers. "We need to be inside Azuri Towers five minutes ago. Pick it up!"

"Coming!" Eni jogged away backward, then called out, "You two get as many out of Ebony as you can, okay?"

TJ and Manny nodded. And despite the healers shouting at them to get themselves safe, the two of them were both back in the towers, saving more people, as many as they could. With each lap back, another wave impacted against the tower. When they were clearing the tenth floor, one of the living rooms was filled with a shark, a few eels, and a pair of turtles, each with glass lodged in their skin and shells.

"They're using sea creatures to fight, too?" Manny asked sadly as they helped another resident escape. They had seen a few fish here and there, but nothing as large as a shark or turtle. "They're just gonna use them and let them die like that? Yemoja would never..."

"Stay focused, Manny," TJ had to remind her as another wave slammed into the tower.

TJ tumbled to one side, flying through the open plan living room and straight into the island in the middle of the kitchen. Were it not for another of Manny's wind walls softening the blow, he would've been concussed. Instead, he just had a raging headache. The entire building was fully leaning now, and the sea creatures on the other end slid straight toward TJ. The shark spread its mouth open wide, revealing endless rows of sharp teeth, ready to swallow TJ whole. But just before that could happen, a hyena bit down on the shark's gills. With an ironclad jaw, the hyena forced the shark's head to the side of the kitchen island where TJ's back was pressed against.

"Hello there, Mr. Young," the hyena seemed to say, but its mouth didn't move. It took TJ too long to realize the back of the hyena was human, and it was Mr. Ikenna who spoke. "Glad to see you lending a helping hand!"

"Help!" Manny called out from across the room. "We're pinned by the couch."

Manny and the woman they were saving were crushed between a leather couch and a broken painting impacted into the wall.

"I've got you!" Mr. Ikenna said as his human side waved a wooden staff and dropped everyone, including TJ, through a portal. They all fell outside the tower on ground level. The streets were flooded with calve-high water now, and the few cars that could escape parking structures were looking for ways out. But that was an impossible task when street lamps and huge billboards were scattered and crumbled along most of the roads. Amid the disarray, Manny got the resident they were helping to a healer.

"There you are!" came the shouting voice of TJ's bodyguard, who waded through the water with his partner not far behind. They were about a block away. TJ waved his hands for them to come over. Their help was greatly needed. But before the guards could get halfway down the block, a fire portal blossomed near the entrance of a shopping mall. From its fiery depths sprang forth a quartet of Keepers, dressed in their typical cream robes. The guards and the Keepers quickly traded spells between one another. Lightning crackled in the air, fire plumes roared in violent lines of attack. The guards were forced to retreat into a water portal, where the Keepers gave chase.

TJ splashed his way to them, shouting to Manny behind him. "We gotta help them. I can turn the fight to their favor."

"No, TJ." Manny grabbed his wrist. "They're professionals. They'll handle themselves. There's still people to save, just like you said." She pointed upward to the creaking skyscrapers.

TJ nodded, knowing she was right. But that didn't help the worry that slithered through him at the thought of the Keepers bringing his guards down. If it wasn't for the snapping of Manny's fingers and a gesture back up to the towers, they might've not been able to save the family they rushed up to a moment after.

TJ preferred this, the simplicity of a search and rescue. No making deals, no meetings, no wondering. Just the work. In the tower, out the tower. That's all he had to think about.

He and Manny were about to head into the nineteenth floor when another wave crashed into the tower, raining debris down on them all. A metal slab came rushing for TJ and he pushed Manny away. It could've been the same metal slab or something TJ didn't see, but something hard impacted on the side of TJ's head and he blacked out momentarily. When he came to again, he found himself falling in the air. To one side of him was Ebony Towers falling into the ocean, to the other, another giant wave, and below him, solid asphalt.

Lifting his sister's staff, he extracted water from the wave and rode it down safely to the street where a pack of cars was backed up in a sea of red brake lights.

"Good save!" Manny called from a totaled delivery truck across the street. "You okay?"

"Just a little woozy, but I'll be all right."

A child screamed from under a collapsed toy shop and Manny went off to save her. Thankfully, that shop was in the opposite direction of Ebony Towers because just as Manny set off, the obsidian skyscraper, the forefront of Eko Atlantic, finally came crashing down on them all with a boom.

Dark storm clouds.

Powerful winds.

Screams.

TJ was back in his dreams, entrapped by the horror he thought was left in his mind.

Huge crashing waves.

Metal creaking.

Death.

TJ's nightmares had turned into reality. The cries for help, the yelps of pain weren't just figments of his imagination. They were real people with real names and real families that would never see them alive again. TJ stood in utter shock. His arms and legs couldn't move anymore, not when they couldn't make sense of how such monstrosities could be allowed in the world.

As the dust settled and the waves receded once more to assault the next set of skyscrapers, a collection of grunting people snapped TJ back into action.

Forget about the nightmare, he told himself. *Just work. Keep working.*

He twisted around to find Umar, Titi, and Emeka trying to pull rubble from the road to clear a path for the cars still functioning. But they were exhausted, their movements weak and sluggish.

"Emeka, Titi, Umar, you got this. Keep going." TJ jogged up to them with his sister's staff raised. "Quick! We don't have long 'til the next wave!"

With TJ boosting his fellow students, the rubble lifted up easily and fell into the dock near the Olokun statue's feet. The clouded that rolled past in their cars thanked the kids and sped off. A few of the passengers gawked and blessed them with words of Christ or Allah, depending on the vehicle.

Emeka signed "good job" to TJ as Titi asked, "Where's Manny?"

It was Umar who pointed a tired finger up above to the Azuri Towers, which were looking like a trio of leaning towers of Pisa. High above on what must've been the twentieth floor or so, Manny was air-stepping up the sides of the building to someone TJ couldn't quite make out. But Manny must've been tired. She wasn't going as fast as TJ knew she could. And the wave out in the ocean had already climbed to two-hundred feet.

"Get yourselves back!" TJ ordered his friends. "Start in on the inland towers. The coast is done for."

Before waiting for an answer, he vaulted off to help Manny, air-stepping the whole way up. His friend was vulnerable, completely exposed to that wave coming in.

TJ had to make it to her.

As he gripped his staff in hand, he realized for the first time that his arms were cut up and bruised. A faint sting of salt water entering his wounds forced painful throbs up his arms, even through his adrenaline. TJ leaned into his power, forcing the pain down with a focus any of his teachers would've been proud of.

As he caught up to Manny, dodging crooked metal fixtures and broken glass all the way, the figure of the person she was trying to save grew in greater definition. It was the old woman with the sunflower hat who'd complained about not being able to watch her Nollywood Movies in peace. The woman hung from her window, her elbows lodged into its sill for support, and she cried out at the tidal wave that started to come in for her tower. "Please, no! I don't want to die! Please, no!"

I won't let you die! I won't!

"Manny, right behind you! On your left!" TJ called out as he continued to bound upward. "I'll grab her, you catch."

"Got it!"

TJ raced past Manny with a boost of wind, his air-steps as solid beneath his feet as cement. He was fifty yards away from the old woman, forty yards, thirty... But the wave that was coming in was smaller, barreling in with less strength. Would it even hit them? He raised his staff to lift her from her window and back down to Manny with wind magic. When the old woman lifted mystically into the air, she screamed at the top of her lungs, flailing wildly.

"Wait, TJ!" Manny bellowed from below. "My leg's caught in something! Wait! Wait!"

It didn't matter that Manny's leg got caught in something, though, because the wave screeched like it was a beast instead of a collection of water. It forced TJ to clamp his palms over his ears; Manny, too. And the woman went into a free fall. Worst yet, the wave would've never reached them if they had done nothing at all. The ferocious waters devoured the woman with the sunflower hat, her screams submerged under the wave.

It happened so fast, TJ couldn't even see where she was under the rush of water. And then, as the ocean rose with that weird screech, as though the sound itself was lifting it from the streets below, up to the towers, TJ was caught in the wave, too.

He tumbled and tumbled, losing his grip on his sister's staff. A lungful of salt water entered his chest. He reflexively took in more and his head went woozy.

Then darkness took him.

TJ GASPED AS WATER WAS PULLED FROM HIS LUNGS. ABOVE HIM stood Emeka with TJ's staff, Titi, and Umar, all backdropped by broken towers full of wails of anguish. To his side, Manny was also coughing up water, her face bruised and bloodied. TJ must've looked just the same.

The nightmare wasn't over yet.

"How long were we out?" TJ asked with a grunt.

"Just a minute or two." Titi took the staff from Emeka and handed it back to TJ.

"We saw you weren't going to make it," Umar said. "So we came to help."

"Where's Eniola?" TJ asked.

"We got split up," Emeka signed. "She's with the older kids clearing out towers to the east."

"What about the woman we were trying to save?" Manny asked, massaging her jaw. "Did you get her, too?"

Emeka shook his head and nodded to the streets around them, flooded with water. They were farther in from where the tidal waves were smashing into skyscrapers, though. Azuri Towers were not among them anymore, and just near a fallen street light, a sunflower hat floated atop lapping water. The heartbreak TJ had felt before resurfaced, threatening to lock his muscles into inaction once more. If he wasn't so bruised and battered, he might've given in to it. He couldn't say the same for Manny, though.

"She just... she just..." Manny shook and stared at the sunflower hat. "I shoulda seen that pipe my foot got caught on. I shoulda never gotten caught up."

"It's not your fault, Manny." TJ helped her stand up as they looked out at the destruction that continued. Oya's storm was barely a wisp, a mere nuisance to the tidal wave, a far cry from the haymakers she was slinging at the start.

There were too many towers, too much land to cover. TJ was foolish to think he could honestly save everyone in the marina, even with the help of the others. But the anger he felt had no business being turned inward.

"It's not any of our faults. We aren't killing these people. They are." He pointed out to the ocean. "That last attack wasn't just a tidal wave." TJ couldn't figure it out before, but now it was clear. He had wondered when one certain Orisha would show himself in the assault. "Those waters had sound magic that made us cover our ears, just like the battlemages on the beach. That sound made me drop that..." TJ took in a deep sigh to cover up a quivering voice. "That woman didn't deserve what happened to her."

Realization rushed through TJ and he turned his eyes to the

ocean that piled up another tidal wave. Through his prism vision, with the help of his sister's staff, an aura pulsated at the tidal wave's center, a signature of energy he was familiar with.

"We have to stop this at the source." TJ narrowed his eyes. "Oya can't keep up. And there's something going on in the ocean. Not just Olokun and Yemoja. They're weakening. Just like Oya said they would without the full praise they wanted. But they're maintaining their energy with some help."

Manny came to his side, squinting in an attempt to see what TJ saw. "What do you sense?"

TJ gulped before answering. "Eshu."

58

A GRAVEYARD OF SAND

"WHAT ARE YOU GONNA DO?" MANNY ASKED AS THEY RACED through the cracked streets with air-stepping, Emeka, Titi, and Umar just at their heels.

"I'm going to drown just like in Camp Olosa," TJ answered.

"Excuse me?" Titi cried out from behind. "Can you say that again?"

"Don't worry," Manny assured her as she hopped off a trashed car, skipped off a puddle, and air-stepped up to a broken traffic sign. "It's not as bad as it sounds. It's just a way to crossover to the Aqua Realm."

TJ used a fire hydrant that had turned into a geyser to lift over a destroyed billboard layered in ice. "Eshu is powerful right now, so I'll use his power to generate the power to crossover... alone." He made sure he directed his last word to Manny.

"Okay," Umar said, his tone not totally convinced. "Say TJ doesn't die from drowning and gets to the Aqua Realm. What then?"

"I make Eshu stop what he's doing," TJ answered plainly. "Olokun and Yemoja are clearly only able to take down a few more towers. But with Eshu, they can take out most of Eko Atlantic. If I convince him to not support Olokun, we can stop more people from dying. If I can't convince him... then we'll have to fight."

"Watch out!" Manny pointed ahead as another tidal wave came in.

TJ stopped his air-stepping and implanted his feet to the ground. "Everyone, on me. Funnel through Manny. We'll make a wind cage like those battlemages to protect ourselves."

"Oh, no, no, no!" Umar quivered and whined. "Omo of Fon always says my wind magic needs work."

Emeka dropped to TJ's side and signed back to Umar. "Just touch TJ's back and follow our lead."

TJ lifted his sister's staff over his head as four hands pressed into his back. A cold chill slithered from his friends' fingers, through his body, and up through his eyes. His pupils lit up, making his vision hazy. TJ mystically attached himself to the wind ball Manny generated for them, then he chained it between Titi and Emeka's twin magic, which enhanced the cyclone howling around them, not unlike the Ibeji twins in the Sky Realm. But Umar was right, his wind magic was far below average. When the wave hit them, the whole of their cage got shunted back.

"Come... on... Umar," Titi gritted. "Pull. Your. Weight."

"I'm. Trying." Umar grunted against the sheer force of the rushing water. "It's. A. Damn. Tidal. Wave."

TJ kept his concentration locked, head throbbing from fatigue, but water always found a way to find the smallest of cracks. One sliver of a gap let in a deluge. Manny tried to repair the cracks, and TJ helped her along, strengthening the wind ball where it was weakest, but that just left other portions of their protection vulnerable. Eventually, ocean overwhelmed wind, and they all went tumbling back into the side of a bus. TJ's back thrummed with pain, but the water was already retreating back to the coast for another attack. Rubbing his back, TJ went over to Umar to help him up.

"Sorry, TJ!" The boy blushed, not making eye contact. "I told you my wind magic sucks. Oya doesn't like me."

TJ shook Umar's shoulder and gave him an encouraging nod. "We're alive and uninjured. That's a win in my book."

"Uninjured?" Manny groaned as she massaged her backside.

Emeka signed, "Speak for yourself."

TJ rolled his eyes and hustled to the beach. "Come on, let's get back to those battlemages before another wave comes."

"Yeah, let's." Titi hunched over like an old woman. "Before we break our spines on the next one."

TJ led the group with vaults of air-steps and water puddles. As they got closer to the beach, they passed by more and more bodies half-buried in muddy sands or sprawled across crumbling asphalt. TJ wanted to throw up. The horror of it was bad enough, but it didn't help that many of the inert bodies were mixed in with rotting kelp, the carcasses of sea creatures, and the copper blend of blood and brine. There were occasional glimpses of hope, though, with diviners and mages healing those who barely clung to life. But even then, the injured cried out in pain as large, gaping wounds were sealed and broken bones were reset.

TJ had to make it stop. He might be the only one who could.

"Wait," Manny said, breathing heavily, "the beach wasn't this far back before. What's going on?"

Unbroken patches of sand had found itself under their feet as they pressed forward, but they shouldn't have made it to the beach yet.

Then TJ realized where they were.

Poking out from lumps of sand were twisted metal and corrugated pipes. Olokun had pushed so far forward, the new beach had literally covered the fallen Ebony Towers.

We're running over a graveyard.

Edging over a sand dune, TJ and the others found the diviners and battlemages on the new beach, holding the new front. They had swapped out their wind cage for a shell of lightning. Where before, their protection was large enough to envelop a group of twenty or so, now it spread wide enough to surround what looked like at least a hundred or more. Above, Oya's storm was barely a few gentle wisps—the likely reason the soldiers switched from air to lighting.

"Crap! Crap!" Umar called out from behind. "Another wave is coming!"

Titi's voice rushed over the chill air. "How are we going to get inside that lightning bubble thing?"

"I got an idea for that!" TJ said as he dashed forward, eyeing the approaching wave all the while. "Everyone run straight for the tunnel. This is gonna be close."

Emeka must've signed something from behind because Titi swore in agreement. "Emeka's right. If we run into that lightning, we'll get fried, TJ."

"Just trust me!" TJ said, a mere hundred yards from the lightning fortress, air-stepping atop the sands. He sunk deep into his mind and thought-spoke. *Elder Adeyemi, it's TJ. Let us in the back of the lightning shield. That wave is gonna drown us.*

The tidal wave loomed high above as the sun finally dipped below the horizon. It was like this latest wave had extinguished all the light from the beach.

Tomori Jomiloju? TJ heard Elder Adeyemi in his head. *Where are you coming from?*

From behind and to the left as you're facing the sea!

The wave was coming down; the lightning cage was fast approaching. It was drown or be fried. TJ couldn't tell which would be worse.

"We're gonna die!" Umar shouted. "We're gonna die!"

TJ bit back. "No, we're not! Everyone, keep air-stepping! Keep air-stepping!"

At the last moment, the arcs of lightning opened up just enough to let them all in, just as the latest wave crashed overhead. TJ tumbled into the sand, the others right behind him. They all ended up in a dogpile, but they were all still alive and breathing. A wrinkled hand hovered over TJ, and TJ took it. He was lifted up by Elder Adeyemi, who said with a smile, "That was a close one, Mr. Young."

"Thank you, Elder Adeyemi." TJ bowed, then took in her new outfit. She wasn't in her pillowcase of a prison outfit anymore. Now she was decked in red and black aso oke with enchanted bangles, shimmering necklaces, and mystical rings. She had pulled off her mask, which was all brass with cowries for eyes. In fact, everyone around them was dressed up like they were cosplaying at some Final Fantasy convention, some with big pointed hats, others with glistening pauldrons, a few with glowing tattoos that bloomed with each spell they cast. Everyone's magical armor glimmered in TJ's Ashe vision.

Besides the crackling of the lightning bubble above, the war drums rung the loudest. At each corner, a grouping of diviners slammed on agba drums, just like the Ibeji in the Sky Realm. The people nearest to them waved electric hands in the air to strengthen the borders of their lightning shell, moving to the beat of the thumping rhythm. Next up for the loudest sound was the war generals, who shouted orders and commanded a reshuffling of the battle lines.

TJ and his friends had found themselves in an all-out magical war zone.

"The clouded actually got the war drum idea from us." Elder Adeyemi closed TJ's hanging jaw, clearly reading his mind, even though she said she couldn't. "What brings you back to the front, Mr. Young?"

"Eshu," TJ shouted over the water that rushed over them again. Each time it passed over, crystals of ice attempted to break through the barrier but were hindered by the bolts of lightning surrounding them. "We can't evacuate the clouded fast enough. We have to stop this at its source. I see Eshu's spirit in the center of the wave. I need to get to him."

"I can't spare anyone to assist you." Elder Adeyemi lifted her staff to bolster a weakening line of bolts that had gone from the shape of thick tubes to thin strips.

"What about them?" Manny pointed to a huddle of diviners in a circle with crossed legs, closed eyes, and hands held aloft in a linked chain.

Adeyemi shook her head. "They are portal masters. They are what's protecting us from outside attacks. The Keepers have been trying to penetrate us this whole time."

"The Keepers are here too?" TJ's chest constricted as he twisted his chin over his shoulders to look for where the Keepers were. "I saw a few throughout the streets. A bunch of them attacked my guards."

"Oh yes, they're very much here, working from the shadows," Elder Adeyemi said. "They're the reason Azuri Towers went down. We couldn't defend ourselves and that skyscraper at the same time. If they get through then—"

"Breach!" one of the diviners, the one closest to TJ and Elder

Adeyemi, bellowed in a voice that didn't entirely sound like his own.

"Breach!" said another with even more terror.

Elder Adeyemi jerked away from TJ to the group. "Where!? Where is the breach?"

"Eastern flank! Eastern flank!"

Eastern flank? That was the same place TJ and the others had come through, wasn't it? TJ pivoted on his heel to see the eastern wall had split open, the fractured and unstable path of the lightning bolts parting like a curtain caught in harsh winds. And through that sliver of an opening, several hooded figures in cream robes and masks with gaping holes for a mouth and eyes stepped through.

General Ito! Elder Adeyemi called out in thought-speak. *Redirect! We need a redirect at the eastern flank!*

But it was too late. The Keepers at the opening held the slit open, and too many of them were piling in, quickly outnumbering the defending group two-to-one. TJ had never seen so many Keepers in one place before, not since his sister's funeral, and even then, there weren't so many. The leader lifted their wooden staff and conjured sand-shaped ropes from the ground. The sand snakes coiled and searched until they latched around something off to the side. Out of the corner of his eye, a body blurred and whipped to the Keeper. It took another second for TJ to realize that the body belonged to Emeka as he thunked into the Keeper's grasp. Emeka had been at the very edge of the group and an easy target. With one hand, the Keeper wrapped their arm around Emeka's chest, and with the other, they pointed their wooden staff to the side of Emeka's head.

"Cease!" the Keeper demanded. It was the voice of Olugbala. Bolawe. Anger roared through TJ's bloodstream and he pounded forward in the sands with his sister's staff raised for an attack.

"Mr. Young, no!" Elder Adeyemi shouted. TJ felt his spine yanked by an invisible force and he fell on his back.

"Let go of my brother!" Titi shouted with tears in her eyes. She probably would've taken off too if she wasn't held tight by Umar's lanky arms.

"Brothers and sisters, please stop!" Bolawe's voice came out muffled under his mask, but more steady than before. "Forfeit your positions. The battle is lost. Eko Atlantic is now Olokun's domain, as it should be."

"Maintain the lightning wall, soldiers!" Elder Adeyemi ordered. "Do not break formation. There will be no concession."

The two or three hundred Keepers were pressed together shoulder to shoulder, all of them wielding staffs pointed in their direction. The tidal waves outside the lightning bubble seemed to cease. But why? If Olokun could wipe them out and reclaim his coastline, there was no reason to give them a warning. There was only one reason they'd be given a chance. It was Bolawe's one weakness, or perhaps his strength. It was just like he told TJ back at the cafe last summer. How he needed to get it right this time, where TJ and the diviners were concerned.

"You're not going to hurt Emeka." TJ voiced the statement with more calm than he expected.

A female Keeper at Bolawe's left stepped forward, brandishing her iron staff like a spear. "You want to bet we wouldn't hurt this little traitor?" She slammed the side of her staff into the boy's side. Not enough to break a rib, but enough to make him keel over in pain. "He's the reason this whole operation almost went under."

"Sister Bisi, enough!" Bolawe commanded. "No more diviner blood needs to be shed this day." He stared her down until she stepped back in line. "To all my brothers and sisters here today. Diviners, mages, sorcerers, clerics, druids, summoners, and magicals all. Put down your weapons. The Keepers are no foes to you."

"You're stalling," TJ said with another challenge in his voice. "Just like Oya said." He peeked through the lightning bubble to the storm above that was beginning to reform. Oya needed this break. "We didn't praise Olokun the full six months like he wanted. He needed *us*, he needed *our* prayer to do what he wanted today. And now his tank is running low, isn't it? That's why you have Eshu helping him along in that wave, right?"

Bolawe's face was covered, but his body language tensed, his grip around his staff tightening. TJ was hitting it right on the mark.

Against Bolawe's hold, Emeka signed, "Get this òlòsí off me."

"Do everyone a favor, Bolawe," TJ said darkly, nodding to his friend to tell him everything would be okay. Bolawe wasn't going to do anything. "If you really don't want any more diviner blood spilled today, get your Keepers to fall back. Leave Emeka alone and—"

A flash of light lanced through the air and burned a still image into TJ's mind. Pain seared behind his eyes as a bright bolt tore straight through Emeka's side and curved, bursting back out of his chest. The crackling of the lightning cage above them seemed to quiet as Emeka's scream pierced the winds. The last sound he would ever make, silencing the world around them. TJ knew he was dead before his head slacked and he fell to the sands like a ragdoll.

TJ knew Emeka was dead because he watched as his spirit left his body.

How could Bolawe actually murder him like that? TJ truly didn't think there was any danger. When he locked eyes with Bolawe's mask, however, he was surprised to find the man on his knees. Was he... crying? Wailing?

It took what felt like several moments before TJ realized he himself was screaming, screaming like all the others around him: Manny, Umar, and especially Titi. They all cried with a fury felt to the very bone.

"Diviners, attack!" Elder Adeyemi roared from the side.

Spells blossomed overhead. Crackled in the air. Impacted. The lightning bubble dissipated. Defense was over. All-out offense was all that mattered now. Fires rushed overhead. Sheets of ice punched into the sands. The crowd merged as one in a vicious cycle of violence.

"Watch out!" Adeyemi cried as a fist of rocks came hurtling straight for TJ's face. The Elder waved her staff and turned the rock into sands that slapped across TJ's cheeks.

TJ spun with the impact and looked for the one who threw the attack his way, ready to fling out the strongest counter he could muster. But Elder Adeyemi stood in his path. "I know you're angry, Mr. Young. But your fight isn't on the Mortal Plane. We'll handle things here. You need to do as you said and stop Eshu."

As a gust of wind flew over her head, she nudged her chin to the ocean, where a new tidal wave was forming. They were all totally exposed. The Keepers. The diviners. All the other magical people who came to help. Olokun didn't care who he was going to drown, didn't care who was in his way, allies or not. They would all have lungs full of salt water soon.

TJ nodded earnestly and set off onto the receding beach with his sister's staff in hand. He air-stepped through the battle, past the hexes and curses, under the tornados of sand being spun from both sides. He ran as fast as he could, dug in his heels and pushed off with wind for all the people who died in those towers, all the people who would die on the beach if he didn't make things right. His hustle was in honor of Ayo, in honor of the woman with the sunflower hat, of all the clouded, but most of all... in honor of Emeka.

If anyone else was going to die, it was going to be TJ.

The wave got closer and closer as he sprinted off steps of wind faster and faster. The waters raised two-hundred feet in the air, three-hundred feet. Would TJ make it in time? Was he even capable of doing it with all the pain he'd endured, outside and within?

Tomori Jomiloju, Oya said in his head. *You won't make it. Use the last of my winds, child. Use them now!*

To his side, wisps of Ashe he knew were the invisible presences of her wind stirred at his flanks. He stood atop them like they were tracks on a skybound railroad. He pushed along the currents until he rose just as high as the tidal wave. When he met his apex, when his nerves swelled into his ears, he dove for the center of the wave. And when he crashed into the middle, when ocean water spread around his whole body, cold as ice, he let water fill his lungs, concentrating hard on the same sensation he felt with Ol' Sally back at Camp Olosa.

And then, with beautiful simplicity...

He drowned.

59

DREDGING THE DECEIVER

TJ SHOT OUT HIS HANDS, LETTING HIS SISTER'S STAFF GUIDE him like the tip of a flying broomstick. His arms were on fire, white-hot and burning raw. Cracks manifested as bright hairlines along his forearms. It hurt so much, like hot pokers set to his skin. The pain threatened to make him stop, but he hadn't crossed over yet. He didn't feel the right sensation. He was between planes, just like that lightning shaft with Ayo. Only now, a tunnel of rushing water surrounded him. Without Ol' Sally, without a golden chain, Ashe resisted him.

"Eshu!" TJ bellowed so harshly his throat went scratchy.

He couldn't let up; he couldn't give in. Damn the resistance; damn the pain. He had to dominate Ashe, make it his own. Searching deep, TJ looked for anything he could latch on to, anything he could sap and enhance for his own use. There was nothing for him to grasp, however. Not when he was in-between worlds.

But he *was* the in-between.

TJ stopped looking for help from the outside and looked within. Omo of Fon was right, Elder Adeyemi, too. He had to look past the Ashe of others, past even the strength Dayo gave him. Here, in the in-between, where he *was* the in-between, stripped back and vulnerable, there was a flicker he'd never managed to find before. Something unfamiliar, something containing an endless pool of Ashe that could power stars. It wasn't his friend's magic; it wasn't his sister's magic. This felt like something primordial. Fundamental. Singular in focus. The power had no questions. It did not hesitate. And that surety is what gave TJ the intensity he needed.

Summoning every bit of energy he could, tapping into that strange well of utter authority, he screamed at the top of his lungs as a radiant white light shot from his sister's staff. It tore the fabrics of reality apart. The water tunnel flooded into itself, sucked into the bright light like an inverted black hole.

It didn't take long before TJ was sucked in, too.

Tumbling head over heel, TJ saw loops of aqua blue and dingy green split by a dark horizon. Blue. Dark. Green. Blue. Dark. Green. The collage of colors didn't stop until he righted himself, clenching his stomach so it wouldn't come up. He was in the middle of an endless ocean floor brimming with fields of kelp. Breathing was easy, despite being surrounded by the murky waters.

"Well, I'll be damned," a familiar voice came from above. TJ peeked overhead to find Eshu at the ocean's "ceiling." The Gate-keeper floated in the waters with crossed legs and his staff in hand. The crystal at its head pulsated a violent crimson. "You crossed over all by yourself, eh?"

"Let the Orishas in your staff go, Eshu!" TJ flung out an angry finger his way, but the gesture was strained. Pulling his fingers from the staff took great effort. His fingers were stuck in a grip, unable to flex fully, almost magnetized in a fist. And the bright fractures on his arm hadn't gone away, embedded in his skin like a bright tattoo. The Eshu symbol had disappeared, too. The imprint of the truce between TJ and Olokun. How long had it been gone? Since the beginning of the battle?

"Oof, that looks painful." Eshu hissed and grimaced. "You look a lot like this one diviner a long while ago." He snapped his fingers. "What was his name? Bankole the Breaker? No, Bolade the Brazen?"

"Eshu!" TJ seethed.

"No, no, no, that's *my* name, kid."

TJ's hand shook as he tried to part his action-figure fingers.

How would he cast spells properly with his hands stuck like that? What would he do now with Eshu a few yards above him? "People are dying on the other side, Eshu! How could you? You said you would help us, not Olokun. This was never part of the deal. You're supposed to be... not this."

Eshu's head twitched with his last words, like something had control of his neck. But in the next moment, the Gatekeeper's expression settled as though it had never shaken before.

"You mortals have defied the Orishas for too long." Eshu dropped his comical tone entirely. "Olokun was right all those centuries ago. A lesson had to be learned."

"The dead can't learn your lessons!"

"But the living will!"

TJ shook his head as he gripped his staff more tightly. "Obatala was right about you."

"Oh, yeah?" Eshu tilted his head, his usually bright irises almost shadowed. "How's that?"

"You've changed. You're unbalanced. Corrupted!" TJ shot out his staff to summon a water bubble to trap Eshu in, but his attack was far too slow. With a sluggish float to one side, Eshu avoided the spell, snapped his fingers, and changed the landscape.

The field of kelps morphed into broken buildings halfway sunk to the ocean floor. Instead of floating in the open sea, TJ drifted in mid-air among stormy clouds.

"Ah, I thought we were friends, TJ." Eshu's voice came from nowhere.

TJ dug deep for his Ashe vision, to find where the Gatekeeper had hidden himself, but his mystical sight was hazy.

"Those mortals had to die, but not you, child."

"Stop hiding!" TJ gripped his staff and flung it around in a three-sixty motion. It was all he could do with his stiff fingers. Fire spit from the end of the wooden shaft and spread in all directions. One of his flames caught Eshu's tunic wrappings, exposing him. "There you are!"

Eshu shook his head. "Don't make me do this." He patted his clothing, then snapped his fingers. The scene changed again. The broken buildings became forest trees on fire, the sky turned red with burning skies. A single rock structure stood in the middle. Oracle Rock.

"If respect will not be given, then it will be earned!"

"Stop this!" TJ screamed. He sent a lightning bolt in the direction of where Eshu was floating before. He hit nothing. Eshu appeared at the top of Oracle Rock, backdropped by fiery clouds. He wasn't alone. In his hand was another figure, one with a lion's mane worth of hair. Manny struggled against Eshu's grip.

"This is the only way you humans learn," Eshu called out. "With the threat of death."

Threat of death? What happened to Eshu's lessons of whimsy? Why and how had he become so radical?

"TJ!" Manny called out, doing her best to elbow the Gatekeeper. "TJ, where am I? What's going on?"

"Manny!" TJ raced toward Oracle Rock—feeling as though he were both swimming and flying—but the Rock was too far away. He cursed at himself. What was he doing? "No, I know this isn't real!"

"Are you sure about that, TJ?" Eshu lifted Manny higher in the air, letting her flailing legs hang over the edge.

"TJ, help me!"

Eshu let her drop into the inferno of a forest.

"Manny!" TJ flew as fast as he could as Manny fell and fell. He wasn't going to make it in time. He wouldn't be able to save her, just like he failed to save the others. Sickness festered in his gut. He hated the feeling, hated the helplessness. Manny's scream was too much to bear. What was worse was the *thunk* of her body smashing into the ground. TJ zoomed for the forest floor, not caring about the fire or the smoke that filled his lungs. He found Manny's legs under a fallen tree covered in flame. Waving his staff with his useless fingers, he pushed the tree aside. But it wasn't Manny's body he found below.

It was Emeka's, bruised, bloodied, and broken.

His t-shirt had a burned hole in the middle where the lightning strike had pierced through his skin. He stood up among the burning trees, his eyes blood-shot and his jaw slack as he uttered with a harsh voice, "How could you let me die, TJ? You had six months." He stepped forward; TJ stepped back. "Six months to fix everything."

Eni stepped out from behind another tree crackling with fire. Her skin was pale, the shadows under her eyes purple, her lips blue. Despite the inferno surrounding them, her clothes were completely drenched in water. Was she dead in reality? Was Eshu showing him what was happening on the other side? TJ couldn't bear to look at her.

"Six months, TJ," Eni croaked. "And you spent it worrying about me."

Manny appeared around another tree with a flaming branch through her shoulder. "Or worrying about how I'd feel about her."

TJ backed away from all of them. "I'm sorry! I'm sorry!"

Watch your step, TJ! Eshu's voice called in his head.

TJ glanced behind him. His heel was at the edge of a cliff leading off into a gorge of lava. He twisted back to his angry friends, and all three of them pushed him over. TJ screamed as he went down, the heat of the lava licking at his spine as he fell and fell. Couldn't he fly just a moment ago? Why couldn't he lift himself up the cliff again? He glanced down to find heavy rocks implanted around his ankles and feet. When had they gotten there? As he dropped, he tried to break the rocks away, but they just grew and grew, all the way up his calves, knees, and thighs.

What sort of twisted lesson was this? The illusions Eshu showed him were just plain nefarious.

When his back crushed against the ground, he didn't burn, but the entire landscape twisted into an all black room. Grunting against the pain, TJ forced himself back to his feet with the help of his staff. Everything was an illusion. None of it was real. He just needed to get his Ashe vision working again; he had to find Eshu in all this mess.

"Our blood is on your hands, young man." The voice came from behind. TJ didn't want to look, but he had to. He had to know who it was. He turned on his heel where a black mirror held the image of the woman with the sunflower hat. Again she croaked. "Our blood is on your hands."

More people entered from different mirrors all around the

circular room: men, women, and children, all with bruised eyes, purple lips, and clothes soaked through with brine and blood. Together, they all said, "Our deaths are on your hands. All you had to do was bring down Eko Atlantic! That's all you had to do!"

A figure stepped through the crowd, tall and haunting. It almost appeared as though it were gliding. Everyone parted for the specter. When TJ got a proper look at it, his entire being seized up, and with shaking lips he murmured, "D-Dayo...?"

Just like the others, she was pale and lifeless, but she didn't chant with the rest. She didn't have to. The disappointment in her eyes was enough.

"*TJ*," a familiar voice said from the side—one TJ hadn't heard in over a month. It was Ayo's. But TJ was done looking, done letting the voices scream freely in his head, done falling for their tricks. "*TJ!*" Ayo's voice came again. "*TJ, we've been looking all over for you! Eshu locked us out of the Aqua Realm.*"

There was something different in Ayo's tone. It wasn't other-worldly like the others. It had real weight to it. TJ lifted his head to his friend's voice. And sure enough, Ayo was there, wearing the same outfit he had when they went to the Sky Realm, his aso oke robes hanging over painted skin, his box braids laying over the sides of his head. He was in the middle of all the other apparitions still chanting, but Ayo passed through them like they were ghosts and he was the real thing.

"*The glass, TJ! Touch the glass! You're the key to break it!*" TJ took slow steps toward Ayo in that dark room of mirrors. As he got closer, the reflection of his friend started to waver like rain on a window pane or the refractions of water in a fish tank. TJ did his best to unlatch the grip that was constricted around his staff. He barely managed it, placing his crooked finger to the glass like Ayo told him to. A click sounded in his head, like a lock being unlatched.

"*Good.*" His friend nodded as the glass began to crack. "*Now get down.*"

"Huh?" TJ questioned, his mouth drier than sand.

Behind Ayo stepped a large man with a bald head and a short, dark beard. His eyes were all-white, and muscles corded his chest and arms, each brawny hand wielding a pair of axes. With an extreme baritone, he spoke, *"He said get down, child."*

Shit, that's the real Shango!

Shango lifted his axes overhead. Red lightning forked into their iron tips and he shot their energy straight at TJ. TJ ducked and the red streaks of crackling power shattered through the mirror and arced overhead. The bolts impacted just behind him. Sparks flared against something unseen, and someone wailed in anguish. When the energy finally let up, it revealed Eshu sprawled along a field of kelp. The mirror room had fallen away, replaced once more with the true Aqua Realm.

"Mortals, behind me!" Shango commanded as his giant form swam forward, sustaining his red lightning. His bolts were utterly concentrated, not forking at all, each flash piercing into the crystal in Eshu's staff. Every second, a new fissure split and TJ could see the spirits of the Orishas trying to force their way out. His belly filled with awe at the astounding display of power.

"Olokun! Yemoja!" Eshu cried out as he dug his heels in against Shango's sustained lightning. "He is here! Shango is here! The Hero is back!"

In the far distance, a great shadow stirred, one TJ hadn't noticed before. Looking at the shadow with fresh eyes, he realized it was a figure in the shape of a giant. No, *two* giants.

Olokun and Yemoja.

Had they been meditating? Concentrating on the tidal wave and frost they terrorized Eko Atlantic with?

"Hurry, TJ!" Ayo shouted from the side. "Help Shango. You gotta bust those Orishas out!"

"Right!" TJ pushed forward and funneled Shango's endless Ashe through his sister's staff. Together they lit the crystal up, cracking it like an ironclad egg. But TJ's arms screamed at him to stop. It was too much. Shango's Ashe was unlike any other he'd leached from before. It burned impossibly hot.

TJ couldn't stop, though. Not when they were this close. Not when Olokun and Yemoja were barreling straight for them. A thousand eyes glowed in the dark waters: two pairs large, the others smaller and in greater number. Fifty, sixty, a hundred? TJ didn't have time to count. Knowing their luck, it was probably a horde of sharks and whales riding in the water deities' wake.

Ayo flung his hands out, too, shooting bolts of energy from each of his fingertips. TJ funneled it all. He said he would take the pain for Ayo back in that shaft of lightning and he meant it. So he took it all in and let it spike through his body no matter how much it hurt.

"Ugh!" TJ groaned. His vision blurred in stark white. He felt his arms rip apart, like invisible claws were tearing away at his skin, his very muscles. He wasn't going to be able to sustain Shango's Ashe like this. The lightning would rip him away from existence; he knew it.

Fear tried to enter his bloodstream, but he wouldn't allow it. The wood in his sister's staff splintered and broke in his hands. Even it couldn't hold in the magic. He'd barely had it an hour and already it was being ruined because he didn't know how to contain the magic within. The wood of the breaking staff bit into his palms and forearms, but the pain was too great for him to feel their bite.

This couldn't be happening. TJ was actually about to let everyone down, even with the help of a lightning deity and his sister's staff. It was all for nothing. The longer TJ held on, the more all these thoughts of doubt assaulted his mind.

But he wouldn't let go, even if he failed, even if it meant permanent damage to his arms... or the ending of his life. Gritting with one more effort, TJ allowed Ashe to enter his body fully, allowed it to course through his staff no matter the destruction. Tears of strain stung his eyes, but that wouldn't slow him.

Eshu's crystal cracked open and out came Olosa of the Lagoons, the Ibeji twins with their drums, Obatala in pure white, and a few others TJ didn't recognize. They all met Olokun and Yemoja in a clash beneath the water. Everything was a blur, a kaleidoscope of lightning, ice, sound waves, fire, earth, and water.

Obatala's giant form rushed over to TJ and Ayo, his pale skin almost glowing in contrast to the shadowy waters. "Quickly, mortals. I must get you back to your realm. Jump into my hand."

TJ couldn't move. He was in too much pain and his hands wouldn't open at all now. Looking down at them, he saw they were devoid of all pigmentation from his fingertips to his elbow. Would they stay like that forever?

"What have I done?" Eshu said from between the kelp fields. He looked wildly between the clashing Orishas and his own hands, where the remains of his staff floated. "What have I done?"

He sounded different then, almost the same as he did when TJ met him properly in the Aqua Realm last summer. What *had* come over him? What could possess an Orisha to do such things that were far outside their character?

Ayo had to swim to TJ to roll him into Obatala's giant hand. The Orisha battle raged on as Obatala raised them higher and higher to the surface of the ocean. TJ was flat on his back, staring up at Ayo, who held him in his arms. The kid looked near to tears under his cracked glasses.

"Good to see you again, Teej." He choked on his words.

TJ could barely get out a response as Obatala pushed them back into the Mortal Realm. "G-good to see you... too... Ayo."

"Only took me and Shango a few days to get back, but we did it."

A few days? Didn't Ayo mean nearly two months? TJ didn't get the chance to ask the question, because when Obatala helped them cross back over, Ayo didn't remember a thing.

60

STREAKS OF WHITE

In the Mortal Realm, the battle only lasted a few minutes more. With Olosa reeling in the waves with the help of the Ibeji's sound waves, and without Olokun and Yemoja empowering tidal waves, the Keepers couldn't keep up their positions, and a majority of them, including Bolawe, escaped through portals to run away from the crimes they had committed that day.

TJ and Ayo had been spit out on the beach, where UCMP officials instantly came to their aid and sent them straight for medical attention at Babalu-Aye Medical. Ayo didn't speak at all, and his eyes stared off into space the whole time they were transported.

The next morning, the healers said he had fallen into a deep coma and they were unsure if he'd ever talk again, to which TJ's heart broke all over again for his friend. And when the healers examined TJ's hands, his condition utterly flabbergasted them. By all accounts, his arms should have been ripped apart by how much Ashe he used. Instead, the streaks of white over his skin glowed whenever he used Ashe.

There were others in the hospital, too. It was like the whole of the Nigerian magical community was packed in that week. Manny, Titi, Umar, Eni, and all the other students that had helped TJ made it out okay.

Everyone except Emeka.

It still didn't feel real that Emeka was gone, but that image of him falling onto the beach haunted TJ's dreams—and his waking hours, too.

Many of TJ's friends and family came to make sure TJ was all right. Eni had filled his entire room with flowers and made sure the nurses had a bowl full of peaches for TJ. Despite their breakup, she was still there for him and that somehow made TJ feel worse, but he was glad she had made it out of the fight alive. Mom was in complete hysterics, Tunde cried, and his father even shed a tear. TJ made sure to keep his arms under his blankets so they wouldn't see his streaks of white skin. When he showed Manny, she said, "I'll get you a nice pair of gloves, don't worry."

Elder Adeyemi, back in her fashionable robes, visited TJ, too. She didn't mention anything or force TJ to speak unless he spoke up first. She had come by only to present the remains of Dayo's staff, which had apparently washed up with him and Ayo when they had gotten back to the beach. It was in complete shambles. The only piece left over was the central wooden double helix.

"They let you out?" TJ asked Adeyemi.

She nodded. "Thanks to your testimony and the little we're reading from Ayo's mind. Though..." She leaned in close to murmur. "A lot of that may have to do with the clean-up. Just about everyone in the council—all the councils across the globe—are assigned to mental reassignment of several thousand clouded who have already hopped online to tell stories of flying people who can shoot lightning from their eyes."

"So..." TJ trailed off. "The clouded know about us?"

"More than usual, but not all. There were contingencies put in place the moment the UCMP knew Olokun was coming. Here, let me show you." She flitted her fingers, and the sole TV that was mounted on the wall in the room sparked to life. Elder Adeyemi had turned to a channel of mundane news. The topic, of course, stemmed from what was being called the largest tidal wave on record. But not much video was provided. The helicopter footage that did make its way across the screen only depicted a great fog that descended across the whole of Eko Atlantic with pockets of lights blooming under the sheets of mist.

"Mr. Windell and his team did good work with that storm,"

Elder Adeyemi went on as she stared up at the screen. "Oya helped a lot with that. But every so often we get a YouTuber or TikToker releasing a problematic video. I've got assignments across the country to deal with this week. We're doing the best we can, but by the end of the month, the uptick in magical believers will go up far more than we'd like."

TJ thought back to those families in their cars, thanking him and his friends for their help. After the UCMP got to them, they wouldn't remember a thing. Perhaps that was for the best.

"Make sure they forget," TJ said hoarsely, darkly. "Whatever clouded you find out there. Make sure they don't just forget the waves. Make sure they forget *everything*. The screams... the blood..."

Elder Adeyemi placed a warm hand over TJ's head. "We will do our best, but..." Her expression took on a sadness. "For our charms to work effectively, some of the horrors will have to remain. It helps reshape their memories. The human mind believes terror above all else."

TJ wanted to argue the point but thought better of it. He was too tired to go against anyone, let alone Elder Adeyemi. She must've realized the turmoil starting in his head, because she removed her hand, stood up, cleared her throat, and said, "You'll get more answers in time, Mr. Young. For now... rest."

A WEEK AFTER TJ WAS ADMITTED TO THE HOSPITAL, ADEOLA visited him with an escort of UCMP officials. They were taking her in to serve a sentence for her association with the Keepers. Before she left, she said something that stuck with TJ that whole night.

"That's the last time I won't be there for someone," she had said, almost with no emotion at all. "First Dayo, now Emeka. That's the last time, TJ. I *promise* you that." The venom she used for "promise" shot straight to TJ's core. He knew the weight behind those words too well.

When TJ regained some semblance of movement in his hands, he was allowed to relocate back to Ifa Academy. Second term exams were, of course, postponed, and many of the students —mostly the exchange students—were pulled from the academy for the rest of the year. Those who remained seemed to avoid TJ's eye contact when they saw him between the paths to classes. TJ was grateful for it. He hadn't felt much like interacting with anyone. The hospital requested he speak with a grief healer, who was essentially a mystical therapist, but TJ didn't want to do that either. He just wanted to go to class, do his work, go to sleep, rinse and repeat.

And that's what he did until he was invited to the memorial at Eko Atlantic on the very day Olokun was originally supposed to show up. Officials gave their speeches, people shed their tears, but TJ was all dried out. Everything was hollow for him. He almost didn't believe the past few weeks had happened at all. It was like it happened to someone else. But the few sunken buildings that still hadn't been cleaned away, surrounded by banners of white, served as a sore reminder of the reality of the lives lost, the damage dealt. What happened that day was all too real, and TJ didn't like the weight it set on his shoulders one bit.

How did Dayo do it? How could she have the strength to deal with all that? Or was TJ's colossal disaster unique to him? After all, Dayo only dealt with lowly mortals or a mystical creature at best, not full-on deities.

Over the past few days, TJ heard whispers of him being some kind of hero. No one ever told you all the grief that came from being one, though.

When Elder Adeyemi got up to say her piece, TJ thought her words would steel some resolve within him, but even her speech felt like empty words to him as well. No one could shake TJ from his stupor, not his brother, not Mom or Dad, not even Manny, as much as she tried.

After the memorial, TJ found himself at the coastline of what was once Eko Atlantic. His jeans were sandy and wet, but he barely paid it any mind. In total, eighteen towers had fallen, two-thirds of the city. The towers further in had significant water damage but still stood tall, right along with the statue of Olokun that TJ thought should've been taken down.

TJ knew they didn't dare bring it down for fear of cosmic retaliation.

No Orisha had made any kind of contact since the ordeal in Eko Atlantic. Not one. TJ would've liked it if he could thank Shango and Oya for their help, Obatala and all the rest, too. Without them, far more than eighteen towers would've gone down. But Adeyemi had said when the tidal wave went away, so too did Oya's storm. She said a curious red streak of lightning was seen in the night sky, intermingling with the storm clouds before it disappeared.

The sun glinted off the edge of something in the sands near his foot. He pulled at it, discovering it was a picture. The photo depicted a family—a grandmother and grandfather in the center, along with a dozen others behind them. It was the grandmother who got TJ the most. She looked so similar to the woman who had fallen out of his grasp. And the ink in the photo was ruined by water damage, making everyone in the picture appear as ghoulish creatures instead of a happy family, just like the images Eshu showed TJ with those illusions.

"I'm sorry," TJ cried to the family who couldn't hear him. "I'm so sorry."

He sat there a long while, tears falling and the photo scrunched in his palm.

"It's okay, TJ," Manny's voice came from behind. TJ didn't turn to look, stuffing the photo under his foot and sniffing away a tear. "Is it okay if I come sit next to you?"

TJ let in a few deep breaths before he replied with a shaky, "S-sure."

Manny sat with TJ shoulder to shoulder, looking out at the destruction as well. She didn't speak. TJ didn't speak. It was often like that since Olokun's attack, and TJ appreciated Manny for it. So they could say much between them without saying anything at all. She knew he'd open up to her when he was ready.

"I'm not okay, Manny," he finally said, solemnly. "I'm not

okay. I can't do this anymore. This isn't me. This can't be my life. I can't be responsible for people's lives like this."

Manny leaned her head on his shoulder, wrapping her arm around his waist to stop his shaking. "Can I share something with you?"

TJ didn't voice a response, but he nodded slowly.

Manny pulled out her phone with her free hand and scrolled to a page of Evocation from a blog titled The Third Eye. The headline read:

TJ YOUNG, THE UNSUNG HERO by Dele Ogunseye

"I don't want to read that," TJ said. "I'm not a hero."

"Listen," Manny replied gently but firmly:

Heroism comes in many forms. For some, it's a sense of duty. For others, an obligation. And then there are those for which it's a necessity.

Nearly one year ago, we lost one of our greatest heroines. You know her as the Hero of Nigeria, the late Ifedayo Young. Few of us know of her younger brother, Tomori Jomiloju Young. Few of us know him because, at this very moment, UCMP officials are going around wiping the battle from the global consciousness. And that's not right. The clouded need to be made aware.

Over the past few days, we've heard valiant stories of diviners and mages, celebrated warriors and service workers. And while these individuals played a vital role in preventing the Great Flooding of Eko Atlantic, they are not the focal point of where our thanks should lie. It was the bravery of a 15-year-old adolescent who fought against the authority and the negligence of the United Council of Magical Peoples. Were it not for the proactive actions of Mr. Young, the number of deaths suffered would have been in the tens of thousands, including my own.

The UCMP doesn't want you to know about this fact. In larger publications like Divination Today and Eshu's Messenger Press,

you'll not hear a peep about Mr. Young's involvement because it
would lean to a line of questioning that would reveal a grievous
mishandling of the situation. So today, for those of us who
always keep our third eye open, I want to say thank you, TJ.

Manny scrolled down to below the blog where several videos
were embedded. Each one featured a different diviner personally
thanking TJ.

"TJ, if you're out there, I want to thank you for saving my
cousin. The UCMP didn't think she was close enough of a family
member to be evacuated."

"Thank you, TJ. I hadn't registered my clouded mother in
years. If you didn't get to Pearl Towers when you did... I don't
know what could've happened."

"I can't put into words how much it means to me that you got
my friend out of Ebony Towers before they went down. She had
no idea what was coming for her."

It went on and on like that, one after the other.

"Thank you, TJ."

"Thank you, TJ."

"Thank you, TJ."

Manny put her phone down and looked TJ full in the face. "I
know this is all hard on you. I can't imagine how much you're
goin' through right now. But you can't just give up. I won't let
you. Those won't be the last people who will need you, TJ. It's
not about the people who were lost. It's about the people who
were saved. You get me?"

TJ chewed on his lip, but nodded. "Yeah, I get you. Thanks,
Manny."

Manny lifted her phone again to share the last video on the
page, a message from Adeola on her hospital bed. When had she
recorded that video, he wondered. She must've recorded it before
she was escorted away. TJ stared at the screen, swore he saw his
sister's face there, overlapping with Adeola's own. When Adeola
spoke, he *knew* he heard Dayo's voice too, as though doubled
along with Adeola as she said, "Thank you, TJ."

TJ sat with his thoughts for a moment, just staring at the
paused image of Adeola on screen until he finally said, "They

shouldn't be thanking just me." He nudged his chin along the top of Manny's head, staring off into the distance, where the crowd of the memorial broke off, where he could see some of the students that assisted him. "I'm nothing without the help I got. I'm nothing without my friends."

"And we'll be there for you." Manny lifted her head to make sure she was looking TJ straight on again. "All of us. We'll all need each other for whatever comes next."

EPILOGUE
A DEITY'S DECREE

MONTHS LATER, AS THE TERM WAS NEARING ITS CLOSE, TJ WAS doing a lot better. He still woke up with nightmares of floods, with creaking metal and the lightning bolt that shot through Emeka, but he got his appetite back, he was able to speak to people who weren't just Manny, and he allowed himself to focus on the good he did. It wasn't perfect. There were bad weeks—a lot of bad weeks—but he got through them by finding the good in the world: the simplicity of a long walk along Ifa Academy's streams, a late-night staring up at the stars in peace, the laughter of students.

A lot of that had to do with his grief healer, who he finally agreed to meet with two times a week. She had suggested that whenever TJ got overwhelmed, he should find a safe place he could retreat into to clear his mind.

During the final week of third term, after he was notified he'd passed enough of his exams to advance to Senior Secondary School, TJ found himself staring at the two empty bunks in his dorm when he returned. He wanted to celebrate with his friends, rub it in Ayo's face that he had done it, gloat with Emeka over a game of Major League Crossover. But he couldn't do that. Ayo was still stuck in his coma, as absent as if he had never returned. And Emeka was buried near his family's compound in New Ile-Ife.

So TJ did just as he was told to do. He retreated to his safe place. Tucked away near the whispering willows just off the lake, TJ carved an area just for him, where most students never went. It was always quiet there. Nothing but the buzzing of insects and the occasional twinkle of adze fairies skimming over the waters. It probably wasn't the healthiest idea, but TJ had gone there to speak to his reflection, to speak to Dayo.

He hadn't seen her face since that video from Adeola in that blog post, but every time he got done talking, he always felt that brush across his neck. And on that day, TJ *did* see a face in the waters that wasn't his own.

It wasn't Dayo's either, though.

The face he saw belonged to a man with a strong jaw and dark skin that looked like it could've been carved from wood. TJ rubbed his eyes to make sure he was still sane.

The man in the lake touched the reflection the same way TJ pressed his finger to the mirror to allow Ayo and Shango to cross-over into the Aqua Realm. TJ outstretched his finger, touched the water, and an ethereal sound filled his ears, followed by a voice.

Tomori Jomiloju? the voice asked.

"H-How are you doing this?" TJ asked. Not even Eshu could speak to him directly with the reflection trick. "I thought communicating with mortals was forbidden?"

The old rules are dying, young mortal, the man said. Who was he? *The Gatekeeper keeps the ways no longer. He hasn't been seen for several moons, in fact. You may see many more Orishas reaching out from now on.*

"Y-you're an Orisha, too?"

Oh, yes! My apologies. I am Oshosi, Orisha of the Hunt. But for our purposes now, your Orisha of Justice.

"Orisha of Justice? What's that supposed to mean?"

You must come with me. The Courts of the Almighty summon you. They claim you are responsible for the death of the Norse God of Thunder. Thor.

What happens when a mortal asks for a deity's help?
They find themselves in the middle of a cosmic war, of course.

Discover the story of how Ayodeji convinced the Orisha, Shango,
to help with the attack on Eko Atlantic, a journey that leads
directly into the events of TJ Young Book 3, *The Hero's Equinox*.

visit this link and read the story:
antoinebandele.com/book-page-an-axe-for-a-hammer

How do you break a god out from a cosmic prison?
You bring a crew and a whole lot of magic.

TJ has already dealt with ancient African gods, and now he's being blamed for the death of Thor!

Last year's conflict with the Orishas of the ocean led to the greatest natural disaster in modern history.

But the Mortal Realm wasn't the only place affected by the destruction. The events of one dimension disturbed another, and now a council of gods accuses TJ of the death of the Norse god of thunder. Worse, the Orisha of Lightning, Shango, has been imprisoned as well for the same charges.

It'll be up to TJ and his friends to clear his name and save Shango. But TJ knows how difficult it is to deal with the Almighty, so he gathers a crew and prepares for a heist for the ages.

Will TJ succeed, or will he be faced with a life sentence in a cosmic prison?

Find out in this young adult fantasy based on the mythology of West Africa, where TJ will encounter cosmic trials, unbreakable prisons, and the ancient secrets of the Orishas.

ALSO BY ANTOINE BANDELE

TJ YOUNG & THE ORISHAS

The Gatekeeper's Staff

The Windweaver's Storm

The Hero's Equinox

ORISHAS AMONG MORTALS

Will of the Mischief Maker

When The Wind Speaks

An Axe for a Hammer

TALES FROM ESOWON

The Kishi

THE SKY PIRATE CHRONICLES

By Sea & Sky

Of Ruin & Silk

For Code & Honor

LOST TALES FROM ESOWON

Demons, Monks, and Lovers

Gods' Glass

ANTHOLOGIES

Chronicles of Underrealm

Tales from the Otherworlds

ABOUT THE AUTHOR

Antoine lives in Los Angeles, CA with his girlfriend and cat.
He is a YouTuber, producing work for his channel "Antoine
Bandele".
He is also an audiobook engineer and publisher.

Whenever he has the time, he's writing books inspired by African
folklore, mythology, and history.

antoinebandele.com

To my beta readers:

Roe Adams, Allison Alexander, Jordan Fortuin, Brian Letang, Negus Lamont, Mary R. Lanni, Francesca McMahon, Chantis Riddle, Andrea S.U.

Thank you for your time and dedication to this project. The story wouldn't be what it is without you delightful diviners.

GLOSSARY

- **Akara:** also known as black-eyed peas fritters, beans fritters, or Acaraje. A very delicious, deep-fried bean cake made from black-eyed pea paste.
- **Àgbádà:** a Yoruba tunic.
- **Algaita:** a double reed wind instrument from West Africa, especially among the Hausa and Kanuri peoples.
- **Ashe:** a Yoruba philosophical concept through which the power to make things happen or produce change is conceived. Within the diviner community, it is known as the source of magic.
- **Aṣọ òké:** a narrow strip-weaving technique and a variety of Yoruban fabric often incorporated into formal wear.
- **Aziza:** fae creatures who once provided early hunters with magic. They are also known to have given practical and spiritual knowledge to people (including knowledge of the use of fire).
- **Bàbálàwò:** a priest of Ifa, also known as the Shepard of Mysteries.
- **Babalu-Aye:** the Healer Orisha, characterized as a protector from death, disease, and cemeteries, but also a contributor of those aspects of life.

- **Bruxa:** the Portuguese word for "witch."
- **Bùbá:** a Yoruba blouse or top.
- **Cara:** the Portuguese word for "guy."
- **Clouded:** a term used to described those of non-magical lineage within the diviner community.
- **Heka:** the Egyptian deity of Creation, also the rough translation of the word "magic."
- **Ibeji:** the Twin Orishas, characterized as rambunctious, childlike spirits that are full of youthful fun.
- **Ìlèkè:** spiritual beads often worn at the neck by devotees of Ifa.
- **Impundulu:** a mythical bird associated with witchcraft, frequently manifested as the secretary bird, also known as a lightning bird.
- **Iroko:** a large hardwood tree from the west coast of tropical Africa that can live up to 500 years
- **Eko Atlantic:** officially Nigeria International Commerce city, also known as Eko Atlantic City, is a planned city of Lagos State, Nigeria, being constructed on land reclaimed from the Atlantic Ocean.
- **Emi:** the Yoruba word for "spirit," also the class title for spiritual guidance at Camp Olosa.
- **Ere Idaraya:** the Yoruba word for "exercise," also the class title for physical training at Camp Olosa and Ifa Academy.
- **Eshu:** the messenger for all Orishas. The Orisha of trickery, crossroads, misfortune, chaos, and death.
- **Ètùtù:** Yoruba ritual in light of propitiatory performances for the Orishas.
- **Evo:** short for "Evocation." An unlisted search engine used by underground diviners for news not savory enough for most publications.
- **Fìlà:** a Yoruba cap.
- **Futebol:** the Portuguese word for "soccer."
- **Garri:** a creamy granular flour obtained by processing the starchy tuberous roots of freshly harvested cassava.

- **Gèlé:** a Yoruba head tie.
- **Ìdẹ:** spiritual beads often worn at the wrist by devotees of Ifa.
- **Ifa:** the name for the system of divination practiced by diviners and devotees. Also the name of the academy for magical students under the guidance of the Orishas.
- **Ile-Ife:** the original city, the homeland of diviners, which in modern times has been moved to New Ile-Ife near Omo Reserve.
- **Irenku:** in Yoruba funeral tradition, this is the final day of observance, often coupled with a small parade for the dead.
- **Ìrènókú:** in Yoruba funeral tradition, this is a day set for games.
- **Ìró:** a Yoruba wrap-around skirt.
- **Ìtàóku:** in Yoruba funeral tradition, this is the day relegated to feasting and celebration of life.
- **Itis:** African American slang meaning the drowsy sleeping feeling one gets after a significant meal, often after Thanksgiving.
- **Itako:** blind women who train to become spiritual mediums in Japan.
- **Ìyá:** the Yoruba word for "mother."
- **Ìyá Àgbá:** the Yoruba word for "grandmother."
- **Jötunn:** Norse giants that are strong, daunting, and often highly misunderstood.
- **Jovem:** the Portuguese word for "young person."
- **Kishi:** a demon creature with an attractive human man's face on the front of its body and a hyena's face on the back. Kishi are said to use their human face as well as smooth talk and other charms to attract young women, who they then eat with the hyena face.
- **Mamãe:** the Portuguese word for "mother."
- **Mami Wata:** a half-human half-snake water spirit venerated in West, Central, and Southern Africa and in the African diaspora in the Americas.
- **Mhamó:** the Scottish word for "grandmother."

- **Naira:** the currency used in Nigeria.
- **Naija:** the term used to refer to "New Nigeria."
- **No Wahala:** the Yoruba phrase for "no problem."
- **Oba:** the Yoruba word for "king."
- **Obatala:** the Architect Orisha, the Healer, or the Shepard of the Imperfect, characterized by his gentle personality and eternal patience.
- **Ode Buruku:** the Yoruba word for "bloody fool."
- **Oduduwa:** the Doted Orisha, the Divine King, characterized by his clear and focused mind.
- **Ogbon:** the Yoruba word for "wisdom," also the class title for Ifa studies at Camp Olosa.
- **Ogiyan:** the Crushed Cassava Orisha, characterized for his ultra specialization of the cassava harvest.
- **Ojo Isinku:** in Yoruba funeral tradition, this is the time relegated to prayer and donation.
- **Oko:** the Agriculture Orishas, the Keeper of the Farm, characterized by his protection of plains, once a hunter turned farmer.
- **Olodumare:** the Almighty Orisha, the Father, or the omnipotent, characterized by his great power and all-knowing pools of knowledge. He is all things.
- **Olokun:** the Orishas of the Deep Blue, the Ruler of the Seas. Husband to Yemoja, and parent to most other water Orishas.
- **Olosa:** the Lagoon Orisha, characterized for her abundance, prosperity, and fertility.
- **Òlòsí:** the Yoruba word for "bastard" or "foolish person."
- **Ọpọn Ìfà:** a divining board of the Ifa divination system, often made of wood and circular in shape.
- **Ori:** sometimes referred to as an Orisha, oftentimes refer to a state of mind relating to spiritual intuition and destiny as it relates to human consciousness.
- **Orunmila:** the Divination Orisha, the Miracle Worker, characterized by his separation from other Orisha. Whereas most Orisha do have some interaction with

the world, Orunmila spends most of his time in the stars.

- **Osain:** the Orisha of the Wood, characterized by his healing nature and distinguished by his Cyclops-looking appearance.
- **Oshosi:** the Orisha of the Hunt and Justice, characterized by his protective nature and strong sense of duty.
- **Oshun:** the Orisha of Rivers, characterized by her sensuality, love, and purity. One of the wives of Shango.
- **Oya:** the Orisha of Storms, characterized by her tenacity and compassion. One of the wives of Shango.
- **Papai:** the Portuguese word for "father."
- **Patakí:** a scared story, song, or myth in the Ifa faith system.
- **Pẹlẹ̀:** a Yoruba shawl.
- **Qi:** the circulating life force whose existence and properties are the basis of much Chinese philosophy and medicine.
- **Shango:** the Thunder Orisha, the Lionhearted, or The Overseer of Masculinity and Masculine Beauty, characterized by his loud personality and substantial presence.
- **Shuku shuku:** a Nigerian-style coconut macaroon.
- **Ṣòkòtò:** Yoruba trousers.
- **Sūrú, ẹrọ, and ètùtù:** in order, patience, gentleness, and coolness needed in Ifa ritual.
- **Tchau:** The Portuguese word for "bye."
- **Tláloc:** the Aztec rain deity.
- **Uziza:** better known as the West African black pepper.
- **Velho:** the Portuguese word for "old person."
- **Yemoja:** the mother of all Orishas. The Orishas of creation, water, motherhood, and moonlight.
- **Yewa:** formerly the Orisha of lagoons, now the Orisha of graveyards.

- **Yumboes:** tall fae creatures at a height of two feet all with the hue of white and silver hair. Spirits of the dead.
- **Zobo:** a Nigerian hibiscus drink of deep red made from Roselle plant flowers.

CPSIA information can be obtained
at www.ICGtesting.com
Printed in the USA
LVHW101610191022
731075LV00021B/615/J